DRAGON'S FANG

The Majaran Trilogy
Book 1

Peter Rogers Stark

EternumPublishing

Eternum • Fantasy

PETER ROGERS STARK

Maps by Peter Rogers Stark
Cover art by MiblArt
Original Cover by Alise Heinrich

ISBN: 0615591167
ISBN-13: 978-0615591162

Published in the United States of America by
Eternum Publishing

Dedication

For

Miku, Mincho, Akane,
Misa, and Saiki

With deepest respect for
five absolutely amazing ladies

私からメイドたちへ

ありがとう ございます

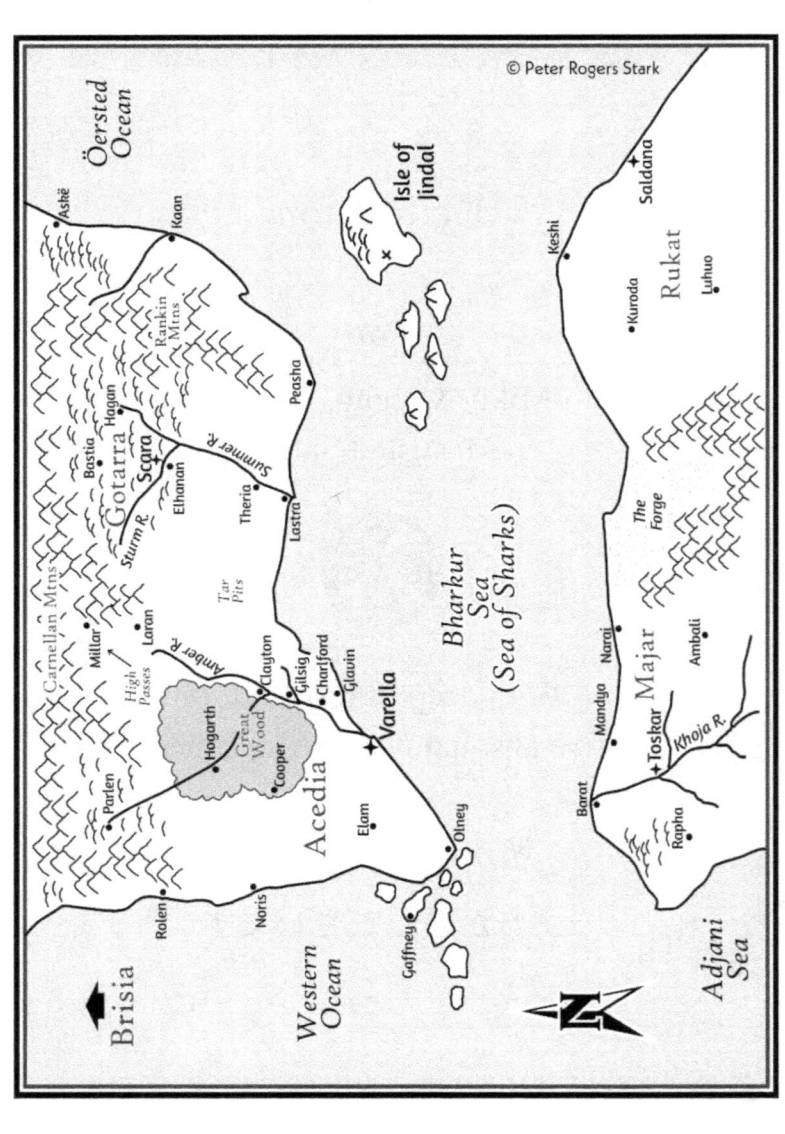

© Peter Rogers Stark

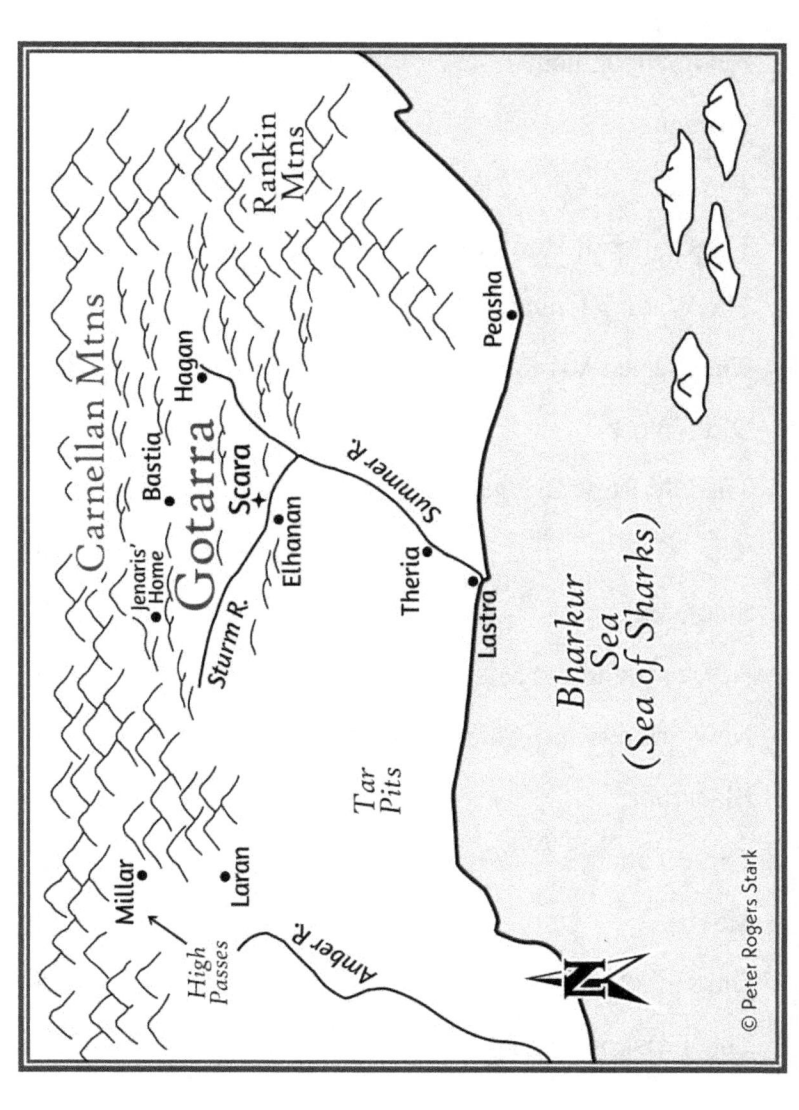

© Peter Rogers Stark

Contents

Peter Rogers Stark

Acknowledgments

A number of people deserve my undying gratitude for their help in the process of writing this book. My thanks to "Yetti" Edwards for helping me write the first ten barbarian jokes in ten minutes, to Don for his research, to Frank for his tireless encouragement (I believe it's called *nagging.*), and to Raymond for keeping me well-fed while I worked. I would also like to express my appreciation to my family for their support and to my parents for their invaluable help, and to those who read the early drafts for helping to make this a better book.

Also, even though most people list Jim Brown "among" the best football players ever (and although Walter Payton will always be my guy), Brown is actually *still* underrated. I just wanted to get that off my chest.

Last but not least, since the original publication of this work, the Chicago Cubs became the 2016 World Series champions (*finally*)! It felt great, guys! I know I can speak for Cubs fans everywhere when I say "Thank you."

Eamus Catuli! (Go, Cubs!)
PeteR Stark (June 29,2020)

Prologue

The flashing steel of the longswords was barely visible behind the snapping and spinning of colorful silk scarves, drawn through the air by the pommels to which they were tied. Seeming to dance as they floated to and fro, the cloth was intended to confuse and misdirect an enemy. Yet Samir wasn't bothered at all by their constant flapping, and he was certain that his opponent wasn't either. Oblivious to the streaming silk, as well as the ring and scrape of steel on steel as the swords struck and slid against one another, each man's attention was focused fully on the sharp, spinning blades and the movements of the warrior he faced.

Caught by the wind of the passing swords and his own movement, the blue brocaded silk of Samir's pants billowed between the waist and tightly gathered ankles as he shifted his weight in defense. But the feel of the smooth material against his skin was lost to him, as was the slow trickle of sweat running down the lightly bronzed skin on his tall, lean frame.

Samir noticed only his opponent—not merely the long blade, but the hands and feet which were at least as dangerous. Against this man, even a slight lapse in concentration would be too much.

Weight always perfectly balanced, Shimei moved deceptively slowly, seeming to flow from one position to the next. Every action deliberate, with no wasted motion or energy, his bare feet seeming to almost caress the floor as they moved, barely lifting at all. The old master's chest still rose and fell in the same steady, even breaths as when the combat began. Even now, skin stretched taut over the corded muscles of his arms and chest, honed from decades of long, hard practice. Only the finest sheen of perspiration gave any hint of exertion from a fight that felt as if it had lasted forever already.

Samir's leading foot lifted as he moved to a high crane-like stance, avoiding the leg sweep even as he guided Shimei's sword off line with his own. Foot already rising, the young warrior snapped his heel forward in a kick, using the movement to reach a more defensible position.

The bodies and weapons of both men wove back and forth in constant motion, each shifting to counter the other—blocks and strikes blended seamlessly together. Samir felt frustration begin to rise as his target vanished before every attack, sword and limbs meeting empty air as the more experienced master dodged aside without apparent effort. Yet his disciplined mind pushed the emotion away, refusing to sacrifice technique in favor of passion.

A sudden flurry of movement nearly caught him off guard, his blade rising only by reflex to push the approaching weapon away. Somehow, the old man's blade came around like a serpent, quick and agile wrists bringing the sharp point back in line and streaking toward its mark. Samir barely managed to turn his body so the long, thin weapon pierced only the air in front of his chest as it slid past.

He almost didn't see it—the barest sliver of an opening in Shimei's defenses left by the attack. Samir's wrist twisted, sword point seeming to leap for the ribs now exposed beneath the outstretched arm.

Too late the younger man realized that he'd been baited, the master's free hand gripping his wrist the instant he was fully committed to the strike. Shimei's foot slid soundlessly over the polished wood of the floor as he shifted his weight back and downward into a lower position—arms sweeping down to draw the much younger warrior with him.

Overbalanced, Samir instinctively pulled back, struggling against the iron grip that held him fast. This was his second mistake.

Without warning, Samir's wrist was released, throwing his balance suddenly backwards as his efforts to escape the hold were given free rein. Once again the other man reversed his direction, this time straight toward Samir. Balance already sabotaged, Samir's body was propelled rapidly backwards as Shimei's palm strike lashed out, smashing into his chest and driving the air from his lungs.

That quickly, the battle was over. Samir landed heavily on his back, gasping, with his opponent standing calmly over him.

Just as calmly, Shimei turned to face the man kneeling in the entrance to the room, the master's long black braid swinging freely to brush against the naturally dark skin of his lower back.

Having arrived during the training session, the servant had knelt to wait quietly in the doorway until the Sòra chose to acknowledge him, knowing better than to ever interrupt. Now, he bowed low over his knees, showing the proper respect to a master teacher in his own training room.

"Yes?" Shimei's soft voice inquired.

"A message for the Prince, Sòra," came the immediate reply. The servant's eyes remained locked on the boards at the master's bare feet, never once glancing toward Samir.

Shimei nodded, his head inclining the merest detectable fraction. It was plainly the only permission he would give.

"His Majesty asks his son's attendance when he is finished here, Sòra," the man concluded.

The request of course, was not for Samir. His presence had just been commanded. It was the old master who had been politely, if obliquely, asked to part with his student as soon as it was convenient.

"Thank you," Shimei returned. "You may go."

Rising, the servant bowed deeply again, then turned and left as quietly as he had come.

Samir had scrambled to his feet as his teacher spoke to the messenger, breath coming under his control as he'd been taught. Now he stood facing the master, sweat plastering long dark hair to his back and neck, posture relaxed in a ready stance.

The weapon in his right hand now pointed casually at the floor, ready at a moment's notice, but in no way intended as a threat. Threatening a friend was, after all, a violation of simple courtesy—and warning an enemy was a violation of common sense.

Shimei tucked his sword behind his back as he turned, its long, narrow blade aligned with his spine and the point peeking just above his head. Wordlessly he studied his student, his sharp, intense stare missing nothing in stance or attitude.

Samir was not bothered by the scrutiny as he once had been. When he had first come to this room as a small boy, the Sòra had frightened him. Now, he was more than a little in awe of the master teacher, but he saw no reason for fear.

Though his master's posture was completely relaxed, Samir wasn't fooled in the least. He knew Shimei could strike, blindingly fast, with hands and feet, or with the sword he still held. Samir had seen it more times than he could count and had needed to defend against it with varying levels of success.

The young Prince paid no attention to the large, windowless room or its contents. He knew them all without the need to look. Hundreds of weapons of all descriptions hung from the dark paneled walls. Most were plain, intended for hard use during practice sessions, yet a few were especially fine examples of their types. These, however, were for use only in serious battle.

Samir could almost have closed his eyes and pointed to them. Broadswords hung, so unlike those used in other lands. Their wide-flaring, curved blades were much heavier than that which he currently held, and they were intended to slice. There were round metal hammers with short handles, used in pairs to batter opponents. Weighted lengths of chain hung ready for capable hands to send swinging rapidly or shooting precisely at a vulnerable target. Racks of spears and long poleaxes stood along the walls, their shafts polished from use. All around, sharp steel points gleamed above the silk and horsehair that most people took to be simple decoration.

Samir was familiar with nearly all and had mastered more than a few. The Sòra, however, had mastered them all. More importantly, he had spent at least as much effort mastering himself.

Aside from Samir's father, King Zahar, Shimei was easily the most impressive man he had ever met. Only a few creases on the master's brow and around his piercing brown eyes marked his face. That, together with the white creeping into the braid and coloring the thin, drooping moustaches which started above the corners of his mouth and dangled to well below his chin, were the only signs that he carried over sixty years. Certainly the hard abdominal muscles and easy, graceful movement gave no hint.

It never occurred to Samir to leave and answer the King's summons. To leave before he was dismissed would show an unthinkable disrespect. Here, his time belonged to his Sòra. In fact, in this place the master had as much authority as the King of Majar himself—in some ways, perhaps more.

Instead, Samir merely stood, calmly, making no assumptions. He had worked with Sòra Shimei virtually every day for the past fifteen years, and experience had taught him that his teacher was as likely to attack as to dismiss him in such situations. In fact, Shimei was certain to work him ceaselessly for hours if the master detected even the slightest hint of impatience or sign the young Prince had tried to second guess him. The Sòra demanded self-discipline and patience, and he would settle for nothing less from those he accepted as students.

Samir apparently met with the Sòra's approval since, as the master brought his longsword from behind his back, he flipped it. The blade now lay cradled between his upturned palm and the crook of his arm, hilt toward Samir.

"Go put the weapons away," he told his student softly. "You're done for the day."

Samir bowed low, acknowledging the dismissal and showing his respect. Straightening, he accepted the offered sword.

The wooden floor, polished by the feet of countless masters and students, felt cool and familiar against his bare soles as he crossed to the empty places among the racks to hang first Shimei's sword, then his own. From habit as much as from intent, he finished by adjusting the red silk of the scarves to drape as smoothly as those on the other weapons in the room.

Finished with the task, he started for the room's only door, a feeling of satisfaction suffusing him as he walked. He had worked hard today, as he always did, which left him pleasantly tired and ready to bathe away the sweat and exhaustion. That would have to wait, however. He hated the idea of coming before his King unwashed and disheveled, but, as ill-mannered as that might be, it would be ruder still to appear any later than necessary.

Reaching the door, Samir turned and bowed—to the room as well as to his Sòra. The formalities done, he slipped his feet into the soft green kidskin boots that sat just outside on the shaded veranda. Adjusting the cuffs of his voluminous trousers to slide just inside the low boot tops, he took his matching shirt from the peg beside the door and stepped out onto the path.

The sun had climbed more than halfway to its zenith since he had arrived for practice at dawn, illuminating a thick haze which blanketed everything in sight. This close to the jungle, the humidity was an almost constant companion, adding an extra layer of discomfort to the rapidly rising temperatures.

The flagstones were warm against his boot soles as he broke into a brisk walk, taking him away from the isolated training room near the outer wall and toward the tall spires of the palace. Beside him the rising rows of plumflower posts, a treacherous test of balance and coordination, lined the path beside wooden men. He had spent many hours walking the levels of the widely spaced posts and performing his katas from a stance on their precarious heights. And he would spend many more.

The Prince responded to occasional waves and greetings as his feet guided him across the well-tended palace grounds. Almost of their own accord they led him down the winding pathways toward the cooler air of the water gardens. At this time of day the polished limestone walls of the massive complex offered deep shade there. Later, the colorful awnings would guard against the worst of the heat. Always, however, there was the refreshing water.

His approach was greeted by the gurgle and splash of fountains—providing an almost musical accompaniment to the laughter that came from within, tugging at him. It was a compelling invitation, more than enough to make him quicken his steps. The view was well worth the haste. Coming around the screen of cattails and rushes, he caught sight of the most beautiful place in the world. It always made him smile, and today was certainly no exception.

After adopting a more seemly pace, he crossed the small arched bridge, following a trail designed to provide visitors with amazing vistas. It didn't disappoint. The path meandered between clusters of stately date palms and lily-filled pools. Cleverly arranged twists and vibrant jungle flora created numerous private areas—inviting exploration and allowing lovers to relax unobserved. In all, it was a marvel of the gardener's art.

He had little time to enjoy it now, however, as he soon came into sight of the central fountain—its large, shallow basin welcoming him, as always. There, a pair of exquisitely carved marble tigers played in the endless streams of water splashing from the mouths of several sea creatures. It was those, rather than the tigers, that drew his attention.

As a small boy, he'd found the strange animals absolutely fascinating. He'd been entranced by the thought of riding one, with the front end of a horse and tail of a fish. Of course, now that he was grown he doubted the existence of such beasts, but the fountain still held a certain allure for him.

Samir laid his shirt atop the low stone rim and bent to push aside the floating lilies, revealing the blue tile beneath. The water was cool and clear as he dipped his hands, quickly washing the morning's sweat from his bronze skin. As good as it felt, it wasn't much, but it was all the time he could afford. He wasn't about to keep the King waiting.

Snatching up the shirt, he hastily pulled it on—fighting it momentarily as it clung to damp skin. But that couldn't be helped. All he could do was try to smooth the light fabric carefully before reaching to pull his long tail of hair free of the collar.

A warmth suffused him as his fingers brushed the gold filigreed clasp that bound his straight black locks. Discovered at his bedside that morning, it had been a gift from his mother. At the moment it was his only jewelry—not that he normally wore much. But, given the Sòra's disapproval of ornamentation, it was best if the signet ring and gold anklet he currently favored awaited him in his room.

With a quick glance, he decided he was as prepared as he was likely to be and moved on. Numerous small trails led from there to other fountains and, eventually, to a large koi pond. Samir, however, chose the most direct route to the audience chamber where he would find his father.

Yet even that path had its distractions.

From the corner of his eye, he glimpsed a figure detaching itself from a group of giggling young women. Even without the glance for confirmation, he knew exactly who approached—the flirtatious laughter had practically announced as much to anyone familiar with his half-brother, Kemal.

Although slightly shorter than Samir, the other man possessed a darker complexion and more muscular build—a fact which seemed to delight the women who frequented the palace. But even this was overshadowed by the man's natural charm, which seemed to make easy friends of nearly everyone he met. There was little to distinguish between the two otherwise, hardly surprising given that they were much the same age—Kemal being just short of Samir's twenty years.

An ever-present carefree smile split Kemal's face as he caught up, strolling easily alongside.

"Good morning, Brother," Samir offered with a nod as they walked.

"Hello, Samir."

The soft whisk of their boot soles and the jingle of Kemal's abundant jewelry at ankles and wrists were the only sounds of their passage for the moment. Clearly, though, his brother had something to say.

Curious, Samir broke the silence. "Anything I can do for you?"

"No," Kemal shook his head in response. "I just wanted to wish you a happy birthday. In case I don't see you later."

He glanced at the man beside him. They weren't close—at least not since Kemal had been banished from Shimei's presence three years earlier. It was inevitable really, after he'd come to train with eyes glazed and reeking of hashish. But, while he had found another Sòra to accept him and wore his whiskers in the warrior's style, the younger man's resentment had never fully abated.

"Thank you," he offered, seeing no reason to be other than gracious. His brother seemed to be making an effort, after all. "I'm afraid I can't stop to talk. Father called."

"That's all right." Kemal's signet ring thumped heavily against his shoulder blade at a clap on the shoulder. "Happy birthday."

Without further comment, the other man strolled back toward the water gardens and his fawning coterie of females. Samir continued, crossing the marble pavement of the royal family's private courtyard.

From there it was only a short walk through a few of the more opulent palace corridors. Although he had seen the displays of finery many times, the incredible beauty wasn't lost on the young Prince. Brilliantly woven carpets cushioned his steps as he passed tall vases—their cobalt blue glazes standing out against their white backgrounds. Gold oil lamps hung from high, arched ceilings, their flickering flames seeming to dance as they reflected from the polished floors and the chains themselves.

But that wasn't all the hallways held. Four Royal Guardsmen resplendent in baggy gold trousers and red vests snapped to attention outside the chamber as Samir turned the final corner. Conical steel helmets gleamed brightly above the red and gold silk bordering the rim. Spears stood straight at their shoulders, long points flashing above the red horsehair streamers and polished wood hafts. Yet they had no need to rely on those, nor on the broadswords hanging at their hips. The men of the royal guard were more than simple ornamentation in a place already filled with it. Each one had the moustaches of a Majaran warrior dangling below his chin, and each had earned them. Every guard ranked among the finest warriors in the kingdom—masters all, who could almost certainly earn the title Sòra. But dedication to their duties left no time for teaching.

He nodded to the men in passing, showing respect for masters of their arts. Their answering nods sent their moustaches swinging.

While their acknowledgment gave him a certain satisfaction, it also reminded him how far his own distinctive whiskers had to go. Though not as fine and sparse as the hair had been at first, time had done little for its length—barely allowing it to reach his chin.

Still, he couldn't afford to let his focus dwell on that when what lay ahead was far more important. Beyond the men and the painted archway they guarded, a wide ribbon of carpet stretched the length of the vast room. At its far end, a low platform piled with cushions held the reclining King.

His father.

An aura of authority surrounded Zahar. Although his own fit warrior's physique was somewhat past its prime, he was nonetheless a man to be reckoned with. A vest of green silk lay open across his chest, displaying muscle honed from a lifetime of effort—all emphasized by the trappings of power. Rings and chains set with large cut gems adorned the King's fingers, wrists and ankles. Yet these drew far less attention than what graced his brow. There, atop his slightly greying braid of hair lay a simple circlet of gold, set with four enormous rubies.

A canopy of blue silk hung above the King, fluttering softly as servants swung fans in broad arcs, stirring the humid air. Sweet-smelling tobacco smoke from a hookah, as well as the familiar odor of burning incense, rose in curls and spread through the room to wrap the Prince in their pleasant aromas. Thankfully, both odors would help to mask the musky smell of sweat from Samir's morning exercise.

The white and grey marble floor seemed to wink at Samir as he passed, the light of hundreds of dangling oil lamps catching the small gold tiles set into its surface. Everywhere golden accents sparkled and shone, adding to the splendor of the chamber.

A broad smile on his father's full lips greeted Samir as he stopped and bowed. "Oh King, live forever," he spoke the ritual greeting with a smile of his own, meaning it.

Zahar patted the plush cushions beside him as Samir rose, a clear invitation to join him. The young Prince complied, sitting beside his father and leaning lightly on one elbow.

"I'm sure the deep perspective of your twenty years must make it seem I'm nearly there," the King said with a chuckle, stroking his long moustache to mask an amused grin. "But none of us lives forever. Nor should we."

"Father..." Samir began to protest.

Zahar held up a hand, forestalling the rest of the comment. "I expect I have a few years left yet," he said with a wink. "I have a present for you." In his other hand, he held out a small box, its black lacquer finish deeply polished. On its lid a painted hummingbird hovered, wings beating in a furious blur as it stopped to drink from trumpet-shaped orange flowers.

Accepting the gift with thanks, Samir opened the box, its lid swinging easily on delicate brass hinges. Nestled inside amid red velvet padding lay a broad gold band set with a flat jade stone, perhaps two inches across. Lifting it gently out, Samir held it up to the light, already knowing what he would see. Carved into the jade, the masterwork of some unknown ancient artisan, a tiger's head roared threateningly in exquisite detail. Samir sat mesmerized by the narrow golden ornament resting in his palm. Once it adorned the Prince's upper arm, it would mark him for all to see as the King's heir.

Samir knew astonishment must have been plain on his face as his father laughed. "Surely this doesn't surprise you," he said.

Looking up at Zahar, Samir found pride and love in the dark brown eyes that met his own. For a moment, a slight shake of his head was all the Prince could manage.

Finally, after a short eternity, he found his voice. "I tried not to anticipate," he explained.

"Your attitude does you credit," the King said softly, "which is precisely what made you the obvious choice."

"Thank you, Father," Samir replied, emotion threatening to take his voice yet again. "I'll try to be worthy of it."

The King smiled indulgently, hand fluttering briefly as if to wave away any concern on his part. "You will be. You're a natural leader, and even Shimei speaks highly of you."

Both men knew that the old Sòra offered praise about as freely as a miser handed out coins. That simple statement from his father was perhaps the greatest compliment he could imagine. A sudden surge of pride flowed through Samir, suffusing his chest to near bursting with glowing warmth.

Zahar placed a gentle calloused hand on his son's. "It won't be official until tonight, of course. But I didn't want to wait. Happy birthday, Samir."

"Thank you, Father." Samir leaned over, kissing the King's cheek. With a quick grin, he added, "Live forever."

Now more than ever, the young Prince looked forward to his birthday feast tonight. Not only would he be served the stuffed pheasant and candied pears that were his favorites, he would also be given the greatest honor any man could hope for. He was about to be named heir to the Kingdom of Majar.

At the moment, however, he needed a bath. Then he would need to hurry to meet Gehazi for their hunt outside the city.

Jenaris once again resisted the urge to pace that had plagued him for the past several weeks. Such impatience was completely unlike him, and it had been decades since he had felt its like. In fact, a wizard's long life had no room for anything but a long view of things, which usually precluded any of the annoyance he now felt.

Slowly, Jenaris schooled himself to stillness and gazed out the bedroom window on the high foothills surrounding his home. In the distance, puffy white clouds obscured the permanent snowcaps of the rocky peaks. Spring in the shadow of the mountains soothed his agitation as the newly melted snows gave rise to the smell of rich, damp earth. Wild flowers had just begun to bloom, scattering reds, blues and yellows among the holly and fir that had been the only color amid the white of winter. Still, Jenaris could not entirely banish the urge to fidget and found himself combing bony fingers through his shoulder-length grey hair.

With a deep sigh, the Mage turned away, stout leather shoes scuffing against the floor's wooden planks. Jenaris had seen none of the movement he had been looking for. There had been so little game as to be almost nonexistent for months, but at least he had seen no sign of what had driven away the deer and rabbits that used to flourish here.

Unfortunately, Jenaris was facing additional trouble at the moment. For nearly a month, he'd tried repeatedly to make contact with Lorn, hoping for advice if not outright assistance. All to no avail. No attempt at scrying could raise even a glimmer, and no connection had yet been formed for a messenger to follow to his location.

In an almost desperate moment he had even tried the most esoteric bit of magic he knew, a Calling; a difficult ritual he didn't even come close to understanding. It was the rite Kirstea had used to "call" new apprentices and, according to her, it *seemed* to use desires in the back of one's mind to entice the *appropriate* person. He had half hoped it would find Lorn for him, but so far he hadn't felt an active response at all.

The Wizard knew he needed to do something soon. And, as much as he hated to admit it even to himself, the two problems seemed to have the same solution. He was going to have to leave what had been a sanctuary.

It brought an almost physical discomfort to even consider it. True, the little log cabin wasn't much—just a large room containing the living area and kitchen, and a smaller bedroom. Most of the living space, and even most of the furniture, was occupied by his extensive library. Yet, between the cedar shingles on the roof and the chinking, it was warm and dry. He had his cozy chair by the fire in which to study, and his own things around him. This had, until now, been a pleasant place to live and work, and he had grown more attached to it than he would have believed.

The very idea of leaving felt so wrong, going against everything inside him—to let anyone or anything chase him from his home. Of course, objectively he knew that wasn't the case. Although he wasn't the most powerful mage by any means, he could still keep himself and his home safe from almost any threat he could imagine. Jenaris wasn't being driven out, but he couldn't help feeling as if he were.

The simple fact was that his new neighbors, wherever they had come from, didn't believe in peace, and that meant the situation *must* be dealt with. For that, he would have to go and find Lorn or, barring that, sufficient help of another kind.

There were a few things he had to do first, though. Glancing at the ornately carved chest at the foot of his bed, he made a brief gesture with one finger, causing the lid to rise smoothly. Jenaris swiftly selected several pairs of good wool pants, much like the ones he was wearing, and tossed them casually onto his quilted bedspread. Thick socks and linen shirts followed, as well as a warm heavy coat he favored when hunting, its green color the perfect shade against the lush backdrop of the thickly forested hills.

It always amused him that people expected robes and a pointy hat when they met a wizard. On very rare occasions he might oblige, though he hadn't done so in decades. Chuckling softly to himself, he selected several undergarments and placed them on the bed with the rest.

From another chest Jenaris chose a few of the patterned blankets woven by the local clans. Finally his roomy saddlebags joined the items on the mattress. Aside from food for the journey, everything else he needed already waited by the front door.

It took only a few minutes to make up his pack and bedroll. It took far longer before the old Wizard could bring himself to pick them up and sling them over his shoulder. When he finally did, he had the sad feeling of having crossed an unseen line, as he had known it would. Some things simply had to be borne, however, and that was that.

Hopefully, there would be game to be had along the way, but under the circumstances, he knew better than to expect it. Once in the kitchen, he gathered a few crusty loaves, cheeses and smoked meats into a sack. Sadly, winter and the recent lack of anything to hunt had seriously depleted his larder, although with no deer or even bears to eat them, berries were plentiful. Surely he would need only enough food to reach the nearest town, and the melting snow would provide plenty of water.

It'll have to do, he told himself. *At least, the horse will have plenty of food.*

Jenaris had done all the research he could. His small square table presently held a good percentage of his extensive library—tome after massive tome—every one that held even the least scrap of information pertaining to the long, bloody fight that almost certainly lay ahead. Unfortunately, most told him virtually nothing. The teetering piles made him imagine the sturdy little table groaning under the weight. Still, he resisted the urge to use a spell to strengthen it. Either it would hold up under the strain or it wouldn't, which struck him as an appropriate metaphor for the current state of affairs in this part of the world.

The Wizard unconsciously caressed the cracked leather cover of one especially thick volume. A treatise on elemental power, it was a particular favorite he'd inherited from Kirstea, the one who had mentored both Lorn and himself, and an especially formidable sorceress until extreme age claimed her. Jenaris had no idea as to her precise age, though he assumed somewhere north of three hundred years, perhaps *far* north. Regardless, it had been much greater than his own one hundred thirteen. Kirstea had been gone nearly fifty years now, but she'd given him the skill and knowledge he'd come to rely on before she passed.

Well, he was in good health and had the strength needed to see his way through. He only wished he had Kirstea's wisdom to call on.

With a deep sigh of resignation Jenaris turned toward the door. Having already set wards, there was nothing left for him to do but saddle Keera and go.

A shadow of regret touched the Mage's blue eyes with an odd, wistful look as he laid his hand on the door latch. Catching himself, he immediately dismissed the feeling. He would miss his home, but only a weak man would be dissuaded by potential homesickness or discomfort, and he was *not* weak. Tripping the latch, he snatched up his sword belt and staff, then took the one step he knew would commit him fully and irrevocably to his chosen course.

The air outside was pleasant, cool rather than cold even this high in the hills. Trills and twitters of birdsong from all directions seemed somehow incongruous given the present threat, yet it also assured him there was nothing untoward in the immediate area. For that, at least, he was thankful.

Seeing his axe next to a pile of firewood yet to be split gave Jenaris a slight twinge of guilt. He didn't like to leave work undone—never had—and the axe had been one of the things which kept him reasonably fit. On reflection, though, he supposed he'd be getting plenty of exercise in the next few weeks. After all, he and the horse had a long walk ahead of them.

Marius ignored the mare's impatient snort as he sat on the hillside gazing down at the quiet village below. Besides the sound of the wind and the soft creak of saddle leather, which he had stopped registering some time ago, it was the first noise to reach him in the last five minutes.

From this vantage, the view was somewhat obscured by the new growth of spring leaves spreading their canopy over the deserted streets. He'd been to Laran many times before in his career, and it had always been quiet, but this time it was different—vastly different.

The skin at the corners of his mouth drew tight as he considered how to report this. After nearly four hours spent among the buildings of the town earlier in the day, Marius still had no real grasp of what *this* even was. Nothing in all his years as a soldier, an officer in the King's guard, had prepared him to ride in and find such an eerie sight.

His thick eyebrows drew down in displeasure. Today had given him none of the enjoyment he usually found on a good ride, none of the sense of rightness of having men at his back and a potential challenge ahead of him.

The urge to come this far north on his patrol had been a response to a long winter cooped up in the castle. Marius had felt the need to move, to breathe in the fresh air and see something besides stone walls. Now, though, he felt the need to ride back and give warning. The only problem was, he didn't have a clue what to warn anyone about.

They had ridden into Laran that morning simply to give the villagers a view of the King's men. The sight of four dozen light cavalry, helmets and breastplates shining in black enamel, pikes held high, was always a reassuring presence, letting people know all was right with the world. Marius' expectation had been that the men would water their horses, have a chance to eat and stretch their legs, and then head south again.

Plans change, I guess, he thought.

There had been a sense of wrongness even before the first houses came into view that morning. Perhaps it had been the lack of smoke from the forge or the chimneys, or the lack of livestock. Maybe something else had alerted him, but it was funny how the mind was sensitive to changes in everyday activities. Marius had immediately urged more speed from his mount, gauntleted hands tightening on the reins to keep from reaching for his sword. His men followed with barely a pause, a double column of cavalry, ranks tight, green and black banners streaming and snapping in the wind of their own passing as they hurried the last long mile through the forest along the packed dirt road.

Finally clearing the last of the elms and maples, they had seen...nothing. No movement, no people, no animals, and no explanation.

Many of the buildings stood entirely undisturbed. Tools lay on workbenches, a bit rusted but otherwise unremarkable. Projects sat unfinished—a half woven basket here, a piece of tack or wagon only partially repaired there. It was as if people had just chosen to abandon their everyday lives and walk away.

Still others among the shops and houses were scenes of bizarre devastation. Doors were barred and furniture piled as though to prevent entry, but always the act had been one of utter futility. Whomever, or whatever, these people had tried to keep out had torn through walls or removed entire roofs to get inside.

The entire company had scoured the area with the expertise of men who had seen their share of violence, but had uncovered nothing but more questions. It was extremely problematic that their best guess was that *whatever* had happened here was at least a month old. Rust and dust tended to accumulate at fairly consistent rates everywhere, after all. Within that month, however, there had been a late snow and several heavy showers.

Any tracks or traces of blood that had been exposed to the weather would have been washed away, and with no bodies to tell the tale, it would be impossible to put together a clear picture.

Certainly they knew that very few people had walked away or, more likely, tried to run. Signs of packing, hurried or otherwise, were few and far between. And a thorough search had revealed that most of the hidey-holes people kept—under loose floorboards and hollow spaces beneath hearthstones—still held what few coins and treasures these people had cached. Very few gave any sign of having been emptied. But the disturbing fact remained that, had they walked away, they would have arrived *somewhere* in the month they'd been gone, and someone would have known why as the news spread.

Marius' first reaction was to suspect a conflict with one of the barbarian tribes, but that idea was too fraught with holes to be worth considering. Although the village was reasonably close to Gotarra, the land here had never been part of any previous dispute, and this hadn't been the work of any raiding party. What's more, *no one* wanted to repeat the bloodshed of the territorial discord. To be honest, though, this just wasn't how they waged war—*ever*. Oh, they would fight if they felt threatened or exploited, he was sure, but only those who bore arms had anything to fear even then.

Marius' fingers drummed on the cool black steel of his helm which rested on the saddle in front of him. He tapped out no particular rhythm. It was merely a way to keep his hands occupied while he considered the situation. He knew, of course, that seeing their commander agitated would be bad for the men's morale, but here on the hilltop only Sergeant Elbrus and his horse would ever see it, and neither of them would say a word.

He patted his dun's neck affectionately. She had carried Marius along many miles of bad road in their time together, and she wouldn't balk even in the toughest battle. Hopefully, she wouldn't need to prove her steadfast nature again soon, but something had happened here, and what happened once could happen again.

This line of thought brought him back to the crux of his present concern. Marius had no doubts about the men whom he had trained, ridden with and fought beside. If these soldiers needed to face whatever had been responsible for this mystery, they would do so with courage and honor as they always did. But as certain as he was of that, he also knew that some of them must be harboring doubts—small, niggling fears that, if left to do their work could cripple confidence and ruin good men. It was, of course, only natural for soldiers to wonder how they would fare against an unknown enemy, especially one with such great destructive capability. But no matter how fierce a foe, surely it was something men had faced before, and if men had, then his could.

Well, Marius had to deal with the present threat to his men—their morale. *Fight the battle in front of you.* His mind echoed one of his father's favorite sayings. *Don't worry about what you can't fight.*

He straightened in his saddle and adjusted his black steel breastplate and the green wool of his uniform beneath it. Only when he was certain that he was squared away did he turn to the old sergeant waiting silently behind him.

"Elbrus." Marius' voice was crisp and sure.

"Yes, Captain?" his sergeant replied, suddenly sitting taller in the saddle himself. He would also know what the soldiers would be thinking and what it could do to their self-assurance. "Sound recall and set a camp for lunch in that clearing outside town." He paused briefly while he considered his next command. Elbrus simply waited, knowing his captain well. "Have the men check themselves and their mounts for ticks."

It was early in the year yet, but the men would need the routine to distract them right now. Somehow, normal work and training tended to calm a man.

"Immediately, sir." Elbrus knew as well as any veteran what to do for anxious troops. "Anything else, sir?"

"You'll know the ones who still need the right word whispered in their ear." Not only did Marius Braden have complete confidence in his men. He also had confidence in the ability of his sergeants to know their jobs. "Carry on."

"Sir!" Elbrus replied with a quick salute, steel gauntlet clanging on the hard cool steel of his armor. With that, he wheeled his mount and went to carry out his orders.

The sound of hooves faded swiftly, leaving Marius alone on the hill overlooking the town. He toyed briefly with the idea of sending some of his scouts to find this unknown enemy or leaving half his troop to continue the patrol. That, though, was just the part of him that wanted to *do* something—to find a way to act rather than merely waiting to react. But it would be the height of foolishness to divide his forces when dealing with an unidentified, and apparently powerful, foe.

Besides, as much as he would love to discover the truth about what was behind the complete disappearance of nearly three hundred souls, he needed to at least report the little he did know. It would be up to King Carlon to decide what action, if any, to take.

In the distance, the bugler sounded recall. In a few minutes, Marius would ride calmly into the camp. As important as it was for the citizens of Acedia to see the King's guard and be reassured, the soldiers themselves needed to see their commander unworried and in control. After all, if the old man wasn't worried, then why should they be?

They would ride back and make a report. If they pushed, they could reach Varella in under two weeks. The men would be tired, but that would be good. Fatigue would serve to distract them in the same way as routine training. Marius just hoped that when they arrived he would have something worthwhile to suggest to the King.

With a grunt, the Captain reined his horse around and rode toward the camp.

Chapter 1

The Long Road

Strands from the flowing black mane whipped at Samir's fingers, streaming from the gracefully arched neck of the gelding as it ran, galloping north across the grassy plains of Majar. Beside the horse, Tirza struggled mightily to keep up the pace set by her master, the coursing hound's long, slender legs churning at desperate speed. Samir knew the animals couldn't maintain this brutal pace for long. Already the packhorse pulled at the lead rope, telling him that he would need to rein in far sooner than he would like. Otherwise, he could injure the horses or the dog, none of which he was willing to part with. Right now, though, Samir needed to put as much distance between himself and Gehazi as possible.

Tears streamed unabashedly from the corners of his deep brown eyes, blown in ragged lines back across his cheeks by the wind of his passage. Samir wanted to scream, to howl and rage against fortune as he felt his heart breaking in his chest. More than anything else, he wanted to turn and race back to the palace as fast as the flagging horse could go, in order to keep his whole world from crashing down around him. But it was already too late for that. It had been too late before he had ever discovered the betrayal that now seared him to the depths of his soul.

Samir felt weak for doing nothing, for running away. It went against every fiber of his being to do anything other than face a crisis on his feet, with courage. To stand and fight instead of running, though, would lose him every possible advantage, the edge he knew that he would need when he *did* return. Sometimes withdrawal for a time was the only prudent course of action.

Someday, hopefully soon, Samir would come back and see things put right. He was owed a blood debt—a big one—and eventually he would collect on it at a time and place of his own choosing. That resolution, and that alone, now kept him moving north away from his home.

Samir had plainly sensed that something was troubling Gehazi deeply as they'd made their way out of the city that morning. The hound trotted happily along behind the horses as they wound haltingly through the same crowded streets that normally evoked an unquenchable excitement in his outgoing friend—a man who even at his young age had lines etched at the corners of his eyes from his irrepressible good humor. At any other time, Samir would practically have to drag his companion away from the stalls of the various food sellers. The man came alive in the presence of the loud flush-faced hawkers with their unending patter, the shoving crowds bargaining for goods and the amazing assortment of foods. The incorrigible Gehazi seemed almost inexorably drawn to the kebabs, confections, meat pies and anything else that captured his attention—the whole time keeping up an unstoppable torrent of jokes, quips and comments about any pretty young woman— and some not so young—who passed nearby.

Today, however, something bleak had evidently gripped his companion. Gehazi had shown none of his typical animation as they rode through the market on the way to the plains. Having known the man since early childhood, Samir couldn't help but sense such an uncharacteristic mood. His friend had sullenly ridden past rows of canopied booths laid out with all manner of wares, peddlers bearing steaming trays of delectable goodies and blankets strewn with assorted bangles. All efforts to draw Gehazi out had failed to produce the typical joking banter that overrode even the shouting and jostling masses of the market. The best the Prince had managed to extract from Gehazi after all his work was a wan smile and a slightly wistful look.

Giving up was not an option, however, and Samir had decided that there would be plenty of time to find answers as afternoon wore on. After all, Gehazi had always done his best to lift Samir's spirits when he was down. That loyalty and affection was a large part of what had made them such fast friends over the years. How could he do any less for his best friend now?

As accustomed as Samir was to life inside the palace, it was always a pleasure to get out onto the plains below the city of Toskar and feel the wind as it sent ripples across the tassels of the long grass waving against the distant backdrop of hazy mountains. Yet, despite the beauty of the day, nothing seemed to make a dent in Gehazi's misery. If anything, it had gotten worse. The man merely withdrew further and further into himself as Samir tried harder to reach him.

Even Tirza had caught the mood and tried to help as they set the horses to graze. The energetic hound nipped playfully at Gehazi's fingers and continually pushed her nose under his hand to elicit at least a quick pat.

For a time, she had managed to evoke a few small smiles as she kept herself entertained. Her short white coat flashed through the long green grass as she chased hares around men and horses with the speed and maneuverability she was built for. Finally, however, even Tirza had given up her attempts to engage the attention of the men. She simply lay watching them, her long lean body stretched out, belly down, head on paws.

Seated on a large rock that had worked its way up through the soil, Samir pulled a foot up to casually lean an elbow on his knee. He had completely given up the idea of doing any hunting some time earlier as he watched Gehazi pacing, sandals slapping at his heels, raising puffs of dust with each step. His friend had obviously been struggling to say something, having stopped and restarted his slow circuit several times already.

Inevitably, his growing impatience got the better of compassion. Samir had waited long enough, he finally decided, for the other man to take the initiative.

"Will you *stop* that and just talk to me?" Samir growled.

Gehazi looked stricken, a plaintive look in his eyes as his head snapped up. Tirza's head rose just as swiftly, ears perked, looking warily for some sudden threat.

"I can't," Gehazi mumbled, plainly avoiding his eyes.

It took a few moments for Samir to process what he'd heard, though understanding still eluded him. "Of course you can. Most days I can't shut you up," he quipped, trying to lighten his friend's mood.

A weak smile briefly managed to take hold, but was gone almost as swiftly. Gehazi just shook his head, sending his long tail of hair swinging and resumed his pacing.

Samir rose, quickly crossing the distance to his horse as an idea seized him. Reaching into his saddlebag, his hand found what it sought by size and shape. Grinning with excitement, he drew out the lacquer box he'd received from his father only that morning.

"You have *got* to see my birthday present," he said, barely managing to contain his eagerness as he turned.

Gehazi had stopped cold, his intent gaze flitting occasionally to the box as if keeping track of a dangerous serpent.

Alarmed, Samir started toward his friend and was surprised when the other man took a single hesitant step backward as if preparing to flee. The Prince halted, confusion fighting with hurt and concern inside him.

"*Damn it,* Gehazi!" he erupted. "What in the hell is going on?" Shimei would never have approved of the loss of control, but all else had failed.

Gehazi drew a deep breath as if to respond, but only mumbled something unintelligible. His head hung as though in defeat.

As it must, compassion finally won out in Samir's internal battle, and he stepped over to lay a comforting hand on his companion's shoulder. Looking down at the slightly shorter man, he sought some clue that would make all of this suddenly clear.

"I won't order you. You know that," he assured. "But I want to know what's bothering you."

"I just wanted one more day." The whispered reply was almost too quiet to hear. "Just one more good day."

Samir waited patiently for more, some clarification. Nothing else came.

Remembering the box in his hand, he flipped back the lid with his thumb and removed its contents. The finger-thick gold band felt cool in the palm of his hand, clinking slightly against his signet ring.

"Look at this." The gold shone brilliantly in the sunlight as he held it up for his friend to see. Samir resisted the urge to slide it onto his arm. "My father gave it to me this morning."

The response he got was the last thing he would ever have expected. Gehazi laughed—a long mournful laugh as if the universe had played some great cosmic joke that only he saw. Tirza chose that moment to pad over, nuzzling Gehazi's hand to offer comfort.

"I'm sorry, Highness," he sobbed. With a muted thud, Gehazi sank to his knees, hand resting on the dog's head, gaze fixed on the ground at Samir's feet. "I'm so sorry."

In all the years they had known each other, his friend had never used formality outside of the King's court. "What are you talking about? If this is about my father naming me heir...." He let the sentence trail off, still wanting answers, but not knowing the right questions to ask.

"It's my sister," Gehazi replied, apparently resigned to talking, but not quite able to gather the courage.

Relief flooded through Samir, as if a giant fist had relaxed its grip on his chest. If that was all it was, some crisis with a teenage girl, then it could be dealt with. After all, she wasn't the type to get into any real trouble. He let out a breath he had been unaware of even holding.

"Listen, Gehazi, if Jhen needs *anything* in my power to grant, you can count on me. You know that."

"*No.*" Gehazi's sudden outburst brought a yelp from Tirza as she jerked away from the hand tightly gripping her fur. The hound eyed him suspiciously for a long moment before moving well away to lie once again in the grass. All energy drained with the unaccountable flash of anger, the man let his hands drop limply to his sides. When he continued, it was in a croaking, tearful voice. "They have her," he finally managed.

"What?" Anger surged in Samir. That someone would dare to do such a thing to any friend of his outraged him. "*Who* has her?" he asked with a tone like cold hard steel.

"You don't understand." Gehazi finally met his eyes, then quickly looked away again.

"I'm still waiting for you to explain it to me," the Prince growled, anger coursing through him. "Who has Jhen?"

"Kemal," Gehazi sobbed. "He'll kill her if I don't help him." Bowed in defeat and shame, he waited, although whether for question or accusation Samir couldn't tell.

Confused, he asked the first thing to occur to him. "Why?"

As meager as the question was, it was enough. Finally the flood gates opened, and what poured out made Samir feel as though he were drowning.

The young warrior felt confusion rapidly give way to anger as Gehazi explained in ugly detail the plans Samir's half-brother had laid. Attempts to shift his friend's allegiance had failed, but had been so subtly done that there could be no accusation of any specific threat. Eventually, however, Kemal had simply gone to the expedient of using Jhen as leverage. Gehazi had tried to bargain, of course, had promised anything and everything if only his sister were released unharmed. In the end, though, there had been little choice but to agree or lose the only family he had.

Deep in Samir's belly anger flared to white-hot fires of rage as Gehazi continued to talk.

Kemal wanted Samir dead, and he wasn't willing to try to do it himself. Naturally, he insisted on seeing proof of his brother's death, but Gehazi had a plan of his own to cover that.

Reaching inside the loose front of his shirt, Gehazi removed a wadded rag and unrolled it to reveal a freshly severed finger. Thieves' hands were routinely forfeited as punishment for their crimes. But he had been lucky, he said, to find a match in complexion and size that morning. All they would have to do, Gehazi insisted, was to place Samir's ring on the rather macabre trophy and the Prince would be free to plan his revenge and await the opportune moment.

Samir had very nearly killed the man then, right where he knelt. Yet the same training that would have easily enabled him to do so, had also allowed him to control his passions. With incredible difficulty, he had taken hold of himself, coldly channeling his fury into deliberate, focused purpose. Without the Sòra's training, Samir would simply have given in to rage and unleashed such terrible violence, he might have taken dozens with him. The fact remained, however, that he would certainly have died as well before he reached Kemal. Instead, he could now act carefully and plan how he would bring to justice anyone who had moved against him or his family.

Samir stood, outwardly calm, as Gehazi tried to finish his tale. The Prince heard none of it as his mind turned furiously, working to grasp the implications of what he had heard.

"What about my father?" Samir's voice snapped like a whip, cutting past the other man's frantic attempts to be heard, which gained intensity and volume by the word.

Eyes squeezed tightly shut, Gehazi swallowed hard, fearing the wrath that must surely be coming. That was all the answer Samir needed.

Kemal hadn't wanted his death to look like an accident, which would have been both simple and effective. An arrow in the back while hunting could easily have caught the Prince off-guard, negating any hope of self-defense. Such a "tragedy" would immediately have cleared the way for his brother to become the heir. The question was why his death wasn't meant to look accidental.

The answer was disturbingly obvious. Kemal had no interest in becoming the heir. He intended to become King—*now*. After all, Zahar had only inherited the crown from his father a little over five years earlier and, in his mid-forties, was still relatively young. Evidently, waiting twenty or thirty years for their father to die chafed Kemal as badly as the idea of Samir becoming King. The only possible reason his death didn't need to appear accidental was that he was not the only intended victim. Kemal was going to kill the King as well!

Samir spun, racing for his horse, needing speed to prevent his father's murder. But somehow desperation had given Gehazi wings. Before Samir had taken two steps, a hand clasped the flapping silk of his pant leg jerking him to a stop.

"No," Gehazi pleaded. "You can't."

Tirza growled, evidently catching Samir's mood as he turned to glare at the offending hand. Hands full, his free foot snapped up to clip the other man's temple with his heel.

"You dare?" Samir shook with pent up anger, longing to strike the craven traitor down. "After all you've done, you dare to lay hands on me?"

He had treated this man like a brother. The King himself had treated him like a *son*. He could have had anything—wealth, authority. Zahar would have put it in his hands gladly.

Although the Prince's blow had clearly stunned him, somehow Gehazi refused to loosen his grip. "You're too late," he cried, tears running freely. "He's already *dead*."

Samir's mind spun dizzily, straining to make sense of what he'd just heard.

Of course he's not dead, he latched onto the thought, clinging to it as if to a lifeline. *He's fine. Anyone who thinks Zahar is defenseless will soon discover differently.* A part of him knew it wasn't that simple, yet he could not accept any other possibility.

Tirza's long wet tongue on his face brought Samir to the awareness that he was somehow, unaccountably, sitting on the ground. The hound's concern was evident as she practically climbed into his lap to offer comfort.

Gehazi was still talking, jabbering away in hopes of making the Prince see reason. His words finally began to seep through as the fog numbing Samir's mind slowly began to dissipate. "...poison," the man insisted, "the same thing I was supposed to give you."

As grateful as he was for Tirza's affection and loyalty, he had no time to indulge her just now. Gently pushing her away, Samir climbed to his feet not even bothering to dust himself off as he forced his mind to review all that he'd heard.

Gehazi's head hung as he wept, kneeling in the grass as he waited for the young Prince to either speak or act. The tension in him was palpable as Samir stood over the man who had been his best friend.

"You know I should kill you," he said coldly, glaring down at the loathsome thing before him. "Of course, Kemal will almost certainly do that for me."

Gehazi didn't even flinch. "I know," he replied. "I don't care about that, as long as Jhen is safe."

Almost Samir could manage to find understanding. Their mother had died giving birth to Jhen, and Gehazi had raised his sister since the death of their father, a highly respected court minister. His sister had been the center of Gehazi's universe for the past three years. It had always been obvious that he would have given his life for hers, just as until only minutes ago Samir would have given his own life for Gehazi's without a second's thought or hesitation. In fact, that selfless dedication had been much of the reason the King had embraced the youth—encouraging his friendship with Samir and granting him a position in the palace that allowed him time for Jhen.

Still, even though Gehazi's motivation was clear enough, Samir could come nowhere *close* to accepting his actions. It was noble, even admirable, to trade one's life for another, but to trade someone else's life—the *King's* life—was the worst sort of cowardice. A warrior like Zahar should have been given the chance to stand and battle for his own life, to determine his fate without excuses. Gehazi had stolen that opportunity from him, and from Samir as well.

The look Samir directed at the kneeling man should have burned him to ash. In that moment, however, the Prince actually did *see* the other man, taking in the cleanly shaven face and registering the difference for the first time.

For most of the time they had known one another, they had both been as smooth cheeked as when they had met as boys. In fact, it had only been within the past few years that shaving had become possible, much less a necessity. So, while he had always longed for the ability to grow the moustaches that would mark him as the Majaran warrior he had trained his entire life to become, he'd only recently been able to grow them. Samir had never truly grasped the fact that Gehazi had begun to shave as well, and that his lack of the drooping whiskers was by choice. The distinguishing symbol of prowess in his people's fighting arts would never adorn the other man's face, because the urge to become a warrior was not in his heart. As alien as it was to Samir, Gehazi had absolutely no desire to be a warrior, and that meant his former companion had a vastly different perspective on life.

It more than disturbed him. It sickened him the way Gehazi had chosen to sacrifice one he claimed to love, even to save one he loved more. Something else bothered Samir even more deeply, however.

Poison.

It was a coward's way of facing any enemy, much less a warrior of his father's ability. Samir would certainly have thought better of his half-brother than to use such a gutless and pathetic method. Then again, he realized he had seen no indication that Kemal was so lacking in even the most basic character as to plot the murders of his own father and brother—and who could say whether the man had chosen to stop there. The facade of natural charm that had hidden Kemal's machinations had apparently been a very effective screen. As much as

Samir hated to admit it, evidently even the King had been completely fooled. And now it was to late.

Too late. The words slammed home, becoming real in a way they hadn't until that moment. The King—his father—was dead, and he was very much alone against his enemies. Certainly there would be those, like Sòra Shimei, who would throw their support behind him immediately. Yet, aside from the old master, he had no idea whom he could trust. Indeed, many would support Kemal simply because he wore the crown.

At last, Samir began to grasp the awful scope of his situation. Kemal would have sweated over the details of this coup, probably for years. Failure to examine every conceivable pitfall along the way would have brought a swift end to his hopes on either the headsman's axe or the point of a spear. Surely Kemal's reason for sending Gehazi, aside from the perverse pleasure of causing the betrayal, had been to keep from losing a close ally to the very real possibility of failure. Doubtless, multiple safeguards had been devised against this eventuality, and it was likely that Kemal even *expected* Gehazi to betray him, sending Samir charging into a trap.

That arrow in the back was clearly still out there, waiting for Samir to return and settle accounts with the usurper.

Obviously, Samir couldn't merely wait a few days, expecting an opportunity to collect on the blood debt that he was owed. It would more likely take months, at least, before Kemal accepted that Samir wouldn't suddenly appear with his heart set on vengeance.

No, Samir would not—could not—waste his one chance on empty bravado or senseless heroics. Even if it took every ounce of self-discipline he could muster, he would have to bide his time and make preparations of his own. Facing his brother and bringing him to justice would require his complete patience as well as his skill.

For his father's sake, and for the sake of Majar, he could afford nothing less.

The resolve brought Samir, if not a sense of peace, then at least an acceptance of the way things were and how they must be done. His Sòra had often insisted that stillness was every bit as important to a warrior as any other weapon he might master. Until just now, Samir had not fully appreciated that fact, his youthful exuberance leading him to think only in terms of action.

Using techniques Shimei had taught him despite his resistance, he schooled his mind and body to a state of calm relaxation. It was time he learned to value inaction.

Scooping the lacquer box from the ground where it had fallen from his grip in his earlier emotional state, Samir opened the lid and nestled the heavy golden armband into its padded velvet lining. With the lid once again closed, he tucked it behind the sash at his waist, making for a snug fit but still allowing for easy movement.

Slowly and deliberately, Samir slid the signet ring from his finger. Sunlight glittered from the thick gold band as he gazed on it one final time, longing to return it to its proper place. The light green jade of its setting, carved with an egret taking flight had always pleased him, but now a sense of determination swelled as he held it before his eyes. One day he would reclaim what was his by right, of that he was certain. For now, though, what must be must be.

With only a brief twinge of regret, he tossed the ring to Gehazi.

"Thank you, Samir," the other man said, obviously relieved as he began to rise.

"You will address me as 'Highness'," the Prince announced, smooth as silk yet hard as steel.

Gehazi froze, halfway to his feet, as the sharp reminder of his sudden change in position made his cheeks redden to a deep crimson. There was no denying that his fortunes had fallen dramatically. Very slowly, he sank to his knees once again, as was proper for a man without status in the presence of royalty.

A look of disgust flitted briefly across Samir's features as he watched Gehazi slide his ring onto the severed finger. He would *definitely* make Kemal pay for this offense, and pay dearly.

Thoroughly sickened by Gehazi's presence, Samir turned smoothly away and walked a short distance, hands clasped in the small of his back. In the distance, the city of Toskar tugged at his heart, her magnificent walls of fitted limestone shining brilliantly in the sunlight. Even the poorer quarters outside the city gates did nothing to detract from the beauty of his home. From here, the Prince could just see the tops of the palace's needle-like spires. He drank in the sight of it all, not knowing when he would be able to return, only that he must.

Seeking some activity to involve herself in, Tirza padded quietly to his side. Samir knew what she wanted, but had too much to consider at the moment to take the time. Hoping to distract the hound, he glanced around for only a moment before realizing the futility of looking for a stick where no trees grew.

"Gehazi," he said without turning, "throw your sandal."

"What?" the other man replied before catching himself, then added hesitantly, "Highness."

"She's bored, Gehazi. Play with her." His tone made it perfectly clear that it was not a request. Without further comment, Gehazi complied. Samir heard a soft thud in the distance, and Tirza tore off in the direction of the sound at breakneck speed.

Satisfied that he could think in peace, the young Prince stopped and looked out at the scenery before him. Far to the south and east, the mountains stood like tall icy sentinels, a hazy blue above the misty jungle that was just visible at a distance. Samir had to admit that in most respects it was a gorgeous day.

Once again, he heard the soft landing of the sandal among the grasses, to the delight of the hound.

Samir loved Majar, unable to imagine that a more beautiful place could even exist anywhere in the world. More than that, he bore a responsibility for his people and their welfare that he was loath to just walk away from. The very thought of leaving them in the hands of a patricidal usurper sent cold chills down his spine, but there was nothing he could do at the moment.

Strangely enough, his family gave him the least concern. As much as he loved them, he had to assume that whoever survived the day was safe enough. After all, his sisters Vesina and Benira would be valuable, if only for their potential in securing alliances when they reached marriageable age. At only twelve, his younger brother Hesed should pose no immediate threat to Kemal—although Samir had no way of knowing exactly how small a threat his half-brother might consider unreasonable. But it was his mother he really wondered about, being quite capable of living through the day only to force Kemal to reconsider his mercy later.

Grudgingly, he admitted that the best thing he could do for all concerned would be to leave. He would need to bide his time someplace where he could practice, plan his return and hopefully find whatever help he might decide he needed. Aside from the very lucrative trade between Majar and the lands north of the Bharkur Sea, there was so little diplomatic contact that he was unlikely to be recognized and betrayed to his brother.

Samir waited until he heard Tirza dashing off again in search of the sandal before he spoke. When he did, he was unable to entirely banish a touch of bitterness.

"I assume the packhorse carries the supplies for my exile."

"Yes, Highness." This time Gehazi remembered to add the proper title when addressing the Prince.

Samir nodded. "I will make you this promise, for the sake of the love I once had for you." He paused, glad of the fact that his back was turned, leaving the other man unable to see the tear he steadfastly refused to wipe away. "When I return, I'll look after Jhen. She will want for nothing."

"Thank you, Highness." There was a definite quiver in Gehazi's voice, though whether from suppressed tears or the stress of the day taking its toll, Samir had no idea.

A part of him resented making that promise, as though he were somehow rewarding Gehazi's betrayal. After all, Jhen's welfare had been his primary motivation and the lever Kemal had used against him. But Samir knew that, in all fairness, he couldn't allow her to suffer on that account. She was every bit as much a victim as Samir and his father had been—although it galled him to think of himself as such—and he would do all he could to care for her when the time came. Besides, he considered her a friend in her own right.

Without another word, Samir took up the long lead rope trailing from the bridle of the packhorse, the chestnut mare's head coming up as if to rebuke him for interrupting her grazing. Mounting his own black gelding, he took up the reins and whistled for Tirza. The horse accelerated quickly to a canter, moving in the direction of the river and the highway that would take them north to the coast. Inside, a part of Samir desperately wanted to turn the horses around, to go home to Toskar where he belonged.

He had to get away, he knew, to escape from the overwhelming temptation to stay and fight. He had to go—*fast*. Without conscious thought, he kicked the gelding, driving it recklessly to a gallop. The lead rope jerked in his grip, skinning the palm of his hand as it pulled tight, but the packhorse followed with barely a pause.

Barking sharply to remind him of her presence, Tirza launched herself after him, refusing to be left behind.

They charged across the plains for what seemed an eternity, but Samir knew it was far too brief a time. Finally, his exhausted mount threatening to stumble, he drew rein, wiping at his tears in a way that only smeared the dust on his cheeks.

The gelding gasped for breath, flecks of white foam trailing from the corners of his mouth across his sleek coat. A quick look at the packhorse confirmed that she too had gone as far as she would for now.

A corner of the lacquer box dug hard into his belly as he dismounted, but Samir was too tired to notice or care. Quickly, more from habit than anything else, he loosened the saddle girth to let his mount breathe deeply, then moved to do the same for the mare.

Managing only a few short steps, he dropped bonelessly to the ground, weary to his soul. Apparently deciding he had chosen a good place to rest, Tirza flopped down beside him, laying her head in his lap as she panted heavily to cool herself.

"We have a long road ahead of us, girl." He stroked her soft white coat, taking comfort in her presence.

His only answer was the slight thump of her tail tiredly slapping the ground.

Chapter 2

The Clatter of Hoofbeats

Sitting his horse patiently just inside the castle gate, Marius Braden watched as the double file of soldiers followed Elbrus toward the barracks for a well-deserved rest. He had pushed the mounts hard, and the men even harder, to reach Varella in under two weeks, but it had been necessary. Thankfully, the men's fatigue had been something of a blessing, keeping fear and wild speculation from taking root among them. Yet, now that they had reached the city, even the deft handling by his best sergeants wouldn't keep rumor from spreading like wildfire in dry grass.

The sound of steel-shod hooves rang from the cobbles of the courtyard and echoed from the surrounding walls as the last of the horses trotted past him. But his attention was fixed on the bustling town below him, gaze sweeping across the slate roofs still damp with the morning's dew. The familiar sounds of commerce vied with the clatter of cartwheels on paving stones as several thousand of Acedia's citizens went about their lives, a bit crowded but congenial, unaware of any cause for concern.

In just a few short hours, Marius knew, an already disturbing truth would inevitably be twisted and embellished until it described a scene of impending doom. He hated the way rumor took wing under normal conditions. This one, however, would grow until it shattered the peace these people took for granted.

Try as they might to contain it, it would happen. After all, soldiers talked. The only way to stop them was to leave the men well outside of the city, and that would have destroyed morale. He could only count on the faith of these people in the guardsmen and their King to protect them.

Marius dismissed such future worries with a brisk shake of his head, having much more pressing problems. With a light touch of his knee, he spun his mount toward the large main doors and broke into a canter. The weathered expanse of oak grew in his vision far more quickly than he wished, but he had never been one to shirk duties merely because they were unpleasant.

Before the mare had even come to a stop, Braden dismounted, leaving grooms hurrying to take hold of the dun's reins and lead her away. In a way, he envied the horse, knowing she would be stabled, rubbed down and fed before he had even reached his destination deep inside the massive stone fortress.

Pulling off his gauntlets as he climbed the wide granite steps, he threw them inside his polished steel helm and handed them to a waiting page as he stepped into the dimly lit entry hall. The large chamber echoed softly with the fall of his boot heels on stone as he walked, trusting his eyes to adjust to the sudden change in light. Still, there wasn't much to see.

Being the oldest part of the castle, the stone here was well worn and poorly worked, yet in his opinion, this gave it a character that was lacking in other parts. In fact, attempts to dress it up with newer, more finely made furniture and polished brass sconces in place of the wrought iron only emphasized the disparity in craftsmanship. But Marius was thankful that whichever of the King's predecessors had built the earliest additions had chosen to leave the original keep and its tower in place.

Built only about seventy-five years ago, the newer corridors of the castle stood in stark contrast to those he had just passed through. The polished marble floors and dark wood paneling were more like those one would expect to find in a citadel. He had to admit that it was tastefully done, though, and would go much farther in impressing visiting dignitaries. Without a doubt, it bespoke his country's burgeoning wealth under the leadership of the King and his forebears.

He followed the hallways with a sure stride, headed directly toward King Carlon's private dining room, where he would be sure to appear soon if he was not already sitting down to eat with his family. Marius hated to drag him away from his wife and children, especially for ill news, but this wouldn't wait.

The two guards flanking the carved and gilded dining room doors were a clear indication of the King's presence, although they spoke more of a desire for privacy than a need for protection. Carlon was too well-loved a ruler to have any reason to fear for his safety—particularly here in his own home. The King was also a man who valued his time with his family, however, and the Captain deeply regretted the need to interrupt. He only hoped his majesty had already eaten enough to tide him over until evening—assuming he managed to have any appetite even then.

The men on duty snapped to attention as their commanding officer approached, their leather boot soles slapping the floor and the long polished staves of their halberds standing straight and proud against their shoulders. More from habit than any need, Marius ran a practiced eye over both men from head to toe. The black leather of boots and sword belts shone with the effort of hard rubbed polish, well creased trousers of black wool tucked neatly into boot tops, and green coats draped across fit torsos, brass buttons gleaming. Not a loose thread or scuff mark caught his notice, as was only appropriate for men on duty before the King.

His soft rap on the door was for courtesy rather than permission. Anyone important enough to come this close without challenge would, of course, be granted entrance on the assumption that the circumstance warranted the disturbance. Still, it was assumed that any conversations within were of a private nature, for the King's ears only.

An answering "Come" sounded from within, the King's voice hardly muffled by the door.

The thick wood swung smoothly open on well-oiled hinges as Marius tripped the latch, revealing that the royal family was indeed dining together as he had expected. Stiffly formal, he bowed first to the King, then to the Queen and finally to the Prince and Princess.

"Majesty," he said. "Your Grace. Highnesses."

"Marius." King Carlon waved him in with a broad wel-coming smile on his well-lined face.

A handsome man with little grey in his curly rust-colored hair and neatly trimmed beard, the King was an expert at putting people at ease—a definite key to his popularity. All that marred the image of jovial humor was an unfortunately prominent bump on his long nose, giving him the appearance of a street brawler.

"Majesty, may I speak with you in private?" the Captain asked plainly, hoping to avoid getting caught up in amenities.

"Yes," Carlon replied, a mild look of concern in his blue eyes. "Of course, Marius."

"Oh, nonsense," Queen Larissa said dismissively. "Surely whatever it is will wait until we've eaten. Will you join us, Captain Braden?"

While phrased as a question, this last was plainly not a request, no matter how friendly and gracious the tone. Of course, the smile accentuating the Queen's mature beauty was genuine, but it was evident that she was less than pleased that her husband was being asked to skip his lunch.

"No, love." Carlon's gentle but firm response was spoken with obvious reluctance. Evidently his majesty had only just sat down to eat, and he knew he would go hungry for a while yet. "This must be important or the Captain would be with his own family now."

Although it was certainly not intentional on the King's part, the statement brought a twinge of guilt—not merely for disturbing a family in a private moment, but also for the delay in greeting his own.

With a deep sigh, Carlon pushed his chair back from the table, shoved a large onion roll into the pocket of his coat and exited through the still open door. Waving at the guardsmen as a signal to remain at their posts, he set off at a brisk pace.

Marius followed the King through a quick succession of hallways, careful to maintain a single pace between himself and his sovereign. Though noticeably shorter, Carlon's stocky build was every bit as broad across the chest and shoulder as the Captain's. As a lifelong soldier, Marius understood the difficulty of remaining fit now that he had passed forty. He couldn't help but be impressed that at fifty King Carlon made the time to keep in fighting trim despite a schedule at least as busy as any subordinate's.

The page on duty outside the King's study leapt to his feet as they rounded the final corner, dropping his book in his haste to open the door. Marius scowled slightly at the young man as he passed, causing the page to blanch. Reading in one's free time he could appreciate—careless treatment of books he could not.

Inside, the Captain stood between a pair of comfortable chairs in front of the King's mahogany desk which, though plain, was impressive due to its highly polished finish and massive size. Marius had been invited here many times before, had played chess with the King at the small table perched below the window. Still, he had always admired the sheer number of volumes in the library lining the many bookshelves around the room. Having read his own collection as well as the more interesting selections in the castle's library, he had always wanted to examine these. Instead, he had to settle for a glance at the titles unless someday invited to peruse them.

The King waved to a sideboard as he sat, indicating the waiting crystal decanters of wine and brandy. "Pour for us and take a seat, Marius."

Quickly selecting two shallow glasses, the Captain unstoppered the brandy and tipped a generous stream of the amber liquid into each. In his peripheral vision, he could just see the King raise an eyebrow at the choice of drink.

"That bad?" Carlon asked.

"I'm afraid so, Sire." Handing a glass to the King, the Captain took a seat and waited for the invitation to speak freely. It didn't take long.

"You may as well go ahead," Carlon told him, taking the roll from his pocket and placing it on the desk in front of him.

Marius would have preferred to stand, but it was the King's preference, not his own, that mattered. Instead, he leaned forward in his seat as he sipped his brandy.

"I'm sorry, Sire, but there's no other way to say this." Only the barest pause marked any hesitation as the soldier drew a deep breath. "Laran is gone."

The King's eyes widened in alarm as he looked to a spot on the wall behind Braden's head. There was no question in the soldier's mind what drew his interest.

Directly above the fireplace hung a detailed map of Acedia, where a small dot near the foot of the Carnellan Mountains marked what had once been a small, pleasant village.

Carlon's eyes narrowed dangerously as they once again met Marius' own. "Gotarrans?"

"No, Sire." The Captain shook his head before quickly amending his response. "At least, I don't think so. Too many things just don't add up."

"Tell me what you know. And leave off the 'Sire,' Marius. It's just us here." Elbows propped on the desk and fingers steepled, King Carlon settled in to listen.

Marius obliged, delivering a report he knew that he would have had a *very* hard time accepting. The King didn't say a word, allowing him to speak without interruption, yet the Captain could gauge the man's reaction easily enough by the tension in his shoulders and the set of his jaw. When he finished, silence stretched for several minutes as he watched Carlon, deep in thought, absently roll the now empty glass between his palms.

"What the hell could've done that?" the King said quietly, obviously speaking to himself. He was also plainly disconcerted.

Marius cleared his throat discreetly, drawing the King's immediate attention and a nod to speak his mind.

"You know how badly I hate to speculate, but in this case, I literally can't." The Captain paused, well aware that frustration was creeping into his tone, but unable to banish it entirely. He'd had nearly two weeks to consider this question—had thought of little else, in fact—and he had no better answer now than when he'd started. "Animals just don't act like this, and neither do any people I've ever heard of. Gerrit's people are hard enemies, but they're honorable. Besides, they leave graves, not mysteries." At a loss, he simply shrugged to demonstrate the lack of any further conclusions.

Carlon didn't consider long. "How fast can you get back there?"

"Me personally," he asked, "or enough men to make a difference?"

"Both, I suppose," the King allowed, sounding less than pleased.

Marius had known the King, and worked closely with him, for too many years not to recognize that he had something else on his mind. Well, whatever it was, if it had any bearing in the question at hand, he would have been informed.

"The men, or most of them, I can dispatch today," he replied easily, having anticipated the need to reassign troops. "If I may suggest, a company each in Milar, Parlen and Elhanan with regular patrols. Another company can sweep the area near Laran and see if they turn up any answers."

"And you?" the King asked.

"I can be ready to ride tomorrow with the men investigating Laran," he said after some consideration. "I *could* go now, Majesty, but my horse needs rest and, begging your pardon, I wouldn't feel good about taking an unfamiliar mount into an unknown situation."

Carlon nodded thoughtfully. He was, after all, a man who understood sensible precautions. "That sounds good except for one thing. You aren't going to Laran." Seeing the Captain's surprise, he added, "You're going to Elhanan to deliver a message to Gerrit."

"As you wish, Sire," he replied smoothly. Inside, however, he fought a slight disappointment at the missed opportunity to discover what had happened. "If I may mention one more point?"

The King waved indulgently, offering permission to continue. From the apprehensive look Marius received, though, he wasn't expecting good news.

Much to the Captain's regret, Carlon was right.

"My men are good soldiers," Marius continued, "but there's one thing soldiers do almost as well as fight, and that's tell war stories. By now I'm afraid you'll have a few circulating in town, and they'll only get worse with each retelling."

Carlon merely grunted. "You're becoming quite a master of understatement, Marius." The thin smile he gave held no humor. "Let it be known that two hundred guardsmen have been sent to deal with the problem, then draw up schedules for double guard patrols in the city before you go."

It was a reasonable response. After all, the men putting the news about would certainly brag about their comrade's abilities, and well protected people would find it hard to feel threatened.

Knowing a dismissal when he heard one, Marius stood and saluted, fist to chest before leaving to draw up the necessary orders.

It was a short walk from his office at the guard barracks to the house tucked into the corner of the castle grounds assigned to Marius' family. Although eager to get home after dealing with the new assignments, he had still delayed long enough for the welcome relief of a hot bath and a fresh change of clothes. He was sure his wife and daughter would have understood if he'd come in smelling like his horse, but he would much rather his homecomings be something to celebrate, not something to be pardoned.

Flowers of several colorful varieties were now blooming in the well-tended beds lining the path to the front door. When he had ridden out, his wife hadn't even begun her spring gardening. He admired her knack for making things grow—a knack he certainly didn't share, but was one of her many qualities he couldn't help but appreciate and admire.

The smell of freshly baked bread wafted over him as he walked through the door, blended with the savory aroma of stewed venison. Looking toward the hearth, Marius could see his wife giving a small kettle a stir as its contents bubbled over the fire.

Short and slender, she always seemed so tiny when he held her, yet their separations always made him feel as if a large part of him were missing. In fact, it was Lawrie's soft breathing as she lay beside him, rather than the warm, comfortable bed that he always looked forward to.

As she glanced over her shoulder to look at him, he could just see the sparkle of her emerald green eyes, almost eclipsed by a fall of strawberry blonde hair. Her welcoming smile nearly stopped his heart. Twenty-one years they'd been married, and she was still as beautiful as the day they met.

Marius quickly crossed the room to her as she straightened, yet as he bent to kiss her, the conspicuous sound of throat clearing came from the corner behind him. Undeterred, he kissed Lawrie anyway. They had never been embarrassed to model genuine love in front of their child—and he was not about to change that to keep from making a seventeen year old a bit uncomfortable.

"Hello, Wife," he grinned, lifting the hair out of her eyes.

"Hello, yourself," she said wryly, a wonderfully inviting smile forming on her full lips.

Giving Lawrie's hand a quick squeeze, he turned to the occupant of the chair in the corner. Morena sat, legs curled beneath her in the large cushioned chair, doing her best to read by the waning sunlight near the window. Her mother's strikingly green eyes gazed out from under a mop of tight red curls as she tried hard to convey disapproval of her parents' display of affection. The effect was spoiled by the warm smile that slowly spread from the creases at the corners of her mouth.

"Hiya, Chipmunk." The use of the old pet name brought exactly the reaction he expected, which both amused and saddened him.

"*Daddy!* I'm too old for that," she scowled slightly, although her voice and features softened as she added, "I missed you."

Still holding his wife's hand, Marius walked with her the few short yards to where their daughter sat. With his free hand, he reached out to draw Morena to her feet.

Rising gracefully, his daughter gently laid the book on the arm of the chair, letting it fall closed as she did so. A little shorter than Marius, even in slippered feet she stood quite a bit taller than her mother. Going quickly up on her toes, she brushed his cheek with a kiss.

A deep sigh of regret escaped him as he took a moment to look at each of the women in turn. When he spoke, it also tinged his voice.

"I missed both of you, too," he told them, "but I'll be leaving again in the morning."

Lawrie's sharply indrawn breath punctuated his statement. Such a response from her was incredibly rare, and a mark of the surprising nature of his announcement. His wife had always made it a point to avoid doing anything that might make him feel guilt over doing his duty. Letting go of her hand, he slipped an arm around her waist, earning him a warm smile.

"But you just got here." A hint of petulance crept into Morena's tone, followed immediately by a slightly abashed look at her mother.

He let it pass without comment, knowing Lawrie would speak to her later. Besides, he didn't like the situation any better than she did.

"Orders," he said resignedly, "and, I think, necessary ones."

Carefully editing out the worst of the details, Marius explained the situation that called for him to leave again almost as soon as he had arrived. He had seriously considered telling them far less; but while he would have preferred to downplay the possible danger to himself, they deserved to know. Besides, it was especially important that they not only understand the brevity of his stay, but also that they be able to counter the rumors he knew would soon be circulating.

"At least we have you for tonight," Lawrie said with a sigh. "I was beginning to feel jealous of the time you spend with your horse."

"Daddy?" His daughter's tone suddenly reminded him of the times when, as a little girl, she would ask him to watch as she danced around the room.

"Yes?" his voice warmed as the memory brought a broad smile to his lips.

"Mom said I have to ask you," Morena began, clearly the lead-up to a major request. "Do you think I could have a horse of my own? I'll take care of him, I *promise*," she rushed the final words out before he could say no.

The hopeful look on Morena's face made it nearly impossible to deny her what she'd set her heart on. It had always been hard to say no to anything that would surely make her smile. But he and Lawrie had always made major decisions together, and this one certainly qualified.

Of course, Marius was *not* about to spend his one night at home discussing this.

"We will sit down and talk about it when I get home," he answered gently. "You are old enough to be responsible, and you're a good rider, but you'll have to wait just a bit more."

He could see the disappointment as her hopes deflated. The hands that had been fidgeting with the blue linen of her dress now lay still. Leaning forward, he softly kissed her forehead to take some of the sting from the decision.

A horse would make it easier to pursue her studies, he thought.

Marius realized he was rationalizing the probable outcome of his and Lawrie's decision, but it was true. Her mother's gift with plants had, for Morena, become a natural talent at herbal medicine. She would undoubtedly benefit from the ability to travel to find the various herbs she needed—to add to the many she already grew in her own small garden behind the house. In fact, he would bet his best saddle that was the subject of the book she'd been reading when he'd come in.

Well, maybe Lawrie and I can spend a few minutes talking about it tonight, he supposed.

Shaking his head in mild amusement, he kissed his two favorite women and headed toward the bedroom to take off his boots. Quiet laughter from his wife and daughter followed him.

"Marius," Lawrie's voice carried gentle amusement, "while you're in there...shave."

He couldn't help but chuckle. He always let his beard grow while he was in the field, and he always had to shave it when he came home. Normally, he would have used his razor at the barracks, but it had seemed a waste of time to shave a beard tonight when he would just start a new one tomorrow. He should have known he would have to do it anyway.

The afternoon had seemed to drag interminably for King Carlon as he sat feeling trapped in the large familiar chair. He had seriously considered canceling court for the day but, now more than ever, people needed to see him conducting business as usual—seeing petitioners and hearing a few appeals. Put together with the rumors that might be starting, any change in routine would soon have some convinced that a crisis existed. But at least the carved and gilded chair had a thick comfortable cushion to make the hours more bearable, and the number of people waiting to be seen was mercifully low. Still, he was eager to be done with the tedium of the day so he could deal with the root of his present irritation.

Carlon's annoyance had actually begun during a break between cases, and from a very unlikely source— his son, Caleb. While it wasn't at all unusual for Caleb to observe proceedings of the court he would one day preside over, he was still an adolescent and was definitely limited where patience was concerned. True, it was far from the worst of possible shortcomings—and it was one the young typically outgrew—yet today it had been just a bit more than the King could accept.

It had always been the boy's habit to joke with whomever was at hand during the brief lulls. Far from being a problem, most people found that it helped to lighten the mood. In fact, the King was often grateful for it.

Today, whether because of the subject matter or due to the unwelcome news Marius had brought, Carlon found it to be terribly inappropriate. Either way, he knew he needed to address what he realized could become a problem if left unchecked. He only hoped his idea for a solution would work.

Gradually the benches lining the walls of the large room emptied as petitioners were heard and disputes were settled. Soon, all that remained, aside from Caleb and the King himself, were a handful of young pages and several of Carlon's ministers seated in the more comfortable chairs near the platform on which he sat.

The session finally finished, the King rose, immediately bringing those present to their feet. Instead of simply turning toward the door behind his seat, however, Carlon motioned to his son to join him.

"Walk with me a while." Throwing an arm across the young man's shoulders, he steered them through his private exit.

While not nearly as broad of chest and shoulder as his father, Caleb was definitely coming into his adult physique. Thanks to regular sword training, he was quickly developing his musculature and his coordination, making him look less the awkward teen he'd been a short time before.

Just short of eighteen, the young Prince was developing the quiet confidence he needed to accomplish what was expected of him—though he still needed a bit of subtle encouragement to get there. Of course, due to the unfortunately prominent nose bump he had inherited, he would never be more than passably handsome. But his wavy red hair and blue-gray eyes were considered striking, and his good-natured humor made him a very likable young man.

Carlon gave his son's shoulder an affectionate squeeze as they walked quietly through the castle corridors. He hadn't given a great deal of thought to what he would say to Caleb, but he didn't anticipate any difficulty convincing a young man who was so eager to be seen and treated as an adult.

Stepping out into one of the numerous gardens, now heavily shadowed as the immense structure of the castle blocked much of the afternoon sunlight, the King stopped. Even in the dim light, he could see the curious expression on Caleb's face out of the corner of his eye.

"I'll understand if it's too much to ask," Carlon began, knowing full well that his son would take it as a challenge," but there's something I need you to do for me. For the Kingdom, actually."

"Of course, Father," Caleb replied quickly, taking the bait. "Anything."

Carlon allowed a wry smile, resisting the urge to laugh. *Almost too easy,* he thought. *I'm going to have to teach him to recognize when he's being manipulated. Not today, though.*

"Don't be in such a rush to agree until you've heard the request," he told Caleb, "But I do think this is something you'll enjoy."

He paused, letting the Prince's curiosity peak before resuming. He knew Caleb was basically sold already, but many years of experience had taught him caution when using persuasion. Sooner than expected, however, he could sense that the younger man was on the verge of asking.

"I want you to take a trip," the King offered at last. He watched his son's face carefully, reading the signs of excitement as well as the slight apprehension there. As he expected, the sense of adventure common to young men soon won out over all other emotions.

"Where?" Caleb asked, eyes sparkling.

"Captain Braden is taking a company to the border," he replied as casually as he could. "I'd like you to go along to Elhanan as an emissary.

"I could do that, Father." Caleb's obvious attempt to be nonchalant was ruined by a mischievous grin.

The King had to fight hard to suppress a victorious smile. "Have one of the servants pack some things for you. I expect Marius wants to leave at first light, so get some sleep."

Carlon actually doubted that his son would sleep at all. The young were resilient, though. If Caleb was anything like he was at that age, a little less sleep would hardly slow him down.

"Go on." The King clapped his son on the shoulder. The friendly dismissal was all the encouragement the young Prince needed, and his father watched as he hustled toward the dim interior of the castle.

Caleb halted at the doorway, turning with an impish smile that lit his face. "Father," he called. "How do you tell a barbarian woman from a bear?"

Carlon groaned inwardly. Such jokes had recently become popular among the young, however much he wished they hadn't.

"How?" the King asked.

Caleb grinned. "The bear has less back hair." Laughing, he turned and went inside.

The first pale pink of the coming sunrise was just beginning to paint the horizon as Caleb reached the milling chaos of the courtyard. Bleary eyed servants hurried, carrying last minute additions for the supply train or running messages for the officers. All around, dozens of horses stomped impatience as they waited the chance to move.

With grooms seeing to his own mount, and no pressing duties to hold his attention, Caleb did his best to imitate the relaxed look of the veterans around him. Still, he found his hand wandering repeatedly to the sword now hanging at his waist.

"Careful with that," Cait's voice bubbled with easy humor. "You don't want to stab your horse when you mount."

Shorter than Caleb and slender, his fraternal twin bore a much closer resemblance to their mother. Where his red hair was wavy, hers fell straight, framing a face that was quite pretty and thankfully lacked the prominent nose of her father and brother.

"Pest," he responded, smiling broadly.

"Brat," she returned.

The nicknames had been a mark of their teasing but clearly affectionate relationship for years. In fact, the habitual taunts were now so ingrained that their actual names felt awkward on the rare occasions when they were forced to use them.

With a glance he took in the dress and slippers his sister wore, plainly unsuitable for riding. "He said no again, I take it."

"You know he did," frustration clear in her tone.

After hearing about his assignment, Cait had immediately asked to go along and had been gently refused. He had known by her expression, however, that she wouldn't give up easily on a chance for an adventure like this. Of course, changing their father's mind could be a long and difficult fight at the best of times.

Well, he would miss his sister, but he wasn't about to weep over it. After all, he was going to Elhanan, the last outpost on the edge of barbarian territory.

"Enough, you two," the King interrupted, though the rebuke held mild amusement rather than heat. In his hand, Carlon held a folded piece of paper and a small sealed package, which he handed over. "For King Gerrit."

Accepting it with a simple nod, Caleb held the packet as if it would try to escape his grasp. He knew it was a grave responsibility being entrusted to him, and he was determined not to let his father down.

Somehow, the Prince failed to notice that his father had placed it in the hand caressing the sword hilt.

"Your commission," Carlon added, handing over the letter. "Technically, this places you in the chain of command. Realistically, you have only the direct authority Captain Braden and Lieutenant Ward give you. Understood?" The King looked steadily at his son, waiting for an acknowledgement.

"Yes, Father," Caleb nodded solemnly.

Apparently satisfied, the King smiled. "You'll do well," he said, his expression conveying his full confidence in his son. "I'm proud of you, Caleb."

"Thank you," he replied, chest swelling at the compliment. Still, in spite of the rush of pride, he allowed himself only a small smile, trying to maintain something resembling proper dignity.

Apparently noticing her brother's internal struggle, Cait slyly stuck out her tongue while the King's attention was focused on the head of the column.

Caleb's barely stifled laughter emerged as a loud snort. Grabbing his handkerchief, he quickly passed it off as a sneeze and managed to hide a slight smile. He could always depend on Cait to keep him humble.

"Bless you," Carlon offered absently, taking each of the teens by an elbow and guiding them to where the Captain stood giving final instructions to several men in the floppy hat and cockade worn by scouts.

"Dismissed." Braden sent the men hustling toward their mounts as he spotted the approaching King. Turning to face Carlon, the officer saluted, right fist over heart. "Majesty. Highnesses."

"Everything ready, Captain?" The King's question was clearly *pro forma*, judging by his casual tone.

"Just waiting for my sergeants to finish their troop inspections, Sire." He indicated the hard looking men now at the end of the lines of horses, checking everything from saddle girths to full canteens. "As soon as they're satisfied, we'll be ready."

"I'm sure they know their jobs," Carlon allowed, unconcerned. "I wondered if I could have a minute of your time before you go."

"Of course, Sire," came the immediate reply. Plainly the Captain was under no illusions that it had been a request.

"Caleb," the King glanced briefly at his son, "why don't you go see to your horse and say your goodbyes to your sister."

Although surprised, the young Prince nevertheless took the obvious brushoff in stride. On the assumption that he would someday be King himself, there were a great many of his father's conversations that Caleb was expected to sit in on. Until he did take the throne, however, he understood that the King's business was still exactly that.

With a quick grin from his sister, they set off to find the grooms waiting with Searcher.

Chapter 3

The Wading Crane

The ride from the fields below Toskar to the port in Barat hadn't been difficult. In fact, it was only a few days' journey along a fairly level stretch of hard packed road. The highway was certainly well-traveled, as men and wagons made their way to and from the capital, yet it was hardly crowded. To Samir's left, the slow rolling River Khoja burbled heedlessly, occasionally inhabited by the fishermen poling their low flat boats near the reeds.

For Samir, however, the entire trip had been a trial. While those who shared the highway seemed friendly and eager to pass a bit of gossip, he shunned their company, welcoming only Tirza's quiet presence. The shock and pain at the loss of his home and family had simply left him exhausted and numb, capable of little more than keeping his horse pointed north as he continued on.

He hadn't bothered to make a camp that first night, completely lacking the energy to exert even the basic effort of laying out a bedroll, much less start a fire. Instead, he had wept until he felt like a wrung out rag.

It hadn't been until Tirza had nuzzled him awake the next morning expecting him to feed her that he had looked to see what supplies Gehazi had given him. The simple task of rising had been a chore, as the emotional hollow of the day before had become a yawning void that resisted any attempt to move. Yet, unlike the horses that grazed placidly, the hound would not be put off.

Samir had immediately found a thick blanket roll atop the supplies beneath the lashed-down covering on the packhorse. The contents of the panniers had been mainly foodstuffs. Fruit, nuts and rice cakes provided the bulk along with bread, cheese and some rather excellent wine. There was also a good amount of jerked meat, most likely lamb, a handful of which quickly appeased the waiting hound and set the long tail wagging contentedly. All told, Samir estimated he could have fed half a dozen people quite well all the way to Barat.

Carefully wrapped bundles held a good many of his own clothes—immaculately tailored silk shirts, pants and sashes, many embroidered with threads of gold and fitted with ivory buttons. Another revealed boots and slippers in soft leather or silk, all in the latest styles. It had all been so important to him, but that may as well have been a lifetime ago. Wadding it up, he stuffed it all back into the pannier and went in search of more important items.

The few weapons Gehazi had provided were easy enough to find. Aside from the short horseman's bow he'd brought on the hunt, he now had a longsword, a broadsword and a pair of knives—each the best from his own exquisite collection. Hardly the selection he was used to, of course, but it would be more than enough in the right hands.

The sacks of gold he found buried at the bottom. At a bit over two hundred ghera in gold, it likely represented all that Gehazi had on hand and perhaps more besides. Certainly a tidy sum, well beyond the means of many.

Sudden anger washed over Samir as he held one of the slightly bulging sacks. If that worm, Gehazi, thought he would be allowed to ease his guilt with *any* amount of money, he would be sadly disabused of the idea if he ever saw the Prince's face again. Whatever Kemal did to the man would be merciful by comparison.

Drawing a deep breath, he relaxed, consciously calling on the discipline and training Shimei had instilled in him. He wasn't so foolish as to think he could lock his grief away and refuse to deal with it, but he couldn't allow it to control him or, worse, keep him from functioning.

Looking over his meager inventory of supplies, he sighed heavily. Flint and steel, some good rope, a razor and some soap were now practically the extent of his worldly goods. Gehazi wasn't the only one who had fallen far in a short time.

A long sip from one of his wineskins felt good to his dry throat, rinsing it clean of road dust, but the relief brought a touch of guilt. If he'd had the presence of mind to push on the few miles to the river before collapsing, he could have watered the horses. Still, in spite of his neglect, at least they'd gotten their share of good grass.

It was that morning that he'd seen his first patrol of the Royal Guard, coming from the north along the highway. The early sun glinting from their burnished conical helms and the plume of dust raised by the hooves of their mounts had made them easily visible in the distance.

Their appearance was no surprise. Patrols moved along the road in both directions, insuring the safety of trade and travelers alike. To most, they were a reassuring presence. For Samir, however, they were trouble.

It failed to occur to him at first that simply meeting these soldiers could be problematic. Having spent his entire life within a few yards of such men, they were so familiar he hardly noticed them much of the time. Yet, suddenly he realized that, for the first time in his life, the familiarity was a liability.

The odds were against any of them recognizing him, since those who guarded the royal family had long since earned their way out of patrol duties. Unfortunately, he couldn't take that chance. Even though these men couldn't possibly be aware that the kingdom had changed hands, it wouldn't do for them to report having seen a dead man once they heard the news.

Snatching the flapping silk scarf from the pommel of his broadsword, he quickly tied the blue cloth over his nose and mouth. Hopefully, the guards would assume he was keeping the dust of the road from his throat, a great deal of which was being kicked up by their mounts. The thin material was scant protection, he realized, but it was all he had.

Several long minutes passed as the eight lean, hard guardsmen drew closer, details growing gradually clearer at each step. Alert eyes scanned the long grass as well as the road ahead, the trained warriors hunting for any threat. Red silk vests flapped and baggy white trousers billowed in the breeze that made pennants of the silk at their sword hilts as the two lines of men passed by on the wide roadway. Samir nodded a greeting, yet hardly dared to breathe as a few returned the gesture, moustaches swinging. They had no reason to stop or question him on a public road, he knew, yet he remained wary until the dust of their passing had fallen far behind him.

For much of that first day he simply rode, letting his horse guide itself along the ribbon of hard packed earth. Lush green plains stretched to the horizon like a sea of grass rippling in the breezes. Beside him, the wide, slow river wound along between reed lined banks, providing a soft accompaniment to the plodding of the gelding's hooves. Only the occasional small farm or rice paddy broke the soothingly hypnotic scene, allowing Samir a blessed relief from his thoughts.

For the most part, Tirza was content to pad silently beside him, making only a few swift forays into the thick grass in response to some hint of sound or movement. Aside from a single pheasant erupting from cover, Samir neither knew nor cared what she chased—whether fox, hare or merely a fancy of the dog's imagination. At some point, usually within moments, she would be panting along beside him again as if she had never left.

Realizing he was terribly hungry, Samir stopped for lunch on a nice easy slope by the riverside where the horses could graze and drink. A snack of fruit and cheese that morning had been his only food since breakfast of the previous day. The thought depressed him, serving as a reminder that the banquet prepared for his birthday had been used to celebrate his brother's treachery. Samir had no memory of his meal, chewing and swallowing automatically, tasting nothing but the ashes of the life stolen from him.

A series of wildly changing emotions assaulted him for the remainder of the day, swinging rapidly through the spectrum from rage to resolve to deep brooding sadness. The young warrior was almost thankful when, finally, fatigue caused him to settle into a kind of functional numbness that brought him an odd sense of relief.

His camp on the bank of the Khoja that evening was fireless, although only from apathy. Dried horse dung was plentiful, since the spot he chose seemed a fairly popular one. The smell of such smoke was unappealing at best, however, and the night was warm enough without it.

Samir found it a welcome distraction to practice forms that evening, with and without weapons. His movements, first sweeping broadly, then subtly, began slowly with every motion graceful and each step perfectly balanced. The katas soon became a deadly dance, punctuated by instants of explosive speed and power. Attacks and wardings flowed smoothly, one into the other, advance into withdrawal, at once hard and soft like water as he moved from high stances to crouches without the need for conscious thought. Hands and feet became a blur of precise motion—strikes and sweeps emulating the crane or serpent, mantis or tiger in combinations never seen in nature. Samir's mind became a perfect blend, completely aware of his surroundings even as he managed to focus on the least detail of position and placement. Emptied of any thought of past or future, the young Prince knew only now, finding his center for the first time since his world had been shattered.

By the time he finished, Samir was comfortably tired, his muscles warm and loose as his breath came in a deep, even rhythm. Settling slowly in the wide circle his feet had torn and beaten in the grass, he opened himself to the pain of loss and regret he had held at bay. Without awareness of passing time, he simply wept, not fighting the terrible surge of emotion as heavy wracking sobs gave way to the gently flowing tears that seemed to wash him clean.

The flood of grief finally began to abate as he watched the setting sun fill the western sky with a wash of pastel colors. It wasn't until then that he became aware of Tirza at his side, his hand gently stroking her soft white coat as she watched him carefully.

For the next two days, he fell into a comfortable routine—ride and rest, eat and practice. The road stretched ahead of him, almost unchanging, leaving him little idea how far he'd gone or how long before he reached the port. Only the rising and setting of the sun in its ceaseless path through the heavens marked any real difference in time or place.

Three more patrols appeared on the highway, forcing him to use the scarf as a feeble disguise. The guardsmen rode past each time, weapons held ready for use with casual ease, apparently indifferent to a single traveler who clearly offered no threat.

Samir rode into Barat with evening fast approaching on the third day, the bustle of commerce fading swiftly as people made their way home or to one of the numerous inns and taverns. These last were easy to spot by the painted signs hanging from brackets above the doors as well as by the music and laughter coming from within.

Samir had little choice but to make his way patiently through the streets as the thinning crowds still allowed nothing more rapid than a slow, plodding walk for the horses. Even at that pace, however, it wasn't long before he was directed to one of the better inns the city had to offer.

The Wading Crane was clean, well lit and obviously kept in a good state of repair—better than the many he had seen missing roof tiles, bearing rotted wood around windows or with cracked and flaking paint. It stood out in other ways as well. Its two upper levels were each skirted by a narrow band of tile roofing in the Rukati style, unlike the onion shaped domes and ornate screens of Majaran buildings. Besides, he had to admit, the image on its sign bore a close enough resemblance to his own egret sigil to make him feel a bit proprietary.

After stabling his horses in the small attached yard and arranging for oats, Samir stepped through a short hallway into the spacious dining room. Well-dressed men and women took their ease at the many low wooden tables, reclining on cushions to eat and drink. Other tables, presumably occupied, had been made private with painted silk screens, their colorful images depicting mountain scenes or animals in exotic poses. A pair of musicians played a soft accompaniment to the muted buzz of polite conversation—the bulbous horn and plucked strings producing a complex quarter-toned music he found rather soothing.

Several of the unoccupied tables appeared suitable, yet he no sooner moved toward one than he was brought to an abrupt halt. The obviously agitated man standing in front of him, bowing and wringing his hands, could only be the proprietor.

Layers of fine, ornately decorated robes, firmly belted at the waist by a wide sash marked him as a Rukati, even if the short cut of his iron grey hair had not. Although of only medium height, the man's slender build and gaunt face made him seem somehow taller as he straightened from his bow. If he was at all surprised that Samir hadn't returned the greeting, even minimally, he gave no sign. Instead, he smiled, clearly making every effort not to give offense to one wearing fine clothes. Regardless of one's dirty, travel-stained appearance, expensive fashion was still an indication of money. The smile, though, was plainly a bit uneasy.

"What an excellent looking animal you have, sir." The wide loose sleeves of the outer robe swung freely as the man gestured to Tirza. "May I offer it the use of my stables for the night?"

"Thank you, no. She can stay with me, Mister...?" Samir trailed off to let the other supply a name.

The proprietor was definitely becoming upset now, yet his years as a successful businessman had evidently taught him customer relations very well. He bowed again.

"My name is Lao, and please forgive me, sir," he said in his best conciliatory tone. "I believe my other customers might be more comfortable if your *magnificent* companion didn't accompany us to your table."

A flash of indignation very nearly caused Samir to strike the man for such audacity. Never in his life had *anyone* refused to accommodate him. No one treated a Prince of Majar like this!

And that was exactly the problem, he realized. He had never been anywhere that people didn't already know precisely who he was. In Lao's eyes, however, Samir was just another customer with money and possible influence. This one wore a warrior's moustaches, true, but that surely couldn't be unusual either.

Anger left him in a rush, along with the well-ingrained certainty that the world would simply bend to his will. The disquieting feeling he was left with was something entirely new to him. He definitely didn't like it, but there was nothing to be done but accept the new order of things, and mark another debt on his list against Kemal.

"Of course, Mister Lao," he replied, hoping the man hadn't noticed the anger in his eyes moments before. "Tirza will be happy to sleep in your stable, which is surely better than the finest room any other inn has to offer. And I would be pleased to be shown to a room and a bath before taking my supper."

This time, the innkeeper's smile was genuine. A sharp clap of his hands brought a boy running to his side.

"Take the gentleman's dog to the stable, and bring her a few slices of roast lamb," Lao instructed without so much as a glance.

At the boy's gentle attempts to coax her, Tirza looked to her master, head cocked to one side. Apparently understanding his quick hand signal toward the door, the hound quickly turned and followed the lad to the stables.

"I'll have your baggage brought up and a change of clothing brought to you in your bath, sir," Lao said smoothly as he led Samir down a narrow hallway and up the stairs.

Aside from the simple courtesy, Samir realized that a bath might actually make him feel somewhat human again. He had washed in the cool water of the Khoja, but he had never felt entirely clean afterwards—especially after putting on the same dirty clothes, seeing no reason to ruin others. A shave would be in order as well, since his razor had been no use without a mirror. Light growth or not, four days was too long.

Smiling for the first time in days, Samir followed Lao down the hall.

The little white mare calmed quickly under Jenaris' soothing attention as he maintained a tight grip on her bridle. The occasional quiver of fear still rippled down her flank, but Keera was much more composed than she had been the first few times—bucking and pulling against the reins in her attempt to run. It had taken all of his efforts to keep that from happening while sustaining his spell, yet had she run she would certainly have died.

Now nearing the plains, they seemed to have left most of the vile creatures behind, judging by the frequency of encounters. Still, even the solitary beast that had just passed by was more than dangerous enough to make Jenaris worry for the safety of travelers. Unfortunately, destroying it would have presented difficulties, not the least of which would have been dividing his energies beyond the magics already in use. He had already done so once, feeling the need for an appraisal that didn't come from a book, and it had been more than enough risk for one journey. Thankfully, he was far enough from anywhere important that any traffic was rare, consisting mostly of an occasional hunter.

Besides, the two weeks he had already spent traveling had been difficult without trying to make the trip while on the brink of exhaustion. He had little choice but to make the best of it, however. What passed for roads here were mainly game trails winding beneath the leafy canopy of old growth. Selecting the ones that headed in the general direction you wanted to go would eventually get you to your destination, but you inevitably fought the terrain along the way.

At least Jenaris had managed to learn a great deal in the time he had taken. Otherwise, he would have felt even more frustrated than he already did.

Of course, the real source of his annoyance was that he had almost no idea where—or how—to find Lorn. Although they had certainly exchanged their fair share of messages in the past fifty years, the Wizard was ashamed to admit he had let communication lapse without giving it a thought. Normally, sending a message was as simple as linking a bird to the other wizard's Marque—if you know the mage well enough to be familiar with the binding. But while he had never heard of such magic failing, he had been unable to make a simple connection. Scrying had been ineffective as well. Sadly, Jenaris had to admit the possibility that his friend was dead, but he would not assume the worst without making every attempt to discover the truth.

At present, though, all he had to guide him was a vague mention Lorn had made, many years ago, of his interest in an animal that lived in the Western Sea. It was a long way from where he stood, but at least travel across the plains would be much faster than struggling through the hills.

For now, though, he would feel better once he had put some distance between himself and the creature that had so recently passed through. Right now, he was nowhere near his full strength, and he would prefer to make his next camp well away from an area where he'd already encountered trouble.

He involuntarily shrugged his shoulders to relieve the odd feeling that had settled between his shoulder blades over the past few days. With a quick pat for the mare's neck, Jenaris swung himself into the saddle. The trail ahead wound between thick trunks and was obscured by scrub, but in a few miles he expected to reach the edge to the forest.

Clucking softly to his mount, he set off toward the plains and the easy roads that would take him west.

Samir had awakened refreshed, but found himself more than a little tempted to stay in bed for just a few minutes longer. The plush down-filled mattress had felt like heaven after three nights on a bed of crushed grass. Still, he knew he needed to get up and begin to put together the pieces of his new life. A long hot bath had actually proved the perfect place to make plans and had left him with a pressing need to get things done.

Dressing quickly, he dropped a small pouch of his gold into the sash at his waist and slipped the sheath of his longsword into place. Having shaved the night before, he did not need to do so again, yet he checked his appearance carefully in the mirror above the washstand. Satisfied, he gathered his long dark hair and bound it with the gold clip he'd received from his mother.

As he left the room, he slid his feet into his soft leather boots and made his way downstairs.

Tirza was clearly eager to escape the gated stall, her barks of greeting spooking a few of the more timid horses, which sent stablehands running to settle them. Lifting the latch, Samir had only to open the gate a few inches before the hound snaked her long, lean body through the gap, tail thrashing wildly. The young warrior found it impossible to completely suppress a chuckle at her excitement which, in a way, closely mirrored his own.

The streets of Barat were already becoming crowded with those hurrying to work as well as those thronging to the markets and shops for the best goods. From the babble of languages being spoken around him, and the vast differences in clothing and hair styles, there had to be nearly as many foreigners as Majarans in the city. But this came as no surprise. After all, trade was the lifeblood of the thriving port city, and trade brought in all kinds. In fact, the only truly unexpected thing about the city's crowds was how well they avoided jostling one another in the swirling chaos of traffic.

One glance at the sheer mass of people assured Samir that riding would only cause him problems and delays navigating on any but the widest boulevards. Leaving Sha'ar in his stall, Samir and Tirza dove into the press of bodies.

Shops and stalls existed somewhere in Barat for anything that could legally be bought or sold—and arrangements could be made for much that wasn't. He passed by most with only a quick scan, causing even the more aggressive salesmen to turn their attention to those more likely to spend their coin.

The hound's prompting did cause him to stop briefly at a small grill where a stooped, elderly woman hawked kebabs loaded with sizzling meats and vegetables. Handing over a few copper coins, Samir gladly tore into one of the skewers, sending runnels of warm juice dripping freely down his chin.

Grinning, he carefully removed several chunks of steaming lamb and tossed them to his waiting companion. Tirza snapped them from the air with ease, tail wagging furiously, making him wish the crowd was thin enough to challenge her speed and agility.

Finishing the contents of the bamboo skewer, Samir wiped his face and hands with a kerchief and resumed his search.

It wasn't hard to find what he needed, beginning with the small silver hand mirror. Although merely a palm-sized rectangle with rounded corners, it would do well enough for shaving as long as it was free of irregularities. Fancy workmanship would get the job done no better.

Samir's brief journey to Barat had already shown him the problem of traveling without certain basic supplies, and it was a lesson he had taken to heart.

A stack of new clothes was hardly more difficult, being only a matter of examining the work samples and available material displayed by the large number of tailors. Samir briefly considered and discarded the idea of trying some of the foreign fashions which, he was continually assured, were all in the latest styles. But a Majaran warrior in a high-collared Brisian coat would surely draw unwanted attention, and he enjoyed the freedom of movement allowed by the loose clothing of his own land.

In the end, he let necessity guide his choices, ordering half a dozen shirts and pants of heavy cotton. Not only would they be much more durable, but it would also be far easier to clean than the delicate silk he had thought nothing of wearing all his life. With a few measurements and a few coins as a deposit, the tailor set to work, promising delivery to his rooms at The Wading Crane before dinner the next day.

Satisfied, Samir set off in search of the most difficult purchases.

The sharp brown eyes of the heavily muscled weapon smith noted everything the instant the young Prince entered the shop—the growth of warrior's whiskers, the fine clothes and especially the sword at his hip. The longsword had been crafted by a master and was worth more than most men could earn with years of hard work. Though its intricately etched blade was hidden by the ornate leather sheath, the carved ivory hilt and the golden sunburst of the narrow semicircular guard said more than enough about its value. For Samir, it had long been the pride of his personal collection and had brought commissions for other work to the smith who had gifted him with it.

A quick flash of avarice showed in the shop owner's eyes as he imagined the kind of money his new favorite customer could spend. A deep and sincere smile of welcome immediately greeted Samir, followed by an equally deep bow.

"Welcome, young master," the man offered smoothly, stopping just short of naming him Sòra. "Be welcome to the house of Lotan."

Naturally, Samir knew the man had no way of measuring his skills, yet he suspected the question of actual mastery was irrelevant. Whether a customer could use a spear or a *kama* without impaling himself would be far less important than his ability to pay for it. With a grand sweeping gesture, the smith invited him to cast his gaze on his vast assortment of wares.

The collection filling the racks and lining the walls was impressive, although more for its quantity than quality. A few here and there would be worthy of his abilities, even if the majority were better suited for common soldiers. Swords of every description, even foreign varieties, filled one wall entirely, allowing him to find several of the proper workmanship. Spears and staves, hammers and knives, and shields of all types awaited his careful inspection. For a moment, Samir was reminded of the array gracing Shimei's walls, causing a brief wave of homesickness that took a moment to dispel.

Samir smiled, swiftly setting aside several examples of each type of weapon. Without a word, he began a much more careful examination, starting with a small round shield that would work well in conjunction with a broadsword. Trusting his instincts, as well as his training, he tested the quality and balance of every item in the only way possible.

When he finally left the shop hours later, he felt as if he had fought half a dozen hard battles against an army of opponents. Calling upon nearly every kata he knew, the young warrior had been back and forth across the open floor more times than he cared to count, seeking just the right length, weight and balance. Eventually, Samir settled on at least one copy of nearly every weapon he knew—excluding only the longsword already in his possession. It was a considerable assortment, causing him to part with a fair amount of his gold. Yet he was satisfied with the result—not least by having left the smith no doubt that Samir *was* very nearly the master he'd been named upon entering.

Like the clothing, the weapons would be delivered to him at the inn. Unlike with his previous purchase, however, extra coin had been needed to pay porters for the work of hauling it. Of course, it would likely cost him still more to have Lao store it for him, but it was well worth the expense. After all, proper weapons would be in short supply outside of Majar.

Samir had only one more search to make, but he was hesitant to even begin to look for what would almost certainly be the most difficult item on his list. After testing so many weapons, his legs felt like lead and his shoulders burned. While he wanted a bath and a place to rest, however, he was reluctant to lose half a day to nothing more than fatigue—an excuse Shimei would have scoffed at. Thankfully, the air so near the sea was cool and far less humid than what he was used to, leaving him somewhat refreshed in the light southerly breeze.

Still, he was willing to make one concession to the exhaustion that now wore at him. Making his way through the crowds to where a man worked frantically over a pair of shallow bowl-shaped skillets, Samir handed over a few small coins and was quickly rewarded with a banana leaf piled high with food. Taking a pair of the tapered bamboo jhoppa sticks, he took a taste of the steaming shrimp and rice and was rewarded with the fiery bite of spices. Flipping a couple of the shrimp to Tirza, the warrior swiftly shoveled the rest down, savoring the flavor as he filled his empty stomach.

Pleasantly stuffed, he strolled toward the harbor, tucking the jhoppa behind his sash and resolving to buy a decent pair.

Making his slow way north along one of the wide boulevards, Samir followed a seemingly endless stream of wagons, as more headed south on the other side, most full of sacks, barrels or bales. Gradually, shops and homes gave way to the enormous warehouses fronting the long wooden docks.

The view that opened up before him was nothing short of spectacular as he finally emerged between a pair of the barn-like structures. A broad wooden wharf stretched for at least half a mile in either direction along the waterfront, punctuated at regular intervals by piers that rose from the surf on massive pilings. Nearly all were occupied by great, high-masted ships, bobbing and rolling as they sat with sails reefed. Everywhere, men and horses scrambled, hauling goods and moving fantastic amounts of cargo in a chaotic dance that he could make little sense of.

Over the next several hours, the harbor master directed Samir to one ship after another—so many that the man was plainly becoming annoyed at the Prince's repeated presence. Time after time, Samir trotted up and down the long wharf with the hound at his heals, ranging east and west in search of passage to wherever the various ships might be bound. In each case, however, he walked away without a deal, followed more than once by the derisive laughter of the crew.

Although what he wanted seemed fairly basic from his point of view, the captains he approached almost invariably stared at him as if he'd sprouted a second head once he started talking. Frustration grew inside him as the afternoon wore on and he knew the list of available vessels must be shrinking rapidly. Yet, while he refused to give in to desperation, he soon became acutely aware that he would have to change his tactics if he were going to get anywhere before running out of ships.

Slowly but surely, Samir began to pare down his requests—beginning with making an effort to phrase them *as* requests. After all, making demands of those used to exercising absolute authority was obviously counterproductive. Even with this approach, however, the young warrior met with failure. Sadly, it appeared he was going to have to accept their terms and not the other way around.

He was definitely becoming weary when he approached a large round-bellied cargo ship bearing the name *Amelia*.

Calling for permission to board had galled at first, accustomed as he was to receiving deference and respect, as much because he was a warrior as because he was part of the royal family. But now, he not only needed to adjust to his sudden lack of station, but also to the fact that other cultures—which this clearly was—had differing ideas of what common courtesy involved.

The slightly rotund man who met him at the top of the gangway seemed rather unimpressive compared to other captains he had met. Perhaps sixty years old and of less than average height, the man with greasy brown hair and frayed cuffs made a poor first impression. Yet, meeting the man's eyes, Samir quickly forgot the stained shirt and scraggly beard as he felt the inescapable aura of power. This, he knew, was that rare individual like his own Sòra, with a deep sense of himself and his own capabilities.

Somewhat in spite of himself, Samir was impressed.

"And you are?" Though spoken in Majaran, the man's accent was awful. Still, the man's tone carried well and gave the distinct impression that he was trying to decide whether his time was being wasted.

Judging from the clothing and the dreadful pallor of his skin, the Captain obviously hailed from the continent north of the Bharkur Sea, most likely Brisia or Acedia. Of course, the lectures he had received from his father's diplomats had given him the impression that the two countries were little different, although the dialects were rather distinct.

"My name is Samir," he answered in the Brisian version, concluding that a sailor, particularly a merchant, would more likely come from that nation. His ability with the language was stiff, but passable.

From his casual perch on the rail, the man slowly scanned Samir, a thoughtful expression on his deeply lined face. The warrior would have been willing to bet that those eyes missed very little. Finally, a small crooked smile quirked the Captain's lips.

"I'm listening," the man said, dropping his crude attempt at the Majaran tongue. He was plainly still unconvinced of Samir's worth, but at least he no longer looked as though he saw mud on his deck.

"I'd like to book passage north." Doing his best to sound humble, the Prince made a point to finger the pouch of coins tucked into his sash. Unfortunately, his earlier purchase of weapons had made it rather lighter than he liked.

"Don't take passengers," the man snorted. "Good luck finding a captain who will."

Samir had actually expected that response, or something very much like it, having heard it many times already. The crews of cargo ships, it seemed, considered the small income of "freeloaders" too small to put up with having people underfoot. His collection of weapons they would be more than happy to haul for him—but they drew the line at live cargo unless it meant *real* money.

Drawing a deep breath, Samir tried a new approach. "Fine, then I'd like to work passage north."

Apparently, the Captain's once-over hadn't left him terribly impressed. "Ever done a day's work in your life?" he shot Samir a look of mild skepticism.

"No, Captain. But you already know that." He paused, forcing a smile. "That doesn't mean I can't or won't."

It was a risk, of course, but at this point he was starting to think a little risk would be necessary. Sadly, it meant giving the other man a great deal of control.

"So why should I take you on?" the Captain chuckled. "I don't do charity, lad."

This would be the answer that mattered, Samir knew. He took a chance on just a bit of audacity. "Because you very badly want to prove to me that I can't handle it," he said.

The laughter that erupted from the older man threatened to topple him over the rail as his entire body shook. Raising a thick, grimy finger to his eye, he wiped away a tear.

"I've decided I like you, lad." The man extended a hand as his humor subsided into chuckles. "Name's Tasca, but you can call me Captain or *Sir*. Deckhands get no privileges." He paused, a wicked gleam in his eye as he fixed the young warrior with his gaze. "And you're right. I *don't* think you can handle it."

Samir looked at the offered hand, unable to take it before settling one more point—one that had ended his chance at passage more than once already. Turning his head, he issued a sharp, shrill whistle in the direction of the pier, causing Tirza to trot up beside him.

"I'll take your hand gladly, Captain Tasca," he answered, "but only if it's passage for two."

Samir had already determined that he would have to sell the horses. He would miss Sha'ar, but the gelding would fetch a fair price. He could not, however, bring himself to part with Tirza. The little Raphan hound had been a gift from his sister, Vesina, and letting Tirza go would mean cutting his final link with who he was. The Prince had lost his home, and even his family. The dog was the one concession he *would* not make. He waited.

Tasca's eyes narrowed slightly in thought. He hadn't refused out of hand, but he hadn't said, "Yes," either. At last, a look of amusement settled on his weather worn features.

"I suppose there's no harm," he allowed, "considering you'll be the one scrubbing my decks anyway. Besides, if I change my mind, dog's good eating." A vicious grin turned up the corner of the man's mouth.

Once again, he held out his hand. This time, Samir took it.

Chapter 4

Unexpected Visitors

Gerrit's head was beginning to throb more painfully as he sat in the massive oak chair at the end of the village hall. He knew the chair hadn't caused his headache—it was actually fairly comfortable—but it was remarkable how often he seemed to get them when he sat in it. One of these days, he would remember to stash some willow bark within easy reach so he would have some to chew at times like this. For the moment, however, he simply had to wait.

Now he sat silently, one of his strong scarred hands gripping the intricately carved arm, a group of ropy pierced-work vines that twined up the legs all the way to the tall back covered in leaves and grape clusters. His father, Galen, had carved it shortly before his death— wanting to ensure that those who came here saw a king rather than some jumped up chieftain. In truth, Gerrit thought his father really wanted to be sure the new King remembered who and what he was. Of course, between the weight of his responsibilities and the blinding headaches that came with them, there was no real danger that he would forget.

His thick shoulders bunched as he leaned forward, sharp brown eyes studying the men in front of him from behind the strands of his wild locks. The Gotarran King had dealt with more than his share of bad news before—it came with any position of authority—but this was unlike any he had ever heard.

"What do you mean by 'gone'?" Gerrit's deep voice came dangerously close to a growl. "Towns can't just *vanish*. I don't care how small they are."

Normally a jovial man, Gerrit's concern and surprise had definitely lent an edge of anger to his attitude. Forcing himself to draw a deep breath, he let it out slowly, relaxing his grip on the chair arm before it broke. He knew his anger wasn't for anyone present here, and it wouldn't do to start treating his friends like enemies in the heat of the moment.

As the unfortunate target of Gerrit's displeasure, Thurl squirmed slightly. Still, he held his ground in front of the throne admirably in the King's estimation. A small flush of guilt washed over the older man, causing him to sit back in his seat with a grunt as his heavy gold torc thudded into his chest.

The young man had enough problems without his King adding to them. Thurl had taken his wife from Hagen to Bastia to visit her family only to discover the town in shambles. The haunted look in the man's eyes as he described a once thriving place that now had no living resident larger than a bird was chilling, but understandable. His wife's family and everyone she had grown up with were missing, after all. But Gerrit would have expected that a span of more than a week since the discovery would have diminished the memory somewhat. Instead, after pushing themselves and their horses to near exhaustion on a hard trek through the hills to Scara, both were still obviously shaken.

Gerrit looked past the men in front of him to a corner near the front of the hall where Thurl's wife sat slumped and disheveled. A group of women surrounded her, offering whatever consolation they could along with cool spring water and hot, damp towels. The same awaited her husband when he was finished here, for which it was now long past time.

"Go see to your wife, Thurl," Gerrit said kindly, offering a sympathetic smile. "My daughter will find you a bed and a hot meal in whichever order you prefer."

"Thank you." Relief was plain in the set of Thurl's shoulders as well as his voice. With quick nods to the other men, he went to join his wife.

"A little hard on him, weren't you?" Kulmar asked arms crossed over his barrel of a chest, stretching the buckskin of his coat across his broad back.

Gerrit had expected the rebuke, or something like it, given the big farrier's presence in the hall. While it was the right of every Gotarran to speak his or her mind, Kulmar had been his friend since childhood and exercised this freedom more than most. But then, the other man was well aware that the King would receive correction far better from him than from almost anyone else.

"Tell me something I *don't* know." Gerrit shot his friend a look of annoyance, although both knew the frustration was really directed at himself. "It's not his fault he can't tell me what happened."

Kulmar's answering grin pulled at the thick scar that ran along the left side of his jaw—an injury that limited him to wearing a goatee, in contrast to the full beards grown by most men.

"He can't be telling us everything," Huldrich broke in.

At nineteen, Gerrit's son was becoming very much like his father in many ways. Though the younger man's physique was just on the edge of powerful, rather than the King's thickly muscled frame, he had the same wild brown hair that somehow looked perpetually windblown. Once Huldrich's thin whiskers grew into his father's mat of curls, he would be the spitting image of the King. Leaning casually on his unstrung bow, he was more an image of confident manhood now than awkward youth.

Gerrit smiled indulgently. Confident young man his son might be, but he was still as impetuous as always.

"A part of me wants to doubt that he looked very hard. After all, it's just too implausible that everyone just vanished." The King shook his head slowly to punctuate his words. "But I won't call him a liar." The look he directed at Huldrich informed the youth he had come close to doing just that.

Huldrich's single nod told him the message had been heard and understood. Before he could take time to consider what Thurl had said, however, some hint of Kulmar's mood drew his attention.

"What are you thinking?" Turning toward his friend, Gerrit used a hand to sweep the hair back out of his eyes. It immediately fell back.

The huge farrier took a moment to frame his answer, a pensive look on his features. When he spoke, his normally boisterous tone revealed that he was deeply troubled.

"Half the houses torn down," the reply came quietly. "Winter snow might collapse one or two if the owners were careless, but what would explain *half*?"

"Acedian soldiers," came an angry reply from somewhere behind Huldrich. A moment later, a short and stocky youth stepped into the space before Gerrit's chair. He looked ready to chew nails. "Soldiers could have destroyed that village and everyone in it."

"That's true, Suppan," the King admitted evenly, his voice carrying considerable forbearance. "But they didn't."

The young man colored slightly, though whether at the rebuke or because he thought Gerrit had missed an obvious truth was anyone's guess. "How do we know that until we see the damage for ourselves?" he asked hotly.

"Two reasons," Kulmar replied firmly, laying a beefy hand on the boy's shoulder in a calming gesture. He waited until he had everyone's full attention before continuing. "No group of soldiers could possibly have ridden that deep into Gotarra—in the dead of winter— and out again without being seen. I assume you excluded Brisia because the mountains would have been impassable." He paused as if expecting contradiction, gazing down at the *much* shorter man. "Secondly, King Carlon is an honorable man, whether *you* think so or not."

The admonition plainly brought Suppan to a slow simmer, but he remained quiet, for which Gerrit was grateful. He had often wondered how Huldrich and his friend Kessel managed to put up with the hot-tempered young warrior. Then again, his own father had probably wondered the same about Kulmar.

"Carlon has always kept his word," Gerrit agreed. "And if so much as a single woodsman ever violated the Acedian end of the treaty, their King would deal with it as harshly as I would." At this, he pinned Suppan with a hard look.

"I think Suppan was right about having a look for ourselves, though," Huldrich said firmly.

Gerrit suspected that his son was merely trying to support his friend, but it was certainly a valid point. He nodded his agreement, bringing a smile to Huldrich's face and a mollified look to Suppan's.

"Which is why you should send us." Kessel stepped forward, gesturing to Huldrich and Suppan in an inclusive way. The tall young man had stood quietly to this point, content to listen and wait for the right moment to speak.

Gerrit definitely approved of his son's choice of friends in Kessel. Mature and confident, he seemed the complete opposite of Suppan. With his sun bleached hair and an already full blond beard, he had many of the young women—and a few of the more mature—dreaming of landing him as a husband. In fact, Gerrit was half-convinced his teenage daughter had once been infatuated with him.

The King stifled a chuckle. He admired the young man's nerve and the air of assurance that was certainly no act, but he wasn't about to send untested warriors into an unknown situation. After all, the sense of immortality that always clung to people of that age did not actually *make* them immortal.

"Kessel, you are a grown man, and if you want to go, I can't stop you. But I'm not about to give you this responsibility and you know it." Now he did allow a soft chuckle at the deflated look on the youth's face. "I'm going myself."

The reactions of the men around him were widely varied, but not at all unexpected. The cocky grin that had recently been frozen on Suppan's lips vanished in an instant. Kessel looked as though Gerrit had just kicked his dog. Although obviously not surprised that he wouldn't be leading the men going to Bastia, Huldrich was obviously disturbed at the implications of his father's plan to go. It didn't take long for the youth to realize that he would be stuck in Scara, acting in the King's place.

Of the entire group, only Kulmar gave any sign of approval. His old friend merely smiled and nodded as if it were the most natural thing in the world.

"That's ridiculous!" Suppan blurted, evidently ready to argue the matter.

"Ridiculous?" Gerrit stood slowly, towering over the youngster once he was at his full height. His left hand rested casually on the long, wide-bladed knife hanging from his tooled leather belt. "Do you think I'm too *old*? Perhaps you think I'm feeble?"

"That's not what I meant," Suppan objected, his voice losing some of its strength as he searched for words. "I just meant that you're....

"Less than a capable warrior?" the King filled in smoothly, gold ring tapping softly on the knife hilt.

"No!" the younger man insisted, obviously flustered and beginning to redden.

"My father is just prodding you." Huldrich stepped in to rescue his friend. With a glance at his father he added, "But are you sure your leadership isn't needed *here*?"

Before Gerrit could reply, he was interrupted by Kulmar's booming laughter. As the muscular giant had probably intended, all eyes were immediately drawn to him.

"Very diplomatic, Hul, but not well thought out," the farrier said gently. "Leaders aren't needed most where things are going *well*. A battlefield is a mass of pure chaos, son, and few men can keep it from ending lives as well as your father."

Huldrich could only nod acceptance of the explanation.

Gerrit knew only too well the truth of that statement. Unlike the younger men and their need for adventure, however, he truly hoped this journey would be a waste of his time.

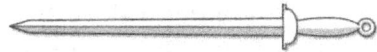

With the matter settled, Huldrich and his friends barely hesitated in making their excuses and leaving the small council. After all, there was little left to discuss beyond simple logistics and suggestions for who should go along.

One thing was certain—Huldrich would not be going. He understood the need to represent his father, and he accepted it, but he was definitely not looking forward to it. If past experience was any indication, it would most likely involve nothing more than listening to complaints for several weeks. Thankfully, Kessel and Suppan had chosen to stay with him when they could be riding out on what was essentially a war party. Given the opportunity, Huldrich wasn't so sure he would've done the same, but he was certainly grateful to his friends.

Outside the hall, the smells of baking bread and roasting meats seemed to fill the air as they wafted from several of the nearby houses. With his bow already in hand, it was almost tempting to go after a nice fat rabbit. But hunting was never any fun if it had to be rushed, and it was too late in the afternoon to take his time. Besides, while Kessel was an excellent hunting companion, Suppan tended to be so loud that he was pure disaster in the woods. Huldrich had found ways to leave the man behind before, of course, but Suppan had just shown him more loyalty than he had a right to expect and he would *not* show his friend less.

Without any particular plan, he found himself following the dusty, winding road that led to the Sturm, a small tributary of the Summer River that served as a natural border between Gotarra and Acedia. It was a pleasant enough place to spend a few hours that, once he realized his direction, he picked up his pace a bit, Suppan and Kessel right beside him.

Turning down a familiar side trail, the trio wound around the side of a steep hill, following a path beaten into the dirt by hundreds of such trips. Still, the route was little more than a deer run through thick brush, yet that and the steepness of the terrain had always ensured privacy at their destination.

They had discovered the immense, ancient oak shortly after the three had started exploring years before and had immediately fallen in love with it. It stood in a small clearing created by its own shade, perhaps a dozen feet above the high water mark on a steep bank of the river. Several thick limbs stretched out over the deep, cold water, one of them supporting a length of heavy rope that was knotted near the frayed end. Three large rocks sat near the base of the tree beneath the sheltering canopy of leaves, placed there after a series of difficult trips with an improvised sling.

Plopping down on his own rock, Huldrich leaned his unstrung bow against the massive trunk and peered down at the slowly churning water below him. The place had been a sort of sanctuary for years—an escape from adult attention at first, and now merely a place to relax with his closest friends. Only the high wooden palisade some distance away on the Acedian side spoiled the view.

The presence of the fort outside Elhanan didn't really bother him.   After all, it was something of an anachronism, having been built before his birth when the conflict between the two lands had been at its height. But that was long past, stopped by Huldrich's father as well as by King Carlon, he had to admit. Both men had come to power at about the same time—Carlon after his father's death in battle, and Gerrit after a long struggle to unite his people behind a single leader. With the bloody conflict ended, the garrison was home to only a token force meant more to give aid to trappers and woodsmen than as a real military presence. Now, the sentries manning the towers watched only for forest fires.

Mostly, Huldrich did his best to ignore it and enjoy the rest of the view.

Kessel gave the thick rope a few hard jerks to test its strength after a long winter of disuse.   Apparently satisfied, the tall youth immediately began unlacing his high buckskin boots and stripping off his woolen shirt.

Suppan was quicker, however, and reached the rope first. With a shout of pure joy, their stout companion dropped away as he swung out over the river, feet on the knotted end that just cleared the surface of water now deep with runoff from melting winter snow. He let go as the rope arced toward its apex and, tucking into a tight ball, performed a surprisingly graceful backflip before splashing into the river.

Whether the loud whoop as Suppan broke the surface was from exhilaration or the shock of the chill water was anyone's guess, but his eyes shone with delight. Shaking back the long wet strands of his hair, the youth grabbed the rope's frayed end and swam it back to the bank.

Huldrich had just removed boots and shirt when Suppan finished climbing the footholds cut into the slope. Handing the rope to Kessel, he used his hands to sluice the cold water from arms and chest covered in goose bumps.

"How is it?" Huldrich asked, already knowing the answer.

Suppan grinned. "Wet," he replied, trying to hide a slight shiver.

It was an old joke that had sprung from their refusal to admit that they were ever affected by the cold, which had seemed unmanly. Although they had outgrown the need for bluster, at least somewhat, they continued to give the familiar reply.

Wondering why he hadn't heard a splash, Huldrich looked up, surprised to see Kessel still standing on the bank. The rope, however, swung freely out over the river without him.

"You knothead." Laughing, Huldrich took a running start and dove into the river to recover the rope swing. Coming to the surface with a gasp, he couldn't resist a friendly dig at Kessel's unaccustomed clumsiness. "What are you doing? Daydreaming?"

In response, Kessel pointed to the Acedian side of the river, staring wordlessly.

Following his friend's finger, Huldrich saw them— two long columns of Acedian soldiers snaking their way through the open gate of the fort, pikes high and banners streaming.　　There had to be over fifty men, with remounts and packhorses to supply a small army. As fighting men went it wasn't a huge number, though it was five times the normal garrison. But if they had decided to rearm the fort, the reason couldn't be good.

Forgetting the dangling rope, Huldrich quickly swam the short distance to the bank and scrambled up. He felt suddenly numb as he tugged at his boots, knowing it wasn't just the chill of the water. It was hard to believe the influx of soldiers was a prelude to any treachery, since his father was a good judge of people and he trusted Carlon.　　Yet it was equally hard to believe anything else. Either way, he had to get back and tell his father what they had seen.

Snatching up his bow and quiver, he started back at a run, letting the others keep up as they could.

Caleb felt oddly constrained as he rode through the gates of the old log fort. Over the past few weeks, he had gotten used to the freedom of riding under wide open skies—no streets, no walls and very few people. This had been especially true on the broad prairie where only an occasional farm had marked the verdant landscape. In fact, his only complaint on the journey had been the horrid smell wafting from the tar fields, where pitch was drawn from the ground for use in the shipyards. It had left him hoping the wind would change direction or stop altogether. It had taken until the following day before he quit imagining he still sensed a lingering odor.

The last few days had been amazing, however, as the troops had gradually made their way into the rolling forested hills. Tier upon tier of high ridges rising in the distance provided a breathtaking view, and the ever-present haze painted the most distant a misty bluish-gray. Caleb found himself wishing that Elhanan, rather than Varella, were the capitol so he could spend the rest of his life near this incredible scenery.

Caleb had needed only a few days to get used to the routine of travel. Captain Braden had made it clear almost as soon as the castle had passed from view that he could not spare anyone, especially not a veteran soldier, to see to the Prince's horse or comfort. It hadn't been a burden, since he wasn't expected to stand watch or dig latrines, but it had taken getting used to not having a groom or someone to see to the little details of life. Yet it felt surprisingly good to be responsible for such things, giving him a sense that he belonged among these men.

But, now that they had arrived, he would need to get used to life indoors again, though he would continue to care for his own horse. He would also have to get ready to visit the barbarian King, Gerrit. The man would probably smell like the stinking tar pits and speak in grunts. He would do his best to represent his father, though, and he doubted even some backward barbarian could spoil his good mood.

Gerrit decided it was best to get on the road as quickly as possible now that he'd made up his mind to go. The four he would be taking with him from Scara wouldn't slow him down but, since he figured to gather more from the villages along the way, he expected plenty of delays.

Khara wasn't best pleased by the decision, of course, always preferring to have things well planned out. Still, she managed to put together supplies to supplement the hunting along the way, which wouldn't be able to support a force the size theirs would eventually reach.

Gerrit was definitely disappointed that Huldrich was nowhere to be found. Not that there was any need for last minute advice—since the worst his son would face was likely to be a dispute over field boundaries—but it would have been nice to say goodbye.

"Take care, Brother." He leaned out of the saddle to briefly grip Kulmar's hand, glad his friend would be around if Hul *did* need advice.

"Take care, yourself," Kulmar returned. A sudden impish smile tugged at his scarred jaw. "What do you call a barbarian man who's married?" he asked.

Gerrit rolled his eyes. He should have known this was coming. Kulmar had been driving him insane with these jokes since he'd heard one in a tavern last fall. He could only imagine how the man's wife put up with it.

"What?" he asked, hoping this would at least be one of the funny ones.

"The slowest runner!"

With his friend's laughter echoing down the street behind him, Gerrit kicked his horse to a ground-eating trot, forcing the others to do the same or be left behind.

Chapter 5

Dirty Work

Samir had assumed that Captain Tasca was serious about wanting to prove he couldn't handle the work of even a simple deckhand. Now he realized that he had definitely underestimated the strength of the Captain's resolve when he decided to prove a point.

From sunup to sundown he coiled lines as thick as his wrist, dragged bulging sacks of sailcloth to and from the hold for replacement or repair, and hung over the side in a sling to scrape the hull free of its crust of barnacles. With breaks only for meals or water, Samir pushed himself as hard as Tasca did, refusing to allow the man the satisfaction of seeing how tired he was or calling him lazy. But while he managed to hide the worst of his fatigue, he ached to the bone from hauling up water to scrub *Amelia's* decks, then hauling more to provide wash water for the crew.

Although there were plenty of other deckhands, he was certainly the most junior, earning him the hardest jobs. More to the point, however, every man aboard knew that the young warrior was the subject of the Captain's special attention—though the rumor differed greatly as to the reason. Yet, if there was work that needed doing, it was Samir who did the lion's share—or was left to do it alone—until sweat ran down his bare chest in streams and he was ready to drop.

Tirza, on the other hand, had taken it all in stride, as she did nearly everything. She spent the nights stretched out on the worn wooden planks beneath his hammock, probably more comfortable than he. During the day, she lay on the deck watching her master work, having given up the idea of trying to stay close amid the heavy traffic of men moving from task to task. It took little time for the hound to claim a spot in the bow where she could nap comfortably well out of the way of the busy crew.

Meanwhile, Samir worked himself to near collapse doing the jobs nobody else wanted as the rest of the crew watched, joked or wagered on his ability to keep up his present pace. Even if he'd been allowed to bet on himself, he wasn't entirely sure *he* believed it was possible to push his endurance much further.

Yet everything else paled compared to the work of cleaning out the bilge—hauling out the most foul smelling slime and brackish water from the lowest part of the ship to be dumped into the sea. Tasca had obviously been saving the task as a rather nasty punishment, since no one was cruel enough to assign it to someone he actually *liked*. If he'd only had to scoop the sludge out, it would hardly have bothered him, but he had needed to slither down into the cramped, awful space in order to do the job right. When he was finally done, after hours of grueling labor, the odor seemed to have seeped into his skin, and he hadn't even tried to clean the clothes he'd worn before he threw them overboard.

There had been moments when he had almost quit, had nearly brought himself to walk up to Tasca and admit he was done. He was certain that the Captain would relieve him of his duties, would tell him to relax and take the easy way out. But he had *never* given

Shimei less than his best, even when the Sòra had worked him until he'd vomited. Those lessons had taught him he had reserves of strength to be tapped, regardless of how exhausted he felt.

Samir had been drawing on those reserves for days and had decided that, when those were gone, he would dig until he found more. In the meantime, the Prince continued to mark his mental tally against Kemal.

Gradually, he saw signs that he was earning the respect of the men around him. Extra rations of meat and bread began quietly appearing on his plate at every meal. A new hammock suddenly replaced the tattered canvas that had threatened to rip and dump him unceremoniously atop the sleeping dog. Nods greeted him more and more frequently from the men around him—first from the other deckhands, then from the senior crewmen. Still, it was Tasca's respect he needed to earn and until he did, at least he would continue to enjoy the deep, hard slumber of the weary.

With a bit of adjustment, and a great deal of fatigue, Samir found the sailcloth hammock a surprisingly comfortable way to sleep as it swung gently from the overhead beams with the motion of the ship. At least he would have found it comfortable if he weren't crammed into a small space with the snoring and farting of dozens of other men. Still, simple necessity allowed him to sleep though all but the worst noises.

Tired as he was, however, there was no way to sleep through the continuous prodding of someone evidently determined to wake him. The offending party was nearly struck from sheer instinct, yet Samir was glad of his restraint when he opened his eyes to find the cabin steward, Wil. He had spotted the good-natured youngster sneaking treats to Tirza more than once and trusted that the boy wouldn't have awakened him without a good reason.

Weariness worked against him as he struggled to focus enough to make out Wil's gestures and sort out its meaning. Eventually, Samir understood he was to follow the boy topside, although he knew it couldn't possibly be time for him to go to work again so soon.

Wiping the slight crust of sleep from his eyes, he swung carefully to the floor, making sure to avoid stepping on Tirza's paws. It felt as though he'd barely slept, with his grogginess making coordination difficult as he wove between the swinging hammocks on the lightly rolling deck. Doing his best to move quietly, he was only vaguely aware of the hound padding along behind him.

The dark sky still carried no hint of a coming sunrise when Samir emerged at the top of the stairs leading to an oddly crowded deck. Normally, the only ones awake would have been a helmsman and whoever held the watch duty. Now though, Captain Tasca, the evening's duty officer—who was entitled to sleep unless needed—and the first officer all crowded the stern castle looking aft through long leather tubes and talking excitedly.

Still following the boy, Samir and Tirza climbed the steps to join the sailors.

Apparently hearing their approach, Tasca spared a quick glance over his shoulder before once again looking aft. "You're about to get more than you bargained for, lad."

"I already have, Captain," he returned, not bothering to hide his sarcasm. While he was definitely suffering the ill effects from their contest of wills, he had accepted what had seemed to be the unspoken terms—the warrior had to work harder than any other crewman, but received plenty of food and the ability to sleep without standing watches. Yet, apparently, Tasca had decided to change those terms once he realized that Samir wouldn't break. That was simply unacceptable.

"Not like this." Tasca stepped from his position at the rail, handing over the tube he had been holding.

Slightly confused, Samir accepted the strange offering, noticing now that brass rings held bubbles of glass at each end. Curious, he held the tube to his eye and immediately jerked back in astonishment at the sight of the Captain's nose, grown to enormous proportions. Returning the tube to his eye, he waved his hand across the other end, causing his fingers to appear the size of sausages.

"It's called a spyglass." Tasca's amused voice intruded on his experiment, drawing the Prince's attention. The Captain stood patiently, pointing in the direction the others faced. "Look that way."

Raising the glass once again, he faced aft and scanned the horizon for several moments, eventually spotting something out of place—sails. Just above the water, far in the distance, canvas sails billowed as the hull beneath them cut through the sea, seemingly headed straight toward them. Though it was hard to say, he thought he could just make out activity on the decks and rigging as the other crew scrambled about.

Even with his mind foggy from lack of sleep, Samir swiftly realized that it was either far too early or far too late for so many men to be working. Lowering the glass, he turned a curious gaze on the Captain.

"Pirates," Tasca explained. "Any normal crew would be asleep right now. Theirs should be as well, but they must have caught sight of us and pushed to catch up."

Pirates. Samir mulled the word over in his mind.

He'd heard merchants in his father's court complain about them and the losses they caused. Yet, somehow, the idea of pirates as anything more than a children's tale had never quite sunk in—until now.

"So why haven't you told the crew?" he asked. But, before the Captain could answer, something else occurred to him. "Why aren't we adding sails to put on speed?"

Tasca smiled indulgently, as if at a child. "Wouldn't do any good," he replied. "*Amelia's* a cargo ship, and she'll never outrun something built for speed. With a narrow prow like that, they'll be on us in a few hours no matter what we do."

Samir nodded as he grasped the truth of that. "And why tell me?"

"Two reasons." The answer came without hesitation, obviously well thought out. "First, the crew knows the risks they face. Pirates are a threat they've all accepted, and they know there won't be quarter given on either side. Right now they need the sleep that other crew is missing."

It made sense. In a battle, any advantage could be important—especially with men not trained to fight. Samir had seen a few brief scuffles between the crewmen, and he wasn't overly impressed by their skills. While he hoped the pirate crew would be no better, it seemed more likely that they would have an edge in both experience and purpose. After all, killing was how they made their living.

"And the other reason?" he asked.

The Captain met his gaze with a steady look. "I know some about your people," he explained. "That moustache you take such care to shave around means you consider yourself a warrior, and you have plenty of steel stored in my hold. I need to know if you're any good."

Samir smiled at the man's misunderstanding. "Actually, the moustache means my Sòra, my *teacher*, considers me a warrior. Trust me, there's a difference," he said plainly. "He would never allow anyone to wear this who might shame him in battle. So, yes, I'm good enough."

Something about Samir's reply must have made an impression on the Captain, because his answering smile showed fresh assurance. "I guess you know you're in this whether you like it or not," he said. "Anyway, it'll be good to have an extra sword."

"As to that," the warrior answered thoughtfully, "I'll have to decide what weapons to use. I'll be in the hold if you need me."

Before he could do more than turn, Tasca's voice stopped him. "What's in there, anyway?"

"Death," Samir replied evenly. Without another word, he walked away, already thinking ahead to what lay in the hold.

It took several minutes of shifting huge bails of silk before Samir found the large canvas bags propped in the corner. Extracting them had taken a bit longer, trying to maneuver his collection of steel weapons atop a stack of crates where there was room to open the sacks.

One at a time, he extracted them, each wrapped carefully in layers of soft cloth. The spear and axe heads he discounted immediately. They would be useless for him or anyone else unless they were properly mounted, and probably even then. Staves and spears would be difficult to use on a crowded deck where he was just as likely to hit his own people. Trying to control spinning chains would cause a similar problem.

No, he would need something that allowed freedom of movement.

Briefly, he considered entering the battle unarmed. Samir had no doubts that he was far more dangerous with hands and feet alone than any pirate could be with a sword. The problem was, while he was confident in his ability to dodge strikes by one or two men without much risk, larger numbers brought a need to parry. For that he would want steel.

He worked quickly, sorting the weapons into two groups almost by instinct. When finished, the ones he had deemed useful were easily the smaller batch.

The rings would work well in the close quarters he was expecting. Sharpened hoops, ten inches across with leather wrapped handles, they were easy to wield and were effective from any angle. They would also work well for disarming opponents. Unfortunately, he just wasn't as proficient with those as he would need to be in this fight.

He considered his longsword as well, but dismissed the idea. It had a fine balance and excellent reach, but was intended as a piercing weapon—easily aimed at precise targets. The longsword would be a good choice against an individual opponent, but not against a ship full of them.

Shimei had taught him well on the subject of weapon selection. After all, those decisions could easily mean life or death for a warrior and were too important to leave to chance. Samir knew there was more to consider than just crowded decks, or even weapon speed, in the battle he was about to enter. For one thing, there was the problem of the decks themselves. He had begun to adjust his walk to the rolling of the ship—a motion that was not exactly side to side and not quite up and down. Keeping his feet wouldn't be an issue, but having been too bone weary to practice, he wasn't optimistic about maintaining his balance with any of the more precise positions. More importantly, he was dead certain that high stances or maneuvers requiring finesse would be completely out of the question.

Ultimately, a double broadsword combination looked to be his best option, allowing multiple fast attacks as well as defense. Slashing or cleaving simply didn't demand precision, or even a deadly strike, to incapacitate an enemy—and he was more than happy to let someone clean up behind him if need be. A fight like this would come down to numbers and brutal efficiency, and he couldn't count on any real support from the crew. That meant he would need to work hard and fast with weapons designed for just that purpose.

The sun had risen by the time Samir repacked his arsenal and came back up on deck, its red-orange glow painting the sky with a beauty that seemed completely at odds with the mood. The rest of the men were awake but definitely subdued as they sat along the rails or hatches eating breakfast—although most merely picked at their food. Still, the sailors held murmured conversations with the people they would soon depend on for their lives, trying and failing to ease the tension.

Samir found the thought of porridge completely unappealing and the idea of company no less so given the current mood of the crew. Grabbing a good chunk of crusty bread and some weak tea, he settled into the bow with Tirza to do the only thing he could under the circumstances—wait.

It was a good spot, although there was quite a bit of movement as the prow climbed slightly against the swells before dropping again. He couldn't see the other ship from his seat on the deck, even though it was now less than a mile behind them and easily visible without a glass, but that was what he wanted. It would do no good to watch them approach or dwell on the fight. Better just to sit and enjoy the last hints of sunrise and the cool spray of the water as the droplets pelted him with each dip of the bow into the sea.

The relaxation was short-lived, however. Tasca was making his slow way in the direction of the foredeck, giving each man a quick word or a clap on the shoulder as he passed. It was what one would expect of a good leader, though it did surprise Samir coming from someone as slovenly as Tasca. More surprising, however, was that the man now looked the part—hair clean and tied back and dressed in a good blue wool coat. From the expressions of the crew, the Captain was doing a fair job of reassuring his sailors, projecting his faith that they would all make him proud.

What really drew Samir's eye was the sword hanging at the Captain's hip. Almost a scimitar, the gently curving basket-hilted weapon appeared well made and, more importantly, very well used.

The warrior nodded his approval to the other man, glad that someone else recognized the value of slashing weapons in a battle like this one.

"Be about another hour," Tasca offered as he covered the last few feet to Samir. "A long wait, I know, but things will happen *fast* after that. The hardest part is trying to keep them from getting charged up too soon." He indicated the crew with a nod as he leaned back against the rail.

Samir knew what the man meant. People seemed to draw energy from impending danger, energy they needed to deal with the crisis. But afterwards they became tired and shaky—and no one could afford to go into battle already in that condition. He assumed that was why weapons hadn't been passed around yet—to keep the excitement to a minimum until it was time.

"Have you thought about just *letting* them catch us?" he asked the Captain.

"You mean furl sails and wait?" Tasca shook his head ruefully. "I would if I could do it without giving them the same advantage. As it is, it would give them too much time to react."

"Maybe when they get closer, then." The suggestion earned Samir another head shake, this time with a sigh that seemed to deflate Tasca's ample belly.

"I forget how little you know about sailing," Tasca said, a slight smile curving his lips and deepening the creases around his eyes. "We won't need to slow ourselves. Once they get close, their sails will steal our wind and we'll stop fast enough."

Samir wasn't sure whether that was good news or bad, but at least now he would know what to watch for. Until then, it was just a matter of finding a comfortable place to sit and wait.

As the other ship drew closer, the men became noticeably more anxious, turning either to animated excitement or sullen silence. Even Samir was not immune to the tension, finding himself on the brink of rising to his feet more than once as the seconds dragged without apparent change. Soon enough, however, Samir could see the other sails clearly from his seat in the bow.

Suddenly, the other ship seemed to accelerate, leaping closer along the port side. A glance at *Amelia's* slack sails told a different story, revealing an abrupt loss of speed.

Men scurried about the deck, passing out more of the curved blades the Captain carried. Others hauled buckets of water, using them to soak the wood of the deck or tying them to lines to be raised into the rigging. While he was curious about some of the preparations, Samir couldn't afford to wonder long. The men knew what needed to be done, and he trusted them to do their jobs, but he had work of his own to do.

Samir stood slowly, using a basic breathing exercise to calm his mind and body, thankful for something to do. Taking his broadswords from where they leaned against the rail, he calmly strode to the main deck and placed himself amidships, poised on the balls of his feet. He hardly noticed a group of his crewmates scrambling up into the rigging armed with tightly strung short bows and bristling quivers. He saw, but would not allow himself to focus on, the men at the rail of the other ship, faces feverish with excitement and eagerness. His mind did note their weapons, however—more of the scimitar-like blades, often paired with daggers, and a good many cudgels as well.

Arrows began arcing rapidly in both directions, those from the other ship trailing fire and smoke as they sped toward *Amelia's* sails. But the warrior gave them only enough attention to see that he wouldn't be struck, completely ignoring the now steady rain of seawater being used to dowse the smoldering canvas. Instead, he turned his focus inward, harnessing whatever strength he could find. As exhausted as he was, it would take every ounce he could muster, and failure to dig deep would spell disaster.

With a long cleansing breath, he was ready.

Grapnels whistled through the air from the other ship, sharpened points biting hard into wooden rails as ropes were pulled tight to draw the hulls together. The men of *Amelia's* crew dashed forward to hack at the tough hemp fibers, axes swinging with desperate strength, but arrows plunged down at them from high above, driving them back or dropping them where they stood. More hooks clattered to the deck and were jerked tight, but Samir paid them no heed. The ships were close now, only feet separating them.

Men leapt from the railings of the other ship, singly at first, then in a flood of bodies. *Amelia's* crew raced forward to meet them with savage cries as the deadly rain of arrows from the rigging ceased abruptly. Without a sound, Tirza dashed off after them.

Men fell, sprawling on the deck as they boarded. Others merely fell, dropping motionless as the two crews collided not far from where Samir stood.

Without warning the warrior moved, flowing across the deck with broadswords moving in swirling counterpoint, drawing figure eights before him. A pair of invaders met him immediately, wicked smiles revealing an eagerness to shed blood and confidence in their ability to make it happen. Yet as they raised their blades to parry his whirling assault, Samir altered his attack—his body turning as he dropped his weight over his left leg in a low, crouching stance, other leg extended. His left hand swept across beneath his opponents blades, opening one belly and scoring a narrow red line across the second. His other sword hovered above his head, ready to attack or defend as needed.

The second man retreated a step, moving cautiously just out of range, circling right. All at once the man swung, striking at the Prince's extended right leg, putting his full weight into the blow as he committed himself to the attack.

Samir wasn't there.

Weight still on his left foot, he pulled his right leg back as the blade whistled past to slam full force into the deck. The warrior countered, the broadsword in his right hand cutting a deep gash across chest and shoulder to drop the man where he stood.

The entire encounter had ended in mere seconds, but Samir took no time to think about his victory as he moved on to engage three more.

He stepped to his right as the men closed in, using the one in the middle to block the enemy on his left, temporarily removing him from the fight. Still, the Prince got no reprieve as the man before him swung from the shoulder, aiming a vicious cut for his neck.

The warrior's left foot arced up, knocking the arm away even as he used a broadsword to sever the biceps. His other blade quickly parried a strike from the man in the center, now one of only two. His weapon engaged, the man failed to block as Samir's right hand sword swept back across to crash hard into his temple.

Stepping left, the warrior threw a double attack at his final opponent, one blade high, the other low. The man leapt back, desperately trying to avoid the strokes, but crashing hard on the deck as he tripped on the body of one of his fallen friends.

Unfortunately, Samir had no chance to finish him. Others rushed in to attack, determined to stop their most dangerous enemy. In moments, nearly a dozen men surrounded him, but he didn't care. This was the response he'd expected, the thing he'd half hoped for.

All around him noise and bodies filled *Amelia's* decks. Steel rang and the screams of the wounded came from every direction, their pain and horror nearly piercing the soul of those who heard. Samir paid it no heed.

He paused for only a moment, reading his opponents and assessing their aggression as well as their skills, then he moved with unbelievable speed. The broadswords whirled and slashed around him as he glided smoothly from position to position, forming a wall of moving steel. Attack and parry almost simultaneous, he spun to face in every direction with all the speed he could dredge up from the depths of his spirit. Blades bit and sliced, flinging droplets of dark crimson blood as they traced silver blurs around him. His feet struck nearly as fast, threading through openings to bash knees or hammer at a solar plexus. Twice, Tirza darted in behind an unsuspecting victim to snap at an ankle or bury her teeth into someone's wrist. All around him, men dropped, but others replaced them as they attempted to overpower him with the sheer weight of numbers, trying to stop the deadly whirlwind that Samir had become.

Back and forth he flowed across the deck, from one target to the next—his strikes whipping out like a serpent then suddenly shifting back the other way to catch an enemy unprepared.

Finally, one man ran, breaking away from Samir, trying to go anywhere else but near the sweeping broadswords. Others wasted no time in following the cowardly example. In seconds the tide of men trying to escape him had become a mad dash, quickly causing a wholesale rout among their crewmates.

Samir stood, swords dripping streams of red on the already bloody deck, bodies dead or barely moving lying in every direction around him. He knew that he was responsible for most of the carnage, although he had no idea how many had fallen because of him—maybe fifteen, perhaps twenty or more. Now he merely watched as those who could jumped for their own vessel, landing clumsily and tripping over rails in their haste to escape.

Men of both crews chopped frantically at the ropes holding the two ships together as one by one they parted under the blows of razor sharp steel. Finally, inexorably, the hulls separated as the other ship accelerated away.

A weak cheer rose from sailors across the ship as *Amelia* heeled to starboard—some crewman throwing the wheel over hard to increase the separation. The Majaran was too tired to celebrate as his fatigue finally slammed home, making him brutally aware of how little he'd slept. Breath came as if dragged from his raw throat as he looked around.

Weary and wounded sailors were beginning to move about the deck, doing their best to help those with even worse injuries. Nearly everyone was covered in blood, though whether their own or someone else's, only a closer examination would tell. Screams slowly subsided, some weakening as death approached to claim another victim, others gaining relief from the care of their shipmates or liberal doses of rum. In a few cases, however, the cries ended with stunning quickness as the pirates who sounded them were either killed or thrown overboard by *Amelia's* crew.

With all the blood in the water, Samir suspected that, if they stayed in the area any length of time, he would see how the Sea of Sharks had earned its name. For a brief moment, he found himself actually feeling sorry for the pirates who had not been killed outright.

The other ship dropped away quickly as she cut off on an eastern tack and *Amelia* picked up speed. With that, the warrior finally let himself relax, shoulders sagging and the weight of his legs dragging down like lead. With an effort, he made his way to the starboard rail and sank back against the low gunwales to sit heavily. His last awareness, as he faded off to sleep, was of Tirza growling with lips curled back the teeth barred, keeping several members of the crew away from him.

When he awoke, it was to find that he was surprisingly comfortable, lying on thickly piled blankets with a pillow under his head. The broadswords, now wiped clean of any trace of blood, had been placed beside him on the deck within easy reach.

A quick glance revealed Tirza, happily gnawing away at what was left of a ham shank, a bowl of water nearby. She appeared content and unhurt, but he expected as much with a remarkably fast breed like a Raphan Hound—dogs that excelled at hunting cats their own size.

Samir knew he'd slept for some time, with the sun now to the port side of the masts, well past its noon peak. The worst of the mess had been cleaned and repairs had begun while he had been blissfully unaware of any work going on around him. The deck would need a furious scrubbing, and one sail flapped loosely in the wind as it waited to be replaced, yet the ship seemed to have nearly returned to its normal pace.

Of course, plenty of jobs were left for him to break his back on. The Prince had done his share and more of every task so far, but he wouldn't be accused of shirking now.

"He's awake, Captain." The high pitched call was surprisingly loud, coming as it did from so small a person.

Samir had noticed the young steward perched casually on the cargo hatch, but had paid him no mind as he took in his surroundings. Wil had clearly been there for a reason—perhaps to make sure the warrior could sleep undisturbed, but more likely to watch for him to wake.

Hopping to his feet, the boy darted to the ladder and vanished below, yet the steward's disappearance didn't hold Samir's attention for long. Tasca descended stiffly from the quarterdeck, limping more than a little from a roughly bandaged wound on his left thigh. Astonishingly, Tirza gave up her fascination with the bone and trotted over to greet the Captain as he came slowly toward them. Judging from the hound's reaction, it had evidently been the old sailor who had given her that tasty little morsel, probably to let the crew near her master.

"Traitor," he chuckled as she padded by. She barely glanced in his direction, not slowing.

She was back moments later, however, as Tasca stopped beside Samir and eased himself down on the rail. He patted the wood beside him in invitation for the warrior to join him.

With a jaw-cracking yawn, Samir threw back the blanket covering him and rose to his feet. Overworked muscles in his legs and shoulders protested slightly, yet he felt better rested than he had in days. A glance at his pants as he sat revealed that the cotton was now more red than blue and was stiffening from the rapidly drying blood. He doubted they were worth saving.

"How many?" he asked, settling in. The Captain seemed to know what he meant.

"Six so far. We may lose another two by tomorrow, and more if infections set in." He sounded understandably grim as he discussed the losses. But his tone quickly changed to one of respect bordering on awe. "*You* on the other hand, tallied *eighteen*."

Samir's eyebrows climbed nearly to his hairline. He certainly wouldn't dispute the possibility that he had at least wounded that many, but he doubted he had killed them all directly. Still, it was an impressive total.

"They're sailing home with a much smaller crew than they brought to the party," Tasca continued with a twinkle in his eye.

Wil chose that moment to return, trotting across the deck carrying a plate piled high with ham, bread and cheese. In his other hand, a cup sloshed what appeared to be ale as the boy hustled over perhaps more quickly than he should. Handing both to Samir, he plopped down beside Tirza and began to scratch her belly.

Famished, the Prince began biting off large chunks of meat and cheese, not bothering to savor the taste. While he chewed and swallowed, the Captain waited silently, letting him take the edge from his hunger before continuing the conversation.

"I'd like you to stay on and train my crew," he said finally, cutting to the heart of the matter. "They'd never be as good as you, of course, but you could make them a match for any boarding party. The dog is welcome to stay, too." He smiled down at the hound, now rolled on her back enjoying the boy's attentions.

It was certainly an interesting offer, and it would give him a place to dedicate himself to training. As far as he knew, his people's hard won skills had never been taught to outsiders, but he wasn't aware of any law against it. There was only one problem with the idea—Majar was a regular trading stop for *Amelia*, and it was the one place Samir couldn't go.

"I'll think about it," was all he could think to say. He would, too, even though he knew it was unlikely he would say yes.

"You do that, lad." Tasca gave the warrior's knee an affectionate pat, then pushed to his feet with a grunt and limped back toward the quarterdeck.

Realizing he had finished the food and ale, Samir set the empty cup and plate at his feet, then grabbed his swords and rose. He needed to wash badly, to rid his body of the sweat and blood that clung to it. After that, he would find his hammock and sleep again.

Bounding over to pick up her bone, Tirza followed close on his heels.

The sitting room was hardly what Jenaris would call luxurious, but it was almost certainly grand compared to what he would find in the fishing village below. No doubt there would be a few of the wealthier merchants who would be able to afford a better quality of craftsmanship, but the local lord's manor would be expected to have the best—as long as he didn't squander their taxes on fripperies. Of course, even with a pleasant home and a few nice things, the lord of a fishing village was still only the lord of a fishing village.

"What can I do for you this fine morning?" The smiling man who entered, Lord Haley, was still busily tying his cravat as he stepped through the door. From the slight odor of fish that clung to him, it was obvious that he had just donned the fine coat and polished boots he now wore. "I hope you'll pardon the delay. I was just seeing after today's catch."

The Mage set down his nearly empty cup of tea on a small side table, returning the friendly smile. He stood quite a bit taller than the rotund, bald man before him, which was unusual since he was only of medium height himself. But, then, he was used to the feeling since being a wizard had a tendency to make people see him as taller than he really was.

"I was actually hoping you could help me find a friend of mine," Jenaris replied hopefully. "He's also a Wizard."

Haley considered for a moment, head shaking slowly. "Hasn't been one of your folk this way since my father's time," he answered. "Maybe twenty years."

"Was his name Lorn, by any chance?" It was a struggle to keep the eagerness out of his voice.

Twenty years was a long time, yet not so long to a wizard. But one effect of being rather long-lived was a tendency to put down deep roots. So, wherever he had gone from here, Lorn was probably still there.

"Yes, I believe that *was* his name," Haley nodded. "Left saying something about sprites or some such. Went to the Great Wood."

Chasing down stories of strange wildlife sounded just like Lorn. The man would climb a mountain to count the eggs in an eagle's nest—but only if it were of some exceedingly rare variety. More than once the man had earned Kirstea's wrath for running off in search of a rumor. But his natural curiosity about such things made him exactly the one who would be able to help him now. If *anyone* could answer Jenaris' questions, it would be Lorn.

"Well, then, I guess I'm off to the Wood," the Mage replied. "I don't suppose he mentioned any particular place?"

"No," Haley said apologetically, "but you might start with Hogarth."

"Thank you." Jenaris offered a smile, although he wanted to cringe at how vague a trail he had to follow. Scooping up his staff from where it leaned against a chair back, he started for the door.

"Um, if you don't mind my asking," the other man broke in hesitantly.

The Wizard said nothing, merely raising his eyebrows as he stopped.

"Do you think you could do anything about my lower back?" Haley finished. "It pains me something awful these days."

Jenaris had to resist the urge to laugh. It had taken the man some genuine courage to ask the question, he was sure, and he didn't need to embarrass him further.

"I'm afraid I'm not that kind of wizard," he answered kindly. He didn't bother to say that kind of wizard didn't actually exist as far as he knew, but herbalists weren't exactly hard to find—not that they could fix the underlying issue, only relieve the pain.

The mage signed. His own nagging sensation, the growing itch between his shoulders, he was now certain was in response to the Calling he had cast. It was really the only good news he'd had in some time now; and he was still uncertain what to make of it. Unfortunately, it was still far too early to tell.

With a final thanks, he went to gather his horse. It was a long ride back to Hogarth.

Chapter 6

The Old Rope Bridge

The gelding frisked a bit, seeming to pick up on Caleb's mood as he rode toward the open gates of the fort. It was already fast becoming one of those amazing spring days he had come to identify with this place, though whether it was due to the altitude or some other cause he neither knew nor cared. All that mattered was that it was a perfect day to ride.

"Morning, Highness." The young guard who emerged from the shade of the guardhouse wore a broad smile as he greeted the Prince. "Time for your morning ride?"

"Morning, Maclin," Caleb returned, halting his mount with a quick jerk of the reins. "You know it is. Nothing else to do around here, and Searcher needs his exercise." He gave the sorrel's neck an affectionate pat.

"I wouldn't mind getting out more often myself," Maclin replied with a touch of longing in his voice. "Patrols just aren't the same."

Caleb nodded his sympathy. He had to admit that as beautiful as the local scenery was, this would be just another post if all you saw was the walls of the fort or the men riding in front of you. Thankfully, he had plenty of time to enjoy himself.

"I've got one for you," he announced, a mischievous light coming into his eyes. "What do you have if twenty barbarians are in one room?"

Maclin considered for a moment, a smile of anticipation on his face. "A ten word vocabulary?"

"No, but that's pretty clever," Caleb grinned. "What you have is a full set of teeth."

Both men burst into a sudden fit of laughter. As it subsided, the young guardsman broke in.

"What's the difference between a barbarian's brain and a large rock?" he asked, smiling.

The Prince shook his head. "I don't know. What?"

"A couple of pounds."

This time the laughter continued until his sides ached, drawing strange looks from those passing in the nearby street. That was what he liked about Maclin—where most of the other soldiers were serious to the point of boredom, he was usually ready with a good joke.

Of course, it was easy to be in a good mood on a day like this. With a wave, Caleb kicked his horse into motion and rode through the gates.

The road split a short distance from the fort, part of it winding south and west out of Elhanan, back to the plains by which he had come. The other fork would soon carry him across the wide stone bridge that spanned the Sturm and linked Acedia to Gotarra—at least as well as any two worlds as different as theirs *could* be linked. But although his father had sent him to deliver a message to King Gerrit, he had yet to cross that bridge. Captain Braden made daily trips across the river into Scara to see if the barbarian King had returned, but so far he hadn't; and Marius would not let Carlon's emissary look foolish by arriving for a meeting that wouldn't happen.

Still, he chose to follow that branch of the road, at least for a time. In sight of the bridge, however, he turned west to follow the river bank away from the town and into the trees that shaded the well-worn trail.

Leaves rustled softly overhead as Searcher followed the path beneath the great oaks without Caleb's guidance, having learned the route well over the past weeks. They had ridden this same route every day since he had discovered that Gerrit had gone and he would need to wait. That first day, he had merely decided to explore the area—to see more of the scenery he'd found so breathtaking when he arrived. The ride had been a short one, less than two miles, but he had encountered a beauty that he was completely unprepared for.

Soon enough, the path opened before him into a small clearing beside the river, well lit and cooled by a soft breeze off the water. Dotted with wildflowers, it was very nearly the perfect place, enough so that someone had built a rough bench here. It was just a thick stone slab perched atop a pair of large rocks, but comfortable enough to sit for hours on end.

It wasn't the bench that caught Caleb's attention as he rode into the little haven, however. It was the bench's occupant. Despite the amazing beauty around him, it paled to insignificance compared to Sorana. He had memorized every line and detail of her heart-shaped face, delicately framed by long hair the color of honey. Caleb could easily have lost himself for days in her deep brown eyes and never even noticed the passage of time. She was, in a word, perfect.

Sorana turned slightly as he dismounted. The smile lighting her face and filling her eyes touched him almost like a physical caress. The Prince couldn't help but smile himself as he covered the short distance to the bench, unconsciously straightening the dark green wool of his coat.

He had anticipated this moment since he had awakened at first light, had thought of little else since he had left her the day before. Her tall, slender figure was warm and supple in his embrace, and the sweetness of their kiss was all too brief. But then, it would have been too brief if it had lasted an hour.

"I don't think I could ever get tired of that," he told her with a satisfied smile, taking her hand as he sat to draw her down beside him.

"I should hope not," Sorana replied, raising an eyebrow slightly. "But if you do, you'll just have to suffer through it, because I intend to do that a lot more."

Somehow, incredibly, the look she gave him was at once brazen and coy.

Caleb had no idea how she managed that, but it absolutely delighted him. *She* delighted him, and from almost the first moment they'd met.

She had been sitting on that same bench, watching as the river rolled slowly past and enjoying the cool breeze that stirred her hair. They had seen each other at the same time, as he had ridden into the clearing and pulled Searcher up, each surprised to find someone in such a remote place. She had almost run then, he knew. He had seen it in the wide eyes and in the hesitant movement of her body. But then her look had changed just as swiftly to fierce determination as she decided that she wouldn't run from him or anyone else. In that instant, he had loved her. He had been captured by Sorana's strength and her spirit, finding them as much a source of her beauty as the soft curve of her lips or the dimples that graced her cheeks.

It seemed impossible that they had known each other such a short time. On the one hand, Caleb knew almost nothing about her—she wouldn't even tell him where she lived, although he could tell her father was fairly well-to-do, probably a merchant. Her clothes, like the blue dress she wore now, were always very well made, of finely spun wool. Her soft leather slippers were durable, but good enough for someone being presented in his father's court. The silver hoops of her earrings, though plain, spoke of some wealth as well. In fact, even the necklace that was a gift from her grandfather—an intricately linked double chain, lovingly and masterfully carved from a deer antler—somehow fit her perfectly.

On the other hand, Caleb knew everything he would ever need to know about her. He knew she had more sweetness and compassion than he thought could exist in a single soul. He knew that her smile was warmth itself, and magical. He knew that her heart was a depthless well that he would be content to spend his life discovering. There were a thousand things about her that he would need to learn—*wanted* to learn. But they had time for that. They would have a lifetime together. After all, there was no doubt in Caleb's mind that she was his soulmate, and he was hers.

The thought made him smile.

Of course, the young Prince hadn't actually told her who he was yet either. It wouldn't change her view of him, he was sure, but at first he hadn't wanted to risk any awkwardness over his rank. After that it just never came up.

"What are you smiling about?" she asked, a quizzical look crossing her features in a way he found endearing.

"Nothing." He gently brushed a stray bit of hair away from her face, his fingertips trailing down he cheek. "I'm just...happy."

Apparently satisfied with the answer, she caught her lower lip briefly between her teeth before leaning in to kiss him.

"And just what makes you think you can do that whenever you want?" he objected with feigned indignation.

"What makes you think you have any say in the matter?" Sorana replied, brown eyes flashing and an impish grin making her dimples appear.

Unable to keep a straight face, all he could do was laugh with delight and shake his head at his good fortune.

"You're amazing." The word didn't seem to even come close to being strong enough, but it was all he could think to say.

"I know," she teased, flipping her hair and adopting a casual pose by leaning back on her hands and turning her face to the sky.

He couldn't help but notice that the arch this put in her back made her breasts do remarkable things. He also couldn't help but stare, just a little.

"Ahem." Sorana cleared her throat loudly and pointed to her face. "I'm up here." The stern look she gave him was spoiled somewhat by her attempts to keep from laughing.

"You're right, of course." Caleb rose smoothly and bowed, executing it with overly dramatic flourishes. "I vow never to look at you again, m'lady."

In reply, Sorana stuck out her tongue at him, causing them both to burst into fits of laughter.

Listening to the musical quality of her voice when she laughed, he wondered how he could *not* love her.

For a few minutes they merely sat in silence, enjoying each other's company and sharing the beauty of their private place. Caleb watched as an eagle spiraled slowly into the sky on the warm updrafts it seemed to find by instinct. Sorana gave his hand a light squeeze.

"I love you, too," he replied simply. From the corner of his eye he could just see her, and the smile she gave him was absolutely radiant.

It was too much.

Scooping up a palmful of small stones from the ground at his feet, Caleb stood and took a few steps toward the river. His right arm whipped back, then forward in a sidearm throw as he let a stone fly, arcing it high to cover the fifty feet to the river. It plunked into the calm water with only a tiny splash and, from that distance, no discernible sound.

"I do love you, you know," he finally said into the silence.

"I know." He could hear the smile in her voice, along with mild concern, as she replied. "And I love you."

"I want to talk to your father." Caleb chunked another stone. "When are you going to let me...."

"*Soon*," Sorana interrupted. "You just need to be patient."

He had known only too well what she would say. After all, they had had almost the exact conversation yesterday *and* the day before. He was growing tired of being patient, feeling as if all he'd done for weeks was to wait for other people. But this had to be done the right way, out of respect for their parents and out of respect for her. He had already dispatched a fast courier to his own parents, telling them about Sorana and seeking their support to pursue an engagement. There was little doubt what their response would be—they would insist on meeting her, of course, but they trusted his judgment enough to give at least a provisional blessing. Until that reply came back, he could do nothing officially, but he still needed to get to know her family and begin to build a relationship with them.

"Can we *please* change the subject?" The frustration in Sorana's voice nearly matched his own.

"Sure," he said, throwing another stone. If they were going to be together forever, then he supposed a few more days wouldn't kill him. He quickly latched onto a new subject. "Hey, why are barbarian women always so angry?"

Behind him, Sorana's gaze snapped up from the river to Caleb's back. "Huh?" Her breath left her in a rush.

"They're jealous," he said, voice bubbling with suppressed laughter. "The men have thicker beards."

The gradual realization that he was laughing alone made Caleb turn and notice the tight, forced smile on her face. He felt like such an *idiot*! Why couldn't he have just let the subject of meeting her father drop instead of pushing the issue again? He couldn't quite understand why it had upset her this badly—which she clearly was—but he shouldn't have brought it up today.

"I'm sorry. I won't mention your father again," he soothed, moving closer and crouching down to take her hands. From here, he could see how pale she suddenly looked. "Are you feeling all right?"

"What?" Sorana seemed briefly confused. "No, I'm really not. I have to go."

Extracting her hands from his, she gently pushed him away, rising on slightly unsteady legs. His brief attempt to reach out and steady her brought a quick head shake as she held him at arm's length.

"At least take my horse," Caleb offered, fighting down alarm. "You shouldn't walk if you're ill."

Without another word, she ran for the gap in the trees that marked the trail toward Elhanan, holding her skirts tightly to keep from tripping.

Caleb merely stood there dumbly for several seconds, then hustled across the clearing to where Searcher grazed calmly amid tufts of clover. It took him only moments to swing up into the saddle and send the horse pelting toward the trail. They should have caught her quickly, he knew, having followed before she could run far. As he pushed on toward the town, however, he began to realize that it was no use. She was gone.

Sorana broke into a dead run as the shadows of the trail swallowed her. Within moments she had reached the small deer run that branched toward the river and took it almost without slowing.

Hateful, hateful man, her mind screamed as she wiped at the bitter tears that flowed freely down her cheeks.

The old rope bridge came into view through the dense cover of scrub, stretching across the river. It had been built before she was born—a span of thick, twisted hemp and closely spaced boards made to allow raiding parties to slip south past the garrison and into Acedia. As far as she knew, only she used it now, although her father made a point of inspecting and repairing it each spring—mostly for her sake.

It barely moved as she crossed, only bouncing a bit under her slight weight. She hardly noticed the few creaking boards, trusting them to hold her as she crossed as quickly as possible, then was off and running again.

Tears continued to flow in an unending stream as Sorana reached the hard packed dirt road and sped past the irrigated fields. By the time she reached her home on the edge of Scara, she was gasping and her sides ached, but she knew it wasn't just from running. Pain tightened her chest, leaving her with the feeling of being unable to breathe.

The thick door shut behind her harder than she had intended, but she paid no attention. Pressing her back to the wall, she slid slowly to the floor as her quivering legs finally gave out, her strength spent. With her arms wrapped tightly around her knees, she wept.

"Mother? Is that you?" Huldrich called, emerging from his bedroom clutching a shirt. "I need you to mend one of my...."

Sorana peeked out from behind a curtain of her long hair to see her brother stopped in the middle of the room, his shirt carelessly dropped at his feet as he looked at her. He was beside her with amazing speed, kneeling on the hard floorboards and lifting her chin to get a close look at her.

"What's wrong?" Concern was plain in his voice as he tenderly lifted her to her feet.

Sorana clutched at him desperately as she buried her face in his shoulder, her body wracked with sobs. He held her quietly, stroking her hair, seeming to accept that she would talk when she was ready. Yet she could also feel the building tension in his back and arms, as if he felt that some unknown threat were out there, needing to be dealt with.

"It'll be all right," he offered soothingly, repeatedly, as the crying gradually eased to quiet sniffles.

Looking up, she gave him a weak smile of thanks, which he seemed to take as a willingness to talk.

"What's wrong, Rana?" Huldrich continued stroking her hair as he had when she was a child afraid of the thunder outside. "What happened?" he urged.

"Caleb." A tremor touched her voice as she answered, the hurt rising all over again at the name.

The muscles of his back and arms went hard as mountain stone. "Did he hurt you?" he demanded, lifting her chin to search her eyes for the answer. "If he touched you...."

"He didn't." Sorana shook her head, feeling her brother gradually begin to relax. "I'm all right, Hul."

But it wasn't true or anywhere near the truth. Caleb *had* hurt her, terribly, and she had given him all the power in the world to do it when she had opened her heart to him. She had allowed herself to be vulnerable, and he had responded to her love by showing utter contempt for everything she was and slandering her people.

She *hated* him!

"Where do I find him?" Huldrich asked softly, loosening his hold on her as if preparing to leave. His voice had held a clear edge of potential violence.

"No, Hul." Sorana gripped his arm hard, digging in her nails to get his full attention. Even with the tears still slowly dripping, her expression was unmistakably serious. "No. It doesn't matter. I never want to see him again."

"Your call," he allowed grudgingly. "Do you want to tell me about it?"

"No," she smiled. "I just want to be alone for a while."

But that wasn't true either. She wanted to be with Caleb, and she hated herself for being so weak.

With a shrug, Huldrich bent down and kissed her forehead before making his way back to his room to give her the privacy she wanted.

Chapter 7

Kir

The end of the long wooden staff emitted a low whistling sound as it sped in a circle above Samir's head to execute a warding maneuver. Faster than an eyeblink he dropped to a crouch to slam the long wooden rod to the deck with a resounding clack, pivoted smoothly on the balls of his bare feet and slapped it down again on his other side, its end a blur. Drawing it back, he centered one hand along the shaft and swept it across in front of him, leaving one end free in space and the other across his back. Without warning, the warrior's body flashed upward in a high spinning kick, legs scissoring before he landed perfectly balanced and centered with the staff spinning in front of him. Almost before he thought to act, the weapon stopped abruptly, its end jabbing out as the air was split with a deafening shout that erupted from his chest.

Amelia's crew had grown used to the grueling practice sessions Samir inflicted on himself, but several of the men still shouted their approval from places along the rails or at work in the rigging as he came to rest, barely winded. It was already his second such workout of the day and he was pleased to find that he could now achieve and maintain any stance or position with little effort—despite the rolling motion of the ship as it rose and fell on the swells of the Bharkur Sea. He wondered briefly how long it would take him to get used to fighting on flat, solid ground again. Still, he would definitely benefit from the improvement to his technique. The pirates were actually lucky they didn't have to face him *now*.

There had been little to do for the past few days except to spend his hours moving through his wide assortment of forms and katas. Not that he would ever complain about having the chance to dedicate himself to training, but it had certainly taken him by surprise.

He had tried to take up his deckhand duties again the morning after the attack. But while he hadn't been told by anyone directly, he was soon made abundantly aware that it was not going to be allowed. When he had tried to grab a brush or a mop to scrub or wash the deck, some other crewman always seemed to need it and got there ahead of him. When a new sail had to be hauled from the locker, he somehow found himself crowded out of the way, purely by chance, by a group trying to "help" him with the job. In fact, the first day he had managed to haul only a single bucket of water to the deck before one of the other deckhands borrowed his bucket and simply never brought it back.

Samir had caught Tasca watching him a few times, or at least he thought he had. It was always deftly handled but, in hindsight, the Captain had always seemed to be on hand and had never so much as implied that Samir might be slacking. Perhaps it was a mark of his fatigue, but it had actually, amazingly taken until the second day before he had fully taken the hint.

Naturally, he was glad to have finally won the respect of the crew, and to a far greater extent than he had thought possible. Yet, even with the seeming insistence that he take his ease for the rest of the voyage, Samir felt uncomfortable with the idea of doing nothing.

So now he practiced, for hours on end several times a day, working himself nearly as hard as Shimei would have. In fact, he might have worked himself *as* hard if he'd had a competent opponent to spar against. The best man available possessed skills Samir had surpassed nearly a decade earlier. The amount of time he now spent honing his technique and improving his fitness was almost triple what he had once considered adequate— and his proficiency had grown accordingly to anyone who knew what to look for. His new routine worked him for nearly as many hours as his deckhand job had. The difference was that, although it still left him weary to the bone, he also felt the thrill that came from doing what he had been made for.

Of course, considering how hard he pushed himself, he was glad that his diet had improved. Not only did the cook regularly slip a meaty bone to Tirza, but Samir's plate also seemed to hold just a little bit extra when he ate with the crew—and he definitely wanted for nothing when he was invited to dine with Tasca and his first officer, Niklas.

Stripping off his shirt, Samir walked the short distance to the barrel of wash water at the base of the forecastle, where the extra sail was stored. Propping the staff against the low bulkhead, he began to lather himself with the small cake of soap, wishing he could dive into the vast expanse of water around them to wash properly. Hearing the heavy tread of footsteps behind him, he knew exactly who he would find when he turned.

"Good afternoon, Captain," he said without looking as he ladled water to rinse himself. "What can I do for you today?"

"Just thought you'd like to know we'll be in Lastra early tomorrow." Tasca's reply gave no hint of where the conversation was headed, yet the man had never sought him out for just a casual chat.

"And what's in Lastra?" Samir turned as he spoke, wanting to see the Captain's face while they talked.

Tasca made a dismissive gesture.

"Not a very interesting place unless you're a sailor or a shipwright," he insisted. "Mostly shipyards and taverns. We'll be there just long enough to take on lumber, sails and pitch...and a few new deckhands."

As brief as it had been, Samir had heard the slight pause in the other man's response. Aside from the men who had died during the attack, one more had of his injuries the next day and another of infection from a belly wound. Even days later, one sailor was still unfit for duty and would be sent ashore with enough money to see him through until he was healthy enough to work. All of these men—including Samir himself, who wasn't actually doing his share—would need to be replaced, though the reality of losing good men obviously bothered Tasca.

"I don't suppose...," the Captain began, but went no further with the thought.

The warrior waited, saying nothing despite his curiosity. It was clear that Tasca wanted something, but it seemed best to wait and find out what, rather than inadvertently commit to anything. After all, while it was true that Samir was thankful for the opportunity to throw himself into his training, he refused to be obligated by it.

After a few uncomfortable seconds, Tasca continued. "Have you given any thought to my invitation?"

The Captain was obviously talking about the offer to stay aboard and train the men to fight. But while he had considered it, as he said he would, there were simply too many difficulties with the idea. Unfortunately, his thoughts had turned in a direction that had made him aware of a problem that would need to be dealt with, and soon. Bringing it up, however, would require him to place a great deal of trust in the man standing before him—and the last person he had trusted had betrayed him completely.

Anger at Gehazi stirred deep in his chest at the memory, bringing a momentary flash of regret that he had let the man walk away. The last thing Samir wanted to do now was to risk having that happen again. Still, there was nothing to be done for it but to take a chance.

"I have," he said finally, shaking his head. "I just don't think it would be possible."

"Well, I'll admit some of them are a bit ham-fisted," Tasca insisted, "but clumsy men don't do well in the rigging. Believe me, they can learn." The man finished with a nod, assured that his faith in the men was well placed.

Again Samir shook his head slowly. "That's not the problem," he told the Captain, knowing that the time had come to make his choice. He chose to trust. "If the crew learns to fight like me and my people, someone will eventually wonder who taught them. As it is, I already need to ask a favor."

Tasca's eyes widened briefly in surprise, then narrowed, but he didn't interrupt.

"I need the crew to forget that I was ever here," he said, meeting the Captain's eyes squarely to convey the urgency of his need.

"They'll forget a lot of things," the other man chuckled, "but they won't forget that fight. In fact, they'll be sure to tell as many as might buy them a drink for the tale."

That was exactly what Samir was afraid of, but he did have a possible solution. "I expect that's true, but what I need is for them to forget my *name*." Seeing the Captain's puzzlement, he explained. "I have an enemy who has to keep thinking I'm dead for a little while. But stories about a warrior named 'Samir' might reach the wrong ears, and I can't risk that."

Tasca was silent for a time while he considered what he'd been told. Finally, he met the Prince's eyes with a penetrating look. "Who's Samir?" he asked seriously. "My deckhand's name is *Kir*, and I'll see that any man who forgets it spends a day in the bilge."

"Thanks," Samir allowed a smile, breathing a deep sigh of relief.

"For what?" Tasca called over his shoulder as he started toward the quarterdeck. "Do you think you're the first sailor who didn't want his real name bandied about?"

Samir laughed, surprised that the possibility hadn't even occurred to him.

Samir, or Kir, as the others were now calling him, had little experience with seaports, having seen only Barat and now Lastra. If those two were any indication, however, he expected they all must be loud, crowded and so chaotic that he could make no sense of what was happening. Ships' crews and stevedores loaded and unloaded goods and supplies with shouted curses and bawdy jokes. Carpenters built and repaired vessels of every description. Teamsters pushed through the crowds driving merchandise in and out of massive warehouses along the waterfront. Well-dressed merchants sweated and swore over the quality and condition of offered goods. Captains made deals for cargoes, gulls shrieked over scraps, and everywhere was the press of sailors seeking ways to part with their money. It was a babbling mob without any apparent direction or logic, and yet somehow it all worked.

The warrior had yet to go ashore, although about half the crew were already making rounds of the town's assortment of taverns and ale houses. Several groups had invited him to go along, but he had never much cared for crowds. Instead, he had watched as Tasca had somehow worked three business deals at once at the foot of the gangway—tea and spices from his hold for gold, and the gold for lumber and pitch. It had actually looked as if he was merely having the others trade among themselves, yet he had ended up with most of the goods. In the end, Samir wasn't sure whether placing the Brisian Captain in charge of Majar's treasury would bring stunning prosperity or complete bankruptcy.

After that came deals for sailcloth and cash in exchange for some of Tasca's silk. Ivory went from *Amelia*'s hold to the docks in trade for enormous casks of wine and still more money. Samir was actually somewhat amazed the ship could hold it all, though room inside the cavernous space always seemed to appear when it was needed. Like a spider spinning a web, Tasca had spoken in the proper ears and the merchants—along with their gold—had come running to him.

All told, it took the Captain less than two days to make his deals and exchange what goods he would. It seemed to take an incredible amount of time, however, to simply hire a handful of new deckhands. Plenty came once they heard there were jobs, but Tasca was clearly very particular about who he took on. Some who appeared to pass muster initially, tripped themselves up with their claims about previous work experience. Samir began to feel fortunate that he had ever managed to convince the man to let him aboard, even if the intention was to prove him inadequate to the task.

In the meantime, the warrior chose the early mornings to walk around the town of Lastra, with generally smaller crowds and much less noise after the evening's revelers made their way home to sleep. Mainly, it allowed Tirza a chance to run more than a handful of yards in one direction—an opportunity she took full advantage of, tearing up and down the long wharf.

As Tasca had said, the place had very little to offer to anyone other than merchants seeking trade or sailors looking for entertainment. Samir had assumed the Captain was exaggerating the situation to make it less attractive as an alternative, but it actually appeared to be the truth. At the moment, neither of those alternatives interested the warrior in the least, but at least it would be possible to do some shopping.

Only a few short weeks ago, he would simply have told one of the higher ranked palace servants to fetch the right kinds of craftsmen and would have commissioned exactly what he needed, and of the first quality. When it was finished he would have paid their bills out of his own considerable funds, and he would never once have needed to *search* for anything at all.

Oddly enough, if he had wanted to buy a hundred or a thousand of almost any item, he would only have had to walk down to the row of warehouses. Any number of merchants would have been happy to find it all for him. But since he wanted only one, he would just have to do it himself. Of course, the problem was that he had no idea where to even begin. Not only was he completely unfamiliar with the town, but he also had much more limited resources than he once had. As long as he missed the worst of the crowds, however, he wouldn't mind a bit of walking.

Still, he wandered for well over an hour before he finally managed to find what he was searching for. He had spoken to stone carvers as well as carpenters, but although they had been willing to make what he wanted—and fairly quickly—none of them kept a stock of such to clutter up their workshops. Eventually, it occurred to him that the inn where he had stayed in Barat, The Wading Crane, had kept a variety of such things available for their guests. From that point, it had taken only a few minutes for an innkeeper to direct him to a tiny shop he would never have noticed on his own. He could have kicked himself for a fool.

The little chess set certainly wasn't much to look at. Nothing like the one he had owned—intricately carved ivory and rhinoceros horn on a gold trimmed board of light and dark jade. That one had cost him enough, he was sure, to buy half of the goods in *Amelia*'s hold, and at the time, the Prince had thought nothing of the price. The set he had just bought was completely unimpressive with the roughly carved pieces and slightly warped board of sloppily painted pine. But as ugly as it might be, he knew that it would play no differently than any other set he had ever used.

Once Samir had started having occasional dinners with the Captain and first officer, he had soon discovered that, while Tasca didn't play, Niklas considered himself a passable player. It had been welcome news. After all, though Samir was enjoying the chance to train in an environment that challenged him more than the plumflower posts, it would be good to have something else to do.

He supposed it was a sign of how accustomed he had become to speaking Brisian that his native tongue had immediately seized his attention. Alerted, he stopped cold and slowly inched forward, moving just far enough to peer around the corner ahead.

There was no way of telling what might have happened if he had walked around that corner, but there was little question that it would have been disastrous. He had no idea who the second speaker of Majaran was, but he definitely knew the merchant who stood at the edge of the street only a few feet away from him. Even here, in the middle of Lastra, he had nearly run into the one person who could have proven his undoing.

Janai was well known to Samir, and more importantly at the moment, the Prince was known to him. The man traded on such a massive scale that he had actually been used as a purchasing agent for the kingdom on several occasions. There would be no way for the merchant to know of the change in the royal succession, since he had to have left ahead of Samir to be here now—but that would only delay the inevitable. Had he seen a member of Majar's royal family, he would certainly have gone straight to the palace on his return, ingratiating himself by carrying word of Samir's excellent health—health that hardly fit someone who was supposed to be dead. Kemal would know the truth as soon as Janai arrived in Toskar, which meant that he couldn't have been allowed to leave Lastra.

Samir backed away quickly and quietly, hustling back the way he had come and watching for a glimpse of fine Majaran clothing or a long tail of greying hair. Circling wide of the street where he had seen the merchant took time, as did checking around corners before moving on. He considered it well worth the effort when he reached the docks with no sign of Janai, however.

The final two days in port passed unbelievably slowly as the warrior remained belowdecks to avoid even the chance of being seen. He found himself thankful to have the little chess set to keep him occupied, helping him ignore the small, dark spaces of the crew's quarters, though Niklas grew tired of play. To the first officer's great relief, however, two more of Samir's crewmates turned out to be fair hands.

Samir was glad when, on the afternoon of his second day below, Tasca announced that the crew had better man their posts to cast off on the departing tide or he would skin the lot of them. *Amelia* was slow to build headway in the sheltered harbor, lumbering around the long stone quay and into the open sea beyond. But go she did.

Samir emerged on deck just in time to watch the town vanish from sight around the headland. It felt good to breathe fresh air again after days in the belly of the stuffy ship. As *Amelia* gained speed in her westward course toward Varella, however, he couldn't escape the strange feeling that he needed to go both north and west, that his purpose somehow lay in both of those directions.

Dismissing the odd idea, he walked out onto the main deck to practice his forms. The cramped cabin had made him restless, and he knew how to deal with that.

Chapter 8

Shattered

Caleb had to admit that spending a few days in the saddle, out in the fresh air with other men, was far better than sitting alone as he had been doing.

He had gone back to the little stone bench in the clearing the next day, certain that he would find Sorana waiting for him there. She wasn't, but if she felt unwell it was better that she stay at home. Yet, with her failure to appear the following day, he felt a small spark of fear that he couldn't quite banish—his mind conjuring images of her lying sick or injured in the woods, waiting for him to find her. Every day he rode to the clearing, waiting for hours on end, and each time his hopes sank lower. Finally he couldn't deny that he had truly done something to offend her, that she simply wasn't coming.

Caleb had no idea why she was avoiding him, but he was sure that if he could only find her, talk to her, apologize for *whatever* he had done, then she would *have* to forgive him. But his attempts to find Sorana, certain that some shopkeeper or goodwife would recognize her name or description, had gotten him nowhere. The Prince had eventually come to the conclusion that she refused to be found, and that her friends and family must be respecting her wishes by helping to hide her. The thought hurt him terribly, but it was the only possible explanation that he could see.

The decision to stop searching for her had been one of the hardest things he had ever done, even with the certainty that she would find him when she was ready. He had made one more trip to the little bench by the river, leaving her a letter wrapped in oilcloth and weighted down with a rock. When she chose to return to that place, whether because she missed him or just to make sure that he no longer went, she would find it and discover how he felt and exactly what she meant to him.

Caleb knew that someday she would find him again or he would find her. When that day came and Sorana could honestly say that she didn't love him, then he would probably be shattered, but he would respect her wishes—although he did hope that she would at least tell him why.

It had been obvious from the start that the patrol they now rode was for Caleb's benefit. Naturally, Captain Braden would have denied it, and the excuse that his men needed training in order to stay sharp made good sense. But it just seemed too unlikely a coincidence that it came now—at exactly the time when Caleb needed a distraction to keep him from sulking. Although a small part of him wanted solitude, he appreciated the Captain's efforts and would have to find a way to thank him.

The slow and winding route, west and slightly north toward Laran, followed a little used route through the hills that could barely be called a road. The journey would have been faster by way of the plains, and much easier going. The constant need to watch the ground in front of Searcher's hooves did an admirable job of keeping him focused, however, so his mind couldn't wander to Sorana overmuch.

"So who is she?" The voice of Marius' lieutenant, Alban Ward, startled the Prince into the realization that he'd been daydreaming about Sorana, bringing a flush of warmth to his face.

"Who?" he replied evasively.

The young lieutenant laughed, obviously not fooled for a moment. "Whoever you've been pining about for the past week." His direct look offered sympathy in spite of the mild amusement in his tone. "Do you think you're the first man who's ever had his heart spun like a top by a woman? Trust me, I know the signs."

"She's not just any woman, Alban. She's special," Caleb told him, slightly defensive.

"They always are," the lieutenant replied. At an angry glare from Caleb, Alban held up his hands. "I don't mean to sound dismissive. What I mean is that *every* woman is special to someone...or, at least, they should be."

Somewhat mollified, the Prince relaxed, biting back a mild rebuke. He knew he could hardly be the only man ever to deal with this, but it wasn't exactly comforting to know that love could bring this kind of pain. After all, walking around feeling like he'd been kicked in the gut was hardly something to look forward to.

"Does she know how you feel?" Alban asked into the silence.

Caleb's gaze dropped to the ground in front of him. "I thought she did. She's disappeared, and I can't find her." A brief glance showed him the compassion in the other man's face. "I just feel like I need to *do* something."

"I know you want to fix this. It's the way we're built. But you'll have to remember that people's emotions are complex at the best of times." The lieutenant met Caleb's frustration with calm certainty, clapping the younger man on the shoulder. "If you made a mistake, you own up to it. If you must, you make amends. After that, either she forgives you or she doesn't." Alban shrugged.

"I guess I can live with that," the Prince admitted. "I just can't stand the thought that she might hate me."

Alban was quiet for a moment, obviously framing his thoughts. "She might," he told Caleb. "Or at least she might feel like she does—and whether the offense was real or perceived, the feelings *are* real, so don't dismiss them. Fortunately, that kind of anger is usually reserved for people we love," the lieutenant smiled reassuringly. "There's hope yet, Caleb."

With that, he trotted up the line to speak briefly with Sergeant Elbrus, leaving the younger man alone with his thoughts. Alban had given him a lot to think about, however.

Caleb knew that Sorana hadn't suddenly become an entirely different person. She was still the same woman he knew and loved, but something in their relationship *had* changed—and he had spent days trying to figure out what. The last thing they had talked about was their hope of an engagement, even though neither had spoken of it directly. True, she hadn't wanted to rehash the subject, but it could hardly be called an argument.

He briefly considered the idea that her father had forbidden her from seeing him again. But it did no good to speculate, and he tried to turn his thoughts in another direction.

She did love him, he was sure. Sorana had been absolutely sincere when she had told him so. And he loved her, which meant that there was no reason why they couldn't work things out.

Searcher snorted, prancing a few steps in agitation. Surprised at the uncharacteristic behavior, Caleb absently patted the gelding's neck as he glanced around for the source of the disturbance. But the horse refused to be calmed, suddenly backing a few steps, forcing the Prince to saw at the reins for control.

It wasn't only Searcher, however. Up and down the line, other mounts began to balk, stamping hooves and tossing manes. Caleb had seen horses behave like this before, when they had caught a strong whiff of smoke. But those mounts had been brought under control easily—these were not.

The reason became clear a moment later.

Whatever the creatures were, they came *fast* as they glided down the hillside, seeming almost to flow around the trees and rocks in their path. Bodies the size of horses, covered in thick black scales were made sinuous by serpentine necks and whiplike tails. His first impression was of enormous lizards charging forward on short legs, yet these were no mere lizards—perhaps two dozen feet long with heads larger than a man's torso. The three of them rushed the line of soldiers, covering the distance to the road before a single man drew steel—a feat made nearly impossible by the bucking and screaming of maddened horses.

Searcher reared, pawing the air with desperation as the Prince fought for control. Caleb clung tightly to the gelding's neck, trying to stay in the saddle and nearly succeeding. But, after several long seconds, his horse went down, jarred as another man's mount brushed past in a headlong flight to escape.

The Prince hit the ground hard but managed to roll, saving himself some of the worst injury. Only a few feet away Searcher thrashed, doing his best to stand amid the chaos. Caleb didn't worry about the horse, however. All he could see was the malevolent gaze of the monstrous thing rapidly bearing down on him. Teeth like daggers lined the wide, open maw that could easily tear him in half. Everything about the beast rushing at him promised pain.

He knew he was about to die, unable to even draw his sword to defend himself. He would never see Sorana again, never tell her he loved her.

The creature suddenly slewed sideways as Marius' charging horse slammed into it, shouldering the thing aside at the last instant. The Captain was clearly rocked by the massive impact, and his horse staggered, but they stood and turned quickly to face the nightmare made flesh that now glared hatred at the soldier.

Caleb struggled to his feet, glad of the chance to draw his sword. All around him he could see armsmen attempting to surround the monsters, having to fight for every inch—struggling against horses nearly as hard as they battled their armor-plated attackers. He dodged aside as, only a few yards away, a soldier was thrown from the saddle by a tail as thick as a tree branch, his steel breastplate crushed. The tail streaked forward, impossibly fast, to impale a horse with the long, flat spade at its tip. The horse fell, knocked sideways from the sheer force of the blow, then struggled only weakly before it lay still.

Determination blended with horror on the faces of veteran soldiers as they did their best to rally against the otherworldly beasts, watching as their brethren fell. Yet, in spite of their skill and their fury, Caleb could see that they were losing.

The Captain's sword flashed hard and fast, barely fending off the teeth of the creature as it battered at him. Others of his men had joined him, more than one discarding a broken lance in favor of a sword—striking at the beast's flanks while defending against a tail that slashed and stabbed among them. Arm-jarring blows struck with a ring of hard steel, doing no discernible damage, even as the monster swung a sweeping claw to eviscerate a horse in a single swipe.

Marius screamed as a fountain of some thick, inky fluid shot from the creature's mouth, splashing across his head and chest. His horse spun and bolted as he jerked the reins reflexively, taking him clear of the battle, but throwing him from the saddle.

Caleb ran to the Captain's side, heedless of the thrashing horses around him. Skidding to a stop as he dropped to his knees, he nearly recoiled as he looked into the older man's face, completely unprepared for what he saw. The exposed skin was a horrible angry red and was already blistered as if burned. The man's hands had begun to swell as he wiped frantically at the viscous liquid in a desperate attempt to get it away from his skin.

"Hold still, Captain Braden," Caleb said in as much of a commanding voice as he could manage. "I'm here."

Despite what was obviously excruciating pain, Marius lay still, allowing the Prince to work. Unsure what else to do, Caleb stripped off his shirt and began to wipe at the awful black slime, taking great care not to touch it himself. Still, the work was too slow, and the liquid clung tenaciously to the other man's flesh.

Searching for something to alleviate the Captain's suffering, he snatched a canteen from one of the fallen horses. The stopper flew as he ripped it free, dumping the contents over Marius' face and hands to wash away what remained of the dark goo. It was all the young Prince could think of.

The Captain lay still, moaning softly, yet evidently in less immediate pain. But something told Caleb that a lesser man would still be screaming as he watched tears leaking from eyes that were swollen shut.

Soldiers around them continued to strike and dodge, doing their best to press near enough to deliver a critical wound. Yet another horse stumbled as the Prince watched, its leg shattered by the blindingly fast sweep of a tail. With a frantic lunge, the rider left the saddle and plunged toward the monster's outstretched neck, sword point leading the way.

A deafening roar erupted from the creature as the blade bit deep between the scales to bury itself into soft flesh. The enormous body thrashed, jarring the soldier loose to tumble away, but the weapon remained deeply embedded. Dark red blood poured from the wound, pooling quickly in the dirt of the road.

With another screeching cry, the beast turned and fled, snaking into the woods above them with impossible speed and agility—especially for an animal bearing what must be a mortal wound. Its fellows followed swiftly in its wake, echoing its call.

"Stand fast," Elbrus bellowed as several men tried to follow, spurring their mounts in pursuit. The soldiers instantly obeyed the piercing voice.

It was ended as suddenly as it had begun, yet men and horses still screamed and bled. Two other men had been struck by the awful, scorching liquid—one badly, the other only glancingly. All told, nine men lay dead in what couldn't have lasted more than three or four minutes. Four more were injured.

Thankfully, enough of the horses survived to carry them, although they had needed to put several down to end their suffering.

Caleb managed to reclaim his own mount, as well as Captain Braden's—the latter having a serious scrape across the shoulder from the initial strike. Sliding Marius' sword into its sheath, Caleb noted the slack muscles and shallow breathing of merciful unconsciousness.

Never hesitating, Elbrus chivvied the other sergeants into action, assigning men to examine horses, care for the wounded and make litters to carry those who couldn't ride. A soldier briefly came to look at Marius, giving him a quick once-over. Unable to check the eyes under the swelling, the man draped loose, damp bandages over the blistering on the Captain's face and hands. Caleb could do nothing but hold the horses and watch.

The ride back to Elhanan was tortuous not only for the roughness of the route while dragging laden travois behind several of the horses, but from the urgency of their desire for medical care for their brethren. None of them wanted to stop for the night and waste valuable time, but neither did they want more horses with broken legs.

Alban had them back in the saddle again the moment the sun broke the horizon, pushing the men and the mounts hard. Somehow, before midday they were once again in sight of the fort outside of Elhanan, causing those with the best horses to take off at a gallop to alert the garrison.

In spite of the fresh hope trying to well up inside him, however, Caleb doubted anyone would be ready to treat Captain Braden.

Huldrich sat slumped at one of the long tables in the village hall, chin resting lazily atop his folded arms while he talked with Suppan and Kessel. His two friends had done their best to keep him calm ever since the day he had seen Sorana so upset, but it had been a near thing more than once. Despite his sister's urging against it, he had came close to crossing the river into Elhanan to track this Caleb down.

Sorana was apparently doing better, at least, seeming to wear her familiar smile as she watched the children who were playing under her care. He still heard her crying at night sometimes, but she was strong and would heal in time.

The opening and closing of the door caused only a few brief glances in that direction, but the purposeful stride of the man who had entered drew a few more. Barlan wasted no time crossing the broad room to Huldrich's table and taking a place on the bench across from him.

Huldrich shot the man a brief look of annoyance at the intrusion, but something in Barlan's demeanor made him pause. Normally, the heavyset woodcarver tended to be placid by temperament. Now though, he leaned forward, excitement sparkling in eyes that held an unusual intensity.

"Just came from the other side," he said, tossing his head unnecessarily toward Elhanan. "Looks like someone poked a stick in a hornet's nest. Soldiers running all over the place."

Huldrich was instantly alert, sitting bolt upright at the man's words, as were his companions. "An attack?" he asked, picking up the excitement himself.

"No. Nothing like." The carver shook his head. "Got a mess of wounded came in from somewhere west. I caught whispers of loads of dead men, but that's not all that's got 'em riled." Barlan grinned knowingly, obviously waiting for Huldrich to take the bait.

"What else?" Kessel broke in.

It was obvious that Barlan was enjoying his moment as the center of attention. He took his time about answering, looking slowly around the table at his listeners.

"They say," the man continued, dragging it out, "one of them that's dead or dying is someone *real* important. You'd think it was the King himself to hear 'em go on about it."

Huldrich's mind raced as he considered what he'd just heard. Anything that could tear through trained soldiers could prove a serious threat to Gotarra. The only thing he knew for sure, though, was that he needed more information.

"Suppan," Huldrich elbowed his friend to get his full attention, "get over there and see what you can find out. Kessel, make sure everyone knows to keep a weapon close at hand. *Go*, both of you."

Huldrich watched as the pair rose and left at a trot, Kessel's longer legs carrying him to the door well ahead of his shorter companion. After that, all he could do was sit and wait for more news.

Despite the exhausting ride back to the fort, Caleb had slept only fitfully, spending most of the night staring at the ceiling. His mind had bounced constantly from one thought to the next—dwelling one minute on the battle, then suddenly lost in memories of Sorana.

He knew he should have done more, should have done *something* besides stand there foolishly holding his sword watching other men fight. Over and over the Prince had to face the thought that, if he hadn't been so useless, the captain wouldn't have needed to come to his rescue and might not have been lying in the infirmary.

And the nagging voices had only gotten worse when morning came. At some point during the night, Braden had died in terrible pain, and the healers simply hadn't known what to do beyond treating his burns. Aside from the obvious damage to his skin, no one could even say what had killed the man.

It didn't matter that Caleb knew that there was probably nothing he could have done that the soldiers hadn't. A part of him couldn't quite shake the idea that he was at least partly responsible for Braden's death.

Now the Prince sat quietly in the saddle with what remained of the company, watching the first light of dawn break the horizon. Still, his eyes continued to drift back down the line to where the Captain's mare, Dawn Rose, was tied to the string of remounts.

It would be a long ride back to Varella, and one that he had no desire to take. He knew they had to get word to his father, of course, and Braden's wife and daughter deserved to hear the news without delay. But he had yet to speak to Gerrit, the one thing he had come to do, and to leave without finding Sorana didn't bear thinking about.

"Highness." Maclin's quiet voice beside him interrupted his thoughts, for which he was grateful. "Why did the barbarian freeze to death?"

"Why?" Caleb asked, hoping for something to lighten his mood.

"He built a new hut and forgot to put in a door." Maclin answered with a tentative smile.

The young Prince found himself actually smiling weakly as he thought of a joke of his own.

"And why did the barbarian starve to death?" he offered.

"Why, Highness?" Maclin asked expectantly.

"He built the hut with himself inside it."

Despite the mood, the two men shared a brief chuckle as they waited to move out.

Sorana knew that she must look as awful as she felt—eyes puffy and red-rimmed from crying and more than a bit red from lack of sleep. But right now it didn't matter to her what she looked like or who saw her as she walked across the great stone bridge between Gotarra and Acedia, a piece of paper clutched in her grip like a talisman.

She had spent the night worrying, dreading what she might find out. Yet, as frightening as the possibilities were, she had to know the truth.

Although no one around her had seemed to notice, Barlan's news had shaken her to the core. All she had done from the moment she had overheard was try to convince herself that it couldn't be Caleb—that it *must* not be him. But she wasn't sure of that at all, and it had taken every ounce of her self-control not to run to the fort and ask who had died. At the same time, however, a part of her had been too afraid.

Sorana hadn't needed to read the letter again to have it occupy her thoughts as she lay awake in the dark. She had already read it more times than she could count since she had found it on the bench—their bench. Now she could have spoken the words by heart, could close her eyes and see the beautiful flowing script of his handwriting.

My Dearest Sorana,

I don't know why you haven't come, but I do know your heart. You are not a woman who could be called fickle, and never could you be called cruel. Whatever your reasons, then, I know and trust your judgment that they must be good ones.

Whether some outside force has conspired to keep us apart, or it is through some action of my own that this has happened, I do not know. But I do know that if our love be a true love—and I believe with all my heart that it is—then there is nothing that we cannot overcome together.

My love, if I have transgressed, I assure you that it was in ignorance, and I humbly ask your forgiveness. If you will but consent to speak with me, I am certain we can find a way to be reconciled. You have but to send word, and I will come to you without delay.

Until then, and I pray it be soon, I remain

Forever yours,

Caleb

She had actually known where to find him since that first day. It had been obvious, from some of his responses, that he was completely unfamiliar with the area, though he had tried to conceal the fact. Since he had arrived at the same time as the new soldiers, that meant he must have been staying at the fort.

So many times she had *almost* gone to him, or asked him to come to her. She had very nearly gone during the night, but there had been no question that Huldrich would have insisted on coming with her then.

It was a short walk from the bridge to the open gates to the fort that stood between her world and his, yet she could feel the fluttering in her stomach grow worse almost by the yard as she approached. Barlan's insistence that someone important had been hurt or killed had tormented her with the thought that it was Caleb. Whatever his reasons for coming to Elhanan, he had been important enough to rate an escort of soldiers. And if he could order someone to carry a message to his father as he had said, then he certainly had more authority than most. Even a look at the way he dressed— in clothing too good for the outdoors, but with no attempt to impress anyone—plainly announced that he was *somebody*.

Sorana came close to turning around and running, though whether she would have gone home or to their little clearing by the river she couldn't have said. But that small voice inside her insisted that, as long as she didn't *know*, then everything was all right. In her heart, though, she accepted that it was better to hear the truth, even if it was unwelcome.

The young soldier on duty in the guardhouse gave a brief but polite nod at her approach, stepping out between the gates. A good look at her worried expression quickly transformed his friendly greeting to a look of concern, however.

"Is something wrong, miss?" he asked kindly. "Can I help?"

"I don't know," she began in a trembling voice, tears again welling in her eyes despite attempts to stop them. Somehow she couldn't make the words come.

"Which, miss?" The guard offered an encouraging smile. "You don't know if something is wrong, or if I can help?"

Sorana merely shook her head, the letter crumpling in her hand.

"If there *is* something wrong, you can't help," she forced out the words, swallowing hard. "Can you tell me if Caleb is here?"

A brief look of confusion crossed the man's brow, causing her heart to quicken its pace.

"His Highness?" he answered after a moment's consideration. "I'm sorry, miss. He's not."

The man's answer made no sense at all. A sudden surge of frustration made her want to smack him.

"*No*," she insisted, speaking slowly. "I mean *Caleb*. Just tell me if he's here."

"Yes, ma'am," the guard nodded, looking at her as if she were simple. "We're talking about the same man. His Royal Highness, Prince Caleb Wagner Cravath, Crown Prince of Acedia. I'm trying to tell you he rode out this morning for Varella."

Prince Caleb? How could he not tell her *that*? Sorana could feel anger and annoyance growing inside her until, a moment later, something else he'd said finally registered in her mind.

"He left?" she asked, stunned, not even listening for his reply.

He was *alive*! And she had missed him by only a few hours. Suddenly she didn't know whether to be elated or distressed, but at least now she knew she would see him again, somehow. It *would* happen—and when it did, Caleb would have a choice to make. Either he could accept her—*all* of her—and love her for who she was, or he could forget about ever loving her. She was Gotarran, and if that wasn't good enough for him, then he wasn't good enough for her.

She was unaware of the new bounce in her step as she walked across the bridge toward home. Caleb *would* choose her. She knew he would.

Chapter 9

A Viewing in the Mist

Jenaris had long since grown tired of the feeling that he was going halfway to nowhere without results. It had taken him weeks to arrive in Rolen in hopes of finding Lorn, only to discover that his friend had gone to Hogarth. Yet when he had retraced his steps to the woodland town, the people there had only vaguely remembered him, thinking he had gone to Varella when he'd left. The optimist in him hoped his journey would end in Acedia's capital but, anticipating the worst, he wondered where he would need to go next. Wherever it was, he hoped it wouldn't take a ship to get him there.

The road from Hogarth through the Great Wood had been pleasant enough. His small satchel now held samples of interesting plants he couldn't find in the hills near his home, and at least the feel of the forest was familiar. Still, he would be glad of a hot bath and a decent bed.

But the farther south the Wizard rode, the more concerned he became. The Acedian people were generally cheerful and open, and yet as he neared Varella, they grew gradually more nervous and uncertain.

Time and deft questioning had allowed Jenaris to piece together a fairly accurate picture of the situation in spite of the way stories changed or became exaggerated in the telling, and he didn't like it at all. There had clearly been trouble of a sort these people were completely unprepared to deal with. Jenaris knew only too well what had destroyed the town of Laran and decimated a company of trained veterans, and as far as he was concerned it was perfectly reasonable for these people to fear it.

The Acedian capital could only be described as subdued—far from the bustling city it should be. In spite of the fact that its citizens went about their daily business, and the markets were reasonably full, there was none of the normal energy he would have expected. Conversations were mumbled and terse, the streets were devoid of children's games, and there was an almost tangible feeling of hopelessness settling over everything around him. The simple fact was that the city of Varella had received too much bad news lately.

The sound of Keera's steel-shod hooves on the cobblestone streets was the loudest sound the Mage heard as he made his way toward the castle. He almost felt self-conscious, as if his noise were somehow intruding on a funeral.

Jenaris found the gates shut tight when he reached the top of the hill and reluctantly brought the mare to a stop in front of the guard.

Although the man acknowledged him, it was with the wary look of a man uncertain what he was dealing with. Still, from the guard's confident stance, at least he appeared unaffected by the fears of the men and women Jenaris had ridden past earlier.

"May I ask your business?" he asked, attitude professional but direct.

The Wizard offered what he hoped was a reassuring smile. "I'm here to help with your problem," he replied.

A quizzical stare greeted the announcement as the soldier gave the Mage a closer look. The gaze very calmly took in the sword, apparently dismissing it as a threat as the guard's mouth quirked in a grin.

"You look harmless enough, Oldtimer." The man offered a friendly smile as he relaxed. "What exactly would you like us to tell His Majesty when we ask if we're to let you in?"

"Don't bother," Jenaris said flatly, shaking his head. "I'll tell him myself."

The other man tensed for only a moment before a wry grin crossed his features. "Not unless you can walk through a locked gate," he replied with more than a little amusement.

"Well, if that's all it takes," the Mage laughed.

Lifting his staff, he pointed it at the gate before him and made a twisting motion. With a loud sharp click that rang through the thick steel, the lock opened allowing the gate to swing wide as if pushed.

In the quickly broadening gap, Jenaris could see a pair of guards staring dumbly as if in shock. After a few seconds, one of the men finally drew his gaze away long enough to notice that they weren't alone and abruptly reached for his sword. From the way the fellow's eyes shifted between the Wizard and the sergeant, it was debatable which man he thought might attack him.

"*We* didn't do it, Sergeant Roland," the guard blurted, removing any doubt as to which man frightened him. His partner merely nodded agreement.

"I know that, Wade. I was here too, remember?" His voice dripped sarcasm. Roland indicated the Mage with a jerk of his head. "Take this man to His Majesty, and don't dawdle."

"Yes, sir." The young guardsman snapped to attention, finally releasing his sword hilt. "This way, sir."

Clucking softly to Keera, Jenaris rode through the open gates to join his escort. Behind him, the sergeant's voice still carried his irritation.

"What are you waiting for, Rayburn?" the man snapped. "Get those gates locked!"

The Wizard couldn't suppress an amused grin as he followed Wade across the broad expanse of courtyard and up to the castle doors. Dismounting, he handed his mount over to the waiting grooms, trusting her to their care.

"King Carlon should be holding court just now, sir," the younger man offered as they wound their way through the corridors. Aside from that one brief comment, however, the journey passed with only the sound of their footsteps to keep them company.

The Mage was fairly certain they couldn't have come by the most direct route, having never seen anything that appeared to be a major corridor. Finally, once he was somewhat disoriented, they entered a large, high-ceilinged chamber by way of a small side door.

Only two of those present appeared to be petitioners, and judging by the way they each tried to speak and continually glared at the other, were plainly attempting to settle a dispute—or to continue one, at least. Several men and women were seated comfortably at the back of a low dais doing their best to look important, clearly marking them as ministers of some sort. A few others sat in various places near the front of the room as well, yet the focus of all attention was the wide man seated at the front of the platform.

Although simply dressed, the King would have stood out even without the large chair and fawning underlings. There was a definite presence that immediately set him apart as a man with an obvious sense of himself, which Jenaris normally only saw in other wizards.

Wade waved the Mage vaguely toward one of the long benches lining the walls as he approached one of the self-important men behind the King. After a brief whispered conversation, the guard returned to stand quietly beside the Wizard.

It was only a short wait before Carlon grew tired of the ongoing argument between the petitioners and stopped them cold by merely clearing his throat. Neither of the men seemed best pleased when the King ordered them to compromise, yet both accepted with murmured thanks before leaving with matching scowls.

Moments later, the minister Wade had spoken to was beside Carlon's chair, bending down to speak in his ear. Giving Jenaris a quick glance, the King gave the man the barest nod. With a slightly oily smile that seemed permanently fixed in place, the minister waved the Wizard toward the front of the dais.

Jenaris approached slowly, each step punctuated by the tap of his staff on the polished stone floor. He halted as he reached the front of the platform, leaning on his staff as he met the broad chested King's gaze evenly.

"What can we do for you, Mister...?" Carlon let the question trail off as he waited for the Mage to supply a name. Behind a pleasant smile designed to place visitors at ease lay an obvious curiosity about the stranger in front of him.

"Excuse me, Sire, but I'm here to help you," the older man supplied with an easy smile of his own. "My name is Jenaris, and I am a Wizard."

He couldn't remember a time when the title had failed to impress, yet the King didn't so much as bat an eye. To say he was surprised would have been a drastic understatement. After all, his kind had never been so common that people would fail to take note on meeting one. Still, at least the others in the room reacted, if not quite as strongly as he had expected.

"Sorry you've wasted your time." Carlon's reddish-brown hair swayed as he shook his head regretfully. "We already have one, and he's not much help." Glancing over Jenaris' shoulder toward the back of the room, he added, "No offense."

Sudden hope surged in the Mage. Lorn *was* here. But, if so, he would surely be able to do *something*. He turned, eager to see his old friend again after so many years.

"*Lorn!*" he whooped excitedly.

But the young man standing there, staff in hand, was a complete stranger.

"I'm afraid not. Jenaris, was it?" The heavyset man standing before him extended a hand. "Lorn has been gone these ten years now. I'm Kordel."

Aside from his evident youth at around thirty-five, the man fit the typical description of a wizard—too much so, if fact. From the long, woolen robes that just swept the floor to the pointed beard stretching down his chest, Kordel simply looked *wizardly*. It was almost as if he were going out of his way to look the part.

Jenaris sighed. "Gone where, Kordel?" he asked, dreading yet another long ride to find Lorn.

The young man's proud expression slipped as he grew uneasy at the question. For a moment he merely stood, knuckles white on the smooth dark wood in his hand.

"Um...perhaps we should speak a bit more privately," Kordel suggested, glancing toward a corner at the far end of the room. "By your leave, Sire."

At Carlon's absent wave, the other man led Jenaris to a bench near the back where Kordel promptly sat, inviting the older Wizard to join him with a sweeping hand gesture that looked like something out of a conjuration. Instead, Jenaris remained standing, forcing his companion to crane his neck awkwardly or stand.

Kordel stood, smiling weakly.

Jenaris simply waited quietly, staring steadily at the youngster as silence stretched, making it obvious that Kordel wasn't about to open the discussion. When he finally spoke, the senior Mage's voice was edged with annoyance.

"Where has he gone?" he asked, almost too softly—a clear signal of his growing annoyance.

"I'm not exactly sure," the other admitted, distinctly uncomfortable.

"Well, what did he say when he *left*?" Jenaris asked, exasperation tinging his voice at the need to ask obvious questions.

Kordel hesitated, briefly breaking eye contact to examine his staff. "Nothing."

The response was clearly evasive, causing anger to rise in Jenaris. He slowly leaned forward, using his height advantage over the other man. Whatever it was that Kordel was hiding, he would dig it out—and it would be far better for the young pup in front of him if he got the truth sooner rather than later.

"I think you'd better explain." The edge in Jenaris voice, and the less than friendly smile, brought almost instant compliance.

"He was working a spell," the younger man began, speaking as if the words were being dragged from him by force. "I'm not sure exactly what it was, but he was looking for information." He paused, looking as if he wanted to run. "Lorn just...*vanished*."

"He *what*!?" Jenaris voice cracked like a whip, causing the focus of his anger to recoil. On the platform, several heads turned.

"I don't think it was anything Lorn did," Kordel continued, offering an ingratiating smile. "One moment he was chanting. The next he was just *gone*."

A sudden, intense fire in the old Wizard's eyes made Kordel look away. The smile faded.

"And you didn't try to trace the magic?" he asked softly.

Something didn't fit. Jenaris knew Lorn's abilities, and they were greater than his own. Any wizard he had chosen to work with should know far more than this *boy* apparently did—especially if he were good enough to finish his training at such a young age. Why, ten years ago he couldn't have been more than....

The final piece clicked into place, and he didn't like it at all. By all rights, the intensity of Jenaris' stare should have burned the young fool to ash.

"You were his apprentice, weren't you?" The Mage's voice was cold when he spoke, a stark contrast to the rage within him.

"Well, yes. But..," Kordel stammered.

"And you've been representing yourself as a wizard." Heat entered Jenaris' tone as he advanced a step, staring down at the man in robes. "These people have been acting on the 'expert' opinion of an untrained poser!"

Kordel paled abruptly, backing away a step. "Now, Jenaris," he began, soothing.

The Wizard cut the pretender off with a sharp hand gesture as his voice filled the hall, drawing every eye. "You may call me 'Master' or 'Magus'. That is, *if* you choose to complete your training." He paused, awaiting an answer. Finally, taking silence as assent, he nodded. "Lorn may have seen some potential in you, but I don't know what it was. Come with me."

With that, Jenaris strode back up the floor, leaving the younger man to follow in his wake. This time, he didn't stop at the edge of the platform, but stepped up without invitation, keeping a slight distance from where Carlon stood speaking with several of his ministers. His position near the edge made it impossible for Kordel to join him, however.

"I believe I can help, Sire," he announced, addressing the King. "Perhaps you should tell me what's happened."

Carlon walked casually to the large chair and sat, the others automatically placing themselves to either side. It was skillfully handled—establishing his authority without the need to say a word—and it spoke well of his leadership skills.

"Captain Ward," Carlon's eyes held a brief hint of pain. "Why don't you start with Laran."

A man just short of his middle years stepped forward and nodded. The black and green wool of his uniform was crisp, but stretched oddly across slouching shoulders.

"Alban Ward, sir," he introduced himself in a clear voice. "We were ending the northern sweep of a long patrol about two months ago when we rode into Laran. A small place of a few hundred—mostly woodcutters and craftsmen with a few small farms," he added by way of explanation. "Anyway, the place was torn up something awful—no people, no bodies, no animals. Best we could figure, the scene was about a month old. If anyone left, they never turned up anywhere, and we didn't have a clue what happened. Until recently, that is."

Ward paused as if considering how to proceed. The momentary silence was interrupted abruptly by a young man to the King's right. From the resemblance, he was obviously Carlon's son, yet at the moment his fidgeting gave him the look of a child waiting to be scolded.

"We were riding about twenty miles west of Elhanan just over two weeks ago when we met what I can only assume destroyed Laran," the Captain finally continued, jaw muscles clenching and unclenching as he spoke. "Three of them came out of the woods above us before we knew it—all scales, claws and teeth, and nearly impossible to hurt. Took out almost half a company of good troops, faster than I could believe. We lost Marius, too." Tears welled in his eyes as he finished, but he held them back by force of will.

Jenaris looked up as the youth beside Carlon mumbled. "I'm sorry," the Wizard offered. "I didn't quite catch that."

"I said you can feel their hate," Caleb answered.

The Mage nodded his understanding. It was one part of the description every source agreed on.

"You know what they are," Carlon said. It wasn't a question.

"Yes," Jenaris nodded sadly. "I'm afraid I do."

The Wizard turned to face the open room, lips moving rapidly in silent speech, head lowered and eyes closed with intense concentration. Slowly he raised the staff in his hand to shoulder level and opened his eyes. Thin tendrils of mist swept across the floor, growing slightly thicker as they drew together. Gradually, almost imperceptibly at first, it began to pile higher rather than spreading out across the polished marble. It darkened, gaining density more quickly as it assumed shape—a scaled black body stood on short legs that ended in wickedly sharp claws. Above the creature's back a tail as thick as a man's leg arced up to end in a long spadelike spike. What held everyone's attention, though, hovered before them at the end of its thick sinuous neck—a head larger than a man's torso stared with baleful eyes, granting it an almost palpable sense of malice, and fangs like daggers dripped with thick saliva.

The thing stood frozen in place, yet it still inspired fear. The rasp of several swords sounded behind the Mage as they were drawn from their sheaths. When Jenaris turned, Carlon, Alban and the young Prince all stood armed and plainly uneasy.

"What *is* that *thing*?" Carlon growled, pointing to the evil-looking creature standing statue-still just a few feet away.

"*That*," Jenaris answered matter-of-factly, "is a dragon."

Shocked silence descended on those assembled as they stared at the monstrosity with expressions ranging from disbelief to anger. Finally, the King's voice broke the trance, sounding incredibly loud after the long silence.

"Can it be killed?" he asked.

"Yes," the Wizard shrugged. As if as an afterthought he added, "If you're good enough."

Carlon smiled knowingly as he turned his penetrating stare on Jenaris. "Men defending their homes and families can be damned good when they need to be."

The Mage considered. It was a valid point—men were as dangerous as badgers and terribly inventive when it came to violence. Having seen a dragon up close, however, he believed humanity may have met its match.

"True," he replied, "but it doesn't hurt to have the right weapon if you want to have anyone left standing at the end of the fight."

At the mention of weapons, Alban's eyes narrowed shrewdly. "And where," he prompted, "do we *get* this weapon?"

Jenaris checked the itch between his shoulder blades. Although it was fairly easy to ignore, when he thought about it he could now feel the magic growing, what... stronger? Tighter? Almost as though he could reach out and touch its source.

"That's the easy part." The Wizard's eyes sparkled as he met the Captain's gaze. "We may have a bit of a wait, but if you'll send someone to the harbor now, I think we can finish this conversation soon enough."

With the gangway firmly in place, the other deckhands made quick work of carrying Samir's belongings to the dock for him. He had no idea how he would manage to haul it all into town, but if he couldn't find porters, he had more than enough to buy a wagon if necessary.

After more than a month in heavy cotton, the silk he had worn his entire life felt slightly odd against his skin.

He luxuriated in the smooth, cool caress of it as he stood on the deck, the breeze rippling the light fabric.

"You're sure about this?" Tasca cast a dubious look at the city that rose up the hillside above the port. From the Captain's descriptions, it was little better than a cesspit. It was strange coming from a man with greasy hair and stained clothing, but the Captain seemed not to notice the inconsistency. "Argol is a much better place to settle. Bigger."

Of course, being Brisian, the Captain would likely favor his own land, and it sounded a pleasant enough place. But somehow Samir was absolutely certain that this was where he needed to be. It was like he could feel the rightness of it.

"I'm sure," he replied, "but thanks for the offer."

Tasca smiled broadly. "Your loss, my friend, but I'll still take that hound off your hands."

"Can't," Samir shook his head sadly. "She's all the family I've got right now."

The admission sent a brief stab of pain through him. All his life, he'd had a strong sense of his place in the world, of belonging. Now, he might not be at sea any longer, but he was still adrift.

The Captain nodded his understanding as he extended his hand to the young warrior. "She's not *all* the family you have, lad," he offered.

"Thanks." Samir was strangely comforted by the man's statement. Taking the offered hand, the Majaran felt his fingers wrapped in the old sailor's strong grip.

"Good luck to 'ya." Tasca winked, turning away quickly to shout orders to the men reefing the sails and leaving Samir to make his way ashore.

The silk against his skin wasn't the only thing that felt odd. As he reached the dock, the absence of motion—of the rolling and pitching of the deck on the swells—caught him completely off guard after so long. For a moment, he merely stood in place feeling the sun's warmth and the strange coldness of the gold armband on his left biceps as he waited for his body to adjust.

Now that he had taken his long straight hair out of the braid he had worn aboard the ship, strands rose and fell on the breeze. For perhaps the fifth time, he unconsciously reached for the golden hair clip binding the tail of hair tightly behind his head.

He supposed the first thing he had to do was find a place to stay. Even in an unfamiliar city, that would be easy enough—although the warrior would need to watch the details carefully to pick out the better parts of town from the worse. While he didn't exactly fear thieves, he had no intention of drawing the attention of the local law, and sharing a room with rats and fleas didn't appeal to him. Of course, before he could look around the city, he would need to hire some strong backs to carry his weapons and his saddle.

With a quick glance down the dock, Samir spotted Tirza sniffing at one of the thick posts that supported the piers along the waterfront. She seemed to be coping well to the sudden lack of motion after the time aboard the ship. If she was affected at all by the transition, it didn't appear to keep the hound from investigating her new surroundings with all of her usual enthusiasm. Dogs, it seemed, coped very well with change.

"Excuse me, sir." Samir slowly became aware of the man seated on the bench of a nearby wagon, shouting over the chaos around them. The teamster smiled as the Prince met his eyes. "Yes, you sir."

The thick bodied man hopped lightly to the wooden planks of the dock, despite his girth. Unarmed, the fellow clearly posed no threat in spite of muscles obviously accustomed to heavy loads. Still, the surprise of being approached by a complete stranger—and one who clearly seemed to think he knew the young Majaran—put Samir on his guard.

"Can I help you?" The warrior adjusted his stance, subtly rising on the balls of his feet as the other man drew closer. It wouldn't be his first choice, having to fight in front of dozens of witnesses, but he would certainly do it if he found it necessary.

"I believe I'm supposed to take you up to the castle, sir." The wagon driver appeared entirely unaware that he was even in jeopardy as he strolled to where Samir stood.

"You must have the wrong man, friend," the warrior offered what he hoped would pass for a reassuring smile as he studied the stranger. "I don't know anyone at the castle."

Samir resisted the temptation to check behind him as the other man glanced up and down the waterfront. Although the fellow sported a nose that had been broken at least once and slightly sunken knuckles, he was plainly nothing more than an occasional brawler. More to the point, nothing in his posture or his eyes so much as hinted at potential violence.

"It must be you, sir," the man explained. "There's no one else here, and you fit the description."

Samir tensed momentarily, before forcing himself to relax. The only people with his description were supposed to think him dead. He had gone to great lengths to make sure of it, in fact. Yet, if this man knew him on sight, it could only mean that there was trouble.

From the corner of his eye, he could see Tirza tense, reacting to her master's sudden suspicion. Trusting the hound to warn of any threat from behind, the warrior focused on the man in front of him.

"What description is that?" he asked. "And who sent you?"

The stranger only shrugged. "It wasn't much to go on. I was told to look for the one who seemed to wonder why he was here. The Wizard said you'd...."

"*Wizard*?" Samir blurted, running over the man's final words. He had only ever met two wizards in his life, and neither had been pleasant if annoyed. In fact, they could hardly have been called pleasant under any circumstances. He had no idea what such a person would want with him, let alone how his presence would be expected, but there was no doubt it would be best not to provoke a mage by ignoring a summons. With a glance at the castle sitting atop a hill, perhaps a half mile away, Samir nodded.

"Name's Ervin, sir, just so you know," the man offered easily as he began casually tossing the heavy load of weapons into the wagon bed and causing the warrior to flinch as the wood and steel within crashed to the boards.

"Kir," the Prince replied, giving the name he'd begun using aboard *Amelia*. After all, while he had no reason to think his real name would mean anything at all to an Acedian, it would be better to let as few people as possible hear it.

As it was, he was beginning to rethink wearing the armband. It had been an impulsive decision, but he'd suddenly needed to feel the connection it gave him to his father. The jade had done it, since his people had long believed the stone to carry something of its previous owners, making it a traditional gift from parent to child. In Majar jade wasn't even considered significant until it had been passed through four or five generations—and this piece had been worn by more of his ancestors than anyone could trace. Right now he needed that, and there should be virtually no risk of it being recognized by anyone here. Still, perhaps long sleeves would be prudent.

The wagon bounced and jostled over the smooth paving stones as it wound its way up the hill. Little traffic was about in Varella, which seemed strange for a city of this size, much less the capital of a nation. It was almost eerie.

"You feel it, don't you, sir?" Ervin broke in before Samir could ask. "Tension you could cut with a knife. But the King will set things right."

That last statement, Samir was sure, had been said with a great deal more confidence than the man had felt. Whether the teamster was trying to convince himself or his passenger was anybody's guess, however.

"I'm sure he will," Samir returned, offering polite reassurances. He was actually certain of no such thing, knowing neither the King nor his problems. But a good ruler would find a way to relieve his people's fears, and often it was merely a matter of being seen *doing* something. He just hoped this man, Carlon, was a good ruler.

The warrior's thoughts turned to his own problems as they drew nearer the castle. Meeting a king in the seat of his power didn't bother Samir in the least. After all, he had grown up in exactly that kind of environment, and this place—really a well-decorated fort—lacked the splendor of his own home. What he didn't like was the fact that a wizard had somehow taken notice of him. From everything he had ever heard, that was definitely *not* recommended for your continued good health.

The wind atop the high crenellated tower continually whipped Caleb's wavy bronze hair into his eyes, but he didn't even notice as he looked out across the rooftops of the city. He could see everything from up here—scores of people, like ants moving through a maze of slate and tile capped buildings; the broad wooden wharves of the port lined with ships and cargo; and the deep blue expanse of the Bharkur Sea that filled the horizon. The oldest and highest point of the castle provided a view that could be found nowhere else, and ever since he was a child this had been his place.

But now, for the first time he could remember, he could find no comfort here. Just the sight of so many people going about their daily lives usually brought an immediate sense of normalcy and rightness. Yet as he stood staring out over the city, he wondered whether his life would ever feel normal again.

"I thought I'd find you up here." His sister's voice carried an unmistakable hint of concern and, although she had masked it well with her typical playful tone, he knew her too well not to hear it. Of course, the fact that she had come *here* to look for him only proved how hard it was for either of them to hide anything from the other.

Putting on his best smile, he turned to face Cait, leaning back against the battlements with a casualness he didn't feel. From the look on her face, she wasn't having any of it—not for a second. In fact, he was certain that if she weren't using both hands to hold her dress down against the wind, her arms would be folded tightly and her foot would be tapping. Even so, the simple arched eyebrow would have done their mother proud.

"What do you want, Pest?" he asked wearily, crossing his arms in front of him. He'd been expecting this, and was actually surprised it had taken her this long to gather the courage to defy their father's order to let him be— something she was *definitely* not used to doing.

Moving to stand beside him, Cait rested her elbows atop one of the walls and gazed out at the calm sea. "Father may insist on letting you 'have time to come to grips with whatever happened,' and I understand if you don't want to talk about Captain Braden, but two days is long enough." She fixed Caleb with a penetrating stare, her eyes sparkling with barely contained excitement. "Now give over, Brat. You send us a letter—by fast messenger, no less—just *gushing* about this woman you *have* to marry, and you haven't said one word about her in the two days you've been back!"

Another wave of now familiar guilt washed over him at the mention of the captain. He had been a man the young Prince had admired greatly, and his horrible death had surely been the stuff of nightmares. Yet, that wasn't what had kept him so distracted the past few days. Even in the face of all that had happened, even with the slaughter of so many good men, Sorana was virtually all he thought about. There had to be something seriously wrong with him, he knew, if he couldn't even take the time to mourn a good man like Marius instead of dwelling on his own loss.

"Let it go," he told her, at the same time wishing *he* could. Caleb had been so sure she had been the one. But he'd long since run out of answers for that nagging voice that told him over and over that, if she *really* was, they would have worked things out. "She wasn't the right one after all. That's all you need to know."

"Why, Brother, of *course* I'll let it go. How could you even *think* I would pry where I wasn't welcome?" Cait's offended tone was completely spoiled by the grin she struggled to suppress. "Now, what happened?"

He shook his head sadly, reluctant to begin, but at the same time glad to have someone to talk to. "That's just it. I don't know. I tried to find her so we could talk, but it's like she just vanished." His voice took on a bitter tone as he glanced over to find her light blue eyes fixed steadily on him. "If she truly loved me, wouldn't she have let me find her?"

For a time Cait said nothing, only standing there thoughtfully studying him. There was no mistaking the genuine compassion she felt for him, but there also seemed to be something in her attitude that plainly said he was being an idiot.

"If you truly loved *her*, would you ever just give up without a fight?" Somehow her tone wasn't the least bit mocking, although the question made him feel as though she'd smacked him. "By the way, Father wants you in the audience hall."

Caleb stood watching mutely as his sister descended through the open trapdoor, smoothing her skirts. At this point, he had no idea what to think, but he knew she was right about one thing—he still needed answers and he couldn't just give up without them. Until he could at least speak to Sorana, he would never be able to let go of the doubts that tormented him or the hopes that still burned inside him.

Chapter 10

New Friends and Ancient Enemies

Samir had just begun to reach into the wagon bed for the heavy canvas bags containing his assortment of weapons when a host of black and green liveried servants came rushing to do the work. He hadn't realized until just that moment how accustomed he'd become to doing things for himself lately. Still, this was one task he was more than happy to surrender to someone else, as long as they treated his things with more care than Ervin had.

At the doors, he was handed over to a young girl who immediately whisked him through the corridors of the massive stone structure. He could practically feel the weight of age as he traversed the halls of the original keep—a place clearly designed to be defensible and no less impressive for its functional purposes. The transition to newer sections was abrupt as they moved deeper inside, yet well executed to blend more decorative elements of wood paneling and artistic glass into the construction. While not nearly as elegant as the palace in Toskar, it was a pleasant enough place.

As they reached a large well-lit chamber, the girl simply waved him inside and, with an added little bob, hurried off down the corridor. The warrior was still trying to figure out the awkward looking gesture when he became aware that he was not alone.

"Welcome." A tall, thin man in his middle years stood just inside the doorway, smiling pleasantly. From the way the man studied Samir without seeming to, he was either a soldier or a diplomat—and the posture, together with a permanent-seeming smile made it the latter. "Markus Silva, Prime Minister of Acedia. Please allow me to make introductions, Mister...?"

"Kir." Samir supplied the name without a pause, now accustomed to the name after several weeks of use. A few more months and he suspected he might even begin to believe it himself.

"Very good, sir." The gentleman inclined his head fractionally in what may have been intended as either a nod or a bow—or perhaps neither.

Waving Tirza to a corner, Samir followed the man to the far end of the chamber and its other occupants.

The room was obviously designed to impress visitors with the wealth and might of Acedia. Polished marble lined the room and composed the pillars supporting the slightly vaulted roof. Golden lamps burned in flickering sconces on the walls illuminating murals of battles long past and causing shadows to dance slightly. At the room's focal point, an ornate padded and gilded chair sat heavily on a raised platform. It was almost certainly built to receive visiting dignitaries and decorated with the best the country had to offer—and it left Samir thoroughly unmoved.

Stopping before the platform, Markus bowed deeply to the broad shouldered man at the center of the group. "Majesty, allow me to present Kir, warrior of Majar," the man intoned, obviously familiar with the telltale signs of various cultures. "Kir, allow me to introduce His Majesty, Carlon Derrek Cravath, Blessed of the Realm, King of Acedia, may he reign in peace and joy."

Samir bowed, more deeply than would be expected of a visiting prince, but appropriately for a mere warrior to a king. In the process, he almost missed the King's flitting look of mild disgust at Markus' mention of peace and joy.

Other introductions followed in rapid order, beginning with Prince Caleb and moving through the guard captain and his under-officers. The posture and stance of every man among them marked them as well-trained soldiers to his warrior's eye, and yet there was something terribly wrong. Although neatly turned out in impeccably tailored clothing, and clean shaven, the group gave the impression of being incredibly harried—especially Captain Ward. The Majaran could only interpret it as an air of *defeat,* as if the confidence that should be present had been beaten out of them all. He had seen it before, and it was dangerous. A warrior who lost faith in himself could cause the deaths of the men beside him—an officer in such a condition would bring swift and certain disaster on his entire command.

Suddenly, any questions he had about the feeling of despair in the city had been answered.

Perhaps the biggest surprise, however, was the man introduced as simply "the Wizard, Jenaris." While the ornately carved, silver-capped staff had marked him already, he hardly fit Samir's expectations at all. From past experience, he had anticipated a long, flowing beard and clothes as rich as those of any prince—yet neatly trimmed whiskers were as close as he'd come. The rustic wool of coat and trousers, together with heavy boots, gave more the impression of a hunter than a wizard. Aside from the age that was apparent in the well-creased skin and an intensity in the clear blue eyes that seemed to miss little, he hardly looked the part of a wizard at all.

The basic courtesies observed, Carlon nodded his thanks to the Prime Minister. "We'll be informal here, Markus. I want everyone to be able to speak freely. But," the King cautioned, sweeping those assembled with a stern gaze, "what is said goes no further than us for now. Understood?"

A series of mumbled acknowledgments seemed to satisfy Carlon, who quickly waved a pair of guardsmen to close the doors. In moments, they were alone.

Seeing no reason not to take the King at his word, Samir spoke up. "Would someone mind telling me exactly why I'm here?" While he asked the question of no one in particular, he turned his gaze on the Wizard, expecting any real answers would be found with him. He wasn't disappointed.

"Not at all," the Mage smiled humorlessly, meeting his gaze stare for stare. "You're here because I drew you here. When you arrived, did you feel as though this was where you *had* to be?"

Samir nodded warily, conscious of having drawn every eye in the room.

"That was because I cast a spell that caused you to find me." Jenaris grinned victoriously, obviously proud of its success. "It was about a month and a half back. A nice bit of...."

The warrior's back fist struck like lightning, catching the Mage in the temple far faster than anyone could react, cutting off the rest of the words as the other man staggered. Samir was only vaguely aware of the sounds of steel being drawn behind him as he focused his anger on the reeling Wizard.

"You!" Samir screamed the accusation as the focus of his gaze landed hard on the stone floor. "You caused all this?"

Leaping, the Majaran launched himself in a furious side kick as the Wizard started to rise. His right foot became a blur as it snapped out, driving toward the fallen man with all the anger inside him before being stopped short of his target by a jarring blow. Pain shot the length of his leg, exploding like fire in his hip as his foot struck the unseen barrier just beyond Jenaris' body. Instead of his usual grace, Samir landed hard as he struggled for balance, giving Captain Ward a chance to interpose himself with sword in hand.

Heedless of the pain, Samir surged forward, fully prepared to go through the soldier in front of him, yet he again fought to remain upright as he found his feet locked in place. Anger mixed with sadness within him as he realized he had failed. He was only vaguely aware of Tirza barking furiously, but he ignored her, focusing on the Mage. Samir had no doubt that he was about to die, but that didn't bother him as much as the knowledge that he had missed a chance to take his revenge. Still glaring his defiance, the young warrior watched as Jenaris stepped smoothly around the Captain.

"It's all right, Alban. We're just having a slight misunderstanding," the Mage offered calmly, patting the Captain's sword arm absently. Stopping well short of Samir's reach, gently fingering a growing lump on his head, Jenaris studied the Majaran with penetrating blue eyes. Finally, he shook his head. "Now, would you like to explain what exactly you're accusing me of?"

Stunned, Samir could only stare mutely at the Mage for a time. That the man could act as casually without even taking notice of the consequences was beyond alarming. It was no wonder wizards had gained such a formidable reputation if they had so little regard for those caught up in their schemes. Suddenly, he couldn't decide whether he should be disgusted or furious—but rage already had its grip on him.

"You destroyed my life," he sneered, wishing the Mage would take one more step forward, but the old man was obviously no fool. "You destroyed my *family!*"

The accusation had no apparent effect on the Wizard beyond a slight lift to the bushy white eyebrows. If anyone else reacted, Samir was oblivious, his attention locked firmly on Jenaris alone as the Wizard studied him calmly. At last, the corners of the Mage's mouth slid into a frown.

"I assume you are referring to whatever circumstances caused you to leave your home?" Jenaris asked, the sympathy in his tone seemingly genuine. Evidently taking the warrior's silence as assent, he continued. "*I* am speaking of the spell that located and drew a willing person with the proper skills—an incredibly difficult bit of magic, I assure you. My spell did not cause you to *suffer*, only to come. Do you understand the distinction, young man?"

Perhaps reading her master's mood, the hound's barking became sporadic, yet she struggled to reach Jenaris.

Now that the initial rush of fury had subsided, Samir forced himself to calm so he could consider what he'd been told. The Wizard's assertion made sense—or at least it seemed to. He knew Kemal's plans to take the crown hadn't simply developed overnight, but had taken months if not years of careful planning. That crime could only be laid at his brother's feet, not the Mage's. At worst, Jenaris' spell had been a remarkable stroke of timing to attach to him just as he was cast loose from his commitments. It did cause him to wonder briefly what would have happened if he hadn't been free to answer, but soon decided that they would never know. The simple fact was that he had no other responsibilities at the moment aside from his own preparations to retake his kingdom.

A brief hand signal caused Tirza to sit where she stood rooted in place. She subsided to only a high-pitched whine.

He nodded, albeit with some reluctance, and he was once again free to move. He had already decided that the Wizard wasn't about to retaliate for the blow Samir had landed—especially if he was necessary to Jenaris' plans. Still, the actions of a Majaran warrior were dictated by courtesy or need, rather than by fear. Without hesitation he dropped to his knees and lowered his head.

"I humbly apologize for striking you," he said, "and I ask your forgiveness."

He was answered by Jenaris' easy chuckle. "Get up," the Mage told him. "It's my own damned fool fault for not being more careful. But I guess reading about your people's reputation didn't quite prepare me for the reality."

Samir rose carefully to his feet, anticipating the twinge of pain in his hip, but steadfastly refusing to let it show. That, he supposed, was the price you paid for underestimating a wizard.

"Now," the Mage continued, "as to the *why* you asked about, you're here to help us with a problem that you are—according to my magic—uniquely equipped to deal with. You're here to fight dragons."

The statement was so matter-of-fact that it took a moment for the words to sink in. Yet, when they did, Samir was certain he hadn't heard the Wizard correctly.

"I'm sorry," he offered with a slightly abashed grin, "I didn't quite catch that. What did you say I was here to do?"

The Wizard wasn't the only one wearing an amused smile. In fact, from the shared glances and suppressed laughter, it was clear that he was the butt of some joke. Well, whatever it was, he supposed he could take a friendly ribbing without offense. With a questioning look around the room, he waited to be let in on the jest.

Jenaris shook his head, sweeping the others with a flat stare that said quite plainly this was no laughing matter. "You are here," the Mage repeated, "to fight dragons."

Samir snorted. Clearly it was a joke, and yet the Wizard still looked as utterly serious as Shimei became with a particularly thickheaded student. But that was impossible.

"You want me to fight a *myth*?" he asked, incredulous.

"Actually," the Mage's tone was more than a bit sarcastic, "it would be more correct to call it a *legend*. But, *yes*, I do."

The warrior bit back the impulse to demand that the other man give up the joke, but Jenaris' expression said plain as day that he believed what he was saying. Before Samir could decide how to reply without being so rude as to call him a liar, the Captain broke in.

"They exist, Majaran." Alban's sober pronouncement was accompanied by an almost haunted look. "I've seen them."

"It's true," Caleb added almost on top of him.

Suddenly, the word 'incredulous' didn't even begin to describe how Samir felt. His head spun like a top. But, from the grave expressions on some of the faces, it was dead certain that this was no joke. Children's tale or not, these men were obviously convinced they knew the truth of it, and the warrior definitely didn't like the strange feeling of uncertainty that gave him.

"All right," Samir offered reluctantly, willing for the moment to at least consider the idea. But his mind flickered through images of the mammoth, impossibly savage creatures that stories described as all but invulnerable. "Let's assume that dragons do exist. Exactly how am I supposed to fight something that's over twenty feet tall, flies, is armor plated, *and*, by the way, breathes fire?"

Samir realized that the sarcasm that had crept into his voice could be taken as rude, but he wasn't about to apologize for it. After all, he could see in their faces— most of them anyway—that they knew precisely how ridiculous it all sounded. The Wizard, on the other hand, merely looked amused.

"Unfortunately, young man, their existence hardly depends on whether you believe it." Jenaris' wry tone was almost cutting and, under normal circumstances, he would have been offended. Apparently sensing the Majaran's mood, the Mage held up his hands as if to forestall an angry reply and took on something of a lecturing manner. "But, as to your description, I used the word 'legend' for a reason, since they're generally based on some kernel of truth. The problem is that tales tend to change with the telling until they're barely recognizable. What I need you to consider is what type of beast could have formed the seed for the stories you've heard.

"In this case," Jenaris continued, his piercing look seeming to add weight to his words as he held up a single finger, "only one of the facts is accurate. Sadly enough, they are armor plated, but the rest is just correct enough to be completely wrong. Dragons are perhaps twenty feet *long*, but certainly not that tall. They could hardly avoid notice if they were the size of a house, now could they?" Jenaris waved away his own question as if to show that it was hardly worthy of consideration. "They can't fly either—no wings—but they are very, *very* fast. And lastly, they do *not* breathe fire, only venom."

"*Only* venom?" Caleb asked accusingly, his fierce stare locked on the Wizard. Still, there was a sense of something haunted behind the Prince's brown eyes. "Is that what it spit at Marius and the others? *Venom?*"

Although Caleb's outburst had drawn his attention, Samir was aware several of the others in the room now watched the Mage intently—particularly Captain Ward and his lieutenant, Gillis. Clearly, whatever it was these men were calling a 'dragon,' it had been responsible for the loss of their confidence—and at least one of their men. Rather than disbelief, he was starting to feel a rising curiosity about this possible new foe. That the monster could have this effect on trained soldiers, yet be somehow vulnerable to his skills was intriguing to say the least.

Jenaris sighed deeply. "That's almost certainly what it was," the Wizard answered with what appeared to be honest sympathy. "I don't mean to be morbid, and I know he was your friend, but I wish I could have examined his body."

Caleb exchanged a quick glance with Captain Ward, the two seeming to decide without words which of them should speak. The Prince paused to take a deep breath, eyes tightly shut. "He looked like he'd been caught in a bonfire. At least, his skin did—all blistered and red. His hair wasn't singed at all."

"I'm sorry. I hope he didn't suffer long." Jenaris nodded, as though he'd expected the description. "The poison is certainly the source of all the stories about fiery breath, and there's very little to be done unless you do it immediately."

Caleb stiffened, hands clenching into fists as if ready to fight. "I washed it off as fast as I could think to," he said defensively.

From the plaintive tone, it almost sounded to Samir as though the young Acedian were trying to convince himself of what he was saying. It was fairly obvious what was behind it—guilt.

"Young man, listen to me." From Jenaris' firm tone, he had evidently noticed Caleb's distress as well and wasn't about to coddle him, Prince or not. The Mage's stare as he approached held the younger man's gaze easily. "I was not referring to any treatment you might have been able to give. What you were dealing with was beyond your ability to cure and it was *not* your fault."

Jenaris laid a hand on Caleb's shoulder, giving a gentle squeeze to take the sting out of his stern words. The other man merely nodded, showing that the assurance had registered even if he didn't fully agree with it.

"The treatment will require some research," Jenaris continued to the entire group, sounding resigned. "I'll need to look through whatever books Lorn left behind. But, without that knowledge, I'm not even certain the venom is survivable.

"It is, Mage," Alban insisted, drawing Jenaris' piercing blue eyes in a way that seemed to search the Captain as if attempting to drag the truth from him. Still, the soldier continued unfazed. "Jether was also struck with a small amount. He was feverish for days before the blackness on his skin began to spread. We finally had to take his arm above the elbow," he finished bleakly.

The silence that followed stretched for long, uncomfortable moments. Finally, mercifully, Gillis found a new course for the discussion.

"No offense, Kir," the lieutenant offered, studying the Majaran curiously, "but why you?"

It was a legitimate question, one that had occurred to Samir almost immediately. But, then, he knew virtually nothing of magic—certainly not enough to question the Wizard as to the subtleties of any spell that may have been cast. Besides, by reputation, those who practiced the magical arts were a tightlipped lot at best.

The warrior shrugged. "To be honest, I don't know. At the risk of sounding arrogant, I'm good. But there are many better—including my own Sòra, Shimei, who may be the best who ever lived."

"Actually," the King supplied thoughtfully, "it makes sense that the Wizard's spell would bring a Majaran, since few will even attempt to dispute that they produce the greatest fighters in the world." He paused to let that sink in, his officers fidgeting but raising no objection. "If any single person can make a difference, it will be a Majaran warrior."

Samir nodded thoughtfully. It was simple truth as far as it went, although the fact that the magic had managed to attach to him at exactly the moment his attachment to his home and training were broken seemed beyond any odds he could imagine. The honor of any warrior, particularly anyone as skilled as a Sòra, would *never* allow him to walk away from his duties, but such a spell would certainly have brought someone—since there were always caravan guards or mercenaries between hires. The Wizard had taken a chance on what he would get for his troubles, but he wouldn't have come up empty-handed. Of course, the young Majaran could always refuse, since it wasn't a fight that affected his people. Yet, it wasn't in him to walk away from a situation where he could make a difference. Now the real question was whether Samir could do the job.

"I have no pressing duties to speak of," he said after a moment, "and that won't be true of any of our genuine masters. I may be the best available for what you need." He didn't add that his only obligation at the moment was to settle Kemal's blood debt, but that was between himself and his brother.

"Forgive me if this sounds rude, Kir," Captain Ward broke in, failing to sound at all like he really meant it, "but if you don't consider yourself a master, what can you actually do?"

King Carlon briefly met the officer's eyes with a look of reproach—though whether it was meant as a rebuke for the lack of courtesy or from fear at offending someone whose help they needed, he wasn't sure. Alban did have the good grace to look abashed, however.

"To be honest, I'm not sure," Samir admitted, doing his best to ignore the interplay. "I would need to see these creatures and their capabilities before I knew what weapons to use, much less my chances of defeating them."

Although he didn't believe in boasting, in this case it was simple pragmatism rather than modesty that moved him to caution. Even if these monsters weren't quite the gargantuan creatures portrayed in the stories, they would no doubt be formidable indeed to have inspired such tales. While the thought of facing creatures with their deadly reputation sent a thrill of excitement through him, it brought more than a little apprehension.

"I believe I can help with that," Jenaris said, stepping smoothly to the front of the platform.

Apparently already knowing what to expect, the others all watched the large open space of the floor as Jenaris began to chant softly. The Mage's voice was just on the edge of hearing, but was strangely powerful—producing an odd resonance, a vibration that almost made Samir's bones hum. Tirza's throaty growl told him he wasn't the only one to feel the disturbing sensation. Mists built quickly as he watched, assuming shape and color in moments to reveal what at first seemed a cross between an enormous bull and some sort of serpent. Yet, the more defined it became the less it resembled anything he had ever seen.

In little more than a minute, the dragon—and there was no doubt that it was exactly that—stood fully formed at the far end of the room, looking as real and solid as he was himself. It was nothing short of astonishing that this *thing* before him was merely a trick of mists and vapors concocted by the Wizard. Now it gave every appearance of being alive as it moved menacingly, broad chest expanding as it breathed with head and eyes tracking back and forth as if seeking some unseen target. The beast was clearly the source of the tales he had heard as a child, and only one word seemed adequate to describe it—*evil*.

"This encounter happened just before I reached the edge of the plains," Jenaris announced. "I believe it to be a fairly good measure of their abilities."

As if on cue, the dragon's glare seemed to lock onto something, or someone, in front of it. The creature lunged, thickly muscled legs driving it forward with unbelievable speed and tail swinging in a jet black blur as it arced toward its target. Without warning the tail's sharp tip jarred to a sudden stop as if striking a wall of air. Immediately the neck snaked to one side, jaws widening to expose gleaming white fangs while at the same time the opposite claw lashed out with a force that would easily disembowel. Both attacks frustrated by the same unseen barrier, the head withdrew just as the tail once again sped forward over the creature's shoulder, plainly seeking to impale its victim with the wicked looking spike.

For several minutes the assault continued unabated, the beast maintaining a constant barrage with no discernible pattern. Nearly black claws shone with a dull light as they raked and snatched. The long sinuous tail danced, one second a club, then suddenly a spear as it sought a target. Dagger sharp teeth tried in vain to rend flesh as the massive head came from every possible angle. Samir's trained eye took in each lightning fast move of the onslaught, approaching a feeling akin to awe at the smooth coordination that took human beings a lifetime of dedication to learn. But what continued to draw his attention was the incredible hatred emanating from the monster's hooded red eyes.

The dragon's increasing frustration obvious, the head cocked back, angling high on the long neck as the jaws snapped open. Samir nearly jumped in spite of himself as a jet of inky fluid shot from the creature's jaws with impressive force and speed to splash against the invisible barrier and flow to the ground.

The illusion froze.

Without a word, the warrior stepped down from the platform, walking a slow circle around the huge scaled form occupying a large portion of the floor. The beast was nothing short of remarkable—with massive haunches and shoulders capable of generating tremendous power, and a supple neck and body which allowed a frightening range of motion for attacks. It was a virtual arsenal on legs, all armor plated for defense as well as offense.

"Can I touch it?" he asked, hands clasped behind his back in an unconscious imitation of his teacher as he continued to scan for weaknesses. There seemed very few that he could exploit.

"It has no solid form, I'm afraid," the Mage replied.

Jenaris' voice came from just behind him, surprising the young warrior. He hadn't even heard the man approach as he studied the dragon. Curious, he swiped a hand casually at the thick muscled neck, feeling a chill as the fingers passed through. The illusion remained but for a gap where the mists temporarily trailed away before reforming. He nodded.

"Your Majesty," Samir faced Carlon, deliberately dragging his gaze from his study of the dragon, "could you have someone bring my bags?"

With a slight smile, the King nodded, gesturing to Gillis. "Send a page," he said sharply.

The lieutenant took only a moment to acknowledge the order before moving quickly to the closed doors at the far end of the room, drawing a brief glance from Tirza.

As the echo of the footsteps faded, Samir turned his attention to the Mage. "Let me see it again," he insisted, mind already racing ahead to anticipate the creature's movements.

At a gesture from the Wizard, the illusory form broke apart as the mists moved back to their original position as if blown by a wind. Once there, they quickly reformed. This time, as the nightmare image moved forward, the Majaran stepped in close, studying its movements and looking for limits to its range of motion. Still not satisfied that he'd seen enough, he asked Jenaris to restart the sequence.

Again and again while the others watched, Samir moved around the rampaging form, gradually fitting strikes and counter moves to those of the dragon. Hands wielding imaginary weapons, he pushed to the limits of his speed and agility as he danced around the head, claws and tail with his stances constantly shifting—first low, then high.

Though focused intently on the dragon, the lack of actual danger allowed him occasional glances at the others in the room, revealing the hope on their faces as they stood mesmerized. Then as always, the jaws opened and the venom spewed out, bringing the illusion to a sudden halt.

"And how do you counter *that*?" Alban asked, worry now etching lines across his features as his shoulders sagged slightly. "It looks like you have everything else figured well enough, but that stuff...."

A small smile twitched at the corners of the Majaran's lips as the Captain's words trailed off into silence. He had already considered the problem and believed he had it solved, although it would take nearly perfect timing.

Within moments a small army of servants arrived, bearing the large canvas bags containing Samir's collection of weapons. Designating a space at the far end of the room for the men to deposit their burdens, he immediately began to sort his gear, eager to find what he needed.

The young warrior unpacked quickly, unwrapping the cloth coverings and arranging the weapons into their familiar categories that, it was obvious, only he could fathom. Moving to place the various selections, the warrior felt an odd mixture of amusement and pride as he noticed the faces of many in the room, particularly the soldiers, changing from initial interest to awe as they began to whisper and point at the sheer variety of deadly implements. When he was finished several minutes later, the assortment covered much of the floor in two somewhat disproportionate groups, and the King was standing only a few feet away gawking at the collection.

"Which ones can you use?" Alban asked, amazement plain on his face.

Surprised at the strangeness of the question, Samir shot the Captain a puzzled look, but could see that the man was serious. "All of them," he replied. Those on the left I am proficient with. The ones on the right I have mastered."

Stark amazement warred with disbelief on many of the faces around him. He had heard that most soldiers outside of Majar mastered perhaps one or two weapons in a lifetime, yet until this moment he hadn't fully appreciated the reality of that situation. Among his own people, warriors were considered lazy and worse than useless who were expert with less than a dozen. Clearly, though, the eighteen or so that Samir *could* claim somehow seemed more remarkable to these people than the forty to fifty remaining. He was suddenly struck with the undeniable fact that this truly was a different sort of place than he was used to.

From the right hand group Samir rapidly selected what he would need—sweeping up a pair of knives and a long tasseled spear in addition to his longsword and broadsword. Stepping to the left side of the floor he picked up a folded silk fan, tucking it into the front of his sash opposite the knives now resting in the small of his back. Giving the other weapons a final scan he nodded to himself, satisfied that the choices felt natural.

"These," he announced, "will kill a dragon. So will many of the others, but these are best—at least in my hands." He flashed a mischievous grin, eyes twinkling. "My teacher, Shimei, could probably kill the creature with his disapproval alone."

A burst of laughter answered the remark, from the King as well as the soldiers. Although none of those present had ever met the Sòra, nearly every well-trained fighter had a similar opinion of his own weapons master—and a similar respect.

Stepping lightly on the balls of his feet, Samir moved a bit apart from the group and set aside the two swords.

Not even bothering to set his feet, he immediately broke into a flurry of motion with the spear. Both ends of the weapon seemed to attack the air in rapid succession as he engaged in an illusory combat with the dragon he had studied minutes before. Fast moving hands guided the sharp steel head to spiral and stab even as the butt wove in subtle counterpoint or swung as if to ward off dangerous jaws or batter aside a tail. The Majaran moved by instinct from front to flank and back again, seeming to attack everywhere at once. With a sudden wordless scream, Samir launched himself to his left, spearhead circling just above the floor as he moved to sweep a scaled leg before plunging the tip into an imaginary red eye. Then, as abruptly as he had begun, he was finished.

The warrior bowed as applause and approving shouts rang from the watching crowd. Still, he did little more than pause to exchange the spear for his broadsword before repeating his previous performance. This time the flashing steel carved precise arcs intended to cleave and slice whatever was found in its deadly path. Colorful silk scarves floated and snapped blindingly around him, but the Majaran paid no attention to anything but the slash of the razor sharp blade.

His knives followed. They flashed, weaving intricate patterns even as the young warrior danced. Although the weapons were obviously far too small to parry anything as sizable as claws or tail, Samir counted on his own speed and dexterity to evade the creature while the blades punctured and cut with a lethal precision born from years of tireless practice.

Finally, he took up the longsword that had been a nearly constant companion from childhood. Almost part of his hand, it swung in a strange rhythm of its own while he himself moved, its point swiveling to dart in from all angles as his wrist and elbow moved in a sinuous counterbalance. In only a few moments, his smooth assault had punctured the imagined foe with a score of precisely placed wounds.

Only a light sheen of sweat covered Samir's chest and arms as he finished, barely winded but pleased. His balance and footwork had definitely improved from his time spent practicing on *Amelia*'s unsteady decks—better by far than even the treacherous plumflower posts. Sheathing the long, narrow blade he strolled across the floor toward the others, only then becoming aware of the whispers and unusual looks passing among them.

"Something wrong?" he asked as the quiet conversations broke off abruptly at his approach, the mood awkward. Whatever the reason, only Carlon and Jenaris seemed able to meet the warrior's gaze without embarrassment.

"Not at all, Kir," Carlon replied, taking only an instant to direct a scathing glare toward the officers. "It was an amazing display, but...well, we were just thinking that some of your maneuvers looked a bit familiar."

Samir nodded, understanding. The forms were such a familiar sight to him, having watched men at practice since he was a toddler that he hadn't considered how strange it might appear to outsiders. Evidently, if he were going to teach these people how to fight these creatures, he would need to start with the basics.

"Our combat forms are based on the movements of certain animals," he explained, adopting a patient tone that he hoped wouldn't seem patronizing. "The mantis forms are the most obvious, but monkey, tiger, snake and crane are distinctive as well."

To his surprise, he saw several heads shake in response.

"That's not it," Alban offered, glancing around, plainly uncertain whether to say more or let someone else speak.

Slightly confused, Samir searched the faces of the other men, hoping to find understanding. It was as if they had somehow all missed the most obvious thing in the world. Quickly he considered several techniques, looking for the best way to demonstrate.

"What we mean," Caleb said thoughtfully, "is that we think there's *another* animal behind some of your techniques.

The King nodded agreement. "Some of your moves looked *exactly* like the dragon's. Especially the spear and that last sword you used." Carlon pointed to the longsword still clutched in the warrior's hand.

It was hardly a stunning revelation. After all, any halfway decent fighter had to be able to make adjustments, adapting to an enemy's style and abilities quickly. He obviously had a lot to teach these people.

Samir shrugged, resisting the urge to sigh. "It's about using moves that will work best against an opponent," he told the King, suddenly wondering how Shimei would explain this.

He never got the chance.

"Sorry, Kir. I know what you're saying, but I can't accept that." Carlon offered a look of mild sympathy as if to take some of the sting out of his words. "Unless you somehow created those maneuvers on the spot that doesn't even begin to make sense of what I just saw."

It had been evident nearly from the start that they weren't communicating clearly. For the first time, however, the Majaran was beginning to realize that *he* was probably the one who didn't understand—and it was not a feeling he liked.

"All right," he allowed, doing his best to set aside what he thought he knew. "What exactly did you see in my style that made you think of the dragon?"

With only a brief glance at the others, the Captain took the lead. "Your spear struck just like that thing's tail," Alban replied, drawing enthusiastic nods all around.

"And your sword arm moved so much like the neck it was almost uncanny," Caleb put in. "But it was in pretty much all of the stuff you did. Like it was just under the surface."

Samir didn't respond immediately, taking a moment to consider. He knew he hadn't really done anything to modify his fighting style or the way the weapons were typically used. But even without taking the time to really break down his technique, he could see some definite similarities. In fact, some of his other weapons could have given these people the same impression.

Glancing at the Wizard, the warrior could see that something deeper had occurred to him that he had yet to voice. Samir waited, expecting that the Mage would speak his mind without prompting. It wasn't a long wait.

"Exactly how old *are* the Majaran combat skills, Kir?" Jenaris' searching expression told him plainly that the question was more than simple curiosity. It wasn't hard to guess where this might be leading.

"No one really knows," Samir admitted easily, "but there are writings and even carvings that must be nearly a thousand years old."

The Wizard nodded as though he'd heard a confirmation of a theory. "I think," he said, watching the younger man for a reaction, "that the movements of those other creatures must have come later—probably *much* later. Your combat style, and especially your weapons skill, is just too similar *not* to have been based on the movements of dragons, which some of the older texts call drakes." The Mage paused to let his words sink in. "It seems to me that, at some point in the distant past, your people must have created those fighting skills in order to kill something a bit more dangerous than a crane or a monkey."

Several chuckles greeted the Wizard's light sarcasm, but died as Gillis burst into uproarious laughter. The lieutenant waved away the curious looks at the seemingly exaggerated reaction.

"It just occurred to me," Gillis explained, straightening his green wool coat somewhat self-consciously under the scrutiny, "that it explains why your people have such a formidable reputation, Kir. If you train to kill *dragons*, facing anything else must be about as threatening as fighting a puppy."

Samir had to grin at the mental image the lieutenant had conjured. Of course, it was never quite that easy in practice. The people Majaran warriors generally faced in combat were other Majaran warriors, or at least those with some experience—like the pirates he'd met. Gillis was close to the truth, though—outsiders weren't usually much of a challenge.

He had to admit that Jenaris' idea made sense, or at least as much sense as believing that dragons were more than the myth he had always thought. And if they really *were* the source of the skills he'd spent his life trying to master, he would need to think long and hard about how to approach the work ahead of him. Making a mistake in spar with a Sòra could get you hurt, but in a fight with one of these creatures it would get you dead.

"I'll need someplace to train," he said after a time, "and to keep my weapons."

"I think we can have a room set aside for you," Carlon assured him. A look at the weapons arrayed across the floor brought a brief grimace to the King's face. "We'll make it a large room."

Samir gave a nod not much short of a bow. It was a generous offer, especially to someone who was a stranger. Still, he hoped the room was big enough for his needs. Some of his forms required a lot of room to perform, and he fully intended to have blacksmiths begin reproducing his weapons using these as examples.

"Thank you, Sire," he replied with genuine gratitude. Samir turned his gaze on Alban. "So when do we hunt these dragons, Captain? Three, did you say?"

"Um, Kir. I think you're under a slight misconception," Jenaris said beside him, the deep creases around his eyes now more pronounced. "There aren't *three* dragons. There are at least *nine* by my personal count."

Samir was speechless. *Nine,* he repeated to himself. *No...at least nine.*

"Excuse me, Mage," Alban broke in, clearly sharing Samir's concern at the number. "We know we saw three because they appeared together. No offense, but how do you know you didn't see some of them multiple times?"

It was a good point, and one that had evidently occurred to some of the others as well, judging by the nods. The Mage plainly wasn't bothered by the scrutiny that followed, meeting each pair of eyes in turn before speaking.

"I *Marqued* them," Jenaris answered with a casual wave. "To put it simply, I placed a magical tag on each one I met. Even a senile old man like me couldn't possibly mistake them after that." The Wizard grinned. "But before we do any dragon hunting, I need to do some research. Hopefully, Kirstea left the necessary books with Lorn."

With that, Samir began to carefully rewrap and pack his weapons. Entrusting his collection to the care of several strong-looking porters, he was soon following a page through the castle's hallways. But he paid little attention to the twists and turns, hardly aware of the comfortable surroundings as he considered the odd irony of his situation. Assuming all of this was true, he was about to become the first Majaran warrior in perhaps a thousand years to use the training as it was originally intended. He only hoped he was up to the challenge.

Chapter 11

Blackthorn

Kordel paced slowly up and down the floor of the spacious study he was now forced to share as Jenaris leafed through the collection of large volumes Lorn had owned. The vast majority had been his share of the inheritance when Kirstea had passed, though his friend had obviously added to their number from other sources. The newer ones seemed to have been copied by Lorn, although the man had apparently written several himself—just none on any topic that interested the current reader in the least.

Jenaris couldn't blame Kordel for having difficulty adjusting to the new arrangement after living with a certain amount of privilege for the past decade. Still, the youngster had deserved to be sharply reined in after claiming what he had never earned.

It could have been much worse, of course. King Carlon had *not* been best pleased to discover that he'd been deceived by someone to whom he'd extended his trust. Perhaps even more troubling, the King had based possibly crucial decisions on the opinion of someone he had believed to be an expert. Thankfully, Carlon had been gracious enough to allow Jenaris to deal out any disciplinary action in the matter.

"Kordel," Jenaris said pointedly, a slight impatience creeping into his voice as he continued scanning the page before him.

"Yes, Magus?" the younger man replied quickly this time, apparently resigned to the sudden loss of autonomy if not the rapid downfall.

The Mage noted that his newly inherited apprentice had chosen to respond with what must have been the less offensive title. Still, he had given the other man the option, so he could hardly find fault when Kordel chose to exercise it. The funny thing was, there were those who would find "Master" far less offensive than "Magus," but he didn't expect his apprentice to understand the distinction yet.

"Either stop that pacing or get out," the Wizard insisted, briefly fixing Kordel with an impatient glare before turning the page. "If you insist on going for a walk, go and fetch me something to eat."

It took several seconds for Jenaris to realize that, while his apprentice had finally ceased the endless pacing, the man still hadn't left the room. Lifting his eyes from the neat script he'd been studying, he found Kordel rooted in place, staring at his master with utter disbelief.

"I did that almost an hour ago, Magus. Right after you asked me to." Kordel pointed a steady finger to an untouched platter of meat and cheese resting on a nearby sideboard. The Mage didn't recall Kordel's return with the food. In fact, he didn't even remember sending for it, but that wasn't surprising given his level of concentration on Lorn's magical library.

Rising to grab the plate, Jenaris had to stretch and work out a few kinks in his lower back. He'd been sitting on that stool for too long, but he had always been one to focus on the task at hand until it was finished.

Unfortunately, he couldn't be sure that what he sought was even there to be found. He'd hardly had the opportunity to look through most of these books when they had belonged to Kirstea, and the ones Lorn added were all obscure. After all, most were far outside his own area of expertise. If the information was anywhere in this library, though, Jenaris knew he would uncover it.

Finding a way through the hopeless clutter of the study was another matter, however. Despite the room's size, the dusty and dented oak of the sideboard seemed to have had the only unoccupied place—other than several now empty bookshelves—on which to set the food. Tables not already covered with jars, canisters or other sorts of odds and ends had swiftly been piled with books over the past several hours. In fact, several chairs and quite a bit of floor space had received their fair share, necessitating an awkward path for the apprentice's pacing.

"If you would just explain what you're looking for, Master, I'm sure we could find it faster together," Kordel insisted for perhaps the fourth time.

It was good that the man was eager to help, of course, but his refusal to take "No" for an answer was becoming more than a little tiresome. Swallowing the bite of sharpish yellow cheese, the Wizard allowed his annoyance at the lack of results to enter the glare he turned on Kordel.

"I've already told you," Jenaris answered with a deep sigh, "I won't know it myself until I see it. That being the case, I don't trust you—or anyone else, for that matter—to recognize it."

Having vented some of his frustration, the Mage forced himself to chew slowly at a piece of corned beef spiced with mustard. He knew that someone must have discovered a way of dealing with the insidious poison these creatures produced. Yet, the number of people who had seen a dragon and lived in the past few centuries was so low that no one seemed to have bothered to study or pass on the relevant information. Only the oldest texts he had seen contained more than the very basics.

At the very least, he would soon be able to remedy that deficiency, however. The material he had been gathering, together with his theories on the origin of the Majaran combat arts, would make a good start on the writing he would need to do. But there was more he would need to learn before they encountered the beasts again, or they might well lose what they couldn't afford to part with. The sad irony was that if they succeeded— *when*, he corrected himself—the information would once again become obsolete, and would pass out of use.

"Get me as much blank parchment as you can find, Kordel," the Mage instructed. "I need to start a new book, and I don't know how thick it will be."

"Yes, Magus," the apprentice replied, already threading his way between the piles on the floor.

"And, Kordel," he called, just as the man vanished through the doorway, "lose the robe and get some real clothes."

Satisfied, Jenaris returned to the table to leaf through the already open book. Someday, he resolved, he would take the time to go through the library properly. There was no telling what gems he had already missed in his hurried scan of the thousands of pages. His only concession to his own preferences had been to set aside several volumes on topics that interested him. *Those* he would do his best to read before "someday."

Having finished the book in front of him, he made an abrupt gesture, sending it drifting to a stack of those already finished. The random volume he selected from the stack beside him turned out to be yet another tome on the subject of herbal medicine—a topic he had always felt was a fine course of study...for someone else. Resisting the urge to set it aside, he forced himself to open the cover and begin turning pages.

It had just occurred to Jenaris to wonder how anyone could possibly care about how to distill blackthorn root when he realized that *he* cared. He had almost missed it entirely as he'd tried to scan the pages faster, wanting badly to move on to something he might actually enjoy. But there it was—a list of ingredients for a "restorative against the expectoration of the great wyrm." It was the final word that had jarred him alert, having found it attached to the oldest description of dragons he had seen.

He could have danced a jig. Instead he immediately marked the page, running to find the King, heedless of the stacked books he sent tumbling in every direction. Briefly it occurred to him to wonder about the time and whether Carlon might be sleeping. But this was far too important to worry about that. The real concern was how to find a good herbalist who could tell him what in the world Blackthorn was.

The Wizard's excitement had made him difficult to understand at first, but once Carlon grasped the need for someone knowledgeable in herb lore, one person had come instantly to mind. He also knew exactly where he would find her.

There were few people out this late, when most people had finished their supper and would be spending time with family or doing evening chores in preparation for tomorrow. Only the tread of the occasional sentry made him aware that anyone else was about as he made his way toward the long brick buildings ahead.

The shadows inside the stable were almost as deep as those without, the few lit lanterns being turned down low by the short staff on duty at the late hour. But he knew where he was going. The young woman he sought would be here—had spent most of her time practically rooted in place over the past few days, in fact.

The silhouette in the flickering light revealed that Morena was indeed perched atop the door to the stall where Dawn Rose was stabled. It was an unusual name for a warrior's horse, to be certain, but the King knew and appreciated how the fallen captain had come by it—how Marius had asked his daughter to name his mount and never hesitated to adopt the one she had given. The bond of affection they had shared had been a strong one, but that had given rise to a grief every bit as deep at the loss.

Carlon understood, of course. Marius Braden had been the kind of man who naturally inspired love and loyalty from others. It was a trait that had helped build a genuine friendship between the King and his Captain, regardless of their relative positions. He only wished he could offer more comfort to those his friend had left behind.

Certainly, he had taken care of their immediate needs. The house on the castle grounds was theirs for as long as they wished to stay, along with a stipend for their living expenses. But, while he knew that Lawrie and Morena were more than grateful, he believed it was the least he could do. The simple fact was that meeting their physical needs hardly began to cover it.

Despite the efforts of the officers, their wives and the King himself to help them through the grief, Morena had begun to take comfort elsewhere. In the stables, Carlon had noticed, and wasn't entirely sure that it was healthy.

It was clear that Dawn Rose had become something of a connection to her father since the funeral. Now, the young woman spent much of everyday in the section where the officers' mounts were kept—and much of every evening as well. In fact, reports had reached him that she had spent the night sleeping in the straw more than once.

Carlon had fully intended to come and speak to her about it before now, and yet circumstances had kept him from it every time. Officially, Morena shouldn't be admitted into these stables, being reserved for the horses of the Royal Guard. No one could bring themselves to tell her that, however. That was fine. If anyone *had* forbidden these visits, the King would have taken that individual to task. Still, everyone's choosing to turn a blind eye didn't alter the fact that Dawn Rose belonged to someone else.

"Morena," Carlon tried to make his tone gentle, but still caused her to nearly jump out of her skin.

Recovering quickly from her fright, Morena climbed down from her perch on the gate to sketch a hasty curtsy as she recognized the unexpected visitor. The look on her face, like a child caught sneaking cookies, told Carlon that she knew very well that she shouldn't be here.

"I'm sorry, Sire," she blurted, finally managing to find her voice. "I just had to come and see her one last time."

Although his heart certainly went out to the young woman before him, he resisted the indulgent smile that tugged briefly at the corners of his mouth.

"And how many last times does this make?" he asked, holding up a hand to forestall a reply.

Morena bit her lip, lowering her head to avoid meeting his searching look. A fall of red, tightly curled hair formed a curtain between them, but he didn't need to read her face to know that the embarrassment she presented was at least something of a front. He would have bet a goodly sum that she was preparing arguments against the near certainty of being told to leave. She was, after all, every bit her father's daughter.

"I spoke with your mother," he continued. "She and I agree that you can't keep coming here to visit Dawn Rose."

She met his eyes now and, while he could see some very real tears forming, there was a fierce determination there as well. It was a look he knew well, having seen it in Marius' eyes often enough—and always before a lively debate. But, as much as he expected that Morena could hold her own if it came to a...friendly exchange of opinions, he had to let her off the hook. After all of her recent pain, it wouldn't be right to tease her.

"You'll just have to visit your horse in her new stall in the royal stable," he told her.

Morena's expression shifted rapidly from confusion to surprise to unadulterated joy as the implications began to sink in.

"*My* horse?" Hope shone in her sparkling green eyes as she searched his face. "You mean I can...oh, thank you!"

Carlon was nearly knocked off his feet as she suddenly threw herself against his chest, hugging him tightly. After a slightly awkward pause while he recovered from his surprise, he briefly and lightly returned the embrace before extricating himself in as gentle a manner as possible, masking a hint of a grin.

A deep scarlet blush suffused Morena's cheeks as she met his eyes, plainly aware of what she'd just done. Lips moving silently, she worked to frame an appropriate apology, which only left her more flustered as the seconds passed.

"It's all right, Morena." The King's booming laugh filled the space, bringing snorts from several of the mounts. "You can consider yourself pardoned for assaulting the King's person...*this* time."

Sight of his grin seemed to dispel the last of her embarrassment, causing her to return his good humor. "I thank His Majesty for not turning me over his royal knee." She dropped into a deeply exaggerated curtsy, green eyes twinkling with mischief. "And thank you again for Dawn Rose."

"You're more than welcome," he replied easily, "but that's not actually why I came to find you. There's a problem I need your help with. More precisely, the Wizard needs your help."

"I'm sorry, Sire," she said, not even bothering to hide her skepticism. "I don't know what I could do if it's beyond a wizard's ability. I mean, I'll help in any way I can, of course, but...."

In a way she was right. There wasn't anything she could provide that he couldn't have gotten from others just as easily. But the truth was that in spite of her youth, Morena was already considered among the best herbalists anywhere in Acedia—both by her teachers and her fellow practitioners. Even without that, though, he simply wouldn't have felt right if he didn't give her this chance to strike back at the monsters that had taken away her father.

To be honest, Carlon would have liked to get some payback himself.

"You might be surprised," he replied. "If you learn one thing about wizards, remember that they are neither all-knowing nor all-powerful. In the case of this particular mage, you know quite a bit more on the subject of herbs," he said with a wink as he turned to go. "I'll expect you after breakfast. And, Morena...."

"Yes, Sire?"

"You can visit Dawn Rose *after* we talk."

With that he made his way back toward the castle, returning to the book and brandy Jenaris had interrupted earlier. There was still time to finish a few more pages before he turned in, but it would be a long day tomorrow, and he intended to get an early start.

Samir stood calmly in the center of the large open room he had been given for training, his bare feet motionless on the smooth white marble of the floor. It was actually fairly chilly against his soles, despite the fact that this land was only weeks away from the beginning of summer, but he could ignore that with little difficulty. Still, while he could appreciate the near absence of humidity, he would hate to actually experience a winter here.

As it was, he was grateful to the rust-haired Prince Caleb for the gift of a jacket to help with the cool night air. The black velvet felt nearly as luxurious as good silk and was nicely accented with silver buttons and welting. Yet, although it fit reasonably well for something tailored for a different frame, it would definitely restrict his movements in combat. At the moment it lay neatly folded beside the door.

Around him, several members of the castle's cleaning staff knelt with brushes and wiping rags cleaning up the last of the sawdust. When he had arrived shortly after dawn, a small army of carpenters was already at work transforming the darkly paneled walls according to the instructions he'd given the previous evening. Now, properly spaced pegs and hooks for hundreds of weapons were fixed to the paneling along two of the walls, and freestanding racks for staves and spears occupied another. It was an impressive transformation in an amazingly short time. And the men had left with promises to deliver the spear hafts and staves to fill the racks in a day or two, and some wooden practice weapons shortly after that.

Regrettably, it would take the blacksmiths he had hired considerably longer to complete the dozens of weapons he had ordered. Of course, the simpler things—like spearheads—should be ready quickly, but producing swords and knives of the proper quality took time. At the moment, extra knives were the most pressing need, since he expected he might lose some in combat. Before long, however, he would need more than a few copies of the larger blades if he were to train King Carlon's men in at least the basics of dragon fighting.

Naturally, even though he would be working with experienced soldiers, he would have his work cut out for him. Assuming the men he was given could somehow manage to forget what they *thought* they knew about fighting, he would still need to teach them everything. Not only would these soldiers know nothing about how to properly strike and defend themselves with hands and feet, they would need to be taught how to *stand*. He hated to disparage good men, but they would never be proper warriors. They should have learned these things as children. The best he could hope for at this point would be to teach them not to get themselves killed.

Then again, he supposed the biggest problem might be convincing them to trade in those heavy, clumsy-looking "broadswords" they carried for something more functional. Twice as wide and twice as heavy as Majaran longswords, they would be far too difficult to maneuver with any kind of precision. From what he had seen, the blades were little more than clubs with sharpened edges.

Samir was glad to see the cleaners pack up their supplies and leave. In his experience, the students were expected to clean the training room, and he had taken his turn alongside everyone else in spite of his station. It was clear that he would be in for a few surprises trying to understand this place. He was still astonished at how scandalized the cleaning staff was when he had asked them to remove their shoes before entering the room. This truly was a different world.

"Excuse me, m'lord?"

The soft voice from the doorway didn't surprise him. He'd heard footsteps approaching. But he was grateful that the young woman hadn't come in. Apparently word had already spread that Samir was...particular about this space.

Turning, he looked a question at the green and black clad page. She bobbed one of those strange curtsies.

"His Majesty asks that you join him after breakfast tomorrow," she reported. "If you'd like, I can leave a message to have someone wake you."

"Thank you, no," Samir shook his head. He had never had any trouble waking himself early. He was aware of one potential problem, however. "I may need someone to show me where to find the dining room, though," he added with a grin.

"Yes, m'lord," she said with a broad smile. "I'll see to it."

With a final curtsy she was gone, leaving Samir to his own thoughts again.

Walking slowly around the room, he trimmed the wicks of the numerous lamps, leaving mere flickers of flame in his wake. Several times he paused momentarily during his circuit to adjust the angle of a blade or the fall of a tassel on the end of a knife. Finally satisfied, he crossed to the door and took a moment to watch the dim lights dance across the metal and stone, thrown by the polished brass mirrors behind the lamps. His training room. *His.*

With a deep final bow, he gathered his jacket and shoes and pulled the door gently closed.

Yawning and stretching, Tirza rose from her place against the opposite wall to join him. She made it nearly impossible to slip into his shoes, trying to lick his face as he sat to put them on his feet.

"All right," he told her, pushing the hound away affectionately. "I'm sorry I neglected you. Now let me get dressed and we'll go outside."

Not very bright, Samir, he thought, suddenly realizing his predicament. *Should have had that page wait.*

He was fairly sure he could find his way to his rooms from here. Unfortunately, he had no clue where to find the closest outside door...or how to find his bed again from there once Tirza had relieved herself.

Well, he would find his way or ask. Regardless, it was almost certainly the least of the many ways that he would need to get his bearings.

The weathered pine boards of the bench creaked slightly as Gerrit shifted his weight. A block of wood in the rough shape of a bear was almost forgotten in his hands, as was the small knife beside him. Only the pile of curled wood shavings at his feet stirred now, blown by the light spring breeze. At the moment, he merely sat and watched as fireflies winked in the dark at the edge of town.

"I know that look," Khara announced from only a few feet away. "There's something bothering you, Gerrit. Out with it."

Although he didn't look, he knew the expression she wore as well. The one that always went with that tone—arms folded and eyebrows raised as she waited, for as long as it took, until he was ready to talk. It was just as well that he kept no secrets from her, since he would have found it extremely difficult to do so without his wife reading it all over his face. But, after nearly twenty-five years of marriage, that was not surprising.

"Several somethings," he replied, moving over to make room for her on the bench.

Without a word she sat, her familiar patient expression telling him she was ready to listen.

"I told you about Bastia," he began. "I still can't figure out what could have destroyed an entire village like that. It just doesn't make sense. But put it together with a few other things and it paints a pretty grim picture."

She waited, aware that he was merely gathering his thoughts. With her usual patience, she took the carving from him and set it aside, sliding her hand into his.

"Sometimes people go out to hunt and just don't come back. It's easy to get careless and maybe break a leg, and plenty of people have tried to take down more than they can handle." Gerrit couldn't help but think of some of his hunting trips with Kulmar, who was nearly as tough as he was brave. "But too many good hunters have gone missing lately. Trackers have found sign nobody's ever seen before, too."

"There's something out there," Khara concluded.

"There's something out there," he agreed. "And it's more dangerous than I care to think about."

She squeezed his hand. "The unknown always seems more dangerous than it really is."

"True," he conceded. "But anything that does all that without leaving any witnesses doesn't just *seem* dangerous. It *is* dangerous."

Khara's soft sigh told him that she conceded the point. Too bad. He would have preferred hearing her disagree.

"So what are you going to do?" she asked.

It was a good question, one that might very well have a high cost in lives either way. He could send out men to gather more information, but that would not only place them at risk, but also any who could encounter this threat in the meantime. On the other hand, blindly sending armed parties to scout without a better understanding of the situation could cost his people every bit as heavily. There was just no way to know which was the wiser course, but to do nothing would surely lead to more disappearances and destruction.

Gerrit shook his head in frustration.

"I'll ask for volunteers to scout," he said finally, not at all pleased at the decision. The alternative seemed no better.

Khara's hand tensed in his for a moment. He knew what bothered her.

"Huldrich is a grown man now, Sweet. He has a right to go if he chooses," Gerrit said gently, giving her hand a light squeeze. "You know it would shame him if we asked him not to go."

"I know," she replied. "He's not my little boy anymore." She turned, eyeing him sternly. "You make sure Kulmar reshoes that horse before our son leaves."

Releasing her hand, Gerrit slipped an arm around her ample waist. The fireflies continued to twinkle in the dark.

Chapter 12

Three Touches

In spite of her best efforts to be careful with the book in her hands, Morena knew that she was fighting a losing battle against age and condition. However the Wizard had managed to read it, she was having nothing but trouble. Even shifting it on the table had caused a section of the cracked leather cover to crumble, and the thread used to sew in the pages gave way as if made of air. It almost made her think twice about trying to turn the page when she reached the bottom, but she was too enthralled to stop. Whatever forgotten corner this volume had come from, it was an absolute treasure. She wanted to *devour* it.

But first, she had to decipher a formula.

Slowly, she rescanned the names of a dozen or so ingredients interspersed among the careful instructions. Only one had caught her unprepared—forcing her to refer to one of her oldest texts for a description to match the archaic name. As it turned out, it was one of the more common plants on her list. Thankfully. A list of unobtainable components would do none of them any good.

"On the bright side, all but three of these are nearly as common as dirt," she began, looking around the table at the expectant faces. "And at least we're sure the others still exist *and* where to find them."

"And the bad news?" Carlon prompted.

She shook her head. "It's not *bad*. Not exactly," Morena answered. "We just need to go find them. Beggar's Wort we can get easily from the Great Wood north of here. Jasper berries, which this text calls "farmer's bane," is fairly plentiful across the plains."

She paused. If some of what she'd discovered could be called bad news, she'd come to it. While none of the herbs was actually unobtainable, one of them could very well present some problems for them.

"That covers two of them," Jenaris prompted. There was something disconcerting about the deep blue eyes the Mage directed at her. Almost as if he looked *through* her. "What of the third?"

"Blackthorn root," she replied. "It grows in Gotarra...and that would be the *easiest* place to get it."

The King nodded his understanding. "Which means it might not be all that easy," he concluded. "We'll need Gerrit's permission to get it, of course, but I've always found him to be a reasonable man. It shouldn't be a problem...unless you're about to tell me it only grows on mountain peaks in the dead of winter?" he added wryly.

"No, Sire." Morena suppressed a laugh. "I can get it now, *and* without walking halfway to the moon in the middle of a blizzard."

King Carlon's eyebrows climbed dramatically at her statement. He leaned forward, his apparent good humor suddenly gone as he studied her across the long table.

"First of all, young woman, *you* aren't going anywhere. You're staying put right here," he said firmly.

"Secondly, why do I get the feeling there's still a problem?"

She'd wondered whether he would make an issue out of her going along. But there was no way she was just going to sit here while everyone else ran in circles trying to find what was needed. She had to *do* something, and if the King thought she was going to be left behind, she would have to make him think again.

Drawing a deep breath, Morena dove in.

"You're right, Sire, there *is* still a problem," she said flatly, just managing to keep the anger out of her tone. "The problem is that you can't find it without me."

She steeled herself, knowing her statement had come very close to the limit of what she could get away with—or at least not too far beyond it. Regardless of any sympathy the King felt over the loss of her father, he wasn't about to put up with disrespect. But he *had* made this an informal session, which gave her a little bit of leeway. *Very* little.

"Morena." Carlon's voice was cool as he spoke, eyes narrowed. He was *definitely* angry. "You are here as a courtesy. I can just as easily get someone else to tell us what we need. Someone every bit as knowledgeable as you. So, do *not* try my patience."

If she hadn't already known he was mad enough to chew nails, his fist pounding on the table announced it clearly. Morena knew she should back down, forget the idea of striking any real blow at these monsters and accept what little she'd been given. But she also knew that she *couldn't*. She didn't know exactly why, yet she *had* to be a part of this—to see it through to the end, danger or no danger. Not that the idea didn't frighten her. To be honest, she was scared to death at the idea of chasing those things. But her father had never let fear keep him from doing what needed to be done, and these dragons needed to be stopped.

Gathering every ounce of courage she could, Morena stood. Too late to turn back now.

"Sire," she met Carlon's eyes, willing him to understand but prepared to argue the point until he did. "I'm sure you *could* find someone as knowledgeable although, at the risk of sounding boastful, that wouldn't be as easy as you make it sound."

His grudging nod told her that he already knew that to be the pure and simple truth. It would take more than that to sway him, of course, but it was a good start.

"If you're afraid I won't be able to defend myself, then you *really* have a problem, because you aren't about to find an herbalist anywhere who knows one end of a sword from another. They're all women and skinny old men who spend all their time buried in books," she asserted. This last wasn't strictly true. Most herbalists spent much of their time in the wilderness and had reasonable survival skills. Still, she had to push on. "At least with me, you have someone who is willing to assume the risk."

"And what do I tell your mother?" Carlon asked gruffly.

"You remind her that my parents raised me with a strong sense of duty," she answered proudly, a sense of triumph only shallowly buried. She knew she had nearly won now.

The King seemed to know it, too, and was not best pleased. "Anything else?"

"Only that nobody will be very safe anywhere unless we succeed."

A snort from the Wizard told her that she had scored, and earned him a glare of reproof from Carlon. The King said nothing for a long moment, however—considering, she hoped, exactly how to explain this to Morena's mother.

"Well, I won't be going, and I won't be the one responsible for your safety," Carlon finally continued, pinning his guard captain with a hard look at the mention of her safety, "so I'll have to leave the decision up to those who will. Who goes, Mage?"

Jenaris studied those at the table with his piercing blue-eyed stare. He settled on Alban.

"How many will you be taking, Captain?"

The question wasn't unexpected, since Alban barely paused before answering. "Half a company," he replied. "Two dozen men. Plus a pack train. If Kir doesn't mind helping, we can handpick them for speed and agility so he can start their training.

"Not at all," the Majaran nodded, the formality of the movement somehow at odds with the amusement on his face. "But that's not what we'll be selecting for. Not primarily, at least. We want men who aren't convinced they already know how to fight."

"I guess that leaves *me* out, then," Alban laughed sharply before turning a more serious look to the King. " as far as taking responsibility for young Morena, Sire. As long as she agrees to do exactly as she's told in an emergency, I will."

A surge of excitement ran through her. Surely, if Captain Ward agreed, then the others had to as well. After all, it would be the Captain and his men who would provide her protection.

She held her breath as the Mage continued.

"Kordel and I will be going, of course," the Wizard observed, " and I have no objection to the young lady joining us. Kordel agrees with me, since he will think exactly what I tell him to."

Beside Jenaris, the apprentice sat looking silently forlorn, winning him Morena's sympathy. Yet it was his nod of agreement that twisted her emotions into a tight knot in the pit of her stomach.

Now her hopes rode on the final two men at the table. Caleb would vote in her favor if asked. She was certain of it. They had known each other too long and, although separated somewhat by their relative stations, they were friends after a fashion. But he would be staying behind, unless she missed her guess entirely, being too valuable to be put at risk.

That left only the Majaran, Kir—the only one she hadn't known all her life. He was the source of her anxiety. She was completely unsure whether she had swayed him in the least, or if he *could* be swayed. And now her future rested in his hands. It wasn't *fair*!

Morena felt sick.

She watched as the Mage turned his attention to Kir, giving the warrior her best smile. The man remained aloof, seeming to ignore the gesture completely. Her heart sank.

"In Majar, a warrior would die to defend even the meanest girl begging on the street, but we would never even consider taking a woman into danger." Even in his strangely melodic accent, his disdain for the situation carried through. Her heart sank even further. "But, as I am growing all too aware, we are not in Majar. If you asked me whether I *want* her along, the answer would be, 'No.' If the question is whether I can and will keep her safe, then I have to say, 'Yes.'" He frowned, clearly uncomfortable, but said nothing more.

She was confused. Was that a yes or a no? He'd actually said *both*. But it *couldn't* be both. She needed a yes.

Morena bit back the question that was on her tongue, struggling against the impulse to ask for some clear statement. But that would only open the door for Kir to question his own response, turning a possible victory into certain defeat. No, she had to keep quiet and hope when she wanted to scream, to reach across the table and shake him right out of his damned propriety.

Protect her?! Who did he think he was? Who did he think *she* was? Some fragile porcelain doll that would shatter without careful handling?

"All right," Carlon said gruffly, jerking her attention back to the present. The King raised a cautionary finger as he met her gaze. "You may go...pending your mother's permission. And I am *not* looking forward to having that conversation."

The heart that had sunk only moments before suddenly leapt into her throat. She could go!

She didn't even *try* to hold back the grin that split her face.

Jenaris was thankful these people didn't know him nearly well enough to see just how troubled he was. Learning to hide such things had been a necessary part of his training, however. After all, if people perceived that a problem was enough to worry a wizard, it could cause even the strong among them to panic. Right now, his job was to instill confidence, especially among those who needed to be leaders. But the unfortunate truth was that he was feeling little enough of that confidence himself at the moment.

Lorn's books *had* contained more information on dragons beyond what he'd already learned. A little. Sadly, it had agreed with his previous assessment of the situation—that there was too much here that simply didn't fit. In every report of previous infestations that he had found, which were regrettably few, the creatures had displayed a consistent pattern of behavior. This time, it was anything but. They almost appeared to be an entirely different species in some respects.

The sources he had consulted painted a picture of creatures that were solitary and aggressive by nature. Pairs would get together only to breed, and that rarely, then immediately separate again. Mothers reportedly even forced their young to find new territories before they were physically mature, ensuring that only the very strongest would survive. Jenaris had no idea where some ancient mage had found the courage to uncover *that* little tidbit.

Ambush hunters, they had typically only been discovered because of the curious number of sudden disappearances they caused. Now, however, at least one large party of armed men—and a sizable town, it seemed—had been attacked by several supposedly solitary drakes working together.

And to top it all off, there seemed to have been no buildup whatsoever. No one had reported seeing a trace of *one* dragon in well over five *hundred* years, and now he had counted nine within a matter of weeks. The world had gone from utter silence to destructive rampage almost overnight.

Too many contradictions, he told himself. *No order at all.*

No, there was an order to it somewhere. There *had* to be. That's what really bothered him—not knowing *why* they were behaving so strangely and whether these people could handle *that* when the time came.

Well, at least they had the right people to see the job done as far as he could tell—even with the limited information they had available. But only time would say for sure.

Most of the small group had made their way back to the table after the short break. Most.

Morena paid no attention, enjoying the companionship of the dog instead. Tirza's master, on the other hand, stood alone by the window, gazing out at the sea. It took very little imagination to guess what was on his mind. In that direction lay Majar and, whatever the young man's reason for leaving, it was obvious he missed his home.

The servant who entered drew few eyes. No one really noticed servants. After a time, they merely became part of the background—like furniture. This one, however, carried something of particular interest to the Mage—a bundle of wooden shingles, lashed with twine. Perfect.

Directing the young man to leave his burden near the table, Jenaris strode smoothly over, finally drawing the attention of the others as he untied the packet. Lifting a short stack of the thin cedar boards from the bundle, he carefully laid eight of them out side by side on the polished marble floor. He was vaguely aware that Morena had wandered over, followed by the little white hound, but he ignored her questioning look. With more shingles in hand, he laid another course atop the first, overlapping about half their length. A third row soon joined the others, and then a fourth as Kir and Caleb joined him. By the time he had exhausted the supply of shakes, seven rows lay neatly overlapped across a large section of floor and every member of the group had joined him.

Jenaris turned to Kir.

"I've been thinking about your choice of weapons," he said simply, causing the young warrior's eyebrows to rise skeptically as if the Mage had intruded by crossing a professional boundary. Jenaris offered a smile to soothe the prickly Majaran. "I'd like you to try something. Put your fingertips under the outside shingles of the bottom row, if you please."

Kir returned a curious look, but knelt smoothly to comply. With Alban's help, they managed to lift the proper boards without dislodging the rest, allowing Kir to slip his fingers into place. In moments, the edges of the wood rested lightly atop the first two joints of his fingers.

"Do you feel the weight of the shingles?" Jenaris asked, eliciting a nod from the Majaran. Lifting his staff, the Wizard placed it at the bottom of the shingle centered in the top row. He pressed down, watching as the warrior's eyes narrowed slightly. "What do you feel now?"

"I feel your added weight." Kir cocked a quizzical smile as if wondering at the need for such an obvious question.

It was a rather simple demonstration. The last thing Jenaris wanted was to question the Majaran's intelligence. But he needed to make an important point.

"Do you know why?" the Wizard pressed.

Kir shrugged, an awkward movement given his need to keep his palms flat to the floor. "Because every board presses down on the pair below it," he responded. "What's your point?"

"My point is that force applied in one place is evenly distributed across a fairly large area," the Mage stated, falling into a lecturing tone. "What do you think would happen if I pressed down on the entire top row?"

Understanding was clear in the warrior's eyes. He was no fool.

Jenaris smiled. "If I apply force to a single scale on a dragon's hide, other scales will help dissipate the force of the blow," he intoned, sweeping the group with his gaze to drive the lesson home. "If I strike several scales at once, the blow is weakened severely." He met Kir's eyes and held them. "I think that broadsword of yours is a waste of time. It will work against you. The best course of action is to focus as much power as you can at a single point."

The silver clad end of the staff lifted a few inches, then rapidly slammed back down on the shingle. With a loud clack, it splintered under the force of the blow. Anger flared briefly in the warrior's features, but was quickly mastered as he jerked his fingers out from under the cedar boards. The reddened digits plainly stung from having been pinched, yet the Majaran gave no more indication of any discomfort as he composed himself.

"You wouldn't happen to have a brother named Shimei, would you?" Kir asked with mild amusement.

"No," Jenaris grinned broadly, "but someday I may have to meet him to compare notes." He pointed to the narrow bladed longsword hanging from the sash at the other man's waist. "I think you should focus on this one weapon. The others won't be nearly as effective." Jenaris paused, expecting some acknowledgement. What he got was far from it. Instead, the Majaran merely threw back his head and laughed, long hair swaying.

"You may be surprised," Kir smiled knowingly. "Scales can't stop knives and spears that come in underneath them. They could be made out of stone for all I care. Your argument makes sense, but all of the weapons I've chosen will be effective. The scales are irrelevant."

Kir could have been a farmer discussing a potato crop for all the emotion in his voice. Said so matter-of-factly, the statement somehow didn't seem arrogant at all. It simply *was* as far as Kir was concerned.

Not everyone was willing to let the comment pass unchallenged, however.

"You think you're that good?" Alban pressed, plainly skeptical.

Incredulity showed on other faces as well. The Majaran seemed completely unaffected by their doubts.

"Yes, I am," he said with complete confidence. "Do you doubt me?"

The guard captain considered briefly, then shook his head. "No," Alban answered honestly. "I've watched you practice, remember? But let's just say I'll need to see it with my own eyes before I admit it's that easy."

Kir chuckled. "I never said it was *easy*."

"Unbelievable!" Morena's voice practically dripped with disdain, the look she directed at the two men one of clear indignation. "One of you boasts about how *great* he is, and the other encourages him to get himself killed proving it." Hands on hips, she stared at the two warriors as if waiting for them to be properly repentant.

The Captain was clearly having difficulty biting back a retort. Kir evidently had no such compunctions.

"It isn't boastful to make an honest assessment of your own abilities—which I believe I am. I would be just as honest about my own weaknesses," the Majaran admitted calmly. Despite his composure, there was a definite tone of annoyance in his voice. "And if you question my ability to protect you, maybe you shouldn't come after all."

"I never said I...," she began, but left the protest unfinished. Obviously she was not about to risk making the situation worse by causing him to withdraw his agreement. Instead she chose to pacify him. " I see no reason not to take you at your word. I only wanted to discourage you from taking unnecessary risks."

Kir cocked a questioning eyebrow, clearly doubtful. He said nothing, however, apparently willing to let the subject drop.

"I *do* have a concern, Kir," Carlon said into the brief silence, drawing all eyes. "I don't doubt your abilities, but I wonder about that sword of yours. It's too thin. Do you honestly think it will hold up to the punishment if you make it your primary weapon?"

The two officers nodded their agreement. They had seen the sword—barely wider than two fingers together and thinner than theirs by a noticeable margin. It made the long blade extremely fast and maneuverable in trained hands, but it did look terribly fragile.

"You think it will break." It was not a question, and confirmation came quickly, written large on the faces of those who knew how to use a sword. Kir shrugged casually. "Very well, let's test it. If you can break it in normal combat before I can score three touches, I'll use one of those clumsy things you call a broadsword. Fair?"

The others considered. Finally, Alban spoke.

"You intend to parry with that blade?" he asked.

"I do." Genuine amusement shaded the Majaran's words.

"*Five* touches," Alban insisted.

"Done."

Without hesitation, the pair stepped clear of the group, moving to the open space at the end of the room. The soft ringing scrape of steel leaving its sheath sounded from both men as they squared off.

The young Majaran bowed deeply from the waist, straightening swiftly, ready to meet his opponent. He stood motionless, calmly poised on the balls of his feet, blade held casually pointed at the floor.

Jenaris could see the tension in the guard captain, a marked contrast to the younger fighter. As the Wizard watched, Alban adopted a classic swordsman's stance—sword up at the ready, right foot forward with weight distributed evenly. It was a time-tested position which allowed for rapid attack as well as defense. The Mage wondered whether Captain Ward knew just how little chance he stood against the man he faced.

Alban lunged, wrist and elbow giving his blade momentum as it swept in a shining blur toward his opponent's belly. He couldn't have believed it would land. Most likely, given the conditions of the wager, the soldier was attempting to force the other man to block his blow and risk snapping his weapon. But the Majaran pivoted smoothly just out of range, evading razor sharp steel by a mere handbreadth as his own sword threaded in on top of Alban's. Kir's narrow blade slid down the length of its heavier opposite, somehow arresting its considerable force and redirecting it down and away. Sword point sweeping near the floor, the Captain tried in vain to bring it back up, but it was too late. The younger man stepped back in, blade darting up to rest at a spot just above Alban's liver.

The two men separated, Kir seeming to flow back and making the Captain appear clumsy by comparison.

This time Alban swung full armed, blade descending straight toward the other man's head. Most swordsmen would have thrown up their weapon to block such a strike, if only from reflex. Yet, Kir glided inside and to the right, his sword's blade meeting the other high, forming a ramp for the larger blade to slide down and away harmlessly. Without warning the Majaran spun, elbow rising as he turned, landing softly against Alban's temple.

The Captain's jaw tightened in obvious frustration as he again stepped back.

"That wasn't a killing blow," Gillis objected, clearly not understanding why his commander had ceded the point.

"Yes, it was," Alban admitted somewhat grimly. "If that had hit me with any force at all, he would never have let me get back up." Sword sweeping up before his eyes, the Captain offered his adversary a jaunty salute, but the set of his jaw spoke of determination.

Again Alban came on, this time jabbing his blade up and inward, attempting to force Kir to batter his sword aside or down. Instead, the Majaran steel dipped in fast and spun as the warrior twisted his wrist. In an instant, the Captain's blade had slid away to the side as the other corkscrewed in to stop above Alban's heart.

It was as if the Majaran were facing a child with a stick. A *very young* child. The Captain seemed to feel it as well.

"You have no intention of taking a strike full on with that blade, do you?" Alban asked wryly, wiping a light film of sweat from his eyes. "We could have agreed to fifty touches, a *hundred*, and all I'd end up with is a good workout."

"Of course not," Kir's answering grin was almost cocky. Yet, somehow, rather than making sport of his opponent, it merely invited the others to share in his amusement. "It takes much less effort to redirect your attacks than it does to *stop* them. I may be young, Captain, but I am not a fool."

Sheathing his blade in one smooth motion, the Captain offered his hand. "In that case," he laughed, "I concede your victory. I'm just wearing myself out for nothing. No matter how I try, I'll never break that sword."

The Wizard nearly laughed himself at the massive understatement. He had once seen a group of dancers from Brisia who had positively awed him with the ease and suppleness of their movements. The way they had leapt and spun on pointed toes, every moment in absolute control as they appeared to defy gravity, had defined beauty for him ever since. He had never believed it possible that he could see anything as graceful, as elegant, as those long-limbed women as they pranced and capered. Until now.

The Majaran warrior was every bit as graceful, every bit in control of his body. Each economical movement exactly what was needed. His focus absolute. The man was the perfect combination of balance, agility and power—danger barely contained. It was like seeing a tiger leashed with a single silk thread. Somehow it seemed impossible that he didn't already consider himself a master, that any amount of training could improve perfection.

But Jenaris knew precisely how to make the warrior better.

"You're quite right, Captain," Jenaris interjected smoothly. "That sword will survive every effort of yours. I'm still not convinced the blade will be up to the task, however."

"How so?" Kir said quietly, his offense evident in his tone as well as his expression.

Danger barely contained, indeed.

"Your sword will need to withstand the strain of being forced *through* the scales of a dragon's hide," Jenaris explained, not unkindly. "Even well forged steel would be under considerable stress."

The young warrior was obviously fighting annoyance, believing his skill sufficient to the challenge and resenting the doubts of those around him. It suddenly occurred to the Wizard that the Majaran *could* stand improvement in at least one area.

"I've already told you. I can come up under the scales with only a little effort," the man insisted, eyes narrowing.

Jenaris nodded, hands held up in an attempt to soothe the ruffled warrior. "I will accept that," he replied gently. "But what if, just once, you can't spare the time to make that happen? What if someone's life is at stake?"

The other man had no reply for a moment, defiance warring with acceptance in his features. "So, what do I use if *both* of my swords are unacceptable?" he asked.

The Mage smiled mischievously, eyes twinkling. "Oh, I think I have a trick or two that might just be good for something."

Chapter 13

Magus

Carlon took a long sip of wine, surreptitiously glancing over the rim at Kir. He was still having trouble believing what he'd just seen. That a man could have that kind of skill. And so *young*.

Alban Ward was one of the most formidable swordsmen he'd ever known. He had sparred against the Captain on more than one occasion and rarely managed to score a touch. But the Majaran had made their contest appear almost embarrassingly simple.

Carlon was just glad that young man was on his side, would be training some of his troops.

"We'll need a blacksmith," Jenaris announced, quickly running his hands over his pockets. Apparently satisfied, the Mage nodded.

Carlon shrugged. "That's not a problem. There are several who do quality work." He looked a question at the Wizard, curious. "What exactly do you want him to do?"

The request was an easy one, certainly, but it made the King nervous. Surely the man wasn't suggesting any alteration to the Majaran's sword. A warrior, *any* warrior, had to live and die by his weapon. It became a part of you, and any change would take time to adjust to—if that would even be *possible* for Kir. That kind of precision could suffer irreparably.

"What do I want him to *do*?" Jenaris asked, bushy grey brows rising toward his hairline. "Nothing at all. I just need to use his forge."

While not exactly frail, the Wizard hardly looked like someone who knew his way around a forge. At his age, most smiths would have handed their hammers over to their sons long since—or, more likely, to their grandsons.

Carlon suppressed a smile at the mental image of the bearded oldtimer bent over an anvil.

"This I have to see." The King set his cup on the sideboard. Without preamble, he walked toward the door, trusting that the others would fall in behind him. A familiar voice halted him.

"Father," Caleb called. " I need to speak with you."

His son hadn't moved, but still stood near the table looking...determined. Whatever was troubling him, it wouldn't wait.

"Of course," Carlon waved the others past. "Captain, go ahead and take them to the barracks forge. We'll meet you all there shortly."

Not waiting to hear the acknowledgement, he turned a searching look on his son. Although obviously uncomfortable under the scrutiny, Caleb met his gaze evenly.

Good.

Carlon waited. Whatever the young man had to say, prompting wouldn't draw it out of him any faster. It would come in due time.

It was a brief wait.

"I need to go, Father," Caleb stated, his tone betraying barely a hint of apprehension.

"Go where?" The King was surprised at the direction of this conversation, but only for a moment. There was little doubt in his mind where this was heading—over ground they had already covered *more* than sufficiently. "Is this about going back to find that young lady again?"

The Prince shook his head. "No, sir," he said with resignation. "We've already established that I'll need to wait, and I accept that decision." Caleb looked less than pleased at the admission, but managed not to sound bitter. "This isn't about Sorana."

Well, that was a relief. Refusing his son's request to go in search of his young woman was not a decision Carlon had made easily. Not at all. The last thing he wanted was to see his child in distress. But their responsibility, their duty, was to the Kingdom rather than to any individual—no matter how precious. Wherever she was, the King hoped she was well, and fully intended to meet her someday, but the current crisis had to come first.

"Then what *is* it about?" Carlon asked, suddenly at a loss to understand the purpose for the conversation. After all, his son was never frivolous with time when something needed to be done.

"This is about me," Caleb answered, making a point of looking him squarely in the eye as he spoke. "I need to be with them when they leave."

"Out of the question," Carlon told his son firmly, expecting that to be an end to the matter. "Now let's join the others. I'd like to see what this...."

"*Why?*"

Carlon stiffened, stopping well short of the door. He was unaccustomed to being questioned—much less interrupted—especially by his children. With great difficulty he pushed down his rising anger. Giving vent to it right now would accomplish nothing, except to discourage Caleb from coming to him in the future.

Drawing a deep breath, he turned to look at his son.

"Why is this so important to you?" he asked softly, wanting to bring the tone of the conversation back to a more reasonable level. "Explain it to me."

Caleb didn't answer immediately, taking a minute to consider his words before responding. That was good. It meant that, whatever this was about, the young man was taking it seriously. When you had one chance to make your case, you wanted to get it right—and a petulant tone could blow it as quickly as the wrong words.

"I'm not exactly sure I *can* explain it," the Prince admitted with obvious reluctance. "But I know what you've always told me. You say people need to fight for the things they're passionate about. That if leaders won't stand up and take action, then nobody will. I guess that's what I'm doing."

Carlon snorted. "I believe at the time I was talking about our duty to people who couldn't defend themselves," he said wryly. "I hardly think that's what's happening here."

"But that's just it, Father," the Prince replied eagerly, eyes suddenly alight. "It *is* about their rights. Our people have a right to feel secure in their homes, to be able to practice their trade or to do business without being threatened."

Carlon looked closely at his son, searching his face for long moments. He wasn't sure what he wanted or expected to find there, but he had spent a lifetime learning to read people. What he found in Caleb's expression now surprised him—a new and unexpected depth that hadn't been there previously.

"I know why we're sending *them*," Carlon allowed, waving vaguely in the direction Alban had recently taken the rest of the group. "What I'm asking is why you think *you* need to go along. I can appreciate your sense of responsibility, but that's not enough. You have responsibilities here."

Caleb's mouth twisted briefly, but he didn't back down. "I know that, and I take that seriously." There was no disguising his frustration as he tried to express whatever it was that was eating at him. "All I know is that this isn't about what I *think*. It just feels like this is something I *need* to do, and that if I don't go, I'll always regret it." Caleb shrugged. "Like I said, I'm not sure I understand it."

Carlon considered. Strangely enough he was fairly certain he *did* understand what was eating at Caleb, and he should have seen it earlier. This was about *the question*—about his son's need to prove something to himself. The Prince had taken Marius' death hard, which was understandable, but he suspected that Caleb was being overly critical of his own performance. From the reports he'd heard, his son had acted properly, trying to give aid in the midst of extraordinary danger. But it wasn't enough that *others* knew Caleb had what it takes— *he* had to know it, too. That meant his son needed the chance to discover it for himself.

Carlon nodded. "I'll tell the Wizard. If he doesn't agree, the Captain will just have to take you as one of *his*."

"Thank you, Father." Caleb smiled broadly. "Now I think we're expected at the forge."

The King slipped an arm around his son's shoulders as they walked toward the door. As if it wasn't bad enough that he had to convince Morena's mother that her daughter should be allowed to go into danger, now he had to explain this to Larissa that Caleb would be going as well. Well, what had to be done....

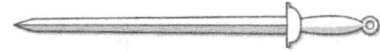

Samir leaned back against the stone wall of the smithy, watching with amusement as the blacksmith tried unsuccessfully to look pleased at the invasion of what he obviously saw as *his* forge. Not that the man was about to refuse the Captain's "request," especially when it was done on the King's instructions. The powerful-looking smith was making the best of it, but the Majaran imagined he could practically hear the man grinding his teeth as he smiled at the trespassers.

The others had found various perches on barrels or tables where they would have a good view of Jenaris once he got started. With only a cursory examination, the Mage had selected a long piece of bar stock, interrupted only by the repeated need to usher the smith away from the bellows.

After clamping the cold unformed steel into a pair of long-handled tongs and choosing a fair sized hammer, he set them beside one of the larger anvils spread through the shop. Slowly and deliberately he drew out two leather drawstring bags—one red and one blue—from a pocket of his coat and laid them gently on the table beside him, keeping them well separated. Apparently satisfied, the Mage nodded and began stripping off coat and shirt, tossing them casually aside in a heap on the soot-covered stone of the floor.

The Wizard was in surprisingly good shape, and not just for one who favored books. Jenaris had to be older than Shimei by at least a decade—although it was nearly impossible to say for certain—but while on the far side of his prime, his muscles were firm. Somehow, seen in this context, he seemed to belong here—or, at least, he wasn't *quite* out of place.

Untying the blue bag, Jenaris poured what looked to be fine coal dust into a pile on his palm. He dropped the pouch, heedless, as he again lifted the tongs to hold the bar stock upright before him.

The Wizard smiled.

Raising the pile of dust to his mouth, he blew out a hard puff of air. Samir expected the powder to fly, dispersing in all directions as it was borne on the wind of the Mage's breath. Instead, it streamed out into the air in a thick smoky line, snaking and twining around almost as if it sought something. The cloud split, then split again, dense tendrils winging through the air around Jenaris as it inched gradually closer to the steel. More than once they nearly touched the bar, needing only a nudge to do so. But the Wizard appeared content to merely watch as he held the stock steady.

Samir risked a swift glance around the room. Every eye was riveted, staring at the scene as though the watchers feared to blink. The warrior understood perfectly, and quickly returned his attention to the strange display.

With a last turn, one arm of the cloud met the steel and clung. Samir watched, rapt, not knowing what he waited for. With almost painful slowness, smoke drifted closer to hover just above the metal until finally settling placidly over the surface of the now black steel.

"Is that *it*?" Alban blurted, at last breaking the tension and allowing the group to blink.

The Majaran had to admit it was somehow a bit of a disappointment. He had expected something much more dramatic.

"Isn't that enough?" Jenaris laughed. "What were you hoping to see? Something like this?"

With a sharp motion, the Mage tapped the steel bar against the anvil to ring resoundingly. In an instant, the metal glowed white hot, looking like it had been freshly pulled from the coals of the forge.

Jenaris took only a moment to savor the stunned looks on the faces around him. Grinning triumphantly, he snatched up the hammer and began to shape the steel, striking furiously but with a sureness and skill born of experience. The Wizard's arm rose and fell rhythmically, the chime of metal on metal ringing through the room. More swiftly than Samir could have believed, the sword took shape as Jenaris worked with astonishing efficiency. Soon the Mage held the steel at arm's length, examining his handiwork with unabashed admiration. Remarkably, the metal still glowed, its internal light undimmed although it had never touched or even come near the coals.

With a self-satisfied nod, Jenaris laid the hot blade across the anvil and reached for the other drawstring bag. Upending the red pouch above his palm, he sent a fine white powder spilling out into a pile.

Drawing back his arm, the Mage cast the dust into the warm coals of the forge beside him and once again took up the glowing blade. Immediately, wisps of grey smoke rose, rolling like dense fog across the surface as they rapidly thickened. Slowly and smoothly, Jenaris waved the newly forged longsword through the smoke, which trailed after the glowing metal as it was lifted free. With a sudden burst, the smoke drew in, coalescing on the steel. As quickly as it had come, the glow vanished from the metal that now appeared cool to the touch.

But what the Mage held looked like no steel Samir had ever seen. Gasps sounded from several throats as the blade caught the light, announcing what the others had noticed as well. The sword shimmered with the opalescent shine of sunlight through a pane of frosty glass, almost as if made of pearl rather than steel.

He hadn't been aware that he'd even moved, yet he suddenly found himself standing beside the Wizard, reaching to touch the strange blade. It was nearly identical in every dimension to the sword at his hip, but that was where the similarity ended. Light reflected in swirling patterns, almost hypnotic as the blade moved. It was beautiful.

"Careful," Jenaris cautioned, laying the narrow tang across Samir's palm. "It's very sharp."

"It *can't* be sharp yet," Alban objected, rising from his perch on a barrel for a better look. "You haven't even tempered it yet, much less honed it."

The Wizard looked mildly amused, shaking his head as he turned his blue-eyed gaze on the approaching soldier. His expression did not speak well of his opinion of Alban at the moment.

"My dear boy," the Mage said, his tone not far short of sarcasm. "What is it you think I just did?"

Alban didn't respond, apparently thinking it wiser to keep his mouth shut.

Samir studied the sword in his hands. It felt far lighter than should be possible and, though lacking a hilt, was somehow comfortable in his hand. As he looked over its sparkling length, the beauty of the unadorned blade left him awestruck. It was the light of a full moon on a cloudless night or sea foam in the dark. But what caught and held his attention was the edge. It was indeed already sharp, as though hours of tremendous care had been spent bringing it to the keenness of a razor. A glint of the fire's reflection skittered cleanly down the very lip of the blade as he twisted it, revealing no imperfections.

Samir couldn't say what made him do it, made him reach out with the sword. He only knew it felt...right when he laid the edge along the side of the anvil and swept it across—producing a long, slender curl of iron hardly thicker than a human hair.

"I told you," the Wizard said proudly, an almost smug smile twisting his lips. "It's very sharp. You'll also find it will prove very hard to break. Give me enough time with it, and I'll make it unbreakable...and a bit more besides."

Before Samir could ask what the Mage had meant by that rather cryptic comment, another voice broke in.

"*You*," the smith said, barely above a whisper. Fear seemed foreign on the muscular man's face, yet plainly that was what it was as he looked at the Wizard. "You're one of them, ain't you?"

"One of what?" Jenaris asked indulgently, as though speaking to a child. "Or is that one of whom?" Despite the question, the expression on his face said he knew *exactly* what the man meant.

His courage obviously spent, the smith was silent under the Wizard's scrutiny. Evidently realizing some response was expected, he finally worked enough saliva into his dry mouth to answer.

"Nothing," the smith replied. "It's just stories. They don't really exist. They couldn't."

Samir couldn't make any sense out of the blacksmith's words. But from the way the Mage hid his smile behind his hand, he could tell the old man found it all terribly funny.

"Of course they don't," Jenaris said with a wink, his voice conspiratorially low. "Nobody ever said they did."

Although the Majaran would have loved to find out just what was going on between the two, he chose to rescue the poor smith, who appeared ready to bolt. Samir laid a hand on his arm, causing a slight flinch.

"What's your name, smith?" Samir asked.

The question seemed to bring the man out of his shock, at least somewhat. Samir did his best to smile reassuringly.

"Hubbard, m'lord," the smith replied nervously.

"All right, Hubbard." Samir rested a firm hand on the other man's shoulder, trying to fix his attention on himself. While it worked after a fashion, Hubbard's gaze continued to wander back to Jenaris. "How long will it take you to make me a hilt for this sword? And not one of those wide crossguards you people favor, mind. You'll make one like mine." He indicated the gold halfmoon shape of his handguard, only slightly wider than the blade.

The smith nodded nervously, looking once again at the Mage. "Um...two days to do it right, maybe. Could be a little sooner. Just leave the blade here and we'll have her fitted out. Scabbard, too."

Samir laid the dazzling blade on the nearby table with exaggerated care, wondering as he did why he worried about scratching the blade. He should have been more concerned about the table.

"Thank you, Hubbard," he offered.

"It's nothing, m'lord. You'll have my best work." The smith gave Samir what was probably meant as a reassuring smile. It made him look ill. "I'll have it delivered just as soon as it's done."

As they reached the great barn doors letting out onto the barracks yard it struck Samir that by nightfall the smith was likely to have his anvil whittled down to nothing. The laugh that escaped him drew several curious looks, but he merely shook his head, seeing no reason to share the source of his mirth.

"A bit flashy even for a wizard, wasn't it?" The King's voice came from beside them as they emerged from the smithy.

Carlon pushed off from the wall where he'd been leaning, evidently watching events through the wide doorway. On the other side, Caleb did the same, walking to join the group with an extra bounce in his step.

"You know how it is, Sire," Jenaris quipped in return. "Anything worth doing is worth doing to excess. It's a requirement in my line of work."

"Well, I think that qualified," Carlon grinned. "You nearly scared that man out of his skin with that little show of yours."

The memory of the blacksmith's discomfort caused more than a few chuckles. It also turned Samir's mind to the strange conversation he had interrupted inside.

"Jenaris," he began, "what exactly did he mean by 'you're one of them'?"

The murmur of conversation died around them as the Wizard rapidly became the focus of attention. Rather than being self-conscious, however, the Mage grinned wickedly, the deep lines around his eyes growing even more pronounced.

"He meant that I'm a Magus," Jenaris replied. The capitalization was clearly audible in his response.

The answer meant nothing to Samir, and judging by the expressions on other faces it failed to register with anyone. Anyone but Kordel, at any rate. The Wizard's apprentice appeared to at least find something of significance in the name, though he seemed puzzled.

The lack of understanding plainly didn't surprise the Wizard, who obviously took an odd delight in the situation. The man held up a finger for patience as they walked past the last of the long brick buildings of the guard barracks. He quickly looked around to ensure that no one else was anywhere in earshot.

"I wouldn't expect any of you to know the name unless you've ever trained as a blacksmith," he said mischievously, blue eyes twinkling. "A Magus is a highly specialized wizard. Well, come to that, *every* wizard is a specialist of some kind. But a Magus is an expert on what one might call items of power. Usually, these items will be weapons or armor, but they can take other forms as well."

Jenaris paused, giving Samir a piercing look, as though expecting the explanation to mean something. Receiving no reaction, he shrugged and continued.

"In the past, some of my brethren have been...less than kind to those who may have given offense. Unfortunately, several blacksmiths once managed to incur the wrath of a rather skilled Magus who cursed their anvils and hammers." Again he flashed that wicked grin. "Parents will often tell children about the bogeyman to get them to behave. Blacksmiths warn apprentices about the *Magus!*"

Just what kind of people have I gotten mixed up with? Samir thought, glancing around at his companions.

They were strange. Yet, in spite of the fact that they were so...different, he felt surprisingly comfortable among them. With Ward and Gillis that was understandable. After all, soldiers tended to be much the same everywhere, and he had spent most of his life around men like these. But even Carlon had a way of putting people at ease, putting *him* at ease. The King had taken him in with remarkably few questions, even giving him rooms in the castle proper when he had little enough reason to expect a place in the barracks they had just passed.

When it came right down to it, these people had no more reason to trust him than he did to trust them. And yet they had offered him precisely that.

Not for the first time, guilt pricked him. They had unquestionably treated him with considerable honor. But, despite the fact that he had done what he had to, he couldn't quite silence the voice that said he was acting dishonorably.

The castle hallways were a cool relief after the time spent inside the smithy. Though Samir was used to a much warmer climate, it occurred to him that the King may have shown considerable wisdom by remaining outside in the breeze. As it was, he definitely needed a bath and to change out of his now sodden silk.

It was certainly no wonder that nearly everyone made straight for the sideboard to pour cups of the fruit punch that waited there. Samir hung back, content to wait his turn.

Watching as the King drew Jenaris aside, the warrior failed to notice the presence at his elbow.

"Kir," Morena's soft voice was just loud enough to be heard above the drone of conversation around them. "How long did it take you to learn to use that sword?"

Turning, he was met by a pair of deep green eyes watching him over the rim of her pewter cup. Although her tone was friendly, there was something about the way she asked that was too...intent to be casual curiosity. But, then, her life would soon depend on his skill and that of those he trained.

"It took me years of practice to master it," he replied, hoping he sounded reassuring. "But I was probably good enough to keep you safe after only a few months of daily practice. You needn't worry. Besides, Alban's men should learn quickly enough."

Morena shrugged, seeming rather unconcerned. "I suppose. After all, they already know quite a lot."

Samir barked a laugh. He had already had that very discussion with the Captain, and it had taken considerable time to convince Alban otherwise. In fact, when they had begun to look at candidates, the Acedian soldier insisted on pointing out the most heavily built men—as if that had anything at all to do with skill. The way the soldiers stood and walked told him a great deal more about their potential.

"Believe it or not, Morena, that may actually work against them." He grinned at the surprise he saw in her face. "It's true. People seem to think that because a man has combat skills already, that should make it easier to learn new ones. All it really proves is that they are willing to apply themselves. But it may be hard for them since they'll have to forget most of what they know in order to learn my techniques."

Morena's eyes narrowed in thought as she considered what she'd just heard. She actually looked pleased rather than bothered by the idea that the Acedians might have difficulty learning.

She pushed back a fall of red curly hair. "So someone without *any* training might learn faster?"

"It's possible," he replied. "It all really depends on the student though. Some people just have a natural aptitude. More grace."

"Like me?"

"I guess," he nodded.

He hadn't really noticed but, now that he thought about it, she was fairly graceful. As attractive as she was, however, he wasn't interested in flirting at the moment. Between preparation for their departure and long term plans for dealing with Kemal....

He would have to let her down easy.

"Kir." The way she drew out the name made it sound like a question. "Will you teach me?"

"Look, Morena, I....What?"

It took a few seconds to finally register. When it did, it *still* made no sense.

"I said, will you teach me how to use a sword? Like you do?" She smiled eagerly. Hopefully.

"Absolutely not," he snorted, dismissing the idea entirely. "Bad enough you ask me to take you into danger in the first place."

Stepping over to the sideboard, he grabbed an empty cup and poured, dashing off half of it in a single gulp. Unbelievable!

"Are you listening to a word I'm saying?" Suddenly, Morena stood face to face with him, green eyes flashing with anger. "*Well?* Are you?"

"No," Samir replied honestly. There was no point in pretending otherwise. Unfortunately, it was too late to feign difficulty understanding the language. "Why? Did you want to talk about something else?"

"No. I *don't*," she said heatedly, color rising in her cheeks. "I want you to tell me *why* you won't teach me."

He could see that she wasn't about to be put off, and he wouldn't be so ill-mannered as to simply walk away. There was little choice but to discuss the matter, no matter how ridiculous.

Taking a deep breath, he met her stare for stare.

"The reason I won't teach you," he said calmly, "is because you're a girl."

"A *woman*."

"Fine," he accepted her correction easily. "Because you're a woman, then. In Majar, women don't learn the art of warfare."

She smiled sweetly. "And as you pointed out just a few hours ago," came the sardonic reply, "we aren't *in* Majar."

He forced himself to stay calm, consciously relaxing as he felt his jaw beginning to clench. After a few moments, he felt ready to reply without shouting. As it was, he knew they were beginning to draw attention to themselves and he saw no reason to make it worse.

"That's true," he said reasonably. "But, from my observation, things are the same here. Or are you going to tell me different?"

Morena's anger flared. "So you just expect a woman to be some bit of fluff who keeps her mouth shut?" she said acidly. "I suppose men are to be waited on hand and foot. Women are just there to look pretty and do your bidding?"

It was all he could do to suppress a laugh. From the dangerous glint in her eyes, he hadn't entirely succeeded.

"If you think that," he replied, attempting to mollify, "then you should meet my mother. You'd like her. She's...formidable."

Samir smiled, trying to at least relieve some of the tension. Morena remained silent, her expression unchanged from the mask of annoyance that had confronted him for the past several minutes. He didn't want to fight, and this was going nowhere.

"Look," he said. "I don't have anything against you or any other woman. Only a fool would think strength is about muscles or the ability to fight, and I am not a fool." He ignored the pointed look she gave him at that. "You can learn anything you want as far as I'm concerned. All I'm saying is that I can't teach you to fight."

"You mean you *won't*," she replied coldly, turning her back under the pretense of pouring more punch.

Clearly the conversation was over.

Samir was willing to admit to himself that she may have been right about the distinction. But as a practical matter, it amounted to the same thing. The fact that she was probably capable of learning—maybe even of mastering—the Majaran techniques was completely irrelevant. He would kiss his horse before he would train a woman to fight.

Whatever the topic of discussion between King Carlon and the Wizard, it ended genially, with the King clapping Jenaris on the back and roaring with laughter. The two strolled over, Carlon grinning ear to ear.

"Get your gear ready," the King announced, his gaze taking in each person in turn. "And give the chamberlain a list of anything you might need. You'll be leaving once Kir's sword is delivered."

Taking that as a dismissal, they began drifting toward the door.

Whistling for Tirza, Samir decided to go and check on the progress of the King's tailor. He didn't know how comfortable the new clothes would be, but at least they would allow him to move.

As he stepped into the hallway, he glanced back into the room and caught a glimpse of emerald green eyes under a veil of curly hair following him with a hurt expression.

Chapter 14

Dragon's Fang

Samir hadn't slept well at all, in spite of the comfort of his goose down mattress. He could have understood if excitement had caused him to lie awake. The blacksmith had sent word that the sword would be finished today, and the need to hold it had him more than a bit on edge. Besides, if the blade arrived early enough, they would be setting out today.

But that wasn't it at all. What had stolen his rest had been guilt, and it wasn't until he had resolved to set things right that he could finally close his eyes and rest. It hadn't been nearly enough, however.

Morning had come awfully early. In fact, he'd actually needed a knock on his door to wake him for the first time in years. This, in turn, had brought Tirza leaping onto the bed as if telling him to hurry.

Still, with his packs already by the door, he had little to do other than wash, dress and shave before heading down to breakfast. It should have taken only a few minutes, even with the extra care to edge around his lengthening moustaches. Tirza had other ideas, however, deciding to play tug-of-war with his new jacket before allowing him to finally put it on.

He had several now. The tailor had done an excellent job all in all. Made of finely spun wool, they would wear well and were quite supple. The fabric also made his skin itch, but he could deal with that. What was important was the way they fit. The tailor had made certain that his ability to move freely would be unrestricted by designing them to resemble his pants. By causing the sleeves to flair widely from the shoulders and regather at the wrists, the man had allowed enough extra material to grant Samir his full range of motion. He was also pleased at the way it ended at the waist, leaving his weapons free. He'd even had trousers made to match.

Sliding the cool band of gold and jade up his arm, he donned his jacket and pulled the long tail of hair free. It would do nicely.

Samir quickly tucked his razor into his saddlebags, grabbing his longsword and a fan as he did so and sliding them snugly behind his sash. A pair of broadswords lay carefully wrapped in soft cloth. Those he would tie behind his saddle, along with the longsword he now carried if the new blade met his expectations. Half a dozen good knives rested among his gear as well, but he would carry those only as needed.

Satisfied, he opened the door, laughing as Tirza snaked through the gap before it was more than a few inches wide. Leaving the door open, he stepped into the hallway. He would send someone for his baggage, but now he had other things on his mind.

Samir didn't go directly to the dining room. Instead, he walked in the opposite direction, taking the turns that led to his training room. A wave of his hand sent the hound to her place against the wall outside, but he wouldn't keep her waiting long.

Bowing to the empty room, he walked along the walls, fingers brushing weapons in the racks as he moved. There were fewer than there had been the day before. Aside from knives and broadswords, he had packed up a dozen spears and several practice weapons. He hoped to find men interested in learning them, but regardless of their training he would be working to master them.

When he returned, many of the empty spaces along the walls would be filled. The smiths would continue producing his weapons while he was away, and they had examples to work from. One smith, he knew, would be absolutely *sure* to do his best work.

A young boy in page's attire waited outside, ready to take Tirza outside for him. He suspected the younger servants competed in some way for the chance to play with the dog since one always managed to show up looking eager. That was fine. It allowed him time to deal with other things without worrying that Tirza was being neglected.

With a nod to the page, Samir headed in the direction of the kitchens and the breakfast that would be waiting for him. There was always an abundant selection—cured ham, eggs, sausages, potatoes and several marvelous varieties of melon. He only wished these people knew how to season food properly. It was all so bland, with almost no spices at all. Still, if that was the only complaint he could muster....

A host of excited faces greeted him as he entered the room, all focused on him. The reason behind it caught his eye almost immediately—a sword rested at his usual place at the long head table. Not bothering to fill a plate from the assortment on the sideboard, he strode directly to his seat.

The hilt was beautifully wrapped in blue leather, wound with twists of silver wire. It fit his hand perfectly.

He found the pommel rather plain—an unadorned thick ring of steel. But scarves or tassels would hang well from it. The blue leather of the scabbard matched the grip and, although plain, was set with silver at both ends. Somehow, the understated treatment seemed elegant and fit well with the overall appearance.

He had to resist the impulse to sweep the blade free of its sheath, well aware that bare steel at the table would certainly be considered rude in any land. With a great deal of restraint, he eased the blade, exposing only a few inches of the frosty steel. Hesitantly, Samir touched the metal. There seemed to be no additional texture, but it *was* cooler than he'd anticipated.

After a last lingering look, he reluctantly jammed the blade home. The motion drew a soft chuckle from beside him.

"Careful," Alban said, sliding a plate of sausage and eggs in front of him. "Looking at your sword like that will make the ladies jealous."

Samir nodded his thanks for the food. Laying the sword across his lap, he speared a bite of sausage with his knife.

"Perhaps they have good reason," he returned, admiration plain in his voice. "It's a beautiful sword. I've never seen its like."

"Have you considered naming her?" Gillis asked.

Samir considered. "It's not a tradition in my country."

"Nor here either," Alban admitted. "But if any weapon deserves the honor, I'd have to say that one does."

It was a good point. The sword that now graced Samir's hip was masterfully rendered—a balance of well executed artistry and perfectly expressed functionality. Despite the fact that he'd been raised in an atmosphere where money flowed freely to purchase the best work, he hadn't thought to find a finer piece of work. Yet his new blade made it appear to be a cheap trinket.

"Very well," he began, considering carefully. "I suppose if my spear is the dragon's tail and my broadsword its claw, then this would be the Dragon's Fang."

Alban nodded, eyes alight and a broad smile on his lips. "A fang to kill a dragon. I like it."

So did Samir. It felt right.

Shoveling the last of the eggs into his mouth, he murmured his excuses and pushed back from the table carrying the new sword. Almost as an afterthought, he stepped over to the buffet, wrapping a number of sausage links in a napkin before leaving. He would share them with Tirza, of course, but if their rations on the road were anything like those aboard ship, he'd best get his fill now. It might be some time before he ate this well again.

The vast courtyard was a mass of barely controlled chaos. Word that the sword had been delivered must have spread quickly, before he'd been rousted out of bed. Most of the group had eaten and were already seeing to their mounts, and the soldiers were taking their turns under the intense scrutiny of inspections.

Those not in military uniforms or livery stood out among the crowd. Jenaris stood calmly, stroking the neck of a small white mare. She was lightly laden, only saddlebags and blankets in place behind the saddle. Yet, given the number of pack animals, the Mage likely had at least one dedicated to whatever equipment or supplies he was taking.

Morena was harder to spot. He barely noticed her, tightening the saddle girth of a dun she would nearly need a mounting block to get aboard. Only her hair had given her away as he scanned the crowd, dressed as she was in shirt and trousers. Although well-made and a good fit, they looked extremely strange given that he had never seen a woman wear pants before. The strange sight held his gaze—until the gradual realization that the belt around her slender waist emphasized her curves in a rather flattering way forced him to deliberately look away.

Kordel sat heavily in the saddle of a sad-looking chestnut mare. It was fairly obvious from his posture that the back of a horse was the last place he wanted to be. But if Jenaris said he was going, then he was going.

A wave from Caleb drew his attention as it was clearly intended to. The other Prince—the *only* Prince now, he supposed—stood looking expectantly, apparently waiting for Samir to join him. He'd been surprised that Carlon had given his heir permission to go along, considering the potential danger on at least one leg of their journey. Still, the Acedian seemed a good sort, and it would be good to have the company on the long ride.

The horse Samir sought waited beside Caleb's mount, in the care of a groom. A gift from Carlon, the black gelding was well conformed with a deep chest, long legs and powerful looking haunches. His blankets and saddlebags were already lashed in place, along with a full water bag hanging from the high cantle. His bridle and saddle were in place as well, silver medallions shining and hung with fringed blue tassels. He had named the gelding Yashar, justice, and while he was no match for the beautiful mount Samir had sold back in Majar, he would do.

Samir pulled his old longsword free from its place under the long silk sash at his waist, shoving it beneath the lashings of his blanket roll. The new sword felt odd as he slid it into place. Its weight seemed far too light compared to the one he had worn for so long.

Unable to resist, he drew the blade fully free of the scabbard with a flourish and held it up to the light. The flat of the sword fairly glowed with a soft white light as it reflected the early morning sun. It was, very likely, the most beautiful sight he had ever seen. He felt as if he could get lost in its surface.

"I'll give you five coppers for it," said a familiar deep voice behind him. "Hell. Make it *ten*."

The King's smile was genuine, but failed to fully conceal a slight touch of envy as he looked at the blade in Samir's hand. It was hard to fault him. If their positions were reversed, he would feel a bit envious himself.

Samir shook his head, sheathing the sword. "Sorry, Sire. I'm pretty sure the Wizard would turn me into a toad if I even *thought* about selling his masterpiece."

"He might at that," Carlon chuckled.

"No doubt about it. That's some of my best work in your hand." Jenaris offered a nod of greeting as he strolled over to join them. He fixed the Majaran with a pointed stare. "I'm not finished with that blade yet. Not nearly. I'll expect you to bring it to me every evening." The Mage held up a hand to forestall protest. "It will be returned to you the moment I'm done."

Samir hated the thought of being separated from the sword. After all, there would be a *very* real threat where they were going, and he seriously doubted the dragons would attack only when it was convenient for him. But he couldn't call it an unreasonable request. When someone offered to do you a favor, you didn't quibble about details. Besides, in a few minutes, it might not matter anyway.

Glancing around, he found that everyone was present—at least, everyone he needed to speak to. Meeting their eyes, he steeled himself.

"Excuse me, Sire," he began, "but I have something I need to say. To all of you."

Not for the first time, he wondered if this would be harder than actually facing dragons. Well, Shimei had always insisted that there were different kinds of courage, and physical danger was often the least part of it.

Carlon nodded, concerned. "Of course, Kir. What's on your mind?"

He drew a deep breath.

"That's just it," he said hesitantly, trying but not quite able to meet anyone's gaze. "My name isn't Kir. It's *Samir*."

A wide range of expressions met his pronouncement, ranging from confusion to surprise to the beginnings of anger. Thankfully, no one spoke, allowing him a chance to explain.

"I'm sorry I didn't trust you with the truth before this." Now he met their stares evenly as he looked from face to face. The hurt he saw there stung, but he continued. "In my defense, I've suffered several betrayals recently and I couldn't afford another. It doesn't excuse what I did, but if you can forgive me, I'll do my best to earn your trust back."

Samir saw uncertainty everywhere he looked, and he couldn't fault them a bit. However unusual the circumstances behind his arrival, he had asked for friendship and trust without giving the same in return.

"If I forgive you," Morena said with a caution indicating the outcome was still in doubt, "will you teach me?"

"I'm sorry, but no," he answered without a moment's pause.

"Well, it was worth a shot," she grinned. "I guess you're forgiven, but I can't speak for anyone else."

"If we can't trust each other," Alban offered, "then I don't think much of our chances." The Captain still looked angry, but he held out his hand.

Samir took it gladly.

"Thank you."

Gillis offered his as well, followed shortly by Caleb. From Jenaris, he merely received a thoughtful look, the deep blue eyes seeming to look through him.

"One question," Carlon said, looking uncertain. "What kind of betrayal were you afraid of?"

He had expected the question, or something much like it. But if he wanted their trust, he would have to be willing to offer specifics. Besides, he felt certain—or near enough—that he *could* trust these people. He nodded.

"My brother betrayed me, using my best friend to do it," he replied, the memory bringing a slight flush of anger. "He stole my birthright and killed my father, and he owes me a debt of blood for that. But until I go back to collect it, he needs to believe me dead. So I changed my name."

Silence greeted the response, but several heads nodded. Finally, the King offered his hand.

"All right, Samir," Carlon said. "But tell me, is the dog's name actually Tirza?"

He was grateful to the man. After all, if the King could make light of the situation so easily—essentially laughing if off—then it couldn't have been that serious in the first place.

"Yes, Sire," the Majaran answered. "She's too smart to lie."

Reminded that the hound was nowhere in sight, Samir gave a high, shrill whistle that soon brought the sound of claws clicking rapidly on the cobblestones. In moments, Tirza was scrambling among the small circle of people, tail frantically wagging as she greeted each one.

"I guess that means we're all ready," Jenaris offered, looking around for signs of disagreement.

"Take care of each other." Carlon briefly gripped his son's shoulder as he met each person's eyes in turn, ending with Morena. "Come back safe," he added.

Samir swung up easily into his saddle, sending the gelding into a frisky little dance as he adjusted to his rider's weight. The Majaran had thought briefly about stopping to give Morena a boost. But considering her comment about his thinking women were some "bit of fluff," he preferred not to seem condescending.

The sound of horseshoes on stone rang around him as riders mounted, the horses anticipating the need to move. He noted that Morena's mare remained stock still as she scrambled up without any assistance.

No. Not just some bit of fluff, he assured himself.

Jenaris wasted no time setting his horse into motion toward the gates, evidently counting on the rest of them to catch up. Alban merely waved his arm overhead, sending a shouted "Forward" from Sergeant Roland. The soldiers started out as a single unit. Caleb, Morena and Samir followed without hesitation, but Kordel looked ready to dismount at the slightest excuse. Finally, the apprentice shook his reins in an awkward motion, causing the docile mare to amble forward as he clung to the leather in his hands. In no time, all of them were clear of the gates and moving through the streets of Varella.

The ride north passed quickly as they wound past farms and cottages, following the river to Charlford and the entrance to the plains. They could as easily have crossed the Amber right away, traveling via the town of Glavin, but the Captain had insisted they resupply in the larger city. Though they paid a fair price for their provisions, it would hardly be right to strip a small town bare.

For whatever reason, they would be starting their search in Gotarra with the Blackthorn root. Samir had no preference in the matter. It was as good a choice as any, as far as he was concerned. But he had noticed a certain anxiety in the air—as if the men were both dreading the trip and eager for it.

"Mind if I ride with you, Highness?" Samir asked, pulling up alongside the Acedian Prince.

"Please do." Caleb returned a weak smile, seeming almost distracted. "It would be good to have a little company. And, by the way, you should call me Caleb."

"All right," Samir agreed.

The pair rode in silence for a time, neither feeling a need to force conversation. It was too pleasant a day, the sun warm on the back of his neck and the breeze tugging his long tail of hair. Eventually, however, he could tell that Caleb had something on his mind. He waited for the other man to choose his words.

"Have you ever had a girlfriend, Samir?"

The awkwardness with which he asked the question seemed unusual for the normally confident Acedian Prince. Sadly, Samir could offer no help on the subject.

"I've had a few who were friends," he said with a shrug. "I never thought about looking for anything more. My parents were supposed to make the arrangements for my wife."

A deep sadness settled in at the thought of his parents. His father was gone now, and he had no idea whether his mother still lived.

"That's the most ridiculous thing I've ever heard." Morena rode up on Samir's other side, looking as if she'd just eaten something particularly sour. "What about *love*?"

He stiffened. "My father loved my mother, and they'd never met before their betrothal," he said defensively. "Of course, my father's feelings about Kemal's mother were...complicated."

Morena gave him a look of sympathy. "So your mother died when you were young?"

"No," Samir replied, surprised. "Kemal might have had her executed by now. I imagine she's been a nightmare if she caused him *half* the trouble she's capable of." Pride swelled in him as he thought of his mother working to undermine his brother's reign. Sudden realization struck him then as he caught Morena's implication. "No. My father didn't marry Zia because my mother *died*. That was political. He was married to both of them."

"What?!" Caleb and Morena said almost in unison, clearly shocked.

"I take back what I said before," Morena added before Samir could respond. "*That's* the most ridiculous thing I've ever heard."

Her mare pulled out of line with theirs as she used her knees to guide the horse toward the Wizard. Samir admired the ease with which she rode, but he definitely thought her tact could use some work.

"Well, I have to admit it sounds strange to me, too," Caleb allowed. He barked an odd laugh. "Apparently *one* woman is more than I can deal with."

The warrior had no real wisdom to offer. Still, he felt the need to say something.

"Is she worth it?" he asked.

Caleb nodded. "*Definitely.*"

"Then you'll find a way to work it out."

Samir was glad to note that, for a while at least, Caleb sat a little straighter in the saddle as they rode.

Chapter 15

The Twist of a Fan

Morena sighed. The cool breezes felt good against her sun-reddened skin. Exposure over the previous several days had begun to bring out a deeper tan, but with her light complexion she would never fully avoid burning. She envied Samir's swarthy color and his ability to endure long periods outdoors.

She wasn't the only one suffering the effects of the sun, however. Nearly everyone else shared her own difficulty—except Jenaris, who somehow appeared to be completely unaffected. Still, with her long loose curls tied back out of the wind, the day was pleasant enough.

So far this morning she had gotten a great deal of amusement from watching the soldiers ride—all of them doing their level best to hide their extreme discomfort. Samir had begun his lessons the previous evening as soon as the camp had been set up, and had evidently worked the men harder than anyone had thought. It had been strange to watch as he seemed mainly to teach them how to stand and had them stretch. But, while they had all found it funny afterwards based on the jokes she'd heard, this morning had been a different story. To a man, they had awakened sore and stiff, moving more like old men than trained fighters.

She had caught Samir more than once wearing a secret smile—each time he heard the groans or saw them shifting in the saddle. From his reaction, it was clear that he had heard the jokes as well and he was *definitely* enjoying this.

She would have liked to try the stances herself, but the open views of the prairie were anything but private. The only time anyone would be out of sight of the others was inside the curtain-enclosed privy. Not a place anyone wished to stay for any length of time.

At least Samir hadn't seemed to mind her watching as he trained the men. She and Tirza had sat together in the long grass, perched on a small rise overlooking the practice area where the men stood in rows. Even if the man chose to be stubborn about refusing a female student, she might be able to learn enough this way to make it useful. After all, once they returned home there would be no one to see if she practiced inside her own room. But it would have been nice to be allowed to learn like everyone else.

Stubborn, pigheaded man! she thought, not for the first time.

But she knew she could hardly blame the Majaran for following Majaran ways. It didn't seem personal in any way. Just incredibly *stupid*.

No. She had to admit that was unfair. The fact that something was inconvenient for her didn't make it stupid. It just meant she would have to find a way to change his mind—even though she wasn't entirely sure why it was so important to her.

But before she could do that, she would have to get him to talk to her. He'd been more than a little bit cool toward her in the past few days. Not that he had ignored her. That would have been rude, and the man would probably have cut off his left arm first. But, whenever she had tried to join the conversation between him and Caleb, he'd been annoyingly formal, aloof. However she chose to describe it, she'd been alone a great deal lately.

Well, maybe she *had* been out of line with her remark about his people's marriage customs. But that was no excuse for him to be childish about it.

With a deep sigh of resignation, she looked up and down the line of riders, finally spotting him—leaning far out of his saddle to take something from Tirza's mouth. She watched him straighten, standing in the stirrups to throw the object far out into the grass. The dog dashed off immediately to retrieve it again.

Almost without her conscious guidance, Dawn Rose moved in his direction, quickly pulling up alongside. Samir spared her only a glance, nodding stiffly, but said nothing.

He was going to make this difficult, she could tell.

"All right," she said with perhaps the *tiniest* bit of reluctance. "I'm sorry."

"What? You'll have to stop mumbling," he replied, an infuriatingly smug smile on his face. "I can't quite hear you."

How *dare* he? Well, maybe she *had* said it quietly— just to keep it between the two of them. It was nobody else's business, after all. But she knew *damned* well he had heard her.

" I *said*, I'm sorry," she repeated loudly, giving him a look that dared him to make her say it again. She refused to look and see if anyone else had heard her.

"For what?" he asked, casually leaning down to Tirza as they rode. This time the throw went a great deal farther, drawing the dog deep into the grass in a headlong sprint.

She very nearly hit him. Taking a deep breath, she forced her jaw muscles to unclench.

"I'm sorry I said what I did...about your parents customs being ridiculous," she admitted, contrition actually coming without difficulty. "I just lost my father, too, and I wouldn't want anyone saying something like that about him."

For the first time, he looked at her, meeting her eyes with genuine sympathy. "I'm sorry. I didn't know," he replied. "How did it happen?"

Morena knew the question was just normal curiosity, but she was still unsure how much, or even if, she should share with him. Beside her, Samir rode in silence while Tirza came and went yet again, giving her the chance to consider. It was this simple courtesy that helped her decide.

"Dragons," she answered, surprised her voice didn't break as she said it. "He was killed just a few weeks ago."

She had expected a response of some kind at the news—like more of the platitudes she'd heard too much lately. Anything but the quiet that answered her. After an uncomfortable few moments she risked a glance out of the corner of her eye, only to find him studying her intently.

The expression on Samir's face was a mixture of wonder and sorrow as he watched her with unblinking brown eyes. There was, perhaps, a touch of respect as well. She looked away, not entirely sure whether to feel flattered or disconcerted.

"Marius Braden was your father," he said finally.

She merely nodded, not fully trusting herself to speak.

"Forgive me if this comes out wrong." He gently placed a hand on her arm. It stung slightly on her burned skin. "Why are you *here*?"

Anger flashed in her green eyes. "Are you saying I don't have a *right* to be here?" she demanded, jerking her arm free of his touch.

He didn't respond to her anger, merely shaking his head. His gaze was so intent on her that he seemed not to see Tirza bounding along beside him.

"Anything but," he asserted. "It's just that most people would rather be as far from these things as possible. *Especially* if they knew how dangerous the creatures are." The frankness of his expression stole all anger from her. "What I'm saying is that you have more courage than I would have thought. And, before you protest, I don't mean 'you're brave for a girl.' I mean you're brave."

"Oh," she replied, unable to think what else to say in response to the compliment. "Thank you."

"And I *am* sorry about your father," he said softly. "I understand how hard it is."

Morena smiled gratefully. She had felt alone in her grief, like no one could possibly know what it was like to suffer this loss. Without warning, tears filled her eyes, spilling down her cheeks and dripping from her lashes. She still cried at night sometimes, when she knew no one could see. Now, in front of someone else, it was embarrassing.

Without a word, he untied the blue silk scarf waving from the hilt of his sword, handing it to her. She almost took it, reaching, but hesitated.

"Please."

She could see the deep compassion in his expression and felt it in his hands as he pressed the silk into her grasp. As he did, he smoothly leaned down toward the dog, granting her a bit of privacy as she hurriedly wiped her face with the makeshift kerchief. When he once again sat upright, he held a small wooden ball.

"Thank you." She handed back the flapping silk, face dry. Morena bit her lower lip. "Um...when you said I had courage.... Does that mean you'll teach me?"

He smiled, amusement dancing in his eyes.

"No," he answered kindly, "but I admire your determination."

"At least you haven't told me to stop asking." Hope shaded her voice.

"You have a right to ask," he admitted. "And I have a right to say no. Besides, you wouldn't stop if I told you to. Or am I wrong?"

"No," she shook her head, laughing softly. "You're not wrong."

"I didn't think so."

Standing up in the stirrups, he threw the ball in a high arc to land well in front of the party. The hound sped after it, a streak of white in the tall grass.

Morena extended her hand. "Friends?"

"Friends," he replied, taking it in a strong, calloused grip.

The time and the waving tassels on the bluestem grass seemed to pass more quickly with someone to talk to. She felt so much easier around Samir now, though he absolutely would not bend in his refusal to teach her. The man wouldn't even answer questions about what she saw, despite the fact that he let her watch every practice. But she had already figured out that—as long as he didn't *teach* her, his sense of honor would be satisfied.

Caleb she had known since childhood, although they hadn't actually been close. While he'd never been formal or standoffish, they'd simply never had much opportunity to spend time together, having different interests. In a way it felt strange calling him by just his first name as he'd asked, rather than calling him "Prince Caleb" as she always had. Still, she appreciated his efforts to put her at ease.

Now that they'd gotten past the initial soreness of stretching and standing as Samir taught, Captain Ward and his men rode much more easily. Morena had been impressed by how rapidly the soldiers had progressed to more advanced positions and the strikes, kicks and blocks Samir used. But they were far from being able to blend them together into the blinding combinations their instructor used. Yet in spite of that fact, the men had begun to swagger about their new abilities until Samir had joked that, in a few months, they *might* be able to do what he could at six. Joking or not, he was, she believed, speaking the simple truth.

Morena was amazed at how soon they reached the forest that signaled their transition into the hills. She was beginning to feel that the broad, flat plains must go on forever. She couldn't have been more wrong. The suddenness of the change to thickly forested hills came as a shock, revealed as they topped a rise shielding the horizon. There was no denying that they were now very close to Gotarra.

With the transition, the group began to move more slowly and, although the rougher terrain was part of the reason, she knew that wasn't all of it. It wasn't hard to sense the caution that now permeated the group like a smothering blanket. A person would have to be blind to miss it. Scouts went out and returned with much greater frequency, riding out in all directions rather than merely ahead. Heads swiveled constantly as eyes scanned the shadows around them. Up and down the line, hands unconsciously drifted toward hilts, or rested there.

Samir showed none of the tension of the other men, riding with a relaxation that appeared completely unconcerned. Yet, riding beside him, she noticed that his eyes moved as ceaselessly as everyone else's.

As much as Morena enjoyed the lush beauty of the trees, she was glad when Alban finally called a halt to the day's travel. The clearing just off the road was the first of any decent size they had come across and, though it was a bit early, still the opportunity was too good to pass up.

Dismounting, she began the process of unsaddling and hobbling her horse. Soon enough, the soldiers would set the picket lines and come to fetch Dawn Rose. But first, she needed to remove her gear.

"Samir," Caleb called to where the Majaran was working to free his blanket roll. "Why don't barbarians eat steak?"

"I don't know," Samir answered. From the odd half-smile, it was clear the warrior was more amused at his friend's fascination with these jokes than with the jokes themselves. "Why?"

"The hooves get stuck in their throats!" Caleb howled with laughter, bringing curious stares from the men setting up the camp.

Samir merely chuckled politely. Morena could just see his head shaking as he bent to work loose the saddle girth.

"Have you ever actually met one of those barbarians?" he asked, straightening so he could see the other man.

"Well, no," Caleb replied, somewhat defensive. "But everyone agrees that they're completely backward. It's common knowledge."

"Really?" Morena teased. "Like the fact that girls can't learn to fight?"

Samir turned, giving her an offended look.

"I never said they *can't*," he objected strenuously.

The slightly sheepish look that followed announced plainly that he realized she was only kidding.

"Glad to know you understand there's no reason to keep refusing," she insisted. Laughing, she couldn't resist adding an impudent grin.

The hobbles in place, she gave Dawn Rose an affectionate pat before walking toward the edge of the trees. She had only gone a few steps before Samir's voice caught up to her.

"Where are you going?"

"It's been a long ride," she called over her shoulder with more than a little annoyance. "I'm not prepared to wait while they dig the privy, if you must know."

Within the space of three steps Tirza had caught her and was padding along happily beside her. Reaching down to scratch the hound's head, she allowed herself a small smile at his concern. It wasn't the first time Tirza had followed her, but somehow she was certain Samir had sent her this time.

The treeline wasn't far, and the underbrush at the edge of the wood was thick enough to block the view and offer privacy. In truth, it was almost enough to block her entry. But watching Tirza snake her way through revealed a passable route. In moments, she stood beneath the cool shadows of the dense canopy.

The hound's deep, throaty growl drew her gaze instantly. Hackles up and half crouched, Tirza stared deep into the trees ahead.

It was the only warning she had.

Morena threw herself to one side, barely aware of the scream escaping her as she placed a large tree between her and the creature. It was unbelievably fast, barely missing her as it barreled through the spot where she'd stood only a second before. With astonishing agility the dragon spun even as it skidded to a stop facing her, red eyes burning with hatred.

The tree saved her, though it took more effort than she could sustain to keep it between them. Fear gripped her. With the tail on one side and its dagger-like teeth on the other, it was all she could do not to run in panic. But she knew she would never survive if she did. It would be on her in an instant.

"Move!" Samir's voice rang as he jumped between Morena and the beast, white blade poised.

She should have done as he said, should have run. But her feet felt as though they were rooted in place. Morena stood frozen clutching the thick, mossy trunk.

Samir had no such problem. He moved—fast! With seeming ease he drew the dragon off, its baleful eyes fixed on him, unblinking.

Somehow, even here in the shadows, the sword appeared to flash with reflected light as he used it to parry and thrust. In his left hand a red silk fan danced in counterpoint to the blade, incongruous with the setting.

Samir turned, perched high on the ball of one foot as the massive tail spike stabbed the air, piercing the place where his chest had been. He dropped low, fan flashing into the creature's eyes, blinding it as his sword sped for the thick, scaly neck. Somehow it knew, head jerking back as it reared, claws slashing for the Majaran's leg.

Samir stepped back smoothly, effortlessly, just out of reach as his weapon carved a bloody line through the back of the dragon's paw. The air split with a terrible scream as again the tail lashed, a massive club as thick as an arm. With perfect timing, the warrior rolled his head under the blow, hair stirred by the wind of its passing as he glided forward to counter.

The monstrous head cocked back with remarkable speed, jaws opening wide. Morena watched, horrified, as a jet of thick black venom splashed toward Samir. Yet his fan spun up to meet it with a deft twist, whipping it away with a casual flick of the wrist.

But in that instant the drake had left itself vulnerable. The longsword swiveled in Samir's hand as his arm directed it, swinging it into line. Without hesitation the sword changed direction, razor sharp point sliding easily into the soft flesh under the creature's jaw and sinking nearly to the hilt before slowing.

Pivoting smoothly on his back foot, Samir withdrew, pulling the blade free as he went. With a shudder, the beast collapsed amid clouds of dust, unmoving.

Samir stood perfectly still, poised on the balls of his feet as he watched the dragon, breath coming fast as his chest rose and fell. Finally satisfied, he spared a glance for his weapons. The frosty blade of his sword ran with dark crimson, giving it a terrible kind of beauty. His fan, however, earned a look of utter disgust as he watched poison drip from the ruined silk to the forest floor. With a grunt of displeasure, he tossed it away.

Feet finally able to move, Morena rushed forward to grip him tightly. Whether relieved for his safety or hers, she didn't know and didn't care, but she couldn't seem to let go. Her heart hammered in her chest.

For a long moment he hugged her tightly, carefully holding the sword's impossibly sharp blade well clear. She felt so stupid, knowing she hadn't even had the courage to run away. How could she have thought she could learn to fight like Samir? And he had believed her *brave*?

With incredible care he gently disengaged, stepping back to look at her. His eyes swept quickly over her body, missing nothing as he checked for injuries. Slowly, the concern etched deeply on his features softened as relief took its place. Satisfied, he let out the breath he'd been holding.

"Are you all right?" he asked, watching her in a way that somehow made her heart beat even faster.

She never got a chance to answer. Jenaris burst through the thick underbrush, Alban and Kordel following in his wake. Beyond them, she could hear others following.

"At least someone around here has some sense," the Mage announced, moving to kneel beside Tirza who stood watching the motionless dragon. He tousled her ears. "Good girl. You would never turn your back on a dragon, would you?"

Morena felt the heat rising in her cheeks as she blushed. She saw Samir's jaw tighten at the implication that he may have been negligent.

Jenaris seemed not to notice either reaction as he approached the enormous corpse, walking a slow circle around it. Not once during his circuit did he blink as he examined the drake from every angle.

For well over a minute she watched the Wizard, waiting for his eyelids to so much as twitch, until Alban blocked her view. The Captain paused in front of her, gaze sweeping over her with the same intensity Samir had only a short time before. With a nod, he turned his attention to the Majaran and, eventually, the area where the battle had taken place.

"What happened to *that*?!" The Captain pointed, astonishment plain on his face as he pointed at the ground near the dragon.

The fan lay in the dust, not a hint of its elegance remaining. What once had been bright red was now uniformly stained the dark purple of a fresh bruise as the venom wicked into the cloth.

"I've always wondered how such an unlikely weapon developed," Samir cocked a charming lopsided smile.

"Not that it isn't useful, mind you, but its hardly the most obvious choice. Seeing Jenaris' illusion spray that stuff gave me the idea. I'm only glad I have five more."

"Well, that's one less that we knew of," Jenaris said as he joined the conversation.

"It was one of the dragons you'd seen before?" Samir asked, quickly grasping the implications of the Wizard's words.

The Mage nodded. "It was Marqued, although it's fading quickly now." He weighed Samir with a long, level look. "I thought you were going to go *under* the scales, not *through* them."

Samir shrugged, grinning wickedly. "I wanted to test your workmanship, Magus. Besides, Morena was so certain I'd take unnecessary risks, I didn't want to disappoint her."

She smacked his arm hard enough to sting her hand. He never even flinched. Instead, he turned the sword over in his hands, studying the drying blood.

"Does anyone have a rag handy?" he asked.

"Don't bother," Jenaris answered quickly, staring with longing at the corpse of the dragon a few feet away. "I'll need to dissect that thing tonight, and I'll need a sharp blade to do it...if you don't mind."

"Of course." The warrior carefully offered Jenaris the hilt.

"Kordel," the Mage called. "Go get my sample jars. We have work to do.

"The shuffle of footsteps and the rustle of brush was the only reply. Jenaris returned to his study of the still form, carefully rolling up his sleeves as he decided where to begin.

"I have work to do, too. There's still a class to teach." Samir offered her a warm smile. "By the way, you start tomorrow."

A gasp escaped her, followed by a grin that made her jaws ache.

"Why not tonight?" she asked, wondering at the delay. After all, he'd already declared his intention to teach this evening.

"You don't want to know," he grimaced.

Whistling for Tirza, Samir walked toward the brush and the clearing beyond, mumbling something she couldn't quite catch. Somehow it had sounded like he'd said something about kissing a horse.

Chapter 16

A Mark in the Steel

It was still dark when Samir rolled out of his blankets, though the sun was just tickling the horizon and the last watchman was quietly waking the rest of the soldiers. As usual, he found his sword beside him when he awoke—hopefully cleaned before Jenaris had returned it to its sheath.

The late crescent of moon gave just enough light to make out the sleeping forms around him. Caleb would sleep until someone, usually Gillis, woke him for breakfast. Morena typically woke when the sky began to lighten, which wasn't far now—as the edge of purple and pink to the east announced. At the moment, however, she was curled up next to Tirza.

He had heard her stirring restlessly during the night. Morena's fitful sleep had been punctuated by frightened moans escaping her as she dreamed. The dog had apparently heard her as well, and had gone to offer a reassuring presence, much as he would have liked to do for his friend. But for her sake he would allow no appearance of impropriety—particularly in front of common soldiers.

After all, he liked these men. He would hate to have to kill any of them for impugning the lady's good name.

Common soldiers or not, they had looked at him with new respect after they had seen the results of the battle in the wood. They had applied themselves harder to their training session as well. Most of these men had been present at the first encounter with dragons, and they remembered only too well how much damage these beasts could do to a troop. Yet their teacher had defeated one, alone, and without suffering so much as a single scratch. Of course, the sword had given him an advantage, but that was a distant consideration to these men.

Several of the soldiers nodded their greetings to him as he made his way through the camp to the privy. Washing quickly, he decided it was too dark to shave, but light enough to satisfy his curiosity.

The thick underbrush rattled and snapped as he pushed through into the heavy shadow of the trees. He didn't need to see to find the place he sought. The smell assaulted him like a nauseating wave, guiding him to the spot where he had killed the dragon the day before. The sight wasn't much better.

Before him the carcass lay half butchered, the dirt around it stained dark with blood and bile. Everywhere he looked he saw evidence of the Mage's work. Powerful muscle stood exposed where the scaled hide had been cut away for study. Entrails lay in loose piles on the ground. Even the top of the head had been removed, leaving only a sizable cavity remaining to show the location of the brain. Samir could only guess what organs had been removed, or even what may have existed inside such a thing. It was clear that Jenaris had done as thorough a job as he could under the circumstances.

Some of what was missing was obvious—like claws, teeth, the tail spike and spines from the neck ridge and face. From the way some areas sagged, however, it seemed many of its bones must also be gone. Glancing around, he noticed that there was no sign of the fan he had used either. It would take a packhorse—a very smelly one—to carry away so much.

Satisfied, he stepped back out into the clearing, deciding to put as much distance as possible between himself and the source of the smell. The Wizard was waiting.

"Did you learn anything?" Samir asked, hooking a thumb back over his shoulder to indicate what was left of the dragon.

"A bit," Jenaris replied with a jaw cracking yawn.

The Mage looked beyond tired, as though he hadn't slept—or even sat—all night. But considering the extent of the work he'd done, that was likely the case. "I would need to examine another one. *At least* one," Jenaris continued. "It may help you to know their supply of toxin is fairly limited. Only enough for about two good shots, I think."

Samir nodded. "That explains why they don't just spray it all over the place and save themselves the trouble of fighting at all."

The Mage offered a brief smile at the insight. He pointed at the sword on the warrior's hip. "Thank you for letting me use the blade. I believe I heard you've named it?"

"Dragon's Fang," Samir answered. "It seemed appropriate."

"Indeed," the Wizard agreed easily. "Have you looked at it yet this morning?"

Shaking his head in answer, Samir reached for the hilt and slid the blade free in one smooth motion. He had been ready to do a thorough examination, but it wasn't necessary. He spotted the change immediately. The once unadorned blade now bore a single mark near the hilt—a strange group of angular lines incised deeply into the steel.

At first glance, it bore a strange resemblance to ancient Rukati writing. Yet somehow he knew this was entirely different from anything he'd ever seen. He stared at the character, feeling as though he was right on the edge of understanding. But it continued to elude him, its meaning frustratingly just out of reach.

"Impressive for a first try."

Jenaris' words broke his concentration, driving away any hope of grasping the meaning.

The world slid back into focus in a mad rush.

"What was *that*?" Samir gasped, attempting to get his bearings. "What just happened?"

Jenaris smiled, blue eyes twinkling. "That was why I came to talk to you," he said. "*Alone.*"

He wasn't quite certain what to make of the Wizard's pronouncement. Still, he had no reason to distrust the man who had, after all, made him the sword in the first place. He waited.

"Maybe you've been wondering why I needed your sword every night," Jenaris said. Unlike his words, the Mage's tone presented it as an absolute certainty. "I won't bore you with details, but let's just say I've been preparing it. Helping it reach its potential. There's more to do, of course, but we have to take it in steps.

"Now that I've begun to add properties to your sword, you'll want to be able to use them." The Wizard watched Samir intently, measuring the effects of his words. "You'll need to...*link* with the sword to do that."

The explanation meant little to the Majaran. Until he'd seen this blade, he had always believed that a weapon was a weapon—some better or worse than others, true, but useful in the right hands. The revelation that his would be something more than it already was...now *that* was a revelation he'd been completely unprepared for.

"Think of it like an unfamiliar horse that someone else has trained. You already know how to ride, but not what this particular animal can do." The lecturing tone Jenaris adopted seemed natural coming from the Mage. "In the case of your sword there isn't a separate personality or will to give you trouble. You simply need to form a bond with it. Get to know it, in a way."

Samir nodded as he considered what he'd just heard. It did make a certain kind of sense, if *anything* about magic could be said to make any sense. The question was...."So, what do I have to do?" he finally asked, earning an approving smile from the Wizard.

Jenaris plopped unceremoniously down into the grass, patting the ground beside him in invitation. Already committed, Samir seated himself beside the Mage and waited.

"What you need to do is much like what you nearly did instinctively already. Clear your thoughts and focus on the blade." Jenaris' voice became quiet, taking on a calming tone as he spoke. "Focus on the blade, not the rune. Just feel it. Let it become familiar."

Samir naturally fell into a pattern of deep, slow breathing as the Wizard spoke, becoming still as the Sòra had taught. He gazed at the blade, focused on nothing as the frosty surface of the steel seemed to tug at him. Compelled, he looked deeper. He could feel it, not precisely within the sword, but not quite anywhere else either. In a way, it *was* the sword.

Comprehension dawned in a rush of sensation as he suddenly understood what had only teased him before. He looked again at the strange symbol cut into the shining metal. He *knew* this symbol, knew it beyond meaning or purpose. And he knew how to use it.

Samir sheathed the sword smoothly as he rose to stand beside the Mage. Jenaris merely sat, watching, excitement in his blue eyes. But the warrior paid him no attention. His focus was on the weapon.

Confidence never wavering, Samir thought about what he wanted—the sword in his right hand—and it was there. There was no need to concentrate, only to *will* it to be there, and it appeared without ever passing through the space in between. Resheathing the blade, he did it again. One moment feeling its weight at his side, the next holding it in front of him.

Amazed, he turned toward the Wizard, unable to find the words to form any of the questions he wanted to ask.

"I have more work to do, but the blade is certainly receptive so far," Jenaris explained. The man obviously needed little urging to talk about his work. "The further I try to go, the trickier it will be. But I can make a few more improvements with no real difficulty."

"It's going to do *more*?" Samir was beyond astonishment.

"Eventually, yes," the Mage said, plainly pleased at the effect his efforts were having. "How much more will depend on how deeply my initial enchantments bonded to the metal. As easily as this one embedded, I believe the potential is...impressive."

"As is the Magus who forged it." Samir offered the compliment with a small bow of respect.

"Of course," Jenaris returned with a laugh.

The Majaran tried to sort through the jumble of questions competing for position in his mind. At the moment, however, there was only one of any pressing concern. He turned a serious expression toward the Mage.

"How far does this work?"

"Now, *that*," Jenaris replied thoughtfully, "I'd like to know myself. The answer depends on the depth of your bond and the strength of your will. Right now I'd guess a few yards. Later, I couldn't say...but farther than you should need."

Samir nodded. He hoped never to need more than the distance from his hip to his hand. But it was always good to know more was available.

"Can anyone make this work?" he asked.

"Only those who have linked to the weapon." The blade was suddenly in the Wizard's hand. "Most wouldn't know how, and I suggest you tell only those you trust implicitly."

The warrior willed the sword to come from Jenaris' hand to his own. It didn't move for a moment, as he felt strong resistance through the bond. Then it was in his grip.

He returned it to the scabbard.

"The stronger will is the one that controls the blade." Jenaris answered the unspoken question. "I imagine that, at some point, you won't need to worry about others linking to the weapon. However, if what you've said about him is any indication, you may wish to avoid allowing *Shimei* that privilege." The piercing stare he leveled at Samir was almost unnerving. "Master yourself."

Evidently considering the conversation at an end, the Mage turned and walked back to camp.

Samir closed his eyes, concentrating. He could feel the link between himself and the sword, even while it rested in the scabbard.

There was a lot to think about now, concerning the blade. He didn't need to hide what it could do, certainly not from his friends. It was less clear, however, whether he should reveal the connection he shared with Dragon's Fang. Not because of any lack of trust, of course, but because he didn't fully know how *he* felt about it yet. After all, it *was* a lot to absorb.

Opening his eyes he, too, walked back to camp. The sun was nearly up now, so he would need to shave and eat quickly before they set out again.

He arrived to find his blankets already rolled and tied and a napkin wrapped around smoked ham, cheese and a crust of hard bread. It would do nicely, but it would have to wait. If necessary, he could eat in the saddle. He couldn't say the same about shaving.

Digging into his saddlebags for his razor and mirror, he offered Morena a grateful smile and a quick "Thanks." He had no doubt who had gathered his breakfast and straightened his gear. Caleb would only have risen a few minutes before, and would still be bleary-eyed. Morena, on the other hand, had everything ready to travel and had finished her own breakfast long since.

"You're welcome," Morena replied wearily.

Tilting the mirror slightly, he could just catch her reflection as she bit her lip until she realized she was being watched. With a quick flick of her eyes, she looked at the mirror to meet his gaze, then quickly looked away.

Something was definitely bothering her, and it wasn't lack of sleep.

"I never did thank you for yesterday," she offered, slightly abashed.

He waved away her concern, dismissing the need for thanks. "Don't worry about it. I'm just glad you're not hurt."

The shy smile she flashed him was an improvement over the apologetic tone a moment earlier. Readjusting the mirror, he carefully laid the razor against his skin and began edging around his slowly lengthening moustache. Shaving dry was hardly his preference, but his whiskers were still soft enough that he could do it without too much trouble.

"You don't have to teach me, Samir," Morena said quietly, almost a whisper. "I know you don't really want to anyway."

His head snapped around, nearly costing him half a moustache. Blood dripped slowly down his cheek, but he was barely aware as he stared at her in utter disbelief.

"What are you talking about? You practically harass me for *weeks* and, when I finally agree, you decide you don't *want* it?" There was something else going on here, he was sure. He took a deep breath and moderated his tone. "What's wrong, Morena? Please just talk to me."

Jaw set, Morena looked at him. She was obviously fighting tears, yet it somehow made her seem...fierce.

"I don't know who I thought I was kidding," she said, suddenly looking somewhat deflated. "I can't learn to fight. Yesterday you told me to run away and I couldn't even do that. So much for you thinking I was brave.

Samir almost had to laugh at how ridiculous Morena's statement was. But he wasn't about to risk having her take it the wrong way. It was clear that she actually believed she'd done something wrong, and that it marked her as a coward. It was all about as far from the truth as you could get, but it wasn't enough that *he* knew that.

"I'm sorry," he said gently. "I must have you confused with someone who survived an attack by a dragon. Did you think that was an accident?"

"Maybe it was," she admitted. "I don't know. I was just so *scared*. All I could think to do was hide behind that tree, and then I was too afraid to even run."

Well, he told himself, *at least she got it half right.*

Laying the razor aside he met her gaze and held it. "I was afraid, too."

She shook her head, her expression one of complete disbelief.

"No, you weren't. You...."

Samir held up a hand, cutting her off. "*Yes*, I was. Or are you calling me a liar?" He took her silence as acceptance and continued. "Fear is part of us. The part that tells us to focus on the problem and *act*. And that's exactly what you did.

"You think fear kept you from running? Your *mind* kept you from running when that thing came after you." Oh yes, he had her attention now. "What would have happened if you ran?"

She sniffed. "I would have been killed."

The look she directed at him had some heat behind it, as if warning him not to talk down to her. Samir almost smiled. It was a vast improvement, seeing a bit of that spirit again. Still, he took the warning.

"Yes, you would have," he agreed, "and you had the presence of mind to know it. Most people wouldn't have. *Most people would have run*...and *died*. After that, you couldn't run because you had already equated that with death."

Morena didn't look *quite* convinced yet, but she was close—or, at least, much closer. "So why did you change your mind? Why teach me?"

Now he *did* smile.

"You move well. Better than most of these trained warriors." He almost hated to admit it, but it was true. The next part, too. "Mostly, I realized something. I promised I would keep you safe, and I will. But sometimes that includes giving you the ability to defend yourself. If you're in danger, you shouldn't have to feel powerless just because you're a woman."

Morena's smile was filled with gratitude, though whatever she was going to say was lost as Caleb returned. Eyes shining with excitement, the Acedian Prince made straight for Samir.

"So, what was it like?" Caleb urged. He grinned broadly as he pointed to Morena. "She won't say much. Kept telling me to ask *you*."

"Not much to tell, really," Samir insisted. "Mostly it was fast. Probably not much more than half a minute, but it felt like forever at the time."

He wanted to pick up the razor and finish, but he knew it would be pointless. Caleb wasn't about to let this go. Not for a second.

"Come on, brother," the other man urged, half pleading in his eagerness to hear the story. "Give over."

"All right," Samir finally relented. He had replayed the fight in his mind several times already, but he wouldn't mind reliving it again. "So I heard Tirza barking and I went into the woods...."

"You heard me scream, you mean," Morena interrupted. She patted the hound lying beside her. "The dog only growled."

Samir shot the woman a mock stern look. "Who's telling this story?"

"I'm just saying you don't need to spare me any embarrassment," she said.

From the look on her face, however, that was precisely what she wanted—or at least hoped for. She was feeling better about herself since their talk, but she evidently didn't share his opinion as to how well she had done in simply surviving. Still, he had no intention of causing her any real discomfort.

"I never let the facts get in the way of a good story," he replied with an exaggerated wink. Grinning, he turned back to Caleb. "Anyway, the first thing I see is this dragon chasing Morena around an oak. All I did was pull my sword and my fan and step in front of it. Then it was just a matter of finding an opening. It's as simple as that, really."

He offered an apologetic shrug.

"Your *fan*?" Confusion was written plainly on Caleb's face as he tried to imagine how a flimsy bit of bamboo and silk could be used against a dragon.

"I'll have to show you later," Samir allowed.

Taking up his razor, the Majaran went back to his careful scraping. The mirror revealed a good deal of rapidly drying blood on his cheek.

"Okay." Caleb clearly refused to be put off. "If you won't tell me what happened, I guess you'll just have to teach me how to do it."

The other man's direct look as he stepped around in front of Samir said he wasn't about to be put off. But he had no particular reservations about teaching Caleb. The young Acedian would never be the most skilled warrior, being built more for strength than speed. Anyone could stand improvement, however, and he was certainly enthusiastic.

"Not a problem," Samir replied, waving vaguely between the two of them with his razor. "As long as you two don't mind sharing a class."

Caleb cocked an eyebrow at Morena, demonstrating his good humor. "Not as long as she doesn't make me look bad," he answered. "I would hate to have her clapped in irons, after all."

"As His Highness commands," Morena replied with a jaunty little bow.

Samir laughed.

"You see that, Samir?" Caleb threw up his hands in surrender. "I can't win now. She'll just claim I ordered her to do badly."

"I never said I would *do* badly." She met Caleb's joke with a challenging stare. "I merely said I wouldn't make you do badly. The only one who can do that is *you*."

"I concede the lady's superior wisdom."

"About time."

The good mood continued as they quickly stowed their gear and saddled their horses. He had finished shaving just as Alban's men were stowing the privy curtains in the supply wagon, so it appeared he would indeed be eating as he rode.

He didn't mind. It was obvious he was having an easier time of things than Kordel, who looked completely unprepared. The man's awful horse-handling skills were only made worse by his obvious exhaustion. As Samir watched, the Wizard's apprentice managed to fumble his saddle and spook his mount. Eventually, however, one of the soldiers retrieved the horse and helped saddle it.

Finally, they were once again raising clouds of dust along the hardpacked road. Alban had estimated another two days to Elhanan, but even this close Samir could tell Caleb was growing anxious. It took no real effort to guess that the cause was the possibility of seeing Sorana again. But try as they might, he and Morena could find no way to distract the man for more than a few minutes at a stretch. Desperate for something to hold Caleb's attention, Samir handed his sword to his friend.

"Hold this for a minute, will you?" he said hastily. "And stay there. I need to try something."

"What? *Hey!*" Caleb had to turn in his saddle to holler as the Majaran dropped his gelding back about a dozen yards. "What are you doing?"

Caleb was twisted around awkwardly, trusting Searcher to keep to the road on its own. The man's expression announced that an explanation had best be forthcoming. Morena's wasn't much different.

Jenaris had said the blade should come to him over a space of several yards even now, but he could make nothing happen at that distance. Vaguely aware of his friends watching, he edged his horse forward slowly. Still nothing.

Will. The Mage had said it depended on will.

Samir focused, demanding that the sword come, and he felt...something. Ten yards from the sword he could feel the bond, feel the weapon *almost* come. He nudged the horse, moving closer. Eight yards.

Come, he practically shouted in his mind.

It came.

With a whoop he rode back to his friends, laughing at the stark amazement on their faces as they stared back at him. *Very* satisfying.

"What in the *hell* just happened?" Caleb asked, shocked, as Samir pulled even with them. "How did you do that?"

"Forget *that*," Morena chimed in on top of him. "When do we get to that lesson in our training?"

Samir barked a laugh that brought a bark from Tirza. "You don't," he replied, his grin causing his jaws to ache. "But if it would make my students more enthusiastic, maybe I should let them think it's an advanced technique."

"Well, if it wasn't *you*, what was it?" Morena demanded.

He was enjoying their reactions as confusion played across their features. But he knew he had drawn out the suspense long enough. With a flourish, he slid the sword back into its sheath, then recalled it to his outstretched hand. He was rewarded by openmouthed stares.

"It's not me. It's the blade," he said quietly, speaking for their ears alone. "I don't know how Jenaris did it, but I needed to see how far away I could make it work."

"Will it do that for anyone?" Caleb asked, lowering his voice. His blue-grey eyes held interest rather than desire.

Samir shook his head. "No," he answered. "At least for the moment. But who knows? By next week, it might even work for Tirza."

"When did you find this out?" Morena's voice fairly dripped with the excitement shining in her eyes.

Samir managed to suppress a chuckle. "Don't worry. I wasn't holding out on you. Jenaris just showed me the trick this morning."

Morena nodded. "So *that's* what he was talking to you about. I saw you when I went to get breakfast, and somehow I didn't think he'd welcome my company."

Samir had to agree. The Mage had been in an...interesting mood this morning. But his mind was on other things at the moment.

"What I'm wondering," he said frankly, "is what the Wizard will do with it next. He's still working on it."

For a moment, he wondered if he should ask the Mage what he had planned for the blade. But perhaps the bigger question was whether Jenaris would even tell him.

The others were silent for a time as the implications sank in. If this was the *easiest*, what might come later?

"I don't know, buddy," Caleb admitted. "I'm just glad he's on our side."

Securing the sword, Samir pulled the wooden ball from the top of his saddlebags and whistled for Tirza. Letting the conversation move on to other subjects, the three took turns sending the hound to retrieve it. Still, none of them could avoid considering the possibilities or an occasional glance at the warrior's sword.

Chapter 17

Comings and Goings

The final day's ride into Elhanan stretched interminably as they passed landmarks that for Caleb, meant he was that much closer to Sorana. He appreciated the efforts of his friends to keep him distracted—and there was no doubt that was what Morena and Samir were trying to do—but it was no use. His stomach was still tying itself in knots with every step as he thought about her. Of course, he fully intended to honor his promises to his father, but while he wouldn't shirk his duty by seeking her out, he did hope to see her.

Somewhere ahead, he knew, lay his very heart.

"Caleb," Samir called once again to get his attention. "How do barbarians kill their game?"

He shook his head. If this joke wasn't any better than the Majaran's other attempts, he almost dreaded the answer. Still, he couldn't just ignore them.

"I don't know," he replied. "How?"

"They get close enough for the animal to smell them."

Caleb offered a polite laugh. It was really more than the joke deserved, but he gave Samir a grin for his troubles.

"Did you hear about the smart barbarian?" Morena cut in.

"No," Caleb answered.

"Neither did I."

Caleb gave her a halfhearted smile, barely holding back a groan. Under normal circumstances the jokes would have brought a laugh, even as bad as they were. Not that he couldn't appreciate their attempts to draw him out—particularly Morena, who he knew disliked barbarian jokes. But now everything seemed to fall flat as they crossed the last few miles and his thoughts dwelled only on one thing.

Just ahead, somewhere, was the woman he was meant to marry.

The problem was that there were just too many well-meaning people around him at the moment, trying to offer help that merely annoyed him. He'd already tried drawing away a bit, riding alone, and it had worked for a time. Yet they inevitably rode over to check on him—although they had claimed a desire for his company. Right now he only wanted to be alone, but he was sure that wasn't about to happen. Silence was a refuge he wouldn't be allowed.

It came as a relief to finally ride into Elhanan. At last, he had an outlet for the nervous energy he'd had to hold inside during the long, tortuous journey. Caleb's eyes darted in every direction as they passed through the streets, careful to catch all the faces in view. Maybe it was a long shot, but he refused to miss any chance to find Sorana, no matter how slim. He missed no one of any description, desperately searching even those who were unmistakably old, male and fat. Yet, despite all of his efforts, she was nowhere to be seen.

Passing in front of the fort, Lieutenant Gillis peeled off with the pack train and all but a small honor guard. The rest continued, riding toward the broad stone bridge to Gotarra. He'd passed close to the weathered boundary many times, but had never crossed it. Always before he had turned down the path through the trees that would take him to the bench where he'd passed so many hours with Sorana. From habit, Searcher tried to follow the familiar path. He wished he could follow it himself, wanted it with every fiber of his being. But, summoning what self-discipline he could, he kept the gelding in line and stayed with the others.

It was only a short journey along the hard packed road once they crossed out of Acedia and into the lands of the barbarians. The trees and the terrain were the same, of course, being separated by only a smallish river, but somehow it was different. It seemed more...tended, with drainage ditches carefully cleared and maintained.

Rounding the hill, he caught his first glimpse of the town where his father had sent him months earlier. A town he had never quite reached—until now.

The sight took a moment to register as the riders emerged from the shadow of the trees. Dozens of homes—ranging from cozy little cottages to large dwellings—spread across the terraced ground of the opposite hillside. Almost all sported slate roofs and finely cut gingerbread trim to accent the well-fitted stone facades. Color was splashed everywhere, from the painted trim of the buildings to the flowers lining the paths and walkways. The quiet little setting was an enormous contrast to the bustling city of Varella.

At the center of Scara lay a broad, flat green. There men and women clad in good wool strolled quietly or sat talking on benches beneath an ivy covered pergola. Nearby, smoke rose from the glowing coals beneath one of three large spits, bearing what appeared to be a nearly finished roast pig.

Yet, the focus of the village was clearly the large building just beyond the green. The weathered wooden structure was small compared to his family's castle, but it would have held a sizable portion of the local population.

The entrance to the village was marked by a shallow stream of sparkling clear water that wound out of sight around the hill. As the horses splashed through, Caleb felt a strong temptation to pause and wash off the dust of the road. After all, he would soon be meeting Gerrit, and he wanted his first impression to be a good one. But they had undoubtedly been spotted already, which meant the delay would be noted as well—and perhaps make them look less than confident.

The road led directly to the center of Scara, allowing him to appreciate the actual size of the hall as they approached. Somehow he had missed the clues from the distance, yet he saw them now. The trees outside were clearly older by far than he had thought, and the rocks decorating the space were actually smallish boulders. Now that he could get a sense of the scale, the building was obviously larger than he'd guessed—perhaps as much as forty feet tall and half again as wide.

In front stood a stone catch basin, into which poured a bubbling spring. This was, he decided, the source of the earlier stream given the water that flowed out over a series of steps and down the hill. Overall, he was forced to admit that it was lovely. It was a shame, in a way, considering it was wasted on a race of simpletons who probably couldn't appreciate it.

The ornately carved oak doors were huge, yet they swung easily on their hinges as the group entered the hall. Enormous tables and long benches were pushed back along the walls, allowing a wide aisle the length of the smooth wooden floor. But it was the cavernous space that drew his eye. The roof beam appeared to be a single, massive trunk that had been cut and carved; and the braces holding its weight would have been from sizable trees themselves.

It was, in a word, impressive.

Heads turned as those at the tables suspended games or conversations to look at the newcomers. Caleb found it difficult not to feel self-conscious. Even though only a few dozen watchers lined the way, every one seemed to be focused on them—including the two large men waiting at the far end of the room.

It was clear that word of their arrival had indeed preceded them, since the chair—which was evidently a throne—held a figure that could only be King Gerrit. Plainly dressed in leather pants and a shirt of finely spun wool, he looked much like the others in the room—though his wild mane of dark hair was pressed down by a thin circlet of gold. A heavy torque at his neck was his only other adornment. But while all of this announced his identity, it was the eyes that marked him as a man to be reckoned with.

They had agreed to let the Wizard speak for them, leaving Caleb free for the moment to study the massive man beside Gerrit. It was impossible *not* to notice him, and not due to his size alone. Unlike every other Gotarran they'd seen, his salt and pepper hair was cropped short, and he wore a goatee instead of a full beard. What grabbed his attention, however, was the thick band of scar tissue covering the left side of his jaw to where his left ear should have been. It somehow made his smile of genuine welcome appear more than slightly sinister.

"Jenaris!" The barbarian King was obviously familiar with the Mage and rose to wrap him in a warm embrace. "Good to see you again. And none too soon I tell you."

"It's been a while, Gerrit." Jenaris met the man's gaze with a look of sadness as he stepped back a pace. "I wish we were here for the pleasure of your company, my friend. Unfortunately, we need to deal with some trouble. You've had some here, I take it?"

Gerrit snorted loudly, a sound like ripping cloth. "You take it rightly. And trouble isn't the half of it. Every attempt to find what's at the root of it results in missing hunters and scouts," he said through gritted teeth. " A lot of good people have just vanished, and I'm no closer to the truth of it."

The Mage wore a look of sympathy in response to the other man's obvious frustration. While not a surprise by any means, the news was still unwelcome. The cost in lives, it seemed, was going to be felt everywhere.

"It's not only happening here," Jenaris informed him with a ragged sigh. "But at least we know what we're up against, and we have some idea how to deal with it."

Gerrit's sharp brown eyes went hard as flint in an instant. "And what is it? What's been killing my people, Jenaris?"

Neither of the barbarians so much as breathed as they waited for an answer to the question. In fact, their attention was so focused on the Wizard that Caleb suspected a halfway competent thief could easily have walked away with the clothes off their backs.

"Dragons," Jenaris answered into the heavy silence.

"Now isn't the time for jokes, Mage," the scarred man replied gruffly, a look of reproach written plainly on his features.

The old Wizard returned the stare evenly, clearly unmoved. "It wasn't a joke."

"How could we not know that a dragon was in the area?" The large man's words left no doubt of his opinion of the matter. "This *hall* could barely hold one...*if* they even exist."

"Kulmar," the King barked, eyes locked on the man beside him. "I know you still haven't mastered wiping your feet, but I expect better manners. These people are guests in our hall. *My* guests."

The massive barbarian merely nodded.

Apparently it was enough for Jenaris, who shrugged as if to say it was unimportant. He directed a penetrating look toward the King.

"First of all, Gerrit, I didn't say *a* dragon," the Mage corrected in a tone that spoke of great patience. "I said *dragons*. Secondly, this hall could hold a great many."

Jenaris accepted a large wrapped bundle from his apprentice, releasing the barbarian's gaze. Slowly, he peeled back the corners, revealing a sharp fang the length of a large man's open hand from fingertip to wrist. Beside it lay the long tail spike of the drake Samir had killed only a few days travel from where they now stood.

The King's eyes shone as he stared fixedly at the items, his face creasing in a smile. He leaned toward the Wizard as if eager to go fight the creatures. From the way the man's hand kneaded his knife hilt, he wanted to do so immediately.

"All right," he said, finally tearing his eyes away from the prizes Jenaris held. "They can be killed. What do we need to do?"

The Mage shook his head sadly. "Right now we need to find several ingredients to counter their venom, including Blackthorn root. Then, if you'll meet us in Varella, we'll need to work out a plan."

The barbarian voiced a loud grunt. "The Blackthorn should be easy enough. But as to the other.... You tell me *dragons* are tearing up my countryside and ask me to leave?" He shook his head, dark locks flying. "You can't honestly expect me to go anywhere *now*."

Jenaris stepped forward, laying a hand on the King's arm. It was obvious the Mage was sympathetic to the man's position, but that made no difference.

"I'm sorry, Gerrit," the Wizard said softly. "I understand your desire to be here, but frankly it's a recipe for disaster. It will take all of us working together to make this work. The beasts are a *plague*, and we can't afford to fail."

The King stood quietly for a time, contemplating. It was clear he didn't like the idea at all, and yet the thought of taking losses through inaction must have been equally distasteful. Finally and reluctantly, he nodded.

"So be it," he said at last. "I'll get you someone to help find the plant. Then I'll make arrangements to go."

Jenaris waved away Gerrit's concern. "Morena is an herbalist," he indicated with a nod, "and an excellent one. I believe you knew her father, Marius."

"I did," the barbarian replied, quickly covering the few paces to stand in front of Morena. With incredible gentleness, he bent to kiss her forehead. "You have my sympathy, and that of my people. As honorable a man as I ever met...in war *or* peace. My own stonecutters carved his stone."

Morena whispered something in reply that Caleb assumed was thanks, a sad smile on her face. At the sight of tears welling in her eyes, he started to step toward her. Samir was there ahead of him, sliding a comforting arm around her shoulders which she accepted gratefully, leaning into him.

Pretending to cough, Caleb hid his smirk behind his hand.

The rest of the meeting involved little more than formalities. Caleb had sat in too many times as his father held court or received diplomats, so he was already familiar with the tedium involved. Timing had to be worked out, and travel plans made. But even so, a few hours remained of the day before it would be necessary to make camp and it was a simple matter to fetch the soldiers and move north.

It was Morena who guided them from that point, after a quick discussion with Kulmar in hushed tones. Although she had never been to Gotarra—only Jenaris and two of the sergeants had—she was still the only one who could find what they sought.

At first, it struck Caleb as strange, if not somewhat reckless, that they dispatched no scouts as they moved deeper into an area where dragons had made their presence known. Yet, after paying close attention to the surrounding terrain and the thickness of the cover through which they travelled, he realized a lone scout would be little more than an easy target for any dragon that might be close. Better to rely on numbers should an issue arise—and on Samir.

Then there was the fact that they were foreigners here. Acedian soldiers seen riding by themselves in Gotarra might not be given the chance to explain that they were actually guests rather than invaders. At least in a group, anyone hostile to their presence would likely decide to talk first.

But once they had gone a few miles from Scara, the roads seemed completely deserted. Certainly there were plenty of places in Acedia, or any other land, where travelers could ride without expecting to see another soul. Except that shouldn't be possible this close to the capitol. A few thin plumes of smoke in the distance showed the location of chimneys or campfires, though the place felt eerily empty as they passed through forests with only birds and the occasional fox for company.

"Where exactly *are* we going?" Caleb asked her as he pulled Searcher up beside her mare at the front of the group. He'd been tempted to ask more than once, but his curiosity had taken time to make him give in.

"The tall hill in front of us," she replied casually, not bothering to look in his direction as she watched the road ahead. "I guess it's more of a small mountain, really. But that's where we're headed."

Looking up, Caleb could see nothing but a solid canopy of leaves. "How can you tell it's still in front of us?" He allowed a hint of sarcasm to color his tone. "All

I've seen for days is a wall of trees and an occasional glimpse of sky. Are you sure you haven't turned us around?"

Morena took a halfhearted swipe at him. He avoided it easily enough, his horse dancing sideways with a mincing step.

"I guess I'm just smarter than you," she teased.

He shrugged. "It's possible. Then again, how do I know your horse isn't actually the one in charge?"

She pointed ahead through a brief gap in the trees. The hill ahead was tall and steep, but not a difficult climb even for the horses. What distinguished it from others they'd seen was its peak. About halfway to its top, the trees became small, stunted, then faded to scrub. The upper third was nearly barren.

The few miles to the base of the gradually rising slope went quickly. But as the grade and the altitude became steadily greater, the mounts labored to climb with riders in the saddle, their breath coming in deep gasps. As the trees began to thin, riders dismounted, leading the horses the rest of the way.

Caleb would have preferred to keep riding, but he realized they would have needed to walk eventually. The footing was rapidly growing treacherous as rocks rose through the thin topsoil—obviously the reason for the lack of vegetation. With fissures and holes that could easily break a horse's leg, it was the kind of place only a mountain goat could ever find appealing.

They stopped well short of the peak where barely enough grass existed to allow the mounts to graze. If they were going to stay, they would need to break out some of their supply of oats and use feedbags.

Breathing heavily, Caleb and the others quickly found perches on the rocks, sitting wearily. Expectant looks began to settle on Morena.

"So," Samir said, sides heaving as he stepped up beside her. "Which one is it?"

About a dozen varieties of hardy looking plant life could be seen scattered around the slope. Eyes darted repeatedly from the ground to Morena, as if searching for some clue to which one was the Blackthorn they'd come for.

"Over there," she pointed to a large rock outcropping that jutted over its surroundings.

At first, it appeared to be nothing but more of the cracked stone that lay exposed everywhere. But as he stepped closer he finally found it, deep in the fissures between the rocks.

"You have *got* to be kidding." Caleb studied her face, looking for a hint that this was, in fact, a joke.

It clearly wasn't.

Sorana watched patiently as her father finished his second piece of pie and pushed back from the table. Predictably, he chose the chair beside the fire to enjoy his pipe after dinner. She smiled. Hopefully, it would continue to be this easy.

Her timing had been less than impressive lately. She had missed Caleb by only about half an hour as he'd passed through with the Wizard. They had heard news of the visitors immediately upon returning home, but it had been the next day before Kulmar had let Caleb's name drop in her hearing. By then, of course, it was far too late to do anything about finding him. Had she refused when Kaylan had practically dragged her off to pick blackberries, or simply returned sooner.... But it was silly to play "what if." That chance was gone.

Thankfully it hadn't taken long for another opportunity to present itself—her father's impending trip to Acedia. The moment she'd heard the news, Sorana had begun to plan and, knowing her father as she did, it was almost guaranteed to work. After all, she had her mother on her side.

They had already fed him his favorite supper of lamb shanks and, now that he was pleasantly stuffed with blackberry pie, all was ready. King or not, Gerrit was pliable enough if you knew what to do. She only wished tricking him weren't necessary to do what she knew she must.

As she finished clearing the table, her mother waited with a steaming cup of tea. Sorana took it carefully, carrying it to the small table beside her father's padded chair.

"Here, Papa." She kissed his cheek as she sat down on the chair arm.

"Thank you, Sweetling," Gerrit replied absently, patting his full belly. "That's a nice little send off the two of you cooked up. Couldn't ask for better."

"You're welcome."

Both were quiet for several minutes. She merely sat, watching the flames and waiting for him to finish his pipe. Finally, the last wisp of smoke rose from the bowl as he laid it aside with a drowsy kind of satisfaction.

"Papa," she said sweetly. "Will you promise me something? Please?"

"Of course." He patted her knee, smiling up at her. "Anything you need, Rana. You know that."

It was the answer she had known would come. The answer he always gave when she asked for something. Why wouldn't he say yes? After all, he trusted her. Well, that trust was about to be damaged, perhaps irreparably, but as much as it pained her it was still worth it. At least, she hoped so.

She took a deep breath, steeling herself.

"I need to go with you to Varella," she said in a rush.

Her father slowly shifted in his chair, moving so he could see her more fully. The look on his face was one she hadn't seen since she and Huldrich had accidentally set the outhouse on fire. It *still* unnerved her.

Sorana broadened her smile, just as she had then.

"You can put *that* idea right out of your head," he announced sternly. His eyes narrowed. "And you can forget thinking that smile will get you anywhere."

Sorana almost apologized. She knew she should, knew he deserved it. But she couldn't. This was just too important. Slowly she let the smile fade.

"You *promised*," she said, as if that settled it. Of course, she didn't for a second believe that.

"Oh, no," he quirked an eyebrow as he met her gaze. "That promise was based on the assumption that you wanted something reasonable. I'll not be bound by a promise obtained through fraud."

Sorana wasn't about to argue that point. He was right. But he *had* left her one opening. Standing, she moved around in front of the chair, arms folded in imitation of a stance that had worked for her mother many times. Her slippered foot tapped lightly on the thick woven rug.

"And why is it so unreasonable?" she demanded.

"It's dangerous." His laughing tone made it plain he thought it the most obvious thing in the world.

"Yes, it is," she replied, being very careful of her tone in the face of his growing irritation. "But you know it's already dangerous *everywhere*. Here, too. That's why *you're* going."

Anger flared briefly in his eyes. She couldn't recall having *ever* talked back to her father, and evidently neither could he. But he had always been willing to listen and that's what she was counting on now.

"Why?" he asked flatly.

Sorana breathed easier, if only for a moment. This wasn't over yet.

"I can't tell you," she offered reluctantly, still meeting his eyes, "But it's important. You'll just have to trust me."

He shook his head sadly. "You know, Sweetling, that would have been much easier to do five minutes ago. But trust requires honesty, and if you can't tell me why, then I can't tell you yes."

It seemed they had reached an impasse. She wished she could tell him *why* she needed to go, but had no idea what to say. That she had to see the man she would marry? Hardly a certainly. That she needed to know where she stood with Caleb? Even to her ears that was too weak to argue. But it was true, all that and more, and she *had* to go.

The only problem was that she'd made a mess of this already. But there was still a chance.

"*Mother,*" she pleaded.

"Sorana," he said warningly. "I told you...."

"Gerrit," her mother broke in, "perhaps you should avoid saying something you'll regret later. If you won't trust her, you'll just have to trust *me*. Our daughter is going with you.

"And Sorana, dear," her mother turned a look of sympathy toward her, "before you see your young man again, you need to learn a thing or two. Honesty works best. Relationships can survive anger, but not a lack of trust." She looked suddenly stern. "Now apologize to your father, and let me handle this."

"Sorry, Papa," Sorana said quietly.

But her father paid her no heed, focusing all his attention on her mother. He stared at his wife as if seeing some strange new animal.

"You *want* her to go, Khara?" Then, becoming aware of something else that had been said, he added, "And what's this about a young man?"

Khara joined Sorana in front of the chair, arms folded beneath her breasts in a proper demonstration of the stance Sorana had merely *attempted*. Her mother stared down from beneath raised brows, foot keeping up a steady rhythm. It was very effective.

"Want has nothing to do with it, Gerrit. She *is* going." Her mother's voice indicated she would brook no argument on the matter. "And, as for the other, we'll discuss it later."

Her father grunted in what might almost have been a laugh. He smiled at his wife, eyes shining with what looked like pride.

"All right," he said, "she goes. But she'll damn well do as she's told."

"Of course," Sorana agreed hurriedly, bending to kiss his cheek. "Thank you, Papa. Thank you, Mama."

Quickly, she kissed her mother as well before bounding from the room. She had to pack her things. They were going to see Caleb.

Chapter 18

Breaks in the Stone

To call the plant completely unimpressive would have been a massive understatement as far as Samir was concerned. The brittle stems rose perhaps six inches, never quite clearing the upper edges of the crack in which it grew. From what he could see, the only possible explanation for the plant's name was found in the small dark burrs on some of the stems. In fact, it was so sickly looking he thought it might die if he stared at it too long...perhaps from shame.

Stepping closer, he pulled a knife from behind his sash, using it to probe at the base of the plant. He expected to find hard soil. Instead, the blade scraped on solid rock, making him flinch as he thought of damage to the well-honed edge. Curious, he carefully took hold of the stems and pulled. The plant popped free, rising easily from the fissure.

Samir stared at the pitiful thing in his hand. It had no root to speak of, only a kind of junction where the stems met which trailed several broken filaments. The Blackthorn *root*, it appeared, did not even exist.

"Something wrong?" Morena's voice fairly chimed with unreleased laughter. If his expression was anything like Alban's, she had ample reason to laugh.

"As a matter of fact," he turned to face her, holding the plant up for her inspection. "Where's the *root*? Isn't that what we're here for?"

"That's right," she told him, flashing a somewhat playful smile. "And you won't get the job done by standing there asking questions. Or don't you think I know what I'm doing?"

He shook his head, making a show of dropping the plant. "I never said that. I just thought it would be nice if you told the rest of us the secret."

Morena's eyebrows rose dramatically. "What's gotten into *you* all of a sudden?" she asked, surprised and plainly a bit hurt.

Samir stopped himself from returning another snide remark. To be honest, he had no idea why he'd been so prickly with her when she had done nothing but try to be nice. Yet, for some reason, he'd felt the need to put distance between them lately, which made no sense. She was a good friend, the best he'd had since Gehazi.

Understanding hit him like a kick to the head, and it shamed him. Yet, at the same time, he felt the tension between his shoulders loosen. A tension he hadn't even really been aware of.

"I'm sorry. I've been an ass," he admitted, redness rising in his cheeks as he forced himself to meet her eyes.

"Yes, you have," she agreed without hesitation. "Want to tell me what's bothering you?"

She studied his face for a moment, concerned. Plainly she was ready to listen, but he wasn't ready to talk about it just yet.

"Later," his tone made it a promise. "I think they're all waiting for you."

From the looks directed her way, everyone was indeed waiting for Morena to offer some explanation.

They could easily see the Blackthorn Samir had dropped and knew there must be more to it.

She pointed to the crack from which he had pulled the plant. "Captain, we'll need some men with shovels or picks to pull these rocks loose."

At his answering nod, Sergeant Roland began directing soldiers as they broke out tools from one of the pack animals. They made quick work of it as sledges pounded at the surface and picks levered open the rapidly widening crack. In no time at all, a large chunk rolled free with a heavy thunk.

Brushing past the men, she knelt at the place where the rock had broken loose, gently lifting a delicate strand of fibrous root with a single swollen node.

"This is Blackthorn root." She held up the thick knot for everyone to examine. "There should be at least one more of these under that other rock. We'll need *a lot* of them."

"You heard her," one of the senior men called out in an earsplitting bellow. "First squad grab some tools. The rest of you, start looking and flag every plant you find." The man swept the soldiers with a hard look. *"Move!"*

As the men began the work, the hilltop became a noisy, shouting, clanging mass of chaos. Before long, white kerchiefs fluttered across the rocky ground, marking the position of Blackthorn to be harvested. Soon all that was left to do was watch the demolition as Jenaris stood collecting the tiny roots one or two at a time.

Feeling less than useful, Samir soon decided to escape the awful noise of picks and hammers. Privacy was easy to find. He merely wandered down into the treeline below and, spotting an outcropping of rock, he took a seat.

Gehazi. It had been weeks since he'd even thought of the man, yet the wound was still too fresh. At the memory of his treachery, anger rose swiftly to the surface—a short journey from where it had lain buried only shallowly. He had thought it had been dealt with long since, but if it caused him to distrust his new friends, his inability to repay the man was obviously still eating at him.

"Share your thoughts?" a soft voice drifted from behind him.

"I suppose this qualifies as later," Samir replied as Morena dusted off the stone and sat beside him.

She offered him a tentative smile, sitting quietly, watching him. He considered for a moment, quickly choosing a place to begin the tale.

"Gehazi was my best friend from when we were children," he told her. "I was closer to him than I was to my own brothers. Of course, considering what happened, neither he nor my oldest brother was worth trusting."

As Morena listened, he spun out the story of his betrayal, explaining how Kemal had leveraged Gehazi's help and how his friend had chosen Jhen's life over his father's. She didn't interrupt, letting him unburden himself as he stared off into the distance—south, toward Majar.

"I guess a part of me was afraid to let you get too close," he said apologetically, still not looking at the young woman beside him. "I mean, if my oldest friend could do that to me, then how could I trust my new ones? It wasn't fair to you or to Caleb, and it won't happen again."

"Samir, I'm so sorry," Morena fairly whispered, pain coming through clearly.

Hearing the quiver in her voice, he turned. Tears dripped slowly, rolling down her cheeks as she stared at him in sympathy. Reaching out with a finger, he carefully wiped away a teardrop from the corner of her eye.

"I'm all right," he assured her. "Or at least I *will* be. It's just...it feels like I let him escape justice. I suppose I had to let him at least *try* to free Jhen. She was a friend, and I couldn't just leave her in danger. But Gehazi had no right to choose her over my father."

His feelings were jumbled. *Worse* than jumbled. A warrior like himself, or his father, should have been allowed to stand or fall by his own skill. Yet *any* Majaran warrior would have risked his life to keep Jhen safe. He despised the entire situation. It made him physically ill. Gehazi had made a mess of everything.

Gently, Morena took his hand. "I'm not condoning what he did, but I think you're missing something very important." She met his gaze intently, green eyes still sparkling with tears. "I don't think he chose his sister. Or at least not *just* her. Samir, I think Gehazi chose Jhen *and* you."

"What are you talking about?" He felt irritation rising and forced it back down as he gave her a long, level look.

Morena paused, but was obviously unfazed by his scrutiny. She met his gaze with tenderness.

"I'm saying," she replied, "that as much as he loved his sister, *and* your father, he loved you, too. From what you told me, I think he may have traded everything to save you if he had to."

He stiffened, jaw clenching. Samir quickly stomped on his temper before speaking. He would not allow himself to snap at her for trying to help...for caring.

"I never *asked* him to save me. He should have allowed me to fight my own battles," he told her, heat still seeping through in his tone, along with disgust. "But it doesn't matter anyway. If nothing else, he's guilty of robbing me of a chance to at least try to save my father."

Morena gave his hand a light squeeze.

"Don't you see what this will do to you?" she fairly pleaded, nearly a whisper. "Bitterness will poison you if you don't let it go. You have to forgive him, Samir."

His eyes flashed dangerously. "I don't *have* to do any such thing. I can never forgive what he did."

Samir seethed inwardly, resenting the idea of letting the traitor go unpunished, and angry at himself for resenting her advice.

"This isn't about him. It's about you," she said into the silence. "The grudge you're carrying around, it isn't hurting Gehazi at all, but it *is* hurting you. Look, all I'm saying is just...think about it. Please?"

She was right, to a point at least. He'd known people who always seemed to be angry at something or someone, and they weren't people he wanted to be around. Now his frustration was turning him into one of those people. The problem was, he didn't know what to do about it since he couldn't stand the thought of leaving this unpunished. Yet the very idea of casting himself as a victim was completely foreign to the warrior's heart within him.

Grudgingly he admitted to himself that maybe, someday, he would be able to forgive Gehazi. But now was not that time.

The silence stretched for minutes as they sat looking out over the treetops several hundred feet below. Gradually, he felt the turmoil in his soul begin to subside and peace return.

"Morena," he finally said, giving her hand a squeeze.

"Hmm?"

"Thanks." He offered a grateful smile.

Samir did feel better for having finally spoken to someone about what had happened. It was good to know he had friends he could trust.

On impulse, he leaned in to kiss her cheek. Instead, he was surprised to meet her soft, yielding lips. A thrill ran through him as he pressed harder, hand coming up to caress her smooth cheek and tangle in her long curls. She returned the kiss hungrily, no longer merely yielding.

After an eternity they pulled back, both breathing hard.

"I'm sorry," he gasped. "I had no right."

Rising quickly, he climbed, scrambling back toward the open air of the crowded hilltop with all the speed he could muster.

"Samir, wait," she called after him. "Samir!"

He barely heard her, never slowing. The Majaran stopped only after he was well clear of the stunted trees and through the scrub.

He didn't know what to think, and his mind was too busy replaying that amazing kiss to consider anything else. Finding the nearest soldier, he took the man's sledge and started swinging. With all the strength he possessed, he threw himself into the task, reducing the stone to rubble and sending chips flying. The hammer continued its steady rise and fall, the warrior completely unaware that those around him had stopped to stare in amazement at the power of his blows.

Morena sat, staring up the hill at the place where Samir had disappeared. Try as she might to understand what had just happened, shock and disbelief made it all but impossible to even think.

Samir had enjoyed it, too. She knew he had. So why was he acting like they'd done something wrong? Or as if it was wrong to kiss *her*?

But her mind refused to work properly right now. It was like the world had been completely spun about and she couldn't quite get her bearings. She had kissed a boy a few times—a stablehand, just to see what it was like. But this had been *nothing* like that. Those kisses had sort of made her tingle, but had been no big deal. But *this*, her first *real* kiss, had been amazing. It was everything she had known it would be.

She had thought more than once about kissing Samir, about what it would be like. Had dreamed about it, in fact, after he had saved her from the dragon. And *he* certainly hadn't hesitated.

Somehow, though, after that wonderful start, it had all gone wrong. Only she had no idea how or why.

But it *had* to have meant something to him. No one could kiss like that and not *mean* it. Could they? So why did she feel like she'd somehow been rejected?

It would be understandable if he had somehow gone beyond what was proper, but it had been innocent enough. The man would sooner cut off his arm than dishonor her. Of that she was certain. So why had he reacted so strangely?

Hastily wiping her face, she took a minute to straighten her hair before walking up the hill. The long climb gave her plenty of time to regain her composure, but his abrupt and wordless departure had stung. Surely he knew that if anything was wrong, he could talk to her about it. After all, he had just been so open a few minutes before.

Mother told me that men are beyond understanding, she thought, *but this is ridiculous!*

It took only a glance around the hilltop to spot Samir, working with the soldiers to pry the rocks apart. They would need to talk, but it would have to wait until they had some privacy. In the meantime, there were other things to occupy her attention.

Jenaris had gathered a good collection of Blackthorn root by the time she found him on the far slope. They had already exceeded the fifty she had set as the minimum needed, yet there was enough of the day left to find more. If Alban sent men ahead to make camp, the rest would need only enough light to get down the hill safely with their horses.

But they didn't stay much longer. With a total of sixty-three, the group made their way cautiously down the hill to a small clearing on the relatively flat ground below. Having plenty of practice, the soldiers readied the camp with astonishing speed and efficiency. Although she had witnessed it many times over, it was no less surprising.

Morena, however, could only sit and wait for her class with Samir. Eating a light supper of roasted potatoes and smoked ham, she watched as the students practiced katas, then practiced attack and defense in pairs. To her eyes at least, the soldiers' skills had improved greatly in only a few short weeks. She and Caleb, on the other hand, were barely beyond the most basic strikes and blocks—having yet to string a pair together. Still, she'd been paying close attention to Samir's lessons since they'd begun, and she felt she had a good grasp of what was ahead in her own training.

With the last group of soldiers finally dismissed to other duties, Morena immediately hurried to talk to Samir. Unfortunately, he saw her coming.

"Wade," he called after one of the guardsmen, who hustled back without hesitation.

"Yes, Teacher?" The man bowed, something they had all adopted when addressing Samir.

At least he hadn't said, "Sòra." Several had tried that, after hearing Samir speak of his own teacher, and had been given a "special workout." As he had told them rather forcefully, Sòra was a title he had not yet earned.

"I want you to concentrate on keeping your back straight, weight centered," Samir directed, demonstrating with a backfist strike. "Don't lean forward and overbalance or you'll be easy meat for anyone who thinks to grab your hand and pull."

"Thank you, Teacher," Wade bowed again before hustling off.

Sadly, Samir's ploy had effectively stopped any attempt to talk, since by then Caleb had arrived. At least it was a challenging session, being their first time working on the long form the soldiers had learned several weeks earlier.

Although Morena had thought she already knew it well enough to get most of it on the first try, she was surprised at how difficult it was in practice. While she could perform either the steps or the hand movements, somehow coordinating them took until the tenth attempt. Even then, it was dead slow. Still, the small victory earned her a comment of "Nice progress so far," which from Samir was high praise indeed.

She didn't even hear him step up behind her as she managed to complete the form for only the second time.

"Morena," he said quietly in her ear as she came to rest. Her heart leapt into her throat as excitement gripped her. "Work on your extension in The White Crane Spreads His Wings."

Then he was gone.

Stunned, she heard him walk toward Caleb and make a suggestion on Part the Wild Horse's Mane. That was *it*?!

No. He was *not* going to get away with this. He *would* talk to her. He would. The only question was whether he would do so voluntarily or if she would have to force the issue.

Morena had just resolved to tell him as much when the barbarians rode into camp.

Chapter 19

A Meeting by Moonlight

There were only three of them, Samir noted, riding with hands empty of all but their reins and offering no challenge. Instantly wary, he scanned the trees and saw the soldiers doing the same, making no overtly hostile moves but certainly not relaxing for a moment.

"Huldrich," Jenaris' voice cut through the tension as he hailed the man in the lead.

"We wondered who it was scrambling around that hill," the young man called in a pleasant baritone. "How are you, Wizard?"

The Mage reached the riders just as they dismounted, clasping the hand of the one who had spoken. At the obvious sign of familiarity, Samir relaxed. Jenaris clearly expected no problems from these men.

"Keeping strange company these days," Huldrich offered far too casually.

"A wizard's prerogative," the other replied.

The young barbarian smiled. "True," he admitted, gesturing to his two companions. "I don't think you know Suppan and Kessel."

The men he indicated were something of a mismatched pair. One was short and wide with a powerful build and a bushy moustache. The other was tall and lean, his blond beard surprisingly full for someone no older than Samir himself. Each not only carried a spear, but also wore the long knives—nearly a short sword—they had seen on men in Scara. Samir smiled. It might be interesting to take a look at their technique if there was time.

Late as it was, the barbarians were invited to share their camp for the night, and didn't hesitate to unsaddle their horses and grab a plate.

Samir said few words to the trio as they settled in. Most of his effort was spent keeping out of Morena's sight. The easy and obvious place would have been the privy, yet simple courtesy kept him from monopolizing it for his own convenience. Instead, he spent much of the evening moving from one campfire to the next.

It wasn't that he was afraid to talk to her. Not exactly, anyway. He knew he and Morena would eventually have to talk about what had happened. Right now, though, he wasn't sure what to say. He also didn't entirely trust himself to keep his resolve when he finally had to look into those green eyes that haunted his dreams. He'd needed to stand behind her just to speak earlier, and he knew that wouldn't work forever.

He had wanted that kiss. It had occupied his thoughts ever since that day in the wood when she had clung to him, but the reality had been more than he was prepared for.

It had taken every ounce of self-discipline to break it off and walk away when all he wanted to do was stay there with her. Not that there was any danger of it going any further, but he would have been happy just to stay there with her a while longer.

Samir wished it could be as simple as giving their friendship a chance to grow and seeing what developed.

But it wasn't a matter of want. It wasn't even about his need to reclaim his birthright. He was certain that, when the time came, he would collect the debt Kemal owed and avenge his father's death.

The problem was that, without knowing whether his mother still lived, he had to act on the assumption—the hope—that she survived. It was certainly possible that Kemal held her as a way to keep Hesed...pliable. Yet, as wonderful as that would be, it meant that she had the right to select his wife. It was a duty his mother took *very* seriously.

Kemal had many failings, and the worst was his unscrupulous use of charm and empty promises—talking women into giving what they could never get back. Samir couldn't do that. It would be offensive, immoral, to lead any woman on. *Especially* Morena.

No, as much as he wanted to find out if she could love him—and he her—he had to walk away. Maybe they could remain friends. He hoped so. But this would definitely make things awkward, and he wasn't at all sure he could stop what he was starting to feel for her. He just knew he didn't *want* it to stop, but he had to be fair to her.

His only choice was to master his emotions and his mind. It wouldn't be easy, but he would do it.

"...should still arrive a bit ahead of us," Jenaris said as Samir walked in from the horse lines.

"Then we should be able to ride along," Huldrich replied. "That is, if you don't mind the company."

"I would have thought you'd ride back home." The Wizard shot the young barbarian a look of mild surprise. "If your father hasn't left yet...."

Huldrich barked a rich laugh. "That's exactly why I'd rather go with you," he winked. "If I go home first, Father will put me in charge, and I'll get left behind. No, much better to ride with you."

Alban shook his head, a wry smile on his face. "That'll be fine, Hul. Be good to have some extra eyes the next few days." His brow furrowed suddenly, humor vanishing. "We'll be taking a road I don't much like. One known to have seen dragon activity."

"Three of them at once nearly overcame two dozen men," Caleb added. "But we didn't have Samir then."

Samir bowed casually at the introduction, then offered Huldrich his hand. The gesture still felt awkward, but he was slowly getting used to it.

"You're not Acedian," Huldrich's words were plainly meant as both statement and question. "One of the southern lands, then."

The man's reference to the "southern lands" probably meant Majar and Rukat. A number of other nations lay beyond the Sea of Sharks, some better viewed as tribal territory than country. Still, he gave the barbarian credit for at least coming close.

"Majaran," he answered the unspoken question. "A long way from here, in any case."

Samir glanced around, looking for an unoccupied patch of ground on which to sit. Gillis quickly shifted, making room on the log beside him. Yet, before he could accept the invitation, Tirza's bark announced the hound's rapid approach. Turning toward the sound, he saw Morena following hard on the dog's heels. Her eyes were fixed on him.

"Good girl, Tirza." Sinking to one knee, she enthusiastically scratched the hound's ears.

The hard stare she directed at him with those magnificent green eyes should have burned him to the ground where he stood. It was very nearly enough to make him give ground, something he hadn't done even in the face of Shimei's anger in some time.

Then again, he hadn't seen the Sòra this upset in a long, long while.

"Don't you *dare* disappear on me again, Samir." All trace of the pleasure she had shown with Tirza was gone now.

Snickers came from several of those seated around the fire behind him. He would rather the others hadn't been here to see this—would *much* rather have put this off—but it was too late now. As he felt heat rise in his cheeks, he was thankful to at least have his back to the firelight so his blush was hidden.

Stepping forward, he tried to speak—to say he was sorry, to say he loved her, to say *anything*. But nothing came when he opened his mouth.

How was this even *possible*? Combat he could handle. Samir knew he was very likely the best warrior in this part of the world. The idea of physical danger didn't even faze him. He had faced a dragon...for *her*. Yet, at the thought of hurting her, of causing Morena the least pain, he was somehow paralyzed.

"Just pretend she's a dragon, Samir," a voice behind him called—half encouragement, half taunting. Laughter erupted. He ignored it.

"Good one, Caleb," someone answered.

Samir glanced back just as all hell broke loose.

Caleb never even saw the blow coming as Huldrich, sitting beside him, swung with everything he had. But, even with the poor leverage of his position, it was still more than enough to knock the smaller man flat. The impact with the ground drove the air from the Acedian's lungs in an audible rush.

The two cavalry officers and the other two barbarians were on their feet in an instant. All clearly wanted to step in, but were fearful of leaving potential enemies at their backs.

It was all the time Huldrich needed.

"You bastard!" the barbarian screamed as he leapt on Caleb's chest, pinning his arms.

Samir was already moving but the fight, such as it was, was on the far side of the fire and the Acedian officers were in his way. He barely slowed as he pushed through, knocking Alban off balance as he went.

Huldrich rained down hammer blows on Caleb's face and head, the Acedian struggling to free an arm and defend himself. But all Caleb could do was move his head, trying to avoid the fists that pounded at him. It was *not* an effective method.

Focused on the fight in front of him, Samir was hardly aware of the hand reaching to grab his arm as he passed one of the Gotarrans. He paid it little attention, deflecting it easily as he threw a backfist into the man's nose. Cartilage cracked as the barbarian was rocked on his heels.

With a leap over Caleb's legs he was there, catching hold of Huldrich's hand as the man reared back for another blow. Samir quickly pressed the barbarian's elbow, straightening the arm behind his back as he twisted and locked the wrist. The man's entire body stiffened in response to sudden pain as the Majaran jerked, holding the hand and applying pressure with only two fingers. Seeking relief, Huldrich bent awkwardly at the waist and rose to his feet as the Majaran maintained the hold, guiding him.

Caleb didn't hesitate, slithering immediately out from under Huldrich as the man's weight came off his chest. Morena was at his side in moments to help, joined swiftly by Jenaris and Kordel. In the flickering light it was nearly impossible to get a sense of his injuries, but they had to be bad considering the pounding he'd endured.

From his one brief glimpse, however, Samir had only the impression of an eye nearly swollen shut. His jaw tightened as anger rose.

He paid no heed to the other two Gotarrans, trusting the others to be able to keep them out of the way. If not, he would deal with them...to the extreme detriment of their incapacitated friend, whose wrist would likely end up broken. At the moment, he was in no mood to be at all cautious.

"Maybe it's none of my business," Samir spoke quietly, voice hard as flint, "but don't you think Caleb has a right to know why you're fighting?"

Bent nearly double, Huldrich had to crane his neck in order to glare at the Majaran. He angrily shook his hair out of his face.

"He hurt my sister!" he screamed, spittle flying.

"I don't even *know* your sister." Caleb's answer came with difficulty, through lips almost certainly swollen and split.

Huldrich fought briefly to straighten, but thought better of it as the movement increased the pressure on his wrist. Doing his best to appear indifferent to the undignified position, he tilted his head back, directing his anger once again at the Acedian Prince.

"So now you deny what you did?!" he raged.

"Did to whom?" Caleb asked thickly. "Who's your sister?"

"*Sorana!* My sister, Sorana."

Huldrich tried to surge forward. More than ready for the move, Samir applied more force, causing the other man to collapse to his knees.

Caleb was silent and far too still following the answer.

"Kordel, go fetch my satchel. It's with my saddlebags," Morena ordered. "*Now!*"

The Mage's apprentice ran.

Caleb mumbled something, or tried to before turning his head to spit out a mouthful of blood. With obvious difficulty he tried again.

"Never," he finally managed. "I'd never hurt her. But she can't be your sister. She's not even Gotarran."

"Are you calling me a *liar?*" Huldrich shot back.

Apparently fitting the pieces together, Caleb shook his head. Stopping the movement abruptly, he put a hand to his temple.

"No," he said miserably. "But I would never hurt her. I love her."

His pleading tone was lost on the other man.

"Too bad," Huldrich's voice was cold and mocking. "You're never going to see her again. I'll make sure of it."

Samir heard a brief scuffle behind him as one of the other Gotarrans finally tried to push through and help his friend. Turning just enough to use his peripheral vision, he could see it was the shorter one, blood trickling from a broken nose. With a thought, Dragon's Fang appeared in the warrior's left hand, aimed directly at the barbarian's solar plexus. The frosty looking metal of the blade threw sparkling reflections in the firelight.

The Gotarran blanched visibly.

"Let him through, Alban," Samir said casually. "Let them both through if they're that stupid."

"Can't." The Captain was plainly tense. "And you don't really want me to. Huldrich there is the Gotarran Prince. This is already nasty enough without more bloodshed."

Samir nodded, understanding the implications of Alban's words. The two Princes may inadvertently have just started, or resumed, a war. *That* he could do nothing about, but he owed it to King Carlon to make sure his actions didn't push this situation any further.

"Caleb," he called. "You all right?"

"Yes," the answer came quickly.

To spare him further humiliation, Samir leaned forward and kept his voice low, for Huldrich's ears alone. "When I let go, I expect you to use your head. If you attack him, I'll make you regret it."

He released the hand.

Huldrich rose slowly to his feet, with all the dignity he could manage. The man was nearly ostentatious in his refusal to rub the sore wrist, yet he did flex his fingers. His only other action was to meet Samir's eyes, making it a point to demonstrate his lack of fear.

"I apologize, Prince Huldrich." Alban's tone carried sincere regret and not a little concern. "We certainly can't ask you to ride out in the dark, but I hope you'll understand if we ask you to make a separate camp tonight."

Samir didn't envy the soldier his sudden need to become a diplomat. Still, the man handled it well.

"Don't worry," Huldrich sneered. "We're leaving. I mean to be in Scara before noon tomorrow."

With that the three Gotarrans walked into the dark to find their horses. They didn't look back. In moments, the sound of hooves could be heard heading south into the forest.

Beside him, Gillis exhaled loudly. The tension was still thick.

"Help me get him over into the light," Morena asked Jenaris.

As the three moved closer, shadowed by Kordel, Caleb's injuries quickly became clear. Drying blood smeared his face where Morena had tried to wipe it from his badly broken nose and split lip. One brow was severely gashed and would need stitching. Blood matted his hair, revealing several places where his scalp was cut deeply. Added to all of that, one eye was indeed swollen shut entirely, and the other not far from it. Overall it was a grotesque picture, but appeared to be mainly superficial as long as the eyes themselves were undamaged. Morena rapidly dug through the large leather bag that held her vast collection of herbs, heedless of the blood on her hands. Retrieving what she sought, she popped it into Caleb's mouth with instructions to chew and swallow. He winced the moment he did so, indicating that loose teeth were also among the Prince's injuries.

"Make me an infusion from this." She handed another herb to Kordel. At his confused look, she let her anger slip. "*Tea!* Make me a weak tea."

The man wisely beat a hasty retreat with a mumbled, "Yes, ma'am."

She worked quickly, focused on Caleb's worst injuries first. Clearly blood didn't bother her, beyond the fact that it was being lost by a friend. Still, she never flinched as she worked. With better light and a canteen, she managed to wipe the last of the dried blood from his face and hair. While the result was less grisly, the underlying bruises weren't much of an improvement. Gently, she probed at the gash above his eye. "Do you feel this?"

"Not really," he replied, his voice a bit dreamy.

The stitches she made were small and tightly spaced, promising only a minimal scar there. It was the deep cuts to the scalp, however, that Samir assumed would be the difficult ones, considering the thick hair around them. But these she painted with the herbal brew brought by Kordel, the flow of blood ceasing immediately as she pinched the edges of the wounds together.

It occurred to Samir to wonder why she hadn't used the infusion on all of Caleb's cuts. The result was certainly much faster than stitches. Yet, considering Morena's present preoccupation, he decided the question would wait.

"Morena," he called.

He hadn't intended to take her attention from Caleb, but she looked up, eyes flashing. Too late he rethought the idea of speaking at all.

"Don't think I've forgotten about *you*," she snapped, turning immediately back to her work. "What do you want? I'm a little busy right now."

"Is there anything I can do?" he asked.

She glanced up again, only for a second.

"No," her tone was considerably softer now. She seemed tired, as if completely drained.

Morena worked for only a few more minutes before she declared the job done. At least as done as possible under the circumstances. Caleb didn't look much different, but she promised he would heal quickly provided he took the herbs she gave him over the next few days.

Samir steeled himself for a confrontation now that she was finished. Realizing he still held his sword, he slid it quickly into its sheath.

The argument never came.

Wiping her bloody hands on a damp cloth, she stood and slowly walked in the direction of her blanket roll. Surprisingly, Tirza followed her, whimpering slightly as they moved into the darkness.

"Kordel," Samir said, causing the other man to jump in surprise. He pointed to the ground at the apprentice's feet. "Make sure she gets that satchel."

For just a moment he considered following her. He strongly suspected she had little energy for anger right now. Unfortunately, he was a bit tired himself, and if he went to her, he was likely to let down his guard.

Somewhat numb, Samir helped Caleb stand, careful of any possible injuries. He needn't have worried. Whatever she had given him had removed his pain almost entirely. Throwing the other man's arm over his shoulder, he headed for Caleb's blankets.

Suddenly, he felt the need to find his own gear and get some rest. Tomorrow promised to be difficult enough without adding lack of sleep to his problems.

Chapter 20

The Laws of Gotarra

Caleb was glad to find that someone had already saddled Searcher for him by the time he awoke. He was sore all over and his head spun, but at least he was able to open both of his eyes. Apparently, Morena's herbs had reduced a great deal of the swelling as she had promised.

Finding the small pouch beside him, he fished out the one she'd given him for pain. The one he'd taken after his fight had left his thoughts fuzzy and his balance practically nonexistent. Still, it *had* relieved all but the worst of his pain and, at the moment, that was good enough for him. He just needed to be able to ride. Now. After his run-in with Huldrich, the last thing he wanted was to stay in Gotarra one second longer than absolutely necessary.

Gotarra. Sorana's home.

It was still a shock, but it did explain a lot. He had wondered how he could have looked so hard for her and never managed to find even an acquaintance. Now, of course, he understood that he'd been looking on the wrong side of the river the entire time.

He also thought he knew why she'd been so evasive about letting him meet her father. While it could be that Gerrit wouldn't have approved of him, it was likely more simple than that. At the time, her father hadn't been anywhere nearby, which had been why Caleb had been free to spend his days with Sorana.

Just the thought of her sent a pang of guilt through him. He finally knew what it was he had done to offend her so badly—a mystery that had driven him to distraction.

A stupid barbarian joke.

He couldn't even remember now which one it was, but that didn't really matter. He had shown contempt for who she was. If he'd known her heritage, he would never have said such a thing. Yet, he was only too well aware that what he had said was an honest reflection of his attitude toward her people—an attitude he now realized had to change.

Actually, although he hadn't really been aware of it until now, his opinion of Gotarrans had begun to change during his few hours in Scara. Not only had the people been little different from those in Acedia, he had been amazed at the degree of sheer craftsmanship displayed in even the common items. Stone work, woodcarving, pottery—it all revealed a level of skill and pride that had left him slightly awed.

Then there was Sorana herself. She was, without a doubt, the most incredible woman he'd ever met— beautiful, caring, smart, funny. She was so unlike anything he had believed about her people that he was forced to admit he'd been completely wrong.

But there was no one to admit it to. From Huldrich's reaction, it was obvious that she must hate him by now. Even if he could get close enough to talk to her—to apologize for what he'd said, she probably wouldn't listen. And the worst part was that he had no one to blame but himself.

As much as he wanted another crack at that cheap shot artist, Huldrich, the man had spoken the truth—Caleb had indeed hurt Sorana. He could have wept.

The mood seemed to fit well with the heavy overcast hanging above the hills. He hoped it didn't rain, which was a miserable prospect when there was no shelter, but a sunny day would feel all wrong somehow. It was ironic, though, that even in bad weather this was some of the most beautiful country he could imagine.

There was little time left for him to enjoy it, however. As soon as the camp was packed up, they would be leaving.

He did have time for breakfast. Just now, though, the idea was somewhat less than appealing—especially with several of his teeth knocked loose. Some hot tea sounded good, however.

No sooner had he thought about it than he spotted Morena approaching with an extra steaming mug. She was plainly exhausted, feet dragging as she walked and heavy-lidded eyes underlined darkly. But although she had put a considerable effort into his healing, he doubted that could be the only reason.

"Thanks," he said, taking the offered mug from a slightly shaky hand. "Do you feel all right this morning?"

"That's what I'm supposed to be asking *you*," she replied in an attempt at humor. The smile she gave him was definitely worn and haggard.

"You look like you didn't sleep at all," he remarked.

She swayed just a bit before steadying herself.

He was half afraid she was going to fall down if she stood much longer. Unfortunately, he was in no condition to try to catch her if she did. He would try, of course, but doubted he would do much good.

"Didn't." She tried to stifle a yawn...and lost.

Perfect. Both of us will fall asleep in the saddle, he thought. Aloud he said, "Would you like to sit?"

"No," she shook her head. "I might not be able to get back up."

He thought it might have been a joke, but maybe not. Unfortunately, it looked like it could be true.

"Morena, I appreciate everything you did for me last night," he insisted, doing his best to convey his genuine gratitude. "If this is because of me, though, I'd rather you'd left me with a few lumps and got more rest."

"I'm okay," she assured him. "It wasn't your fault. It's that...*jackass*, Samir."

In spite of his dizziness while she'd been working on his injuries, Caleb had heard her voice when she'd spoken to Samir. Whatever had caused it, Morena had sounded absolutely furious.

He sighed. "Want to talk about it?"

"No."

He could tell from the tone that her denial was no more than half-hearted. Caleb waited and wasn't disappointed.

"I thought everything was going so *well*," she said, tears threatening to spill. "He kissed me. And it was *so* nice, but he just walked away." The look in her eyes as she paused was painful even to see. "And now he won't even *talk* to me."

The tears did flow then.

Careful not to spill the contents, he took the mug from her hand, setting it down along with his own. As gently as he could, he put his arms around her and let her cry. "It'll be okay," he told her quietly. "He's too good a man to be an idiot forever, right?"

The small laugh he caused came out as more of a hiccough as she sobbed. Her brief hug before letting him go told him she felt at least slightly better, however.

Scooping up her nearly finished tea, he set it in her hands. With a grateful smile, she walked away. He watched for a moment before sitting and grabbing his own mug.

Somehow he doubted anything else could possibly go wrong. Still, he was glad there was at least one problem he could do something about.

Making up his bedroll, he secured it in its place, silently thanking whoever had saddled his horse for him. The herbs were already making him foggy.

Pouring the rest of his now cold tea on the ground, he walked carefully off to find the privy before it was dismantled.

Huldrich was relieved to finally ride into Scara after a long, hard ride. Now that they'd arrived, he was willing to admit it had been a bad idea, driven by anger and pride. To even try such a journey in the dark was foolish, and only familiarity with the road had kept them from crippling their mounts before the sun rose.

His knuckles ached and his wrist was swollen, but at least he'd had the satisfaction of pounding Caleb. If that Samir would've had the courage to come at him openly, he'd be wearing his share of lumps now, too. A slow smile split his face. Let him run into the Majaran again and things would go very differently.

For all his present fatigue, Huldrich felt good as he dismounted outside his home. He felt slightly guilty about letting his horse's care wait as he went inside, but he would be out again soon enough. Right now, he needed to let Sorana know she didn't need to worry about Caleb bothering her again.

His sister looked up from her book as he came through the front door. He couldn't resist a broad grin of anticipation as he thought of her reaction.

"What?" she asked, a quizzical look crossing her features.

"I ran into someone you know, Rana," he answered, drawing out the surprise. "Caleb."

The book hit the floor, unnoticed, as she jumped to her feet. He found it impossible to read the rapidly shifting emotions he saw, but happiness would appear soon enough. "You'll never have to see him again." He bent to kiss her cheek, but was stopped by a hand on his chest. Drawing back, he read the concern in her eyes.

"What did you do, Hul?" she demanded.

"Don't worry. I'm fine," he reassured her, rubbing the knuckles of his closed fist suggestively. "I just convinced him...strongly...that he wasn't allowed anywhere near you. *Ever.*"

As tired as he was, her full armed slap caught him completely off guard. Head ringing, Huldrich rubbed at his stinging cheek in confusion. Judging from the exaggerated way she shook her head, Sorana had felt the blow every bit as much as he.

She stared at him, livid with anger.

"How *could* you?!" she shouted. At her step forward, he stepped back. "I told you not to. I *told* you! And now he's going to *hate* me."

The sound of the door slamming behind Sorana as she stormed out pulled Huldrich out of his shock. For one brief moment he thought to go after her, but it was too late. He hesitated, unsure what to do.

"Well, *that* answers a few questions," his father's voice drifted from the corner of the room, causing him to jump.

Gerrit's face was a mask of grim amusement as he watched Huldrich from a place near the bookshelf. Now, as he smelled the fresh pipe smoke filling the air, he realized his father's presence should have been obvious.

"There are only two things you need to know," the King continued, walking slowly in Huldrich's direction. "The first is that, although we *love* to dig our hands in and fix things, a wise man keeps out of a woman's business unless he's *sure* it's what she wants."

Huldrich nodded ruefully. "I think I just figured that one out for myself. What's the other one?"

"The second thing is this," his father put a hand on his shoulder as grimness drove the amusement from his features. "That young man you were just talking about was the Prince of Acedia...and was here as my guest under the laws of hospitality." He paused, letting the words sink in as his gaze hardened. "You just violated my sacred word."

Huldrich could practically feel the color drain from his face. He had just broken not one, but *two* laws. Failure to provide for the safety of someone to whom hospitality had been provided was one thing, but he had also caused his father to stand as an oath-breaker. As bad as it was that he'd beaten a foreign Prince and possible ended a truce, the shame of this was far, far worse.

"I'm sorry, Father." The sentiment was completely inadequate, but it was all he could think to say.

Gerrit took a long pull on his pipe, a habit that allowed him time to think. He shook his head sadly.

"What's done is done," he said, mouth twisted slightly as if he'd eaten something sour. "I was hoping to leave you in charge while I went to see Carlon. Now you'll just have to come along and see if we can find a way to make things right."

"Yes, sir." Huldrich lowered his gaze, knowing that his punishment would be determined entirely by the offended party. "I understand, and I'll do whatever is necessary."

It never occurred to him to do anything other than take full responsibility for his actions, but he was definitely not looking forward to it.

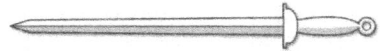

Caleb had been quiet during the entire long ride since leaving camp. Not that Samir took it amiss. He could tell that his friend was bothered by something and wanted to be alone with his thoughts. That was fine. He had concerns of his own.

Of the numerous people who had come to check on Caleb, Morena had not. In a way it was a relief, and yet.... Samir supposed he should make some excuse to ride over and speak to Alban or Jenaris so she would feel more comfortable. But he had actually hoped that she would show up just to prove she could. At least then he could hear her voice and, perhaps, sneak a glimpse or two. "I have enough problems of my own, Samir. You know that, right?"

Caleb's words were more than a little slurred from the bit of swelling that remained. Between that and the surprise of hearing the man speak after so long, Samir needed a few seconds to realize he'd missed what was just said.

"What?"

"I said, you know I have enough problems without getting caught in the middle of yours," Caleb spoke carefully, making sure to pronounce each word. "I'm in love with someone who now hates me, and I just got smashed by her brother. On top of that, I can barely stay awake in the saddle, and Morena is crying on my shoulder about you."

"Sorry," Samir replied, embarrassed. "She shouldn't be bothering you with that."

"Bothering me? You misunderstand." Caleb turned to face him directly, punctuating his words. "You're my friends and I don't mind listening to your problems. What I *mind* is that, from what I hear, you're being an imbecile. I haven't seen Sorana in over a month, and I might never get to speak to her again. You, on the other hand, have Morena right here and you won't even *talk* to her. Well, if I'm going to be in the middle of this, you're *at least* going to make an effort. You *will* go talk to her. Do I make myself *clear*?"

Samir was impressed. The man had managed to command without ever raising his voice. Caleb would almost certainly make a fine king one day.

Samir bowed low in the saddle with genuine respect. "Immediately, Highness." Without another word, he urged his mount toward the front of the line, where Morena rode slightly apart from the others.

It was Tirza's excited bark that made her turn and look. She appeared to be past mere exhaustion, shoulders sagging and bloodshot eyes unfocused.

Guilt hammered him as he saw her. It was his fault, his doing. He should never have kissed her, but he hadn't been strong enough—or wise enough—to leave her alone. And, instead of honesty, he'd made it worse by avoiding her. Now he had the feeling he was about to make it worse again.

"What do you want?" she asked wearily as he drew closer.

"We need to talk," he answered.

She swayed slightly as she turned to look at him. It was a wonder she stayed on Dawn Rose's back at all.

"What a brilliant observation," she said, voice dripping with sarcasm. "How did you ever figure *that* one out?"

He deserved that, he knew.

Pulling even, Samir reached out to touch her arm. She jerked back as if burned. "Morena," he pleaded.

"Just go away, Samir. I don't have the energy for this right now." Turning her attention back to the road, she flicked her reins, drawing more speed from the mare and leaving him behind again.

With a resigned sigh, he followed. He would simply have to keep at this for as long as it took to get this done.

This time, as he moved Yashar up beside her, she reined her horse to the other side of the road. He let her have the space. They didn't need to be that close to be near enough to talk.

"I'm sorry, Morena." he called over, fairly certain that at least Alban and Gillis could hear him. He didn't care.

"Fine," she answered. "You're forgiven. Now go away."

He only wished it were that simple. But it wasn't just forgiveness he wanted—even if he believed she'd actually given it. Well, he hadn't expected her to make this easy. He only wished she wasn't going to make him do *all* the work.

"Will you please just let me explain?" The question brought him close to begging, but he'd humbled himself before and almost certainly would again. In fact, in this situation it was almost a guarantee.

"All right." She pulled her horse off the road and stopped, forcing him to circle around the head of the column and ride back. "Explain. Tell me why you've been treating me like dirt since yesterday. Let me hear the reason you won't even look at me."

Alban slowed, looking a question at him as he passed. Samir shook his head. He didn't need the kind of help the Captain could provide, and there was no reason for anyone else to witness this. When he and Morena were finished, they would just have to catch up.

He forced himself to meet her tired eyes. Hurt shone through the fatigue as she stared back at him, as if expecting this to go badly. But even like this, she was so beautiful it nearly took his breath. Why couldn't he just tell her he wanted them to be together and forget everything else?

He knew the answer, of course. And he understood his responsibilities—a duty to collect a debt on his father's behalf as well as a duty to his mother.

"I have no excuse for the way I've treated you," he said finally. "I wanted to talk to you about this...to say something. I just didn't know what to say."

She sniffed. "How about something like, 'Morena, that was a *huge* mistake. I'm sorry I kissed you'?"

"It *wasn't* a mistake," he replied a bit too loudly, bringing interested gazes from the soldiers guarding the pack train. He knew he was blushing.

"Well, if it meant that much to you, why have you been running away from me? Why wouldn't you look at me?"

Moisture formed in the corners of her eyes, threatening to spill. She fought down the tears, not bothering to wipe them away.

He knew he owed her an honest answer, and he could feel himself tensing. Drawing a deep breath, he tried a relaxation technique Shimei had taught him years before. It almost worked.

Samir swallowed hard. "Because if I look at you, I'll only want to kiss you again."

"Are you *trying* to confuse me, Samir?" she asked, shaking her head. "If that's what you want, then what's the problem?"

"The problem is I *can't*. I don't have the right."

He wanted to make her understand—needed it—but he didn't think he fully understood it himself. In that moment, looking at her, he could almost have walked away from his responsibilities to be with her. Almost. But he knew that, if he did, he would come to resent her. *That* he couldn't allow to happen.

Unfortunately, it might just bring him to resent his mother.

"As much as I want this relationship, it wouldn't be fair to let it start," he said sadly. "I can't make any promises, any commitments. Legally, I'm bound to the woman chosen for me by my parents...my mother, now. So I had to do the honorable thing. I decided I had to give up what I want."

"You decided?" she shot back. "*You* decided? What about what *I* want? Or don't I have any say in the matter?"

Samir opened his mouth to speak, but no words came. His jaw hung open stupidly.

"I guess it's settled, then," Morena announced. With that, she turned Dawn Rose and followed the dust cloud left behind by the soldiers' passing.

"I still want to be friends," he called after her, hoping to preserve *something* of a relationship he valued.

"Don't do me any favors," she spat back. Then she was gone.

Samir stared at her retreating back, curls bouncing wildly. It was hard to believe that could have gone any worse.

Chapter 21

Hidden Among the Bluestem

Two days it had taken to reach the plains after that *stupidity* Samir had called an explanation, and she was still no closer to understanding him. After all, if he really wanted to be together, they would be. And how *dare* he say that what she wanted didn't matter. Ugh! She wanted to smack him.

In fact, she'd imagined it many times during the training sessions the past two nights—pretending every strike was aimed at him. Oddly enough, it seemed to have improved her technique a great deal, based on the number of comments he'd made. Of course, some of that was doubtless an attempt to mend fences, but she could tell which compliments were genuine. Once or twice he'd even seemed impressed.

She was more motivated now as well—fully determined to force him to admit his mistake, to make him *beg* for another chance. A part of her could admit to a certain amount of pettiness. But as much as she wanted him to change his mind—and confess he'd been an utter fool—she would still make him squirm just a little when he did. He owed her that much.

Though it pained Morena to do so, she'd made it a point to spend plenty of time around him. After all, Caleb was her friend too, and she wasn't about to stop talking to him just because Samir was there. Besides, if he said merely seeing her made him want to kiss her again, she intended to be where he would notice her—usually riding on Caleb's other side. He would act sensibly eventually, or he would just have to get used to her being around as a reminder of what he could have had.

But, to be honest, she wanted to see him, too. She missed his jokes and his laugh. As strange as it was, she even missed the way his accent sometimes made him sound like some arrogant foreign prince.

But, even though she wanted to hate him right now, she did love him. And while it would have been tempting to choose more kisses with the promise of pain later, Morena knew that he had made the right—and honorable—choice.

Reluctantly, she decided she'd had enough of feeling sorry for herself. Her father had always scorned self-pity, considered it a form of weakness, and at the moment she had a job to do.

As Dawn Rose walked easily through the waist high grass she scanned the area around the horse, glancing down through green leaves and long lavender stems. What she sought was short by comparison, but common enough that she was confident of finding it before she went far. The rest of the group merely trailed after her for now, trusting her knowledge and ability.

It took about ten minutes to spot the first clusters of small purple berries through the grass. Dismounting, she waited for the others to gather around, still sitting their mounts for a better view. With so many people, they would need to rotate in order to let everyone see, but she could at least speak to them all at once.

"This is Jasper Berry," she announced loudly, pointing down to focus their attention. "It isn't rare. Birds drop the seeds all over the plains. Unless you're careful, though, it's easy to pass by without seeing it from any distance."

Glancing around, she found every eye either on her or the plant. Satisfied, she continued. "We need as many berries as we can get, so it would be best if we spread out to cover more ground." She paused to push Dawn Rose away from the plant. "Do *not* let your horses eat any of these berries. There's something about them that makes horses sick, sometimes to death. And maybe dogs," she added, looking over her shoulder to where she knew she would find Samir.

Finished, she nodded to Captain Ward, who spoke briefly to one of the other soldiers.

"All right," the sergeant's voice boomed. "I want a line abreast with five yard spacing. We ride dead slow, so look around and don't worry about falling behind. Just find 'em, strip 'em, and move on. Now *spread out!*"

The mounted men immediately rode north and south, fanning out across the plains. Only those tending the pack animals and the carter were exempted, clearly having other duties to keep them occupied.

Dead slow was an apt description of their pace, the horses barely plodding along. She was fairly certain that, at this rate, they would all die of boredom before they came in sight of the Amber River at the far end of the grasslands. Even a couple of days of this, while they gathered the berries forming the bulk of the recipe, might make her wish to be *anywhere* else.

They covered a broad swath of land, stretching in a line nearly a hundred yards wide. Periodically, someone would stop and dismount, leaving a gap. At the end of an hour the straight line had become staggered beyond belief as people stopped and moved seemingly at random. Still, Morena took it as a sign that everyone must have found at least one plant and more likely several. The problem was, she had focused so long and hard that she was having trouble concentrating. In fact, more than once she'd found her eyes wandering the twenty yards to where Samir sat his black gelding. Once she had caught him looking back at her.

She couldn't help but wonder how many berries they had missed just from simple inattention. Not that they wouldn't find enough, but every plant they passed by only meant more time doing this.

It was a relief when they finally stopped to make camp late in the afternoon. Their rest was delayed slightly, however. The fact that the horses had to be kept from accidentally ingesting any berries while they grazed, forced them to do an intensive examination of the site. The worst part was that the sweep failed to turn up so much as a single plant.

There was another problem with where they had chosen to pitch their camp—water. Wells were dug at fairly regular intervals along the roads, yet their slow search had left them somewhere between water sources. Now, aside from a few stream beds that stayed dry unless filled by runoff from a heavy rain, they had only an occasional pond to supplement what they carried. Sadly, for the moment this meant limiting what was available for washing, which did nothing to improve her mood.

She couldn't even water her horse if she did come across a pond. At least not right away.

"It shouldn't be a problem here," she'd been told by one of the soldiers, "but closer to the tar fields it can be dangerous to approach standing water without investigating first."

Apparently, even away from the places pitch was harvested, new pools occasionally bubbled to the surface. Covered with a layer of standing water, they soon became a trap for the unwary. As rare as it was to discover one,

Morena did *not* want to fall victim just for trying to get her horse a drink.

It was almost enough to make her paranoid about riding anywhere on the plains but the road itself. After all, what if she crossed an area where the pitch hadn't *quite* risen to the surface? That, she was told, was simply a matter of watching for "bald spots"—places where the grass was dead or dying, but with the soil not yet eroded. Dawn Rose would likely break through in such spots, but they were easily avoided.

Somehow, such assurances provided small comfort.

Caleb and Samir were already laying out saddles and blanket rolls by the time she found them. Of course, had she thought to look for that flashy bridle Samir used, she could have saved a few minutes of walking. In her present mood, it almost felt like *that* should have been his fault as well.

"Bad enough I've had to cross this stinking grass four times already this summer," Caleb was saying. "But having to stare down at it all day makes me want to get as far from it as I can. What do you think, Samir? Maybe I should go to Majar."

Samir laughed, shaking his head. "Different place, but the same scenery," he replied. "I rode for three days from Toskar to Barat, and the only real difference was that I saw rice paddies instead of farms. Worst three days of my life."

Samir's posture revealed an abrupt sadness. She knew exactly what he was thinking about, and it made her want to go to him, if only to hold him for a few minutes. Morena hated to see him so heartbroken, even though it was he who had broken hers.

"So maybe we'll go somewhere else," Caleb asserted. "What was it like at sea?"

"Pirates," Samir answered without embellishment. The single word forced her mind to fill in images that a story would never have provided.

"You're kidding," Caleb challenged, laughing softly.

Instead of answering, the other man merely looked at the Prince with a serious expression. The laughter stopped.

Caleb whistled. "Is there anything you *can't* fight?"

"Just one thing," Samir said with a sigh, then remained silent.

It finally occurred to Morena that they were still unaware of her presence, having walked up from behind the pair. She coughed loudly.

By the time she reached the clear patch of ground in front of him, Samir wore a convincing smile. His eyes told a different story, however. A slight tightness at the corners announced that, in spite of his calm demeanor, he was obviously wondering how much she had just heard.

As tempting as it was to let her own smile tell him *exactly* what she'd heard, she chose to let him believe he'd kept his feelings hidden. But she knew.

Someday he *would* beg her to take him back.

Samir was glad when, by the time they broke off their search to eat lunch, Morena determined they had enough berries for their purposes. Not only did he feel certain that another hour of staring at grass would drive him completely insane, he had also found it difficult to teach a class of mentally exhausted students the previous night. He only hoped an afternoon of normal travel would give them enough time to recover before tonight's session.

The Wizard had seemed tired as well, merely nodding distractedly when Samir had, as requested, delivered the sword before bed. It had caused him no real concern at the time, of course. Jenaris knew what he was about.

His feelings changed on waking, however. Always before, the blade had been right beside him when morning came. Today, only an empty scabbard had greeted him. While he was surprised, it was hardly disturbing. Yet, when he had sought out the Mage, he had received no reassurance whatsoever, only a terse "Patience."

Samir found his hand drifting repeatedly to where the hilt normally sat as he rode, somehow surprising him each time he found nothing. It was nearly enough to make him wear his old sword just to feel the familiar weight on his hip. But it wasn't the weight he missed, he realized. It was the bond he had with the weapon. Over the past few days, he had grown so used to the feeling that now he was only aware of its absence.

In a strange way, it was similar to the way he longed for Morena's presence. The difference was, he was confident that his link to the sword was absolutely unbreakable. His relationship with her, on the other hand, seemed so tenuous he thought it could blow away in a puff of wind. Hopefully, he would find a way to keep that from happening. But short of nullifying his mother's rights, he didn't know what he could do.

An odd sense of relief suddenly washed over him, putting a smile on his face. Without turning to look, he could feel the Mage drawing closer. More importantly, the sword was with him.

"I was beginning to wonder," he said as the Wizard's little mare came abreast of him. "I thought maybe I'd have to wait until morning."

"No," Jenaris replied, "only until we had a chance to talk. I had to make sure you didn't access the blade's new property when you were surrounded by sleeping men and horses."

Samir shot the Mage a quizzical look. The old man's face revealed nothing.

"What's it going to do, set the grass on fire?"

"Not a bad idea," Jenaris laughed. "The fire, I mean. Not the grass. But this isn't anything dangerous exactly. It would just be rude to use it around your friends until you have control of it." He quirked a bushy white brow at Samir. "I suggest you walk well away from the others before you test this one."

Without another word, the Wizard handed him the hilt and rode back to the tail of the column where Kordel waited. Not for the first time, Samir wondered what the apprentice did besides fetch for the Mage. So far, it was all he'd seen the man do.

The thought didn't last long, however. Curiosity about the sword became a constant distraction. There was little he could do. In his hand or its sheath, its presence was enough to ensure his continued frustration.

He had no doubt what Shimei would think of his student's recent state of mind. After all the Sòra's teaching on patience, focus and self-discipline, he would be more than merely disappointed that Samir still had trouble with all three. Then again, he wondered whether Shimei had ever met a woman like Morena.

But that would make no difference. Shimei would never allow anything to master him—not a sword and not a woman. Briefly he envied his teacher's strength, and yet....

Surely the Sòra had given him the skills he needed to do the same. All he had to do was apply them, focusing on the solutions rather than the problems. Not that he wouldn't value his bond with Dragon's Fang or cherish his relationship with Morena—whatever form it eventually took. It was simply that he could not dwell on what he could do nothing about. He could only control himself, and it was high time he did so.

Resting his hands on the saddle in front of him, reins held loosely in his fingers, he concentrated on one of the first things his master had taught him—a deep breathing exercise that would relax him while he cleared his mind of his concerns. There was nothing so pressing that it required his conscious thought. His horse would continue without his attention, following the ones in front. The wind, the grass, the birds, and even his balance passed beyond his notice and were banished to a corner of his awareness. He had no concept of passing time, and no idea how long he merely let himself be in the moment. Even had someone tried speaking to him, he might not have noticed. The next thing he was truly aware of was that his horse had stopped, though from some action of his or because the others had, he didn't know.

Still, he felt refreshed as he dismounted and, although he could tell that his concerns were ready to force their way back in, he was almost content. Tirza seemed to sense it as well, sitting quietly as she watched him care for his horse. That took little time, however, and with supper still some while off he found himself without any immediate responsibilities.

Waving Tirza away, Samir left the growing camp behind and wandered into the tall grass. It was slow going with the stems wrapping around his ankles as he went. But he was in no hurry. Finally, beyond the sounds of men and horses, he stopped, calling the sword to his hand as he sat.

A new symbol now stood above the first on the flat of the blade. But, where he now understood the original set of lines etched into the steel, these others meant nothing to him.

Once again, he focused on the shimmering blade resting lightly on his knees, focused on the bond he already shared with it. This time, the knowledge came almost instantly, and it intrigued him.

Considering for only a second, he triggered it. Sounds of rustling grass came from several directions as, around him, creatures ran for their lives. Whether foxes, rabbits, or even mice, he could only imagine, but he knew that they were all suddenly and unaccountably afraid.

Jenaris had been right to warn him to be careful, at least until he had sufficient command. It would come. Eventually, he would be able to dictate the intensity— anywhere from mild uneasiness to wild panic at the sight of him. Of course, not everyone would flee such a thing. People dealt with their fears with vastly different levels of success, but those nearby would *feel* it even if they stood their ground.

He remained seated as he focused again on the sword. One proud part of him thought briefly of dismissing this function of the blade as unworthy of a warrior's skill. Many times, however, Shimei had insisted that a true warrior makes use of *every* weapon.

This was something he needed to master, and there was no time like the present.

Chapter 22

A Trophy On A String

Thirty Gotarran warriors made an impressive sight as they wound their way down out of the hills and approached the plains. It was a different sort of company than those of Acedian soldiers Suppan had seen. There were no uniforms here. Each man made his own choices, carrying the weapons—or perhaps shields—he personally favored. Every one of these men had proven himself many times over and against every kind of hazard—or *almost* every man.

Suppan had noticed more than a few questioning looks as the other men wondered about his presence. He knew what lay behind the gazes, the assumption that he was only here because he was Huldrich's friend. It was true, though, just as it was true of Kessel. But somehow no one seemed to think twice about Kessel's presence, or about Huldrich's.

He'd grown used to it in the last few years. He'd had to.

It had become obvious early on that he wouldn't be as tall as most, although how much shorter he was had been a surprise. Even Huldrich wasn't as tall as Kessel, of course. Few were. But the King's son still topped him by nearly a full foot.

He wasn't as agile as he'd like either. True, spending so much time around Hul and Kessel, both natural athletes, caused him to suffer by comparison. But it wasn't only that. With his heavy build on such a small frame, he just wasn't quite as coordinated. *They* had always accepted him as an equal in spite of that. No one else did.

Oh, he knew he wasn't along as a charity case. He was as strong as any man here—except maybe Kulmar—and could probably outwrestle any of them as well. Some of the others knew it, too. He just wished they would give him the same respect they gave his friends.

Yet Suppan knew he was accepted by those whose opinions really mattered. His place riding in the van wasn't about who his friends were, but about the fact that Gerrit and Kulmar wanted him there. And if *they* thought him worthy, then no one else could say otherwise. At least not openly.

Ahead of him, Kulmar sat his stallion with a casual ease he could only admire. In fact, Suppan admired a great many things about the giant farrier, who had been respected for his toughness at an early age. Now greying, he was considered almost a legend for the things he'd done, but he wore only a single trophy of the many he'd earned—hanging on a leather thong around his bull-like neck.

One day, Suppan hoped, he would have a fraction of the older man's respect.

"You know you brought the wrong weapon," Kessel told him, pointing to Suppan's spear. His friend's own spear was propped on his shoulder, occasionally brushing leaves on the low hanging branches. "You can't kill a dragon with that."

"It's the same thing you have," Suppan reminded him.

The tall man shook his head. "I've got my axe. All you have is the spear and your knife." He grinned. "Who do you think you are? *Kulmar*?"

Unconsciously, he reached for the hilt of the long knife hanging from his belt. The wide, single-edged blade was over a foot of sharpened steel. In the hands of a Gotarran it was hardly inconsequential as a weapon, but it did call for close quarters to use it effectively.

"It's not the only weapon I've got," Suppan insisted, thumping a fist over his heart. "But I like my knife better than that axe of yours. It's so blade-heavy that if you miss you're dead."

"I'll take my chances," the other replied with his normal confidence.

"I don't know why either of you is even arguing about it," Huldrich said from Kessel's other side. "If any of us is going to kill a dragon, it's going to be me."

Suppan opened his mouth to respond, but a loud snort interrupted him. In front of them, Kulmar turned in his saddle, the movement causing his horse to turn nearly a full flank toward the younger men—its prancing steps taking it sideways along the road.

"Any one man who can best a dragon alone is a man I'd like to meet. Better still, I'll buy that man a good mug of ale," the farrier announced with a wry look. "Game like that will take a group to bring down."

"Like a bear, you mean?" Kessel interjected.

Kulmar grinned, his thick scar giving it the look of a grimace. "Like *me* if you don't mind your manners, pup."

Suppan erupted in laughter as he saw color rise in Kessel's cheeks. Hul only just managed to fight down his amusement.

It was a point well taken, however. They knew from reports about the Acedian patrol, as well as the Wizard's information, exactly how dangerous these creatures could be. It would definitely take a group of them to stop even one. But Suppan fully intended to do his share of the damage when that time came.

Still dreaming about the possibilities, he casually turned up the collar of his coat as the rain began to drip from the leaves overhead. It wasn't exactly welcome, but no Gotarran was about to complain about something so predictable. Close to the mountains, winter was cold; and, in the forest, summer was punctuated by rain showers. That was just the way things were.

Unfortunately, it made for slippery footing as they set the evening camp, and dry firewood was in short supply. But this land didn't produce people so weak they would die without a fire. Everyone present had spent a cold night outside before—including Sorana. They would make do.

The worst problem was mud. By the time the horse lines were secured and everyone fed, the ground had become a boot-sucking mire. Even a brief glance around the clearing revealed more than one spear haft being used as a walking stick.

For those who brought hammocks to sling between the trees, the night would merely be uncomfortable. The rest, however, would need to find another way to stay off the sodden ground. As far as Suppan was concerned, a deadfall was hardly the most comfortable perch, but it kept their feet out of the mud as the trio sat tented beneath their blankets. Sleeping like this, though, would be nearly impossible.

Next time, he would bring a hammock.

The sudden agitation of the horses sent several men running to get them under control. They stamped excitedly, tossing their manes and snorting as if seeking to escape a fire. But there *was* no fire.

Suppan was on his feet instantly, blanket sliding into the muck, already forgotten. Beside him, Kessel and Huldrich were also alert.

All around them, in fact, men stood hefting weapons and seeking the source of the horses' distress.

It broke through the brush only forty feet away, the sound of snapping branches allowing surprisingly little time to react. The sinuous black shape moved with unbelievable speed. *They* did not. Under normal conditions they could have covered the ground in moments, surrounding the dragon with enough men to overwhelm it. But the slick, deep mud made it an absolute nightmare to reach the fighting.

Suppan spared one brief glance to check on Sorana, who was being quickly herded behind a group of experienced warriors. Nothing would get past that, he was sure, but it was up to the rest of them to keep it from getting that far. Putting her out of his mind, he turned back to the battle.

Of the four men who had reached the beast, two already had broken spears and a third was trying to keep his entrails from spilling onto the ground. The last, a hunter named Anton, was holding his own for the moment with sword and shield. He wouldn't hold the dragon at bay for long from the looks of it.

Men scrambled to help, to force the creature to divide its attention, but those few feet might as well have been a chasm. The dragon's tail lashed toward the man, who instinctively raised his shield at the last moment. Wood splintered under the force of the blow, tossing Anton aside to land in a motionless heap.

Others arrived then, including his two companions, who were faster by far than Suppan. Most had discarded spears, having seen how they shattered against the thick black scales. Only Kulmar still carried one as he met the creature face to face.

Jaws snapped shut on empty air as Kulmar jumped aside, spear angling in from the side. The dragon's deafening scream announced a hit, as did the beast's sudden recoil. As the enormous head whipped away from the source of pain, Suppan could see the injury. The farrier had taken an eye.

The dragon didn't slow for even a second. Claws raked for Kessel's chest, catching his axe head as he blocked the deadly slash and ripping it from his hands. The weapon flew, sliding in the mud far from its owner until it came to rest at Suppan's feet.

Scooping it up, he ran on.

With a flash of steel, one of the older men drew his knife, leaping onto the beast's back. It was a tenuous perch judging by the way the warrior slid, but he somehow managed to stay aboard. Knife angled to drive up under the scales of the neck, he braced himself for the thrust, then suddenly sagged as the spiked tail impaled him.

Huldrich swung his own knife, aiming for the other eye. He was too slow. The sharp point of the blade found only thick armor plating as the head of the beast cocked back, jaws opening wide.

Jenaris had warned them what to expect. Kessel and Huldrich dove aside as venom streamed out, missing both. Kulmar bore in, spear driving for the soft skin at the back of the creature's throat. But the dragon was ready. With incredible speed, the mouth slammed shut on the weapon, splintering the shaft.

Time seemed to slow for Suppan as he covered the few remaining feet. He watched the beast turn, its malevolent gaze falling on Kessel who still struggled to stand. The dragon's head streaked toward his friend's exposed back.

Despite the mud-slicked handle, Suppan gripped the axe tightly and swung with every ounce of strength he possessed. Momentum carried him forward, placing him directly between the monster and Kessel. With a dull sense of dread he knew he'd been right about the axe—if he missed, he would die. He would probably die anyway, but he was committed. In a wordless battle cry, he screamed, pouring out all his fear, all his rage, and all the love he had for his friends.

His arms jarred, pain shooting all the way to his shoulders as the heavy blade bit deep into the skull, but his own blow couldn't stop the creature's attack. Force carrying it forward, the massive head slammed into his chest, knocking him aside and sprawling him face down in the mud.

Desperate, Suppan dug his hands into the mud as he sought the axe. Nothing. Precious seconds slipped away as his dazed mind fought for direction. Finally, drawing his knife he climbed to his feet to face the beast again.

It lay still, Kessel's axe buried deeply in the side of its head. Around him men still struggled to cross the morass, yet now they ran toward him screaming approval at the top of their lungs.

He was nearly battered to the miry ground as hands slapped Suppan's back and shoulders. Air was crushed from his lungs, shooting sharp pain through his chest as Kulmar lifted him in an enthusiastic bear hug.

"Well done, lad," the gravelly voice said in his ear. "*Very* well done."

Finally, the rush of realization hit him, pushing through the confusion and pain. He had killed the dragon. *He* had. Exhaustion he hadn't even been aware of was washed away in a sudden surge of joy.

No, not joy. *Elation.*

"What took you so long?" a familiar voice appeared beside him. "You almost missed all the fun."

"I had to pick up the axe *you* dropped, you clumsy oaf," he replied, turning to face Kessel.

The claws that had stripped the weapon from the taller man hadn't missed. Long bloody gashes ran across his mud-smeared chest, trailing thin runnels of pink as rain washed the wounds. They were shallow, but would definitely need treatment soon.

Looking himself over, Suppan saw only slick brown muck coating him. His chest throbbed, aching from where the dragon's head, or possibly the axe handle, had been driven into him. Otherwise, he felt fine.

"Count on Kessel," Hul put in behind him. "He gets a fine set of scars to impress the ladies and we just get a few bruises."

"Naw," Suppan grinned. "He just wants them so he can get out of standing watch."

They became aware of the silence then. Following the other men's gazes the reason became apparent. Near the creature's still form, several warriors bent to arrange the bodies of four of their own, spears laid across chests and blankets ready to cover them.

In silence, Suppan sheathed his knife as Kessel went to reclaim his axe. Suddenly, a celebration seemed inappropriate.

Although it had stopped raining before full dark, Suppan still spent an uncomfortable night atop a fallen log in an effort to stay out of the mud. As it was, the stuff was crusted in his thin beard and covered nearly every inch of exposed skin when he awoke. He wasn't at all sure how much of his stiffness was due to the battle and how much just from sleeping so awkwardly. Still, it could have been much, much worse.

Several men had taken injuries, Kessel's far from the worst. While Anton's shield had almost certainly saved his life, he'd still taken a nasty blow. His shoulder was badly damaged, and vomiting indicated a serious blow to the head. Added to the splinters driven into his face and arm, he was definitely in for an uncomfortable ride. He would live, though, and others had not.

No one injured worse had been so lucky. Dragons, it seemed, didn't leave wounds. They left corpses.

Grabbing his spear, Suppan levered himself to his feet. The unexpected smell of roasting meat called to him, although he wasn't entirely sure he wanted to find the source. He'd been ready for a meal of hardtack and jerked lamb, but they wouldn't need a fire for that—only for fresh meat, and they hadn't lost any mounts.

The grit that had worked its way into his clothing chafed as he walked, bits of dried mud flaking. He needed to wash...*badly*. Looking around, he was sure he wasn't the only one planning to jump into the first stream they saw.

He was right about the meat. The spit was large, and it was loaded almost till it bowed with what could only be the haunch of the dragon he'd killed. Although the smell wasn't bad, he somehow found that less than reassuring. True, his people hated the thought of letting good meat go to waste, but "good" could be a *very* relative thing. Still, he had to eat.

A pair of men stood by the fire pit—one turning the spit, the other slicing chunks of sizzling flesh onto tin plates. Both greeted him with welcoming nods as he approached.

"Any good?" he asked.

The man at the spit smiled. "It has its points."

"A bit tough and sinewy," the other man said, handing him a plate. "Definitely greasy, like bear. But it's not half bad."

Hot grease burned his fingers as he lifted a chunk warily. It smelled all right and looked close enough to beef. Tentatively he took a bite and was pleasantly surprised. A little gamey, but better than horse. It was a shame they lacked the time to smoke the rest of the meat.

He ate as he walked.

Hails greeted him as he crossed the camp, coming from men who had recently wondered about his presence or, worse, ignored him. In only a short distance, however, he'd been addressed, slapped, or nodded to by half the men in the camp. He felt...taller.

It was Gerrit and Kulmar who hailed him as he approached the still corpse of the dragon, curious to see it in the light of day. It was a fearsome looking thing. Cruel. Yet, somehow it didn't seem quite as large with the two Gotarrans sitting, arms crossed, on its outstretched neck.

"I thought you might come this way," Gerrit said solemnly.

"They can never resist, can they?" Kulmar asked.

The King shook his head sadly. "And, of course, the poor ladies will never hear the end of this."

"Never," Kulmar intoned. He looked up at Suppan. "I suppose you'll be wanting some proof of the deed, too?"

Suppan looked back and forth between the two. Both now appeared to be plotting some kind of mischief.

"Here, son," Gerrit unfolded his arms and held out a hand. Dangling in his grip was a long rawhide thong, strung with a few wooden beads and one great black claw.

The four inch talon hooked wickedly as it tapered to a very sharp point. It looked to be designed to eviscerate. Now, though, it had a different purpose. Near the root, a hole had been carefully bored to allow the leather to be threaded through.

Suppan's hand almost shook with excitement as he accepted the trophy, holding it up before looping it over his head.

"Careful with that point," Kulmar said wryly. "Don't want the thing poking holes in you *now*, do you?"

The King stood to leave, clapping him on the shoulder.

"Good job, young warrior," Gerrit said quietly.

Kulmar followed, hesitating just long enough to place a leather wrapped package in Suppan's hand. "In case you need spares," he said. "If that one breaks, it won't exactly be easy to replace."

The contents of the package slid against each other as he carefully unwrapped it. Inside, seven more daggerlike claws gleamed dully in the morning light.

Chapter 23

Lost in the Wood

The transition from the bright sunlight of the plains to the deep shadow of the Great Wood was abrupt, requiring a few minutes' pause for their eyes to fully adjust to the gloom. After the warmth of early summer, Jenaris found it almost chilly in the shade of the giant trees. Still, it took little time to adapt as they followed the road from Clayton.

It was only a short ride to where the road branched. To the northwest lay Hogarth. The southern route led back to Varella. He had taken this road south not too many weeks ago in his search for Lorn and would do so again soon. For now, though, they would forego the roads and ride deeper into the forest.

Jenaris sat patiently, waiting for Morena to lead them on their search. She had assured him, as they'd waited for the ferry across the river, that it wouldn't be hard to find. He had no reason to doubt her. So far, he had to admit, Morena knew what she was about. It still made him nervous, though.

Not that he was one of those mages—common though they were—who detested relying on someone else's knowledge or ability. After all, even a person as old as he couldn't know *everything*. But, as competent as Morena obviously was, the consequences of failure were simply too high.

Yet, where they had managed to find the first two plants with no trouble, this one seemed to elude them. For well over an hour, the group rode up and down trails and over hills, finding nothing. Finally, at Captain Ward's discreet suggestion, she thought to tell the scouts what they sought and merely waited for their return.

It didn't take long.

The path they took led gradually downhill until they arrived at a small pond. From the sheer volume of tracks at the water's edge, it was clearly a popular watering hole for local wildlife. There were also, he noted, a number of types of vegetation.

Once again confident in her abilities, Morena quickly dismounted and walked to the verge of the small stream that fed the pond. The plant she plucked from the soil was nothing to attract attention. Its thin woody branches were covered in knotty growths. At their ends lay small round leaves, now brown, with something of the look of copper coins. It was from these, he supposed, that Beggar's Wort took its name.

Several grew on either bank, making it easy enough to collect what was here. But it was obvious there was a problem. This small amount wouldn't be anywhere near enough to meet their needs.

Twice more the scouts were dispatched, and twice the harvest was far too meager. Eventually, in frustration, Alban had the men make camp as he sent the scouts with instructions to return the next day with as much as they could gather. After all, he said, there was no reason the rest of them needed to go traipsing all over creation. A few fast riders could easily spread out and do the job more efficiently.

Although sensible, this had the unfortunate effect of making the Wizard extraordinarily *bored*. Under ideal conditions, Jenaris would simply have immersed himself in study. But in the middle of nowhere there were no books to keep him occupied, leaving his mind free to wander in strange directions. Not that this was a bad thing. Not exactly. Still, as he considered certain courses of action, he strongly suspected that at least one person would find it unpleasant.

"Kordel," he called the heavy set young man. "Come here a moment."

With a shrug, the apprentice wandered over.

Jenaris would have preferred more enthusiasm from someone looking to become an adept. But his evident apathy was exactly the attitude that made the man perfect for this experiment. Had he shown a bit more eagerness, the Mage would have felt at least a little guilty for what he was about to do.

"Yes, Magus," Kordel finally replied.

"Just stand there a second," Jenaris instructed.

The brief words and gestures of the incantation weren't at all complicated, merely unfamiliar. It wasn't a spell he'd used more than a bare handful of times. In fact, he couldn't actually recall any specific instance beyond the time he'd learned it decades before.

When he was done, Kordel's eyes had the mildly unfocused look the Mage remembered.

"Why don't you go for a walk?" he asked with a friendly smile.

"Okay," the apprentice responded happily before wandering off in no particular direction.

"Where's he going?" Samir jerked a thumb at Kordel's retreating back as the man entered the woods.

If it was time for the Majaran to deliver his sword, then Jenaris estimated there should be sufficient daylight left for his purposes. Provided his plan worked, that is.

"I have absolutely no idea," the Wizard replied honestly, "and neither does he."

It was clear Samir believed it was a joke, until he saw that the Mage was perfectly serious. Realizing it must be the simple truth, he looked a question at the older man.

"Won't he get lost?" the Majaran asked.

Jenaris smiled reassurance.

"I have no doubt that he already is," the Mage answered, unfazed by the situation. Of course, he wasn't the one ambling through the woods. "By the time the confusion spell wears off, he shouldn't even know what country he's in. The spell lasts about half an hour."

"Um," Samir was clearly concerned, but seemed sensibly hesitant to tell a wizard off. "Mind if I ask why?"

As it happened, Jenaris didn't mind at all. In fact, he considered it a rather clever experiment.

"It was necessary to see if I could draw a Marque to me," he shrugged. Seeing concern in the young man's face, he quickly waved it away. "Don't worry. I'm fairly sure he's aware enough not to hurt himself."

As briefly as he could, he explained the problem, taking the opportunity to organize his thoughts.

There were, he told Samir, things he knew how to do. He knew, for instance, how to send a message using a link between two known Marques. He could also, under the right circumstances, bring the right person to him at need—as Samir's presence attested. What he didn't know, because as far as he knew it had never been tried, was whether one Marque could be *drawn* to another. He had some notions of what to try. Many spells could, in fact, be successfully reversed. But, although he had hope of finding something he could use, they would never know until they tried it.

"So what happens if you can't bring him back?" Samir asked, fascination warring with disapproval on his features.

"Then I'll have to let Tirza find him," Jenaris chuckled. "I know I can send her Marque to his."

With more than a little annoyance, the Majaran nodded toward the water's edge where Tirza and Morena played. "You'll have to pry those two apart, but I don't mind."

The Wizard laughed at the young warrior's evident discomfort. He wondered if the man even realized it was the dog he was jealous of and not the young herbalist. Then again, he might not even have been aware that he *was* jealous.

"What's so funny?" Samir asked, not offended but certainly guarded.

"Perhaps you're too young to have figured it out," the Mage replied with a grin, "but women will *always* team up against a man."

The Majaran returned his grin. "Well, good luck," he offered. "I have a class to teach."

"Samir," Jenaris called before the other man could leave. "The sword."

With an embarrassed smile, the warrior handed him the weapon, then trotted off to where the guardsmen were quickly forming up in well-spaced ranks. The Wizard envied the man the chance to do something constructive, something meaningful. His present task needed to be done, but it was still make-work in an attempt to keep boredom at bay. Of course, he didn't envy the young warrior his problems. As much as he sympathized, no one could make Samir's choices for him.

Dismissing the lad from his well-disciplined mind, he focused his attention on the sword in his hands. There was no need to hurry. Focus building, he cleared his thoughts and concentrated all of his attention on the task. While it was an elementary procedure to expand an item's capacity, pushing it toward its potential, he didn't dare make a mistake. A failure at any point would set him back, forcing him to repeat days or weeks of effort from the last Fixed Element imbued into the weapon. Better to make an error early than late, of course, when the work became harder for diminishing returns. But best not to make one at all.

Jenaris began his soft chant, making certain to enunciate perfectly the syllables that were a part of no spoken language. Slowly his hands traced their way up and down the smooth metal, feeling as he did so the depth that lay beyond what was visible to the eye. He didn't allow himself to experience satisfaction. It would only be a distraction as he fed magical power into the blade, stretching the limits toward the next plateau and hardening the metal in the process.

An odd pleasure came over him as his chanting ceased, knowing he was that much closer to the next step, but still anxious about a job unfinished. He always enjoyed the process of making an item—often more than its conclusion. But this one, when finished, would be special.

Of course, he also enjoyed investigating the work of others. It was a rare opportunity given that the heyday of his craft was long past. Most items were now lost— buried, hung above a mantle, or merely collecting dust in an attic. But he had seen—had sensed—that curious object in Samir's possession. At first, he had assumed the Majaran was aware of its nature, but lately he'd begun to think otherwise, and he positively itched to get his hands on it. Without a chance to examine it, he could only feel the extreme weight of antiquity in its presence. Still, he sensed no danger. The time would come, he was sure, and he could afford to be patient.

Setting the blade aside, he estimated that Kordel's confusion was past. At least, the confusion induced by magic should be. It was unlikely that, wherever he'd gotten to, he would be able to track his way back to the camp. So far on this trip he had shown absolutely no ability at woodcraft. Certainly, he could make magical fire, but that could very well be the extent of his survival skills.

With a rueful shake of his head, Jenaris considered leaving Kordel where he was. It wasn't a serious thought, of course. He would never have actually gone through with it. But a man was allowed to dream.

Time to get on with it, he told himself.

As he was about to call the hound, he looked down, spotting what he needed on the rock beside him. It wasn't meant as a commentary on his feeling toward Kordel, merely a matter of convenience. But using a snail was almost poetic in a way.

Not that it should make any difference. It wasn't a matter of any intrinsic value or even consciousness that allowed Marques to be formed and linked. All that was necessary was that it be laid on a living creature.

The spell itself took only a few seconds and less than half his attention to do. It was the next part that would be tricky. Although he had done it before, creating something unstudied and unrehearsed from an existing enchantment was...uncertain at best. Only the fact that he knew the original so well, and that it was so basic, made him believe it could succeed. Still, he figured his odds at nearly even, which was good enough.

Not for the first time, he wished Kirstea were present.

The link was identical in every respect. It had to be. But that one thing was all that would remain unchanged.

Normally, it was the one on the local end that was given what amounted to a sense of weight. Just as a stone *wanted* to roll downhill under the impetus of gravity, the *object* of the link wanted to move toward its *subject*. The connection merely served as a guide. Yet in this instance, the snail required a certain sense of *downhill-ness*, and it was this that had taken a great deal of thought.

It wasn't simply a matter of altering polarity, as if two lodestones were involved. The attraction was based in something else. Likewise, there was no way he knew to merely reverse the relative positions by adding weight to the other end. At present, it was too remote to access.

No, the only way he could see was to alter the degree at this end of the effect, and to do it so drastically that *weight* became *magnitude*. In theory the Marque at the other end would be captured and pulled in. Yet the sheer volume of power needed meant the construction would break down. Hopefully, it would last long enough.

Slowly he added to the link, as he would normally do. Instead of ceasing with a mere drop, however, he opened the tap. The "stone" this usually created to roll downhill grew rapidly, becoming a boulder, then a *world* which would force the other to roll toward its ponderous, unmoving mass. Finally, shutting off the flow of energy, he waited.

It should take time for Kordel to begin moving in response to the pull of the snail's gravity. It would surely take time for him to get here when he did. If this worked, though, he would know soon enough. Picking up the snail, he held it lightly in the palm of his hand. Until he knew one way or the other, he would have to protect the little creature. After all his work, it would hardly do for someone to step on it and destroy the Marque it carried.

Jenaris had decided to let Kordel sleep much of the morning, considering how worn and weary he'd been on his return the previous night. At some point after dark he had actually come *jogging* in, as if responding to a strong sense of urgency, going straight to where the Mage sat with the snail.

The apprentice was hardly the worse for wear. Scrapes and bruises had been the extent of his injuries, though he certainly needed a bath. Luckily, he hadn't stumbled into a hornet's nest.

There was one interesting effect of the reversal, however. Most of Kordel's fatigue had come as a result of proximity to the link's subject as they waited for the spell to break down. Odd, to be sure, but well worth noting.

The important thing was that the experiment had worked and would prove useful. Its duration might be a limitation, of course, but that could be worked around— within certain limits.

Scouts began to return well before noon, sacks filled with plants ripped root and all from the ground. Jenaris estimated that, by the time the last man returned, they would have nearly twice what Morena had called for. Of course, that was assuming every scout had found what they sought—and it didn't do to make assumptions on something as critical as the fate of nations. At least none had come in empty handed. In fact, there appeared to be a little friendly competition going on, which could only help.

As the day wore on into afternoon, he could tell the Captain was becoming agitated as he watched for riders to return. It had been hours since one had entered the camp, a fact that caused an almost palpable tension as it continued to stretch toward supper. Alban clearly felt the worst of it. The man's mind was evidently beginning to spin out scenarios of a man injured or, worse, killed by a drake that could even now be approaching the camp.

It was a sign of a good officer to be concerned for the welfare of his troops, but too much imagination without facts could lead to poor decisions.

"How many?" Jenaris asked flatly as he approached the Captain.

"Just one," Alban sighed deeply. "Dane's a good soldier and a good rider. All my scouts are."

The Wizard could picture the man. A tall, slender youth with a mop of curly hair. Along with that knowledge came what was needed now—his memory of the Marque placed on the rider. Jenaris was briefly tempted to try his modified version of the link again, but thought better of it. If the man were able, he would already be coming.

Lifting a finger toward one of the surrounding trees, the Mage called down a bird. The robin responded immediately, calmly alighting on the offered perch and watching him, head cocked in expectant curiosity.

"Would you like to send a note," Jenaris inquired, a slight smile on his lips, "or do you just want to know if he's alive?"

It took the Captain only an instant to call for paper and a pen.

The fact that the scout still lived was established as the bird took flight, heading south rather than back to its nest. The note said simply, "Stand fast. We're coming."

If anything, volunteers for the rescue party were too easy to come by. Although all of the soldiers stepped forward, Alban selected only two other scouts, leaving Gillis in charge of the rest. As the only trained healer, Morena insisted on going, as did both Caleb and Samir— the first seeming to feel responsible for every Acedian; the latter, for one in particular.

This time, the link was attached to the Captain, whose look of pure astonishment at the sudden surge of feeling was priceless. Without a word, he kicked his horse into motion, leaving the others to catch up or fall behind.

The ride to find the missing scout took longer by far than it took the bird to fly out and return. The Captain was forced into a meandering route around gullies, thickets and fallen trees. The game trails they followed took them south only indirectly, but always generally south. That Alban knew where he wanted to go was obvious, if just from the way he continually glanced in the same direction.

As he crossed a small stream, Alban tugged on the reins, halting the group in the middle of the trail. He looked thoughtfully around him.

"Is there something wrong?" the Wizard asked, surprised and not a little concerned. If the link had broken, it meant Dane had died.

"No," the Captain answered easily. "I just wondered whether this could be resisted. I still *want* to go on. I guess I'm not uncomfortable about stopping, but I don't feel right about it either."

"You aren't being coerced, Captain," the Mage laughed. "It's more like a sense of purpose."

Alban grunted, but continued on. "I just don't like the idea that I could be *forced* to do something."

Jenaris nodded. He'd been concerned about the same thing as an apprentice.

"You aren't an animal, Alban," he assured the Captain. "Men have free will."

The soldier's face wasn't the only one to show relief.

Minutes later, the group rounded a low hill and came face to face with the missing scout perched calmly on a large rock, saddle and bedroll at his feet. Rising, he offered a jaunty salute, clearly glad to see them.

His horse, it seemed, had broken a leg and sadly needed to be put down. By Dane's estimate, he had covered nearly five miles on foot before the bird arrived with the message.

It was a relief that the man was unhurt, but there was one problem. In all the rush to bring help, no one had thought to bring a spare horse.

Chapter 24

Ill News

The easy ride south passed in only a few short days as the road left the forest and carried them beside the Amber River. So close to the capital, farms were almost constant, and the smell of livestock was a regular presence on the breeze. The river rolled lazily by, carrying the occasional small boat or raft of logs cut in the Wood and bound for Charlford or Varella.

Samir paid little attention to any of it, concentrating instead on developing and honing the ability to focus mind and will. Lately he was aware of everything. More aware, in fact, than he would have believed. But he simply allowed the details to flow past him, deeming them unimportant.

Unlike his first attempt, he no longer thought of interactions with others as a distraction. Rather, he was now able to give others his full attention without worrying that his peace would be stolen. The sense of control he experienced—over his mind, his emotions, and even his body—was a welcome change from the turmoil he'd gone through over Morena. He only regretted the necessity. As much as he wanted the love he felt for her, he preferred to avoid the pain of loss.

Still, he was nearly unprepared for the intensity of his feelings as they covered the last few miles to Varella. He had known, of course, that gathering the last of the necessary herbs would bring a quick end to their travels.

What had failed to register had been the fact that, once that happened, Morena might vanish from his life. As much as he hated to admit it, he had taken her for granted.

The truth was that without the mission to bring them together every day, he might never see her again. The realization was more than enough to shatter his focus entirely.

Samir knew he couldn't let things stay like this. Eventually, he would have to deal with the root of the problem instead of ignoring it—which is exactly what he'd been trying to do. And under the circumstances, it would be better if he did so sooner rather than later.

Of course, his need to return to Majar still presented problems. His sense of honor required him to settle matters with Kemal, and he had to discover whether his mother lived. Yet, he'd made a commitment to Carlon and the others as well. However important his ultimate plans, he would not be shamed by breaking his word.

But there was one possible solution. It should be possible for him to sail south when winter began. Although it hadn't been mentioned to this point, he got the impression it would put a halt to their plans anyway. Surely it wouldn't take more than a few months to set things right and return.

Of course, he would need to discuss this with wiser heads to see what they advised. It was still hard to allow himself to trust at times, but he believed Carlon and Jenaris would be discreet and he valued their opinions. Besides, only the King could release him, albeit temporarily, from his promise to see this through.

Once it came down to action, he was fairly confident of his ability to reach Kemal, especially with the advantage Dragon's Fang would give. After that, he should have no real difficulty besting his brother. The only real drawback was his lack of knowledge about Kemal's security. Anyone who had gained his position by treachery would certainly expect others to attempt the same thing, after all.

Well, there was no sense worrying about it just yet. He had other things to deal with first.

Samir felt better as they came within sight of the city, as if a weight had been lifted. A genuine feeling of peace came over him at the thought of finally doing something about his problems instead of worrying about them.

"What are you grinning about?" Caleb asked as they rode.

"A man can't be happy?" Samir returned.

His friend shook his head. "No offense, brother, but lately I've wondered."

There was nothing he could say to that. He had to admit he'd been poor company lately. Either he'd been moody over his relationship with Morena or seeking escape in his mental exercises. But, then, his present lighter mood was just as much a result of his feelings for her. In this case, however, it was hope that he felt, rather than despair.

"Fair enough," he answered. "But I'm beginning to think things might actually work out. It's been a while since that's been true."

"Mm-hmm." Caleb looked more than a little doubtful. "Look, I don't know what's happening between you two, and it's none of my affair. But do me a favor, will you?"

"What's that?"

Caleb met his eyes with a serious expression, but was silent for a long moment. Thoughtful.

"If you think you have a real chance to be happy," he finally replied, "take it."

With that his friend once again lapsed into silence, lost in thought. Samir could easily guess what was on his mind—Sorana. They had discussed the problem more than once on the long trip, and the Acedian Prince was understandably anxious. In perhaps as little as half an hour Caleb could come face to face with her father—who had certainly learned of the encounter with Huldrich. It was bad enough he had fought a potential brother-in-law, and might again, but it would be disastrous if Gerrit shared his son's hatred. Worse still, what if Sorana did as well?

Samir understood how Caleb must feel and respected his desire for silence. The city of Varella refused to cooperate, however. A flurry of activity pressed in on them as they rode toward the castle, the sound of commerce almost like a heartbeat, a far healthier one than he'd experienced the last time he arrived in the city. All around buyers and sellers, carts and craftsmen raised a clamor loud enough to feel.

It was exhilarating.

But, within minutes, the party had swept through the gates of the keep and into the broad courtyard. Word of their arrival had obviously preceded them as they were met by an army of grooms and servants, crowding forward to take horses and baggage. The staff was overseen by Carlon himself who smiled a welcome as he approached.

"All well, I see." The King's eyes swept the small group as they mounted the steps to the enormous front doors.

His gaze stopped, widening slightly as he saw his son. Caleb's injuries had almost disappeared entirely. *Almost.* A definite pattern of yellow blotches remained from the terrible bruises he'd suffered, and the stitches had only just been removed.

"Something happen?" he asked.

Caleb steeled himself visibly. "I'd prefer to tell you later, if you don't mind, Father. Privately," he answered. "Have the Gotarrans arrived yet?"

"Later's fine." The King's slow nod made it plain the agreement was somewhat reluctant, but he was willing to wait. "And, no, they haven't. But enough of that. Did you find everything?"

A slight anxiety showed in Carlon's tone, though he hid it well. He turned his gaze on Jenaris.

The Wizard immediately looked to Morena, inviting her to answer. It was she who had been responsible for their success, after all.

"Yes, Sire, and with plenty to spare." Her satisfied smile echoed her words. "If I could have a room to work and a few apothecary supplies, we should have what we need in a few hours." Looking down at her clothes, she made a small expression of distaste. "After I've gotten a bath, of course."

"Of course," Carlon replied with an easy laugh. "I sent a page to tell your mother you're home. No doubt she's waiting for you."

"Thank you, Sire. I'll make a list of the necessary equipment." With a quick curtsy, she was gone.

Samir watched her disappear into the crowd before turning his attention back to Carlon. "Majesty, I'd like a few minutes with you when there's time," he said. "With you as well, Jenaris."

The Mage merely nodded his assent. The king, however, studied him for several moments before responding.

"Certainly, Samir," he allowed. "I imagine you'd like to get cleaned up, as well. Your rooms are ready."

"Thank you, Sire." Samir took the dismissal, bowing deeply before heading toward his rooms. He was almost surprised to hear Tirza padding along behind him.

Spotting a page he recognized, the Majaran waved the boy over.

"See if the cook can spare a few sausages, will you?" he indicated the dog. "I'll be in my chambers."

"Right away, sir." The lad trotted off, vanishing rapidly around a corner.

It seemed an age since he'd passed through these halls, which were somehow familiar despite the brief time he'd spent here. Finding his way was easy. After only a few twists and turns, he stood before the carved door.

The sight of a large steaming copper tub greeted him as he pushed the door open. He wasted no time, slipping off his boots before stepping inside.

It took only an instant to shed his stained and travel-worn clothes and sink gratefully into the hot water. He could easily have fallen asleep as the warmth soaked into him, but he resisted the impulse. Instead, he considered what he needed to say to the King. His thoughts scattered in half a dozen directions, unable to fit together in a coherent whole. Ultimately, all he could think to do was to begin at the beginning.

Toweling himself off, he pulled his good silk from the wardrobe and dressed hurriedly. Still, he was careful about his appearance. He left his hair loose, tucking the hair clip behind his sash. Although it meant nothing here, among his people it was a sign of familiarity—an indication of comfort. It felt appropriate to wear the armband, which he retrieved from his saddlebags. By the time he was done, the page had arrived with the sausages—an entire plate of links.

"I thought you might be hungry, too, sir," he said with a grin, disappearing once again at Samir's nod of thanks.

Sitting back on the bed, he tossed Tirza one of the links before biting into one himself. He really wasn't especially hungry, but at least his appetite wasn't blunted by worry. In no time at all the contents of the plate were gone—mostly into his own belly.

With a sigh, he grabbed his sword and stood as a light knock sounded at the door. He opened it to find a young page in livery.

"Good afternoon, sir," she curtsied. "The King will see you now."

It was only a short walk through the hallways as he and Tirza followed the girl to the second floor library. Samir had been there before, finding the well padded chairs by the tall windows a comfortable place to enjoy a book or a conversation. Now Carlon and Jenaris sat talking quietly near the cold fireplace, enjoying a glass of wine. A nearby table held a silver tray with a pitcher and several empty glasses.

"Help yourself, Samir," the King waved graciously toward the wine.

Carlon fell silent then, allowing him enough time to pour and move to the indicated seat. Bowing, Samir sat and waited on the other man's pleasure. Although he had asked for the meeting, it would still be up to the King to open the discussion when and as he chose.

"Jenaris has been telling me about your fight with the dragon," Carlon began. "He made it sound easy."

Samir smiled at the hint of a question in that last statement, as well as the choice of subject. Combat was a welcome topic—one he strongly suspected the man had deliberately chosen to help him relax. If so, he appreciated the gesture.

"Quick doesn't necessarily mean easy, Sire," he replied. "I'd be a fool to think I won't need to stretch myself more the next time. At this point, we don't even know how a *typical* dragon fights...if such a thing exists."

Carlon nodded. "It'll be interesting to see how much difference you find in their skills." He paused, indicating a change of subject. "What about my soldiers? Their abilities?"

He'd known the question would come, and it was important to his plans. Unless the men made good progress, it was unlikely he would have time to return to Majar.

"They all seem well motivated, and a few have real potential," he answered honestly. It was no surprise since the handpicked men probably represented Carlon's best. "They'll be good enough to teach the basics soon. A few more months and some could stand against a dragon with reasonable odds."

"But the odds improve if they work as a team," the King observed. It wasn't a question. The man knew something of combat.

"Yes," the Majaran nodded. "We've been working on that. I've been working with Caleb as well. He has some good skills."

Carlon allowed a grin of paternal pride. "I appreciate that, Samir, and I hope he continues to learn from you. But I would prefer to keep him out of any more danger from dragons."

Samir nodded. He understood the man's desire to protect his heir. It wasn't a comment on Caleb's ability to handle himself—or didn't seem to be.

"That's between you and His Highness, of course, Sire," he allowed, not at all interested in appearing to take sides.

"Very diplomatic," Carlon chuckled. "Now, what's on your mind?"

It was an abrupt change of topic, almost catching the young warrior off guard. He made it a point to remember the tactic.

Samir took a long sip of wine to gather his thoughts.

"I'd like to get your advice, Sire," he said, making sure to include the Wizard with a glance.

Carlon nodded. "About the young lady or your claim to Majar's throne?"

Samir nearly choked on his wine. For the second time in as many minutes, the King had managed to surprise him. But this time surprise didn't half cover it. He was *stunned,* and it wasn't a feeling he enjoyed at all.

"What?" he blurted, trying to think what to say—or to think at all. "How...?"

Carlon's look seemed to weigh Samir to the ounce. "If you mean how did I know, I didn't." He smiled, very much as a cat might smile at a very plump rabbit. "I just put a few things together."

Samir schooled himself to remain still. "You've had news," he said, fishing for information.

The man gave nothing away, merely meeting the warrior's gaze for a moment. "I've had news," he allowed with a nod, then suddenly warmed. "Relax, *Prince* Samir. You're among friends here. But I can't give advice without all the facts."

It was clearly an invitation. The Majaran Prince complied, describing his brother's treachery, the events of his birthday, and the significance of the gold band he wore on his left arm.

"Highness," said a voice in his ear. He'd forgotten the Mage entirely until the man appeared at his elbow, pouring wine to refill the empty cup in Samir's hand.

Carlon, on the other hand, stared thoughtfully out the window as he digested what he'd just heard. He absently held out his cup for the Wizard to refill. Finally, after several minutes, he sat forward in his chair to look intently at the young Prince.

"It was the timing that gave you away," the King informed him. "You had already mentioned that your brother had killed your father. Of course, that's not the official story in Toskar, but an illness that kills the King and his oldest son on the same day?" Carlon shot him a dubious expression. "With the timing of your arrival and the false name, it just fit too well."

Samir's opinion of Carlon rose several notches. He appeared to miss very little and could put together seemingly unrelated facts. One thing was certain—with a mind like that, King Carlon Cravath would be either a valuable ally or a terrible enemy.

"I mean to get my crown back," he announced, cutting immediately to the point. "I would be willing to wait, but there's something forcing my hand."

The King nodded sagely. "I understand," he said. "But exactly how *does* Morena fit into this?"

Samir's jaw dropped. How did the man keep *doing* that? Somewhat chagrined, he resigned himself to the idea that he could keep nothing hidden.

"Majaran law gives my mother the right to choose my bride for me. But, until I know if she lives, I'm not free to make any promises," he answered, frustrated. "I can't pursue a relationship right now. Not without that information."

The Mage laughed softly, earning him a puzzled look from Samir.

"I hate to ask," Jenaris said wryly, "but how does *she* feel about that?"

He shrugged. "I don't know exactly. She didn't seem very happy about it, though."

"You didn't *ask* her?" Carlon wondered. He and the Mage shared a brief look of amusement.

"Young man," Jenaris shook his head, "I'm sure your father taught you how to rule, but you obviously have a lot to learn."

Put so plainly, Samir could hardly argue. He'd been so concerned with making the right choice, doing the proper thing, that he hadn't thought to discuss it with Morena. Not that they could have made any other decision in the end, but at least she would have been heard, felt valued.

"I may be able to find about your mother." Carlon's voice broke through his introspection as he pinned the warrior with a penetrating stare. "My emissary can ask a few discreet questions, but you *can't* go back right now."

Samir accepted the declaration. He had hoped to receive a different answer, but Carlon had the right to hold him to his promise.

"I understand, Sire," he said. "Be assured, I'll fulfill my obligations to you first."

The King looked at him sadly. "You don't understand at all," he insisted. "The news I hear isn't good. Majar's borders are all but completely closed now. The army is being expanded, and *all* ships are being searched."

Confusion gripped Samir. "It sounds like he's expecting an attack."

"It does," Carlon agreed, leaning forward. "Every report I've heard points to the same thing. They also say he's acting...irrationally. "Samir, I understand how badly you want to do this," the King said with genuine sympathy. "I just don't think it can be done. There's no way in."

He sat silently for a moment, trying to absorb what he'd just heard. Kemal had always been irresponsible, but the worst he'd expected was that his brother would squander money, take advantage of the people. But, while he had anticipated that there would be some safeguards against possible treachery, this was...*crazy*.

Now he *had* to do something. There was no way he could allow the usurper to remain in power one second longer than necessary. Especially an unstable or irrational usurper. If he waited too long, there would be nothing left to return to.

"I have to go back." An edge of despair touched his voice. "I don't have a choice now."

Carlon stood, stepping in front of Samir and forcing him to look up. "I don't think you're hearing me," the King insisted. "There's *no way in*. Especially for you. You'd be recognized."

"I can make it," he replied quickly. "There's a crossing through the desert from Rukat."

But even as he said it, he knew it wouldn't work. The Forge killed everyone who didn't know how to survive there—and many who *did*. He wouldn't last a day on his own, and no caravan would take anyone they thought might be a burden.

He dropped his head into his hands. There *had* to be a way. To simply abandon Majar to the control of a maniac was unthinkable. And he wouldn't, he *couldn't*, leave Kemal unpunished. For now, however, he could see no way to do anything about it.

Carlon's hand fell onto his shoulder, a gesture that reminded him of his father for a moment. He looked up into the King's eyes.

"I'll make you a promise, Samir," he offered gently. "We'll help you any way we can. Just promise me you won't try anything reckless or foolish. Deal?"

"Deal," he nodded. "In the meantime, could we keep this between us?"

Jenaris and Carlon agreed easily, adding reassurances of support.

The need to wait was unwelcome, to be sure. But at least he wouldn't have to do it alone.

Chapter 25

Alliances

From his vantage at the second floor window, Caleb could see the frenzied activity in the courtyard clearly as servants rushed to meet the Gotarrans and see to their needs. Of the two dozen or so, he recognized only a few. King Gerrit and Kulmar had been welcomed by his father and swept inside to enjoy a hot bath and a cool drink.

It had come as no surprise to see Huldrich and his two friends milling about with the others. He'd been hoping they had been too late to come along, or that Huldrich would need to stay behind in Gerrit's place. But considering what had happened, it had been a fair guess that they would be here.

His father had said almost nothing when he'd heard the story, but Caleb could tell he'd immediately begun planning how to handle the situation. Not that he hadn't given his son the rough side of his tongue. News that the fight had been about Sorana had definitely set him on edge. Still, he hadn't been able to fault Caleb's actions—at least not beyond the bad judgment of telling barbarian jokes to the daughter of the barbarian King.

Of those who had ridden into the courtyard, however, only one held his attention. After nearly two months, that first glimpse of Sorana had been a shock, his heart leaping into his throat. He'd been unable to look away since.

"I can see from here that she's too good for you," Cait said mockingly from her perch on the window seat.

He knew she expected some sort of retort, and normally he'd have been happy to oblige. Yet, at the moment he couldn't.

"I know she is," he answered.

Cait studied him for a moment, then gracefully rose to stand beside him, a slight look of envy in her eyes. "If someone ever feels *half* as much for me, I'll be truly happy," she said seriously. "Do you want me to talk to her?"

Caleb considered, but swiftly discarded the idea. He knew his sister would advocate strongly for him, and he loved her dearly for the offer. He just couldn't let himself take the easy way out. This was something he would have to do for himself, and if he had to take a few more lumps, then so be it. But first he needed to figure out a plan.

"Thanks, Pest, but no." He slipped an arm around her to give her a squeeze. "And don't you dare settle for half."

"I was wrong, Brat. You do deserve her." She gave his cheek a quick peck, then made a face. "Now get out of here and get cleaned up. Trust me, if you show up looking like that, she'll say, 'no' for sure."

Sticking out his tongue, he headed for his rooms. He probably didn't want to wear his finest clothes—especially if he had to face Huldrich again at some point. At the very least, though, he needed to look presentable.

He didn't really see any of the finery displayed in the castle's halls as he swept past. Caleb had seen them a thousand times and rarely took any real notice anymore.

Tapestries, portraits and tables laden with crystal or fine silver seemed drab as he recalled the wood and stonework of Scara. Yet, even that paled next to the image of Sorana captured by his mind's eye.

Even with her face covered in road dust and her hair in disarray from the wind, she was beautiful. Sadly, he could read almost nothing of her mood from his earlier vantage. Did she hate him? Miss him? But he couldn't make her love him or even forgive him. All he could do was tell her how he felt, apologize and accept whatever answer she chose to give.

He was as nervous as a cat in a leaky boat trying to think his way through this. It always came back to the same problem. Even if her response was everything he hoped—which was by no means a guarantee—there was still a very real possibility of a confrontation with her brother. Or her father.

At least he would have Samir at his back when the meeting happened. The man could probably face every Gotarran unarmed and never wrinkle his silk or muss his hair. Caleb knew his friend wouldn't fight his battles for him, and he wouldn't want him to, but it was good to know the Majaran was solidly on his side.

There were several hours yet before dinner. But Caleb knew his father enough to anticipate that there would be a reception as soon as it could be arranged, and that the two Kings would be meeting over a pipe and a drink. Whether good or bad, everything would almost certainly be settled before the evening meal.

He washed quickly and shaved. There wasn't much else he could do, though it would have been nice to have something to keep him occupied. The selection of clothes was a practical matter—finely spun wool of a decent cut, and dark enough not to show stains if he had to fight. Something sturdy.

A sword, he decided, would be a bad idea. While he was sure decorum would have allowed it, he refused to let Huldrich or anyone else assume he was hiding behind steel. His small belt knife was the most he would allow himself, and he would need that to eat.

Running a comb through his wavy rust-colored hair, he tied it back. He was ready. Succeed or fail, he would soon have his answers.

With the last buttons of her dress fastened, Sorana clasped her hands tightly to her belly in another vain attempt to settle her stomach. It had felt as if it were doing somersaults since coming in view of the city, but now it was growing steadily worse. Her Caleb was somewhere in the castle.

Her Caleb. Well, he wasn't hers yet. In fact, no matter how badly she wanted it, he might never be hers thanks to her *oaf* of a brother. As much as she loved Huldrich, she could happily have skinned him for doing something so stupid.

Caleb must despise her entire family now, she knew, but she had to at least try. Still, if he had a spark of love left for her, then there was a chance they could salvage this. After all, if she could forgive, then surely he could too.

Forcing herself to relax, she smoothed the bright blue fabric of her dress for perhaps the tenth time. She had already tried on several, and hadn't been truly satisfied with any of them. They were her best, all of good wool or linen, and well made. But suddenly they seemed so shabby and plain compared to the wealth of this place. Gold and silver were displayed in the halls. Servants were dressed in clothes as fine as any she owned. Now she even stood before a full-length mirror, when the largest she'd ever seen had been a quarter the size. It was no wonder he had thought her people backward.

She hoped he would eventually see that he'd misjudged them. First, though, there were some bridges that needed to be rebuilt.

Hopefully, Caleb wouldn't be too hard on Huldrich when he decided the punishment for her brother's crimes. But whatever the penalty, she knew Hul would face it without flinching—for their father's honor as well as his own.

The plain silver hoops swung from her ears as she gathered her long hair to tie it back. She hoped he would recognize the ribbon she used—a length of dark blue she'd once stolen from his own hair. Perhaps it was a touch too sly, but she was prepared to do anything within the bounds of propriety to remind him of what they'd shared.

With a final glance in the mirror, she decided she was ready.

Once in the hallway, she wandered for several minutes before finally asking one of the maids for directions. The place was just so *huge*, bigger than any building she'd ever thought to see. But, then, she'd caught sight of several along the waterfront that could have swallowed the community hall in Scara. In fact, her entire village would probably fit inside the castle's grounds. Together with the city outside, with its thousands of people, the size of this one place was staggering. It was hard to believe anyone could find their way without becoming lost.

The reception hall she was led to was already beginning to fill. Perhaps sixty feet on a side, the room was beautiful. Polished marble in several shades patterned the floor. Tiered chandeliers hung with cut crystal cast sparkling highlights on walls painted with well-executed hunting scenes. Even the padded chairs along the walls were gilded. The room made her want to dance.

She must have been among the last to arrive, since the hall was nearly full. The Gotarrans kept to themselves, hanging near the back and trying very hard not to be obvious about staring at the splendor. As a result, the lot of them looked like nervous hens surrounded by foxes.

The Acedians in the room circulated freely among themselves, all the while casting discreet glances at her father's warriors. As a group, they were more successful at keeping their uncertainty hidden—but only slightly. Only the black and green clad servants moved between the two groups, bearing platters of cheese and fruit as well as wine and ale. Sorana actually admired the way the servers carried out their duties without a sideways glance at either group. They simply went about their work with a composure she envied.

Drawing a deep breath, she stepped inside and almost immediately stopped. It would have been easy to move to where her own people stood. But she steadfastly refused to appear frightened, as if she were merely taking refuge. Unfortunately, the momentary indecision left her standing alone, squarely between the two groups as those on both sides cast curious glances her way. Acutely self-conscious, all she could think to do was take a cup from a passing tray and try to look as though she was exactly where she meant to be.

It was then that she caught her first sight of Caleb through the milling crowd. He was standing at the front of the room, speaking with a longhaired man and a pair whose green uniforms and gold braid marked them as military men.

His appearance surprised her. While he had always dressed nicely, and was now, the style was completely unexpected. He looked so somber—coat and trousers a blue so dark they were nearly black, and even his shirt was grey. With her he'd always worn such bright colors that she wouldn't have believed he owned anything so *bleak*. Caleb's expression was serious as well.

How could he have changed so much in so short a time?

"Men are idiots," a sympathetic voice said beside her. "And neither of them deserves us."

The woman who slipped an arm through hers was on the cute side of striking with green eyes and a pert nose. Somehow she felt an immediate sense of kinship.

"I'm Sorana," she offered with a grateful smile.

"I know. I'm Morena," her companion replied. At Sorana's questioning look the young woman continued, laughing softly. "Caleb's a friend of mine, but sometimes he's a fool. He's been brooding about you for weeks, and he still doesn't have enough sense to come over and *talk* to you."

Sorana's stomach did a flip. If Caleb was brooding, then surely he felt *something* for her. She offered her unexpected new ally a grin as her mind tried to form the questions that all seemed to come at her at once. But it was Morena's opening comment that registered first.

"Neither of them?"

"Mmm, Samir," the other woman nodded toward Caleb's group. "The one in silk. He can battle a ship full of pirates, but somehow he's afraid to risk letting me in."

She hadn't been aware of it right away, but they had started walking slowly toward the front of the room. The spot they were headed for was well to the side of the men, but still entirely too close. Sorana hesitated, but was pulled along gently.

"Trust me, you look beautiful," Morena whispered, "But I think we need to make sure Caleb keeps that in mind. Just let him see you and I'll be surprised if he doesn't come over.

Sorana could just see Caleb in her peripheral vision as they came into his line of sight. She couldn't hear what he said to Samir above the buzz of conversation, but the other man glanced briefly over his shoulder to lock his eyes on Morena, his long hair swaying.

"You got Samir's attention, too," Sorana said quietly.

Morena sighed. "I've *had* his attention. What I want is for him to do something about it."

"You're right," Sorana replied. "Men *are* idiots."

Morena had just opened her mouth to speak when three sharp raps sounded from the doorway, stilling the room. Every head turned toward the lean, balding man who stood just inside holding a staff.

"Prime Minister Silva," Morena whispered in her ear.

She smiled her thanks.

Behind Silva, she could just glimpse her father in the hallway with another man. King Carlon?

"Ladies and gentlemen," the Prime Minister intoned in a ringing baritone. "I present His Majesty, King Gerrit den Galen, Lord of the Highlands of Gotarra. And His Majesty, King Carlon Derrek Cravath, Blessed of the Realm, Lord of Acedia."

As the two Kings strode into the room together, polite applause sounded from the Acedians in the room. The thought struck Sorana that they were praising Carlon for his gracious gesture—allowing the barbarian to enter as an equal. But that was uncharitable of her. It *was* gracious to present a foreign King as an equal.

The Gotarrans whistled loudly, clapping like wild men and drawing a smile from their King.

King Carlon was impressive, even at a glance. Although powerfully built, he wasn't a tall man. Probably close in height and strength to Suppan. Yet, somehow, Caleb's father exuded what could only be called *presence*, which strangely made him seem the tallest man in the room. Like her own father, he gave the sense that following where he led was simply the sensible thing to do.

The two Kings immediately set to work, separating to approach small groups on either side of the hall, paying no heed to nationality. As they crisscrossed the room from group to group, they invariably drew one or two with them, depositing Gotarrans among Acedians and vice versa. Within a matter of minutes the people had become so interspersed, it was hard to imagine things had been any other way.

At the same time, her father and Carlon began gathering another group at the front of the room. A whispered word in passing, a subtle nod of the head, and people wandered to the indicated spot near where Sorana already stood.

Caleb and Samir, Huldrich and Kulmar all came slowly together. The tension between the two Princes was obvious, though somehow Hul seemed more wary of Samir.

Another woman of about their own age joined the growing group, close enough in certain features that she could only be Cait. Finally, Sorana's father caught her eye with a subtle gesture, sending her and Morena the few short steps to the others.

There was an odd feeling to the little gathering as Caleb watched both Huldrich and Sorana, Samir watched Morena while standing between the Princes, and Cait casually studied her. It was as if the Kings had managed to disarm the tension between their two peoples only to drop it all among their families. Yet, remarkably, neither man gave the impression of having noticed anything unusual.

Carlon and Gerrit seemed to finish their rounds at nearly the same time, approaching from different directions.

Wordlessly, the Acedian King led them to a small side room.

"That went well," her father gave Carlon a sly grin.

The Acedian King waved it away as if denying there was ever any problem. "People are pretty much the same anywhere you go, Gerrit. We just had to show *them* that." He paused, looking around the small circle. "Now I think we need to do something about maintaining the peace here."

Both Huldrich and Caleb paled noticeably as their fathers turned their attention to the two young men. The Princes were more than a little anxious as they stood under the intense scrutiny.

"We've decided it would be best to make sure there are no more...incidents," the Gotarran King insisted. "Our two families need to be allied a bit more permanently from now on."

Sorana's mouth went suddenly dry as she tried to take in what she'd just heard. *Surely* that had to mean.... Across from her she could see Caleb considering the implications as well, although she wasn't at all sure what he was thinking. Her own mind was spinning as she raced through every imaginable emotion—from anger at her father for not asking her to unbridled joy.

"Huldrich," Carlon gave her brother a warm smile, "Cait, we've decided the two of you will marry."

The breath left her as if she'd been kicked in the belly. This was all *wrong*! She was supposed to marry Caleb. She *knew* she was. Stark confusion gripped Sorana as she tried hard to understand. Surely Carlon had simply said the wrong names...unless Caleb had refused already.

Her stomach turned to a ball of ice at the thought, tears stinging her eyes.

Around the circle, others responded with equal surprise. Cait merely stared, swallowing hard and looking like a trapped animal that wanted to bolt. Huldrich wore resignation like a cloak, shoulders sagging and gaze lowered as he nodded agreement without argument. Caleb, however, appeared to be furious as he stared at Huldrich, teeth clenched and fists balled so tightly his knuckles were white.

"No," he said firmly without raising his voice.

"What was that, Caleb?" Carlon asked his son. He had clearly heard, and was not at all pleased to be gainsaid in his own keep.

Caleb met his father's hard stare evenly. "I said, 'No,' Father. That man is *not* going to marry my sister."

In spite of her muddled emotions, Sorana's own anger rose quickly as she looked on in disbelief. How *dare* he?! It was one thing if he didn't want to marry her, but to refuse her brother because of some stupid grudge. She took a firm step toward him, forcing herself forward.

"What?" she asked, tone rising. "My brother isn't *good* enough for her?"

Caleb stared at her, amazement plain as he sought to find his voice. "I don't know anything about your brother," he replied. "Or *you* apparently. If you think this is a good idea, then you've evidently decided you don't want to marry *me*."

Hurt filled his eyes as he looked at her. With obvious difficulty, he bit back whatever he'd intended to say next.

"And another thing," she continued. "Wait...*what*?"

Sorana paused as her thoughts leapt back to what he'd just said. "Don't you put that on me. It's *you* who doesn't want to get married."

"What are you talking about?" he demanded. "Of course I want to marry you."

Both were shocked into silence as everyone in the group burst into sudden laughter. Her father's booming guffaw nearly drowning out the rest.

The sudden scrutiny caused her to blush scarlet. Caleb did as well.

"See," Cait crowed, exultant, as she faced the two Kings. "I *told* you he would fight for her."

"Right you were, lass," Gerrit replied with a wink.

A disbelieving expression on his still red face, Caleb rounded on his sister. "Pest! I told you to stay out of this."

His sister was unperturbed by his tone. She smiled.

"I love you too, Brat," Cait said softly. "Too much to sit and watch you mess things up."

It was all too much to try to take in—except for one thing. He *did* want to marry her! Warmth spread through her at the thought, thawing the cold that had recently gripped her. She really did want to dance.

Excitement growing, she took another step toward Caleb, although this time with very different intent. He held up a hand to stop her, clearly apologetic.

"There's something I need to do first," he told her, love in his voice like a caress. Turning to her father, he dropped immediately to his knees. "Your Majesty, I owe you an apology. I've been guilty of looking down on your people. Belittling you. I was wrong, and I ask your forgiveness for disrespecting you, your daughter and all the Gotarran people."

Gerrit took only a moment to recover from his initial surprise. He laid a calloused hand on Caleb's head.

"Forgiven," he said easily, smiling.

"In that case, Sire," the young Prince rose, "would you give me permission to ask your daughter's hand in marriage?"

"I suppose so," her father grinned. "I'd hate to think we went through all of this for nothing."

Joy surged in her, heart pounding as Caleb again turned toward her, eyes shining. As his mouth opened to form the question, however, she couldn't wait.

"*Yes!*" the answer burst from her as she threw herself at him in a rush, nearly knocking them both to the floor. Tears flowed uncontrollably, but she didn't care. All that mattered was that they were together.

Congratulations came from all around as their families surrounded them, showering them with hugs and pats of affection. Sorana barely noticed any of it. Her eyes saw only the man in front of her, as if only they existed.

"I hate to interrupt, son," her father said gently, directing the remark to Caleb. "We still have unfinished business to deal with."

The look of mild confusion on Caleb's face brought reality crashing back to her. Huldrich's crimes. All the happiness that had filled her only moments before felt like ashes. Why did they have to do this *now*?

But she knew the answer. Her people's laws wouldn't allow this to wait. Caleb's rights were clear—he was entitled to decide her brother's punishment at the earliest opportunity. His presence, along with Huldrich and someone to act as judge, made this the proper time.

"Huldrich den Gerritt," the King said gravely, "you stand guilty by your own admission of the crime of assaulting Caleb, a guest under the laws of hospitality. You are also guilty of causing my oath of hospitality to be broken." He turned to his future son-in-law as he continued. "As the aggrieved party, you have the right to decide his punishment."

Caleb nodded, understanding. "I forgive him, then. No punishment needs to be given."

Sorana's breath caught. It was a generous gesture, but obviously he didn't know what was required.

"You can't," she whispered urgently. "You can only forgive the assault. No punishment for the other means you don't value my father's word. He would be shamed."

"For the assault, I mean," Caleb amended hastily, frantically wracking his brains for an appropriate sentence to punish the other crime. Unfortunately, he had no experience with Gotarran law and had nothing by which to measure the severity of the offense.

Huldrich evidently saw the problem, too. He stepped forward, shooting Caleb a look of sympathy in the face of his consternation.

"Thank you for the forgiveness, Brother." He grinned, plainly aware of the strangeness of their new relationship. "I would help you if I could, but it wouldn't be proper for you to transfer your rights to me."

She saw Caleb's eyes brighten at Huldrich's words. He had obviously caught her brother's implication.

"You mean these rights are transferable?"

"Yes," Huldrich and her father said almost at once.

"In that case," Caleb smiled at her, "I'll let Sorana choose your punishment...as an engagement present."

She gave his hand an affectionate squeeze.

Everything was fine now. This she could handle.

"Did you know," she said to Caleb, "that Hul is an excellent woodcarver? We're going to need a wedding arbor. And he can gather flowers, too, when the time comes." Sorana gave her brother a wink, smiling sweetly. "I'm sure I'll think of a few other things between now and then."

Caleb slipped an arm around her waist, pulling her tightly against him. Yes, everything was fine now.

Samir could have kicked himself for his inattention as he wove his way rapidly through the still crowded reception hall. He forced himself to move carefully, not wanting to be rude and jostle anyone just because he was in a hurry. Besides, he knew where she had to be going and which way that would take her.

It had been obvious that Morena felt genuine happiness for Caleb and Sorana, and had plainly wanted to share the moment with them. But Samir could see that underneath was also a heartbreak that tugged at his own.

He had wanted to go to her then, but had chosen to wait for a more private moment. He'd waited too long. The second he had looked away, Morena had been gone.

After that, the time it had taken to work his way around to the door had given her more than enough of a lead to reach the hallway.

Clearing the doors, he turned left and broke into a trot, leather soles slapping the stone floor. He picked up speed as he went, eyes straining at every turn. Yet, after several corners had come and gone without a glimpse, he began to worry. What if he'd gone the wrong way? Where else could she have gone?

He put on more speed, determined to catch her.

Finally, he spotted her as he reached the last stretch to the eastern door. He was almost right behind her.

"Morena," he called. "Wait. *Please.*"

She stopped, hand on the door latch. Still, she didn't turn as he approached.

"What do you want?" The question was soft, but couldn't disguise a quiver in her voice.

Steps making no sound, he moved up behind her, reaching out to touch her arm cautiously. She didn't pull away, as he'd half expected she would. Instead, she seemed to sag in weary resignation.

"Morena," he said, the weight of guilt heavy. "I'm sorry."

Even as he said it, he knew it was inadequate.

The words made her flinch in a way his touch hadn't.

"What are you sorry for this time?" Bitterness tinged her words as she finally turned to look at him, tears streaming. "Tell me."

"All right. I'm sorry I didn't ask what you wanted. I'm sorry I shut you out and let you think I didn't want to be with you." Samir cupped her chin, bringing her eyes up to meet his. "And I'm sorry I waited so long to do this."

He was committed now, but he'd already made his choice. His loyalties lay with her.

The kiss was electric as he let it say everything he felt for her, and there was nothing hesitant or tentative about it.

Morena didn't hesitate either, leaning into him for a long, delicious moment. Without warning she tensed, shoving him away so hard he nearly stumbled.

Quickly catching his balance, he looked up to find her glaring at him, stiff backed and arms crossed. The look in her eyes should have bored holes through him.

"No," she said heatedly, shaking her head with a slow, deliberate motion. "You're not going to do this to me again. Either you're in or you're out. *Right now.*"

He smiled. "Don't worry, I'm not running. Not this time, and not ever again."

She tensed as he put his hands on her shoulders, but didn't pull away as he bent to kiss her—softly this time. Slowly, her tension melted away.

"I have something for you," he said as they broke, breath coming quickly.

Lower lip caught between her teeth, she watched as he reached into the sash at his waist. Finding what he sought, he drew out the golden clip with his fingers and held it up for her examination.

It was a wonder of finely woven wire looped in intricate knots and spirals. Although she had seen it before, many times, somehow she seemed surprised by it now.

His fingertips brushed her neck, bringing a shiver as he gathered her loose curls behind her. Setting it in place, he snapped the clasp shut with a soft click.

It was still early afternoon, and it would be several hours yet before the engagement feast. He drew a deep breath.

"Morena," he said, "there are a few things I need to tell you."

Chapter 26

What a Wizard Can Do

The council chambers seemed almost small with all the places occupied—especially with Kulmar at the table. Still, with only a little rearranging, they managed to accommodate everyone without complaint.

Jenaris now held the head of the table, where Carlon would normally sit while his ministers met. Instead, the King sat in the center of the long expanse of oak, opposite Gerrit, where he could preside more easily without the need to raise his voice—a bad idea considering the prodigious amounts of wine consumed by several of these men the previous evening.

It had been, by all accounts, a particularly fine banquet.

Bleary eyes and throbbing heads could be found all around the table, announced by the queasy looks on their faces. The Wizard knew there was a simple herbal remedy, yet from her self-satisfied expression, Morena had chosen not to inform those who were suffering. Of course, had Samir been hungover, he suspected she might have offered to help. But the Majaran had been far too disciplined to overindulge—unlike Caleb, who received plenty of sympathetic looks from Sorana. Well, perhaps they would learn the lesson she seemed to be trying to teach, although he thought it incredibly unlikely.

Overall, the Mage considered it a good sign that those on both sides had set aside differences, even if the reason *was* a party. The fact that there had been no fights he attributed to Kulmar and Samir—who had each made it perfectly clear that the winner of even the smallest scuffle would face them. After that, voices had only been raised twice.

Besides, it was hard to speak ill of former enemies when it also meant insulting your new Prince or Princess.

Among the members of the council there had been no problems, but he'd expected as much. Hopefully, the example set here would be enough to forge lasting peace among the people.

"I guess I just don't understand," Kessel insisted from his place near Jenaris' end of the table. "If we have a wizard, why do we need to risk men in the first place?"

Gerrit shot him an apologetic look, which he waved off. At least the boy had asked an honest question. Most people seemed to think along those lines, expecting a wizard to be capable of anything. He was actually surprised it hadn't come up before now.

"I think what you *really* want to know is what exactly I do." Jenaris leaned forward slightly, hands flat on the table. This would only require minimal gestures, and no one would be watching his hands. "Why don't I merely conjure fire and burn them all to ash?"

Heads all around the table snapped up as a thin ribbon of fire flashed into existence, spinning and twisting near the ceiling. As the ends joined, it swelled, thickening rapidly until it formed a ring a foot thick and ten feet across. Several of the men—those with hangovers—shielded their eyes from the intense light. Nothing could be done about the heat.

"Or perhaps," Jenaris continued, "I should freeze them and make them easy targets for anyone with a sword?"

The fire above them instantly turned to a frozen ring of snow and ice that sparkled as it caught the light of the many lamps around the room. Slowly, snowflakes drifted down, barely landing before melting to leave behind tiny droplets of water.

"Maybe," the Mage wondered, "I should call lightning from the heavens to blast them to pieces?"

Several chairs scraped quickly back from the table, as if to escape the coming onslaught. Instead, the ice vanished at a wave of his hand.

People gradually settled back into their seats as they realized the Wizard intended no demonstration. The show had produced its desired effect, however. "Elemental magics are powerful and happen to be one of my particular specialties." Jenaris swept his gaze around the table, preparing to drive home the lesson of the display. "They are also nearly *useless* against our current enemies. The hide of a wyrm and its scales are essentially several thick layers of insulation with air spaces trapped in between. Fire, ice and even lightning have almost no effect...unless you have prolonged exposure."

"Prolonged? For how long?" Carlon took the bait, asking the question Jenaris had wanted.

He paused for only a moment, pretending to consider.

"I'm fairly certain I could burn a drake to death in about two minutes," he replied casually. "That's *if* I use power at a rate that will exhaust me in little more than that.

Sober expressions met his as he looked around the table again. *Very* satisfactory. He let the implications sink in as he took a sip of his tea.

"That's not to say I won't be able to help in other ways," he said with an easy grin. "I still have at least seven of the devils Marqued, which will allow us to find them. Or them to find *us*."

"Seven?" Alban jumped in. "I thought you knew of *nine*. If Samir killed one...?"

The Mage almost laughed. The Captain was an intelligent man, and a capable leader, but clearly he was far from the most perceptive.

"No offense to Samir's abilities, but he's obviously not the only one capable of killing a drake." He pointed, drawing the other man's attention to the leather thong around Suppan's neck—or, more importantly, the claw hanging from it.

From his place almost directly across from the young Gotarran, the soldier had a good view of the trophy. Judging by the rapid widening of Alban's eyes, recognition wasn't long in coming.

Suppan looked only slightly smug.

"So that's from one of the nine you know?" Carlon asked, nodding toward the young barbarian with new respect.

"I have no way of knowing unless I try to form links to all eight—which I suppose I could." The admission that he might have overlooked something so basic was a bit distasteful, but the experiment would be easy to do. "Any residue from a Marque will disappear within an hour of the creature's death. If that was one of them, any trace of the magic is now long gone."

"What I want to know," Kulmar insisted, voice booming from the far end of the table, "is what you meant about them finding us. Do you mean they're tracking you somehow?"

Kulmar's scowl was soon echoed by others as the question took root in other minds. But Jenaris paid little heed, his attention focused on Kordel. For the first time, the Wizard saw excitement in the apprentice's eyes as awareness dawned. He nodded permission for the younger man to address the question. He had earned it, after all.

"No, sir, they're not," Kordel replied, plainly unnerved as attention focused on him. "But they can be *made* to come to us when and if we choose."

Nods and smiles began to appear around the table as the warriors took in the statement. It would be easy to track each of the Marqued beasts through a link, but that would require facing them on their own ground. Bringing the dragons to them would allow the choice of *time* and terrain, which was always preferable to those fighting the battle.

Gillis slapped the thick polished oak of the table, causing heads to snap around. A gleam of excitement lit his brown eyes.

"Bring them down to the plains and let them walk right into a cavalry charge," he whooped. "Let's see them survive a dozen lances right down their throats!"

The lieutenant's enthusiasm quickly began to catch hold of Alban and Carlon as they considered the possibility. Immediately discussion started as they put their heads together. The exhilaration was short lived, however. "I think horses are a bad idea." Samir's assertive tone cut through the discussion like a knife. "I've heard Caleb talk about the battle he witnessed, and a man fighting a battle shouldn't have to fight his mount as well. If horses panic, people will die." Recalling how Morena's father had died, he took her hand under the table, receiving a light squeeze in return.

"But horses give the advantage of size and speed," Alban objected, plainly defensive.

The Majaran laughed, causing the Captain to redden. "I'm sorry, Alban," he offered, attempting to mollify.

"Against a normal enemy, you'd be right. Crowded in against a dragon, a horse is just a large, slow-moving target. A man can react faster on foot against one of those things than on horseback."

Thoughtful expressions greeted Samir's words. Even the Captain seemed to realize the other man was right.

"Besides," Morena added, "we know horses can't tolerate Jasper berries, and they're the primary component in *this*."

As she spoke, she set a large flask on the table in front of her. Inside swirled a thick, sickly purple liquid the color of bruised flesh. With a nudge she slid it across the polished wood so it came to rest precisely between the two Kings. Gerrit grunted. "So *we* wouldn't have to worry about their poison, but our horses would?"

Morena merely nodded, point made.

"On foot, then," Jenaris said. "But where?"

The council immediately degenerated into a raucous debate as everyone threw in opinions, seeking the best place to meet the beasts head on. Always an obvious counter-argument seemed to present itself. This end of the plains would likely mean the drakes would arrive tired, but anyone living or working along their route would be put in jeopardy. On the other hand, the Gotarran hills would be a short distance to bring the beasts, but they would be unable to anticipate the direction of the attacks, and dense cover worked against them. Finding a way to drive them into the sea was tempting. Unfortunately, no one could quite reason out how to do it, or knew whether the dragons would drown or swim if they succeeded.

Argument continued unabated for nearly an hour with no real sign of a resolution. The only feasible plan appeared to be Kessel's idea of huge bear traps dug into the plains. As the eager youth pointed out, causing a dragon to come to them could just as easily be done with a trap between them. Even this was not without its problems, however.

"They're too cunning to ever fall for something like that," the Mage asserted. "Huge piles of dirt and a covering of blankets? It's just too obvious for any creature smarter than a dog."

"You haven't seen how well we hide out bear pits," Huldrich said with pride. "We can make it work."

Suppan and Kessel chimed in quickly with their agreement. Gerrit and Kulmar looked thoughtful. It was evident the two older men could see it from both sides.

Discussions seemingly exhausted, silence fell as people waited for another suggestion. No one looked very hopeful about the possibility that a better suggestion would come.

Upending a now empty pitcher over his cup, Carlon's rapidly souring mood was beginning to show—a huge contrast to his normally composed demeanor. His deep sigh as much as shouted his frustration.

"Morena, dear, would you ask the page to bring more water?" he asked through a forced smile.

She didn't move.

"Morena?" The King tried again, a bit more loudly.

Even from his place at the opposite end of the table, Jenaris could see that some idea had just burst into the young woman's mind. From the depth of her focus, it was going to be good. Questions popped up, but quickly vanished as it became evident that any discussion would only pose a distraction. Morena sat silently as her mind wove through the ins and outs of the plan.

In the meantime, Samir did the only constructive thing he could. He stepped into the hall to ask for more water.

"We don't have to dig anything," she finally said into the silence. "The traps are already there."

Carlon leaned forward, craning his neck around Caleb and Samir. "What traps? There aren't any traps dug into the plains."

"Yes, there are," the Wizard nodded, catching the gist of her thoughts.

"And with a little dirt or water, the dragons will never see them." She was excited now, thoughts and words gaining momentum as she spoke. "In fact, you don't even need to do *that* much for some of them."

"The pitch fields?" Alban asked, understanding.

Morena's expression was nothing short of triumphant. "Let them step one foot in them and they'll be stuck fast!"

"Fair game for archers or spears," Alban added.

"Or fire for that matter," Jenaris replied. "Set the tar ablaze and it would be enough to kill one eventually."

The discussion that followed was just as frenzied as the previous debate, but entirely different in tone. This time, no one doubted the plan, and the only argument involved the hundreds of details to be ironed out. While the emerging idea wasn't foolproof, it was still almost certain to work with a minimal loss of human life.

Alban and Gillis immediately dashed off, making arrangements for supplies and troop dispositions. Fast riders would be sent out at once, carrying word to anyone between Gotarra and the pitch fields to move south or west. The population there was small, but there would be plenty of farmers to order out of harm's way.

Other riders would be sent to those who worked at harvesting the pitch. Their assistance, especially their knowledge of the region, would be invaluable.

"Would somebody explain to me," Carlon said seriously as the discussion ended, "why I haven't elevated that young woman to the nobility yet?"

"I was wondering the same thing myself," Gerrit snorted. "I may have to *create* an aristocracy just so *I* can grant her a title."

Morena had the good grace to blush at the compliments, but it seemed she stood just a little taller as everyone rose. In Jenaris' opinion, she would have made a far better apprentice than Kordel.

"Are you sure you don't want to marry Huldrich?" Gerrit continued, plainly only half joking.

Huldrich gaped, eyes wide. Morena merely threaded her arm through the Majaran's as they exited the room.

"I'm sure," she replied playfully. "But if this one makes me change my mind, I'll let you know."

As the last of the others filed from the room, Jenaris turned toward Kordel, who waited quietly near the door. The punishment had lasted long enough, and it would be good to have someone else at least capable of utility spells.

"Kordel, I think it's time to begin your instruction," the Wizard said casually. "Come with me."

Without waiting for a reply, he stepped into the hallway, leaving a stunned young apprentice in his wake.

Chapter 27

Under Gotarran Law

The library was pleasantly cool as the sea breeze fluttered the light curtains. It had actually been quite an enjoyable evening as Caleb and his family had gotten to know his future in-laws—except for Sorana's mother, Khara, of course.

The fact that Khara was acting in place of her husband had actually surprised him. Somehow he'd expected Gotarran women to be...more subservient. But that couldn't have been further from the truth. In Gotarra, as in Acedia, men and women had the same rights and the same authority.

So much for the stories of shield wives, he thought.

All he'd really known about Gerrit's people, aside from the jokes he'd been so fond of, had come from stories. But it seemed much had changed.

The Gotarrans were several generations from the days when wives went to battle with their husbands, holding their shields and taking up the weapons of the fallen. The last of the clan feuds had vanished as well— ending along with the raids into Acedia when Gerrit had come to power.

That, in itself, had been an enormous change. The man had gone from chief of the strongest clan to the king of a unified land in only a few years. It was an impressive achievement, building a nation from a bunch of squabbling tribes.

Caleb had come to genuinely admire his future father-in-law, not only as a strong leader, but also as a man of real vision. Without that, his reign would certainly have been incredibly short lived. But prosperity had a tendency to make even the oldest grudges disappear, and Gerrit had definitely made trade flow.

"I don't see why we have to wait so long," Sorana grumbled, pouting in a way Caleb found absolutely adorable. She snuggled a little closer under his arm as she pulled her feet onto the sofa to curl up beside him.

Given his preference, he would have chosen to wait no longer than completely necessary. Yet he understood everyone's insistence on a longer engagement. After all, not only did they have things to learn about each other, they needed to learn about each other's people—he more than she, he supposed.

"A year isn't that long to wait," her father replied gently, evidently familiar with her moods.

"Besides, dear," Caleb's mother offered with a conspiratorial wink, "it gives us more time to plan the wedding. I'm sure you'll want everything just so, and your mother will have to be consulted."

As the pair dove into discussions about colors and decorations and every possible minute detail for the ceremony, Caleb tuned it out. It wasn't that he didn't care. He *wanted* everything to be perfect for Sorana. By now, though, he understood she already had an image of their day he could only interfere with. Oh, he could make a suggestion or two, but the best way to ensure her happiness was to let her plan and keep himself out of it. All that really mattered to him was that they were together.

Instead, he turned his mind to what he could, hopefully, do something about. It was only a matter of hours now before everyone would set out for the pitch fields to meet the dragons.

His father's desire to keep him safe at home was no surprise, nor was it entirely unreasonable. The King had to consider the heir and not merely the danger to his son. But Caleb couldn't just sit in safety while his friends— Morena included—rode into harm's way. It would be pure torture to stay behind wondering whether all was well or if a messenger was coming with news of a friend's death. Of course, he knew his father would experience exactly that, but it was no comfort. He had to go.

Thankfully, Huldrich had given him the information he needed to make that happen. The only problem was that he was seriously pressed for time, with only a few hours to make use of it. He had little doubt he would need Hul's help.

"But, Gerrit," his father said adamantly, "if you let them in to mine your copper, not only do you get the taxes, they'll probably marry Gotarran women and the next generation will be your own people. Sure, they'll bring some foreign ways, but most likely it would be minimal."

Gerrit shook his head insistently. "I know you mean well, Carlon, and I appreciate that you have to speak for your people, but I don't think so," he replied. "Those 'foreign ways' tend to be drunkenness and fighting every time they leave the mountains with a load to sell. Trust me, I had men ask around."

Caleb's father nodded, knowing the problem only too well from his own reports. Such issues were exactly the sort Caleb was forced to study and discuss in depth, preparing for the day he would take the throne.

"Do you know what the problem with hereditary nobility is, Gerrit?" Carlon leaned forward in a posture his son had come to know well after countless lectures.

"The problem is that an accident of birth doesn't keep anyone from suffering from normal human failings and weaknesses. Lady Euna maintained good order. Her son, Kris, takes a lax hand because he's afraid to face labor troubles."

The Gotarran King quirked an eyebrow. "I'd have thought you'd handle the situation."

Carlon smiled.

"It would be easy enough to station a company or two where they could keep order," he replied with a chuckle. "The man's even *eager* to pay for their upkeep after the trouble he's been having. Unfortunately, those soldiers have spent the summer chasing dragons."

Gerrit couldn't resist a laugh himself. "So what you're saying is that someone with a strong enough hand could keep the trouble down?" he asked, nodding. "I think I know just the man for the job."

"Oh, I think you're missing your biggest advantage," Carlon said shrewdly. "Once they understand your laws, they'll behave. Restitution they can afford. Risking indentured servitude they might find a bit hard to swallow."

"That law is rarely invoked," the other corrected, waving away any real threat of that possibility.

Carlon shrugged. "You don't have to tell *them* that."

The turn of the conversation had definitely snagged Caleb's attention. It had been almost inevitable that they would come near enough to the topic that he could steer the conversation where he wanted. Now they had practically handed it to him in a neat little package.

"Excuse me, sir," he addressed Gerrit. "If you don't actually *use* the law, why do you still have it?"

Surprised at the unexpected question, the Gotarran King studied his new son-in-law. "First off, you may as well call me 'Da'," he responded easily. "But to answer your question, we leave it there in case it's needed. If a man is maimed in a fight and he can't support his family, most times the other pays the bloodgeld and it's done. But sometimes indenture to the family is the only way they can make amends."

Caleb nodded, doing his best to keep his expression thoughtfully neutral. It wouldn't do to appear too enthusiastic. After all, his father wasn't a stupid man.

"I don't think I'm in much danger there," the Prince allowed, "But I've already come close to making a mistake once, and I'd rather not do that again."

He paused for a moment, then sighed. Both were real, since he'd come to the pivotal moment, but they worked just as well for dramatic effect.

"If I'm going to know your people...*our* people, then I need to know more about your laws," he said with as little enthusiasm as he could muster. "At least the ones that will keep me from offending anyone."

"The best way to learn," Huldrich broke in from his seat by the window, "is to live under them for a while. They're as much about social interaction as anything else."

Caleb was impressed at how neatly his new brother had planted the seed. He was quickly learning that Huldrich could make a valuable ally.

Now he just had to keep from ruining Hul's careful work.

"I don't know, Brother," Caleb said dubiously. "I'm still trying to learn the finer points of Acedian law. I don't think I'd have time for anything else."

"Nonsense," his father snorted. "You already know enough to hold court here, son. What you need is to gain a good understanding of Gotarran culture. I think it's a fine idea."

It took all of his efforts to hold back a victorious smile. He couldn't believe it had been so easy.

"What?" he asked, incredulous. "Live under their laws?"

The King stopped to consider. Caleb relaxed, knowing his father well enough to recognize his success. "That's exactly what I mean," his father said. "As long as Gerrit doesn't mind."

The Gotarran King shrugged. "Fine by me. Rana should be able to teach you what you need to know."

Caleb nodded, wearing a mask of resignation. Behind it he was ecstatic. Glancing at Huldrich, he caught his brother's wink. He was now officially under Gotarran law.

Of course, he hated to think how he'd manipulated his father into the decision, but he'd gotten what he wanted.

Samir checked the knot in the green silk cord binding his long braid. He was well aware he'd done so four or five times in as many minutes, and it annoyed him that he seemed unable to stop. But relaxation eluded him.

Normally, he would have sought a good, strenuous workout, practicing until he was warm and loose. Under the circumstances, however, he had to forego that idea. Arriving sweaty and disheveled now would be completely unacceptable.

He looked fine, he knew, with pale blue silk and green sash draped perfectly and his warrior's moustache groomed. But making the right first impression was about far more than his clothes, and this was too important to risk it going badly.

Samir barely caught himself before checking his fingernails for the third time.

Closing his eyes, he forced several slow breaths, concentrating on relaxing one body part at a time. The process normally took only a couple of minutes, but he took his time. When he had finished, the nervous energy seemed to have abated—for the moment at least.

He opened his eyes.

The paper covering the tall package crinkled slightly as he scooped it up to nestle it safely in the crook of his arm. It wasn't heavy, but its fragile contents called for extremely careful handling.

He almost whistled for Tirza as he left the room and closed the door. But she was with Morena, as she had been for most of the day and a great deal of time lately besides. Not that he minded. The dog had been doing so for weeks while they traveled, and now that they were together it seemed appropriate. Of course, it might not have mattered if he *did* mind, since Tirza seemed to come and go between them as she wished.

The hallways were much quieter this late in the day. Much of the daytime staff had gone off duty by now, and everyone else would be enjoying their supper or digesting it. As it was, he saw only one or two of the late staff and a single sentry before reaching the outside door.

Sunset painted the bottoms of the clouds in purples and bright pinks as he stepped out into the evening breeze. He couldn't resist a small smile. Only two days before he'd stopped Morena by that very door, and his life had changed.

He didn't regret his choice.

It was only a short walk around the large brick buildings of the barracks complex to the cottage tucked into the corner of the wall. The rows of flowers lining the path told him immediately that he had the right place. They also told him he'd chosen an appropriate gift for his hostess.

Tirza's excited bark announced his arrival before he could even reach for the heavy brass knocker. With a soft chuckle, he let his hand drop back to his side and took another deep, calming breath.

He didn't have long to wait. The door was flung open by a beaming Morena, eyes sparkling as she ran an approving gaze over him. She herself was beautiful in what he was sure must be her best dress, its pink linen embroidered with flowers and adorned with wavy frills.

Taking his hand, she pulled him inside.

It felt odd, stepping into a family's private space without first removing his shoes. He'd almost gotten used to it now, having visited Caleb in his rooms more than once, but the strangeness did nothing to help him relax. Thankfully, the warm feel of the cottage did.

More flowers in small clay pots graced every windowsill, adding splashes of color to the cozy main room. Other pots appeared to hold herbs, though whether for cooking or Morena's healing he couldn't have said.

The furnishings were sturdy, but looked comfortable with their well stuffed pillows. Not exactly like the couches he was used to, but still a pleasant place to spend an evening. If only there were more carpets covering the hardwood floors.

But, overall, the effect was certainly cheerful with only one real exception. Above the mantle, draped in a length of black cloth, hung an ornate sword. Marius' sword. Almost, he went to examine it and touch its well worn hilt, feeling as if he were drawn to it. Now, though, was not the proper time.

"Mother is in the kitchen," Morena smiled, standing on tiptoe to kiss him. "Dinner will be ready in a few minutes."

With that, she darted off through a doorway to the left. Now that he wasn't so preoccupied, he noticed the smell of roasting meat wafting from that direction. He thought it was lamb, which had been a favorite since childhood. It smelled wonderful, and he was definitely looking forward to the taste, even with the limited number of spices they used here.

"Is there anything I can do to help?" he called, trying to make his voice carry to the back of the house.

"Don't be silly, Samir." The gentle, laughing voice came from much closer than he'd expected. "You're a guest."

The woman who emerged, a steaming platter in her hands, was clearly Morena's mother. With the same brilliant green eyes and hair shading toward her daughter's red, the resemblance was marked. If Laurie was any indication, Morena would mature into a much deeper kind of beauty than what she now possessed.

He bowed deeply as his hostess set the plate on a table already draped with a cloth and set for three. As he straightened, her mildly amused smile told him where she stood on the subject of formality in her home. It was a nice smile—warm—and somehow it made it hard for Samir to recall why he had ever been so nervous.

It would be easy to set aside formality, but he did believe in bringing a gift when visiting someone's home. With an answering smile, he held out the package to her.

"Thank you for the invitation," he said simply, catching himself before he could offer another bow.

"You're welcome, Samir." Laurie set the gift on a small table and began working on the string. "And thank you."

At first he hadn't been sure what was appropriate for the occasion. In Majar, it would have been nothing to present a string of horses, gold or jewels. But the homes he'd visited there had invariably belonged to wealthy or high ranking citizens. The question of what to bring a girlfriend's mother, on the other hand, was a complete mystery to him. Peeling back the paper, she gasped. The artistry of the delicate silver orchid made it seem almost alive—its stem, leaves and petals flawlessly worked. Only a master could have produced such exquisite beauty.

Laurie stood mesmerized by the sight, and he couldn't blame her. He'd had almost the same reaction when he saw it in the silversmith's shop—awed by the nearly perfect replica of the jungle flowers of his native land. He had known the moment he saw it that it was the perfect gift, and it was more than worth the gold it cost.

"So you'll always have a least one flower through the winter," he told her.

Turning from the orchid, she wrapped him tightly in an embrace, leaving no doubt he'd made a good impression. Behind her, he could see Morena wearing a smile he'd have gladly walked through fire for.

Caleb felt both excitement and dread as he walked among the saddled mounts, surreptitiously looking for his own gelding. It would be waiting here, somewhere.

The talk he'd had with Sorana when they'd said goodnight had been harder than he'd expected. She had understood, of course, but had been anticipating time together they wouldn't have now. Suddenly, she would be forced to wait alone as Caleb left with her brother and "Uncle Kulmar." The tears hadn't lasted long, but it had been heart wrenching in a way he hadn't thought possible.

His father wouldn't be crying when Caleb explained his plans. Though it was rare to see the King genuinely angry, this had the potential to cause exactly that. It was not a conversation he looked forward to.

But there was no way to simply avoid the situation. Not at this point. Even knowing the words would be unpleasant and the tone harsh, he had too much respect for his father to just sneak away. Then again, until now he'd have thought himself beyond manipulating the man. Plainly, that wasn't the case.

Searcher was indeed saddled and ready with bedroll and saddlebags in place. Still, he made a quick check of his gear after hanging his canteens. All seemed in order. He was glad at least one thing would be easy this morning. Hopefully *more* than one.

With a quick pat of the gelding's neck, he went to find his father. It wasn't a long search.

Caleb found his father near the gates, exactly where he'd known he would. It had been a safe bet the man would be speaking with either Alban or Jenaris, both of whom were at the head of the column. But, having located him, the Prince was still in absolutely no hurry to get his attention—waiting to one side for several minutes without notice.

Inevitably, he was spotted, however. At Samir's hail the King turned, forcing him to join the conversation or ask his father for a few minutes privately. He chose the former.

"I am *not* making fun of you," Samir soothed, directing a somewhat pleading look at Morena. "It's just...why in the world would you *want* to find where the city sewers drain?"

Her light punch in his ribs seemed not to faze the Majaran in the least. "I was looking for twitch weed for *you*, you ungrateful wretch. And it was well downstream of the sewer drain."

Samir's look went beyond dubious. Of course, he was wise enough not to actually question Morena in her area of expertise.

"Look," he replied. "I appreciate your effort, but...."

"Oh, stop it." A look of annoyance was beginning to form as she stared up at Samir. "I still have to process it, and it won't hurt you to use it as long as you follow my instructions."

Although Caleb could sympathize with his friend, it was evident the warrior would never win this argument without completely offending Morena—which he would consider bad manners. The only option was to bow out gracefully, which he finally did. Unfortunately, this kept

Caleb from asking about her worrisome closing comment.

"Where's Sorana?" the king asked, scanning the faces around him.

"Seeing Huldrich off," Caleb said easily. "King Gerrit's there, too."

"I should really go over and say something. He's family now." Carlon gave a slow parting nod. "If there's nothing else?"

Now was the time to speak up, he knew. Unconsciously, he gripped the hilt of his sword before speaking.

"A word, Father?"

Already turning to leave, Carlon checked his movement. "Of course."

They walked only a short distance, to the only empty space in view. Caleb would have preferred a place where their words—or, more precisely, his father's—wouldn't carry to the others. As it was, a voice raised here would reach a lot of ears in spite of the noise. That was something he would just have to deal with.

His father waited quietly, a curious expression on his face. It was time. Taking a deep breath, Caleb plunged in.

"Father, I need to apologize to you," he said, somehow managing to meet the King's eyes. "I believe I'm doing the right thing, but I went about it the wrong way."

Carlon's penetrating stare finally made him lower his gaze slightly. "What exactly have you done?" the King asked quietly.

Caleb knew the look and the tone were designed to make people uncomfortable—though they were intended for use on contentious diplomats. Strangely enough, they seemed to work just as well on him at the moment. It was a fact he could have gone his whole life without learning.

He swallowed hard.

"I took advantage of Gotarran law," he made an effort to sound contrite. "The law that says any adult male has a right to join a war party, and even the King cannot forbid it."

Caleb straightened, steeling himself for the inevitable explosion, knowing he would need to stand up and take what came. As bad as it was bound to be, though, he believed he was ready.

Nothing. Carlon was silent as he considered what he'd heard.

"You didn't take advantage of the law, Caleb. You took advantage of me...of my trust," his father finally answered. A look of extreme pain was etched deeply into his features. "I would never have thought you'd ever disappoint me."

Caleb had never seen his father like this, and it was the last reaction he would have expected. No look of accusation. No anger. Just *hurt*—and it was because of him. He would rather his father had slapped him instead. But, then, the King plainly felt the same way.

The Prince hung his head, taking a moment to find the words. No, he knew the words. What he needed was the courage to speak them.

"I'm sorry, Father," he said. "I'll stay here."

"No," Carlon replied almost too softly to hear. "You're going. I don't think I could face you right now if you stayed."

Without another word, his father turned and walked away, moving slowly through the crowded courtyard with shoulders slumped. Caleb could only stand dumbly, watching the King's retreating back until it was lost to sight.

Chapter 28

Twitch Weed

The ride through the heart of the pitch fields took far longer than Jenaris would have anticipated. He expected perhaps eight or ten miles from the western end to the eastern. Instead, they had needed to stop for the night halfway through, then continue past noon the next day. Plainly, a few trips past the edges had given him no real idea of its scope.

Although often spaced a long distance from one another, the individual pools were occasionally clustered tightly together with no apparent standard between one and the next. Whether a vast lake or a tiny pool, the contents could vary from the consistency of tar to something nearly as thin as water in the space of only a few feet.

The harvesting methods, too, seemed incredibly diverse. Several times they passed pairs of workers slowly turning a wheel that scooped viscous fluid into a long sluice. Others used long handled dippers or even shovels to scrape and cut the dark surface deposits.

One thing did seem to be a common factor in the fields, however. Every man was clean shaven from scalp to chin. No whiskers could be seen and nothing longer than stubble was present on even a single head. Anyone who wondered at the strange custom, however, had only to look at the sticky black smears on their exposed flesh to understand. The Wizard could imagine the frustration of trying to clean any amount of the substance out of his hair. It left him no doubt he'd have chosen to shave as well.

While the foreman, Jak, had not so much as a single spot of pitch on his clothes or skin, he shaved as carefully as any of his men. In fact, riding this close it was plain that the man shaved his forearms as well.

Alerted to their coming by Carlon's messengers, Jak had met them as they entered the fields, hoping to discover their exact needs. Given the size of the area in question, though, they would clearly need a guide to find the most suitable place to lay their trap.

After only a few minutes' conversation, the man bobbed his head in a quick, jerky nod and set off. Even though they had the entire length of the region to cover, they turned north after only a handful of miles, leaving the larger road behind in favor of narrow lanes that crisscrossed without discernible logic. Their route was certainly indirect, moving at times a bit north, then south. Always the ride took them further east, however.

Jenaris had no doubt whatsoever that their guide knew where he was going. The fact that he had consulted no maps indicated that he knew each and every pool on the prairie. What concerned him was whether the wagons could carry their critical supplies over some of the narrow, rutted paths that passed for roads. That they had, at one time, carried carts and wagons was evident from the ruts themselves, but maintenance clearly wasn't a priority. Still, he supposed that if these men could haul loads of pitch out, then their own wagons could make the journey as well.

Whatever the criteria for choosing one pool over another as a site for harvest, most of the hundreds they passed were entirely unoccupied. At those that were, though, it became apparent that no one *ever* worked alone near the edge of the pools. Jak always watched carefully when workers came into view—eyeing the safety lines staked into the ground, and once yelling at someone lacking the loose, thigh length leather boots all men wore.

The place where Jak drew rein on the second day was a string of five long pools separated by distances anywhere from a few yards of hard packed soil to just over a dozen. It gave them a good killing ground—nearly seventy yards of thick black ooze overlooking the broad plains and backed by a good stretch of level ground on which to post archers and stage their supplies.

"These should do you all right," the foreman announced, speaking nearly his first words in two days, aside from shouted comments. "Two of these are a bit on the thin side, but the others have a firm grip on whatever happens to step a wrong foot."

His expression indicated that this could mean men as easily as dragons. Either way, he would take no responsibility for anyone foolish enough to prove his point. So saying, he took his leave, riding south at a good clip.

At a word from Alban, the sergeants wasted no time chivying the soldiers to the work of setting the camp and preparing the ground. Aside from their usual arrangements, Jenaris could see several groups at work in entirely new ways.

Hammers, shovels and scythes with long, sweeping blades quickly came from one of the wagons along with over a hundred three-foot wooden stakes. Men rushed to their tasks—some clearing the grass along a wide perimeter while others pounded stakes to mark the edges of the pools. They were remarkably fast, with two men driving the thin lengths of wood for each one dropping them at intervals. By the time they were finished and the final stake was set, those working the scythes had cut back a ten yard stretch on each side.

It was well done and had been impressive to watch. The rest would be for Jenaris himself to do. But first, he would have to see about getting the dragons moving as soon as possible. After all, they were at least two days hard travel from the hills and forests where the beasts were hidden, and there was no reason to assume they were even that close. Besides, it would probably take considerable time—and certainly many renewals of the links—to even begin to draw them with the modified spell. At least, he hoped that was all it would take.

The problem was that the force of a dragon's will was an unknown quantity. While he had no doubt it would be a good deal stronger than a bird or a dog, he had to admit the possibility that it could match even a human will. Worse still, was the thought that they might exceed it. Regardless, if they chose to resist—as they very well might when it came to leaving the cover of the forests— the plan would virtually collapse, and the only recourse would be to use people as bait.

There was no doubt such a tactic would work. The hatred of these creatures for human beings bordered on obsession. Any lone rider would surely bring a dragon to leave the shadows in order to run him down and kill him. Jenaris knew there would be no shortage of volunteers, even with the near certainly of death, and the help he could provide would only prolong a chase temporarily. If the situation demanded, they would all do what was needed—himself included—but he might never sleep soundly again afterwards.

Better not to think of that possibility just yet. At least he had volunteers for the links to bring the wyrms into their trap.

Pulling Suppan aside, he quickly formed the first link, making sure Kordel watched closely as he did so. Magical energy flowed freely into the young Gotarran as if the Mage had opened a tap. As with his previous experiment, time was the only real factor—allowing enough power to flow to make the warrior attract the beast at a distance. Finished, he moved on to Kessel.

As he worked, filling the stocky Kessel with more than enough power to form a tornado, he spied Suppan out of the corner of his eye. The barbarian continually glanced over his shoulder, yet seemed completely unaware of having done so. Northwest. It would be interesting to see whether his awareness would grow as the drake drew closer.

Huldrich was next, then Kulmar. Ever so slowly, the desire to rest grew, but so did the need to finish the process. In a matter of hours these links would need to be refreshed, and again every few hours after that—probably for several days. Although Kordel couldn't help him now, having never seen the Marques placed on the dragons, he would be necessary later. Jenaris would never be able to maintain the bonds alone once they were established.

Moving on to Samir, the Wizard estimated he'd been working for nearly an hour. Still, even fatigue couldn't cause him to make a mistake in such a simple spell. No, the risk would come later, as he tried to focus on the Majaran's sword. Then mistakes would not only be easy, but could cost him weeks of work.

As the Mage reached Gillis, he distractedly made the minuscule effort to form yet another link. Nothing happened. Focusing more fully on the simple spell, he tried again, yet with the same result. Smiling, he tried a third time, linking the lieutenant to a different Marque. Almost as he thought it, the bond snapped into place.

Seven. The young Gotarran had indeed killed one of the nine he had encountered, just as Samir had. There were now only seven that they knew of. *Only* seven dragons was still the stuff of nightmares, however, and they couldn't even guess how many more were out there. But at least now they knew how many they would be waiting for. With a new bounce in his step, he went to find Alban to forge the final bond.

"Why do you keep doing that?" Morena asked as Samir once again looked over her head to stare at nothing.

The first few times he'd done it, she had turned to see what had drawn his attention. She had found only more grass and an empty sky. After that, she'd done her best to ignore it. It hadn't worked.

"Doing what?" he said, a look of concern on his face.

Unbelievable, she thought. *He stares at nothing, then looks at me as if* I'm *imagining things.*

"You keep staring," she answered, hands on hips and eyebrows arched in as good an imitation of her mother as she could manage.

He responded with a blank look. "You know I think you're beautiful, but I don't think I was staring."

"Not at *me*." Frustration made her voice rise at least an octave in pitch.

"I'm sorry," he answered, shaking his head in confusion, "but you aren't making any sense. I'm not staring at anything."

"*Exactly!*" she cried.

The blank look was back. This time, though, he seemed to think better of opening his mouth to respond. No doubt he preferred not to add to the confusion he was already suffering. She didn't blame him in the least.

Taking hold of his arms, she turned him around, moving with him to remain in his view. Wisely, he remained silent. After their last exchange, she might have accused him of being deliberately obtuse.

It took a moment to remember where their conversation had left off but, before she could speak, he quickly glanced over his shoulder. When he turned back, his own face registered surprise.

"I have no idea why I just did that," he admitted. "It was like I couldn't help it."

Gently laying a hand on his arm, she scanned the camp for the Wizard. What she saw instead surprised her.

"Look at Huldrich and Kulmar," she told him.

"What am I...?"

"Shhh," she cut him off. "Just watch."

The two barbarians sat twenty feet off, joking and laughing uproariously. As they watched, it quickly became apparent that, every few seconds, one or the other would turn his head in roughly the same direction Samir had.

"It's Suppan and Kessel, too," he said a short time later.

Morena continued her sweep of the area. "Alban," she pointed out.

"And Gillis," he finished.

Several minutes of continued observation failed to turn up anyone else who had suddenly developed the strange, repetitious stare. Once again she sought the Wizard, suspecting she already knew what he would say.

A brief talk confirmed it.

"I'll grant you that it's distracting," he offered, "but it's completely harmless. I do want you to let me know if you become aware of any...impulses, however."

"You mean like a desire to go running off after the dragons before they get here?" the Majaran deadpanned.

Jenaris chuckled. "Something like that."

Turning her attention back to Samir, Morena again held out the small leather pouch they'd been discussing.

She still couldn't see why he was being so stubborn, but it was clear she'd made a mistake telling him the herb's origin. Still, she wasn't about to give up on this when it might very well keep him alive.

"Just *try* it, Samir," she asked, nearly pleading.

He held up his hands. "I'm not eating anything that came out of a sewer," he insisted.

She sighed heavily. Now he was just being *pigheaded*!

"It didn't come out of a sewer," she said through gritted teeth. "And it's been thoroughly washed...in *alcohol*. Just try it and I promise I'll never ask you again."

Samir merely stood for a moment, quietly eyeing her as he considered. She'd been tempted to ask him to do it for the sake of his love for her, but she wouldn't resort to manipulation. Especially after the way Caleb had been kicking himself lately.

Finally he nodded, holding out a hand. "All right. Let me have it."

Opening the pouch, she fished out a thick cluster of small blue-green leaves and dropped it into his palm. She steadfastly resisted the impulse to wipe her fingers after handling it.

"What is that?" Jenaris asked, studying the curious plant.

"Just something I want Samir to try," Morena said, somewhat evasive.

The Wizard quirked an eyebrow, but said nothing more about it as the warrior walked a few paces away and turned to face them. After only a moment's hesitation, he popped the leaves into his mouth, chewing and swallowing reluctantly.

"Bitter," his lips twisted in distaste.

Without pause, he broke smoothly into one of his weaponless forms, hands and feet sweeping in circles. Morena had seen him work the movements many times and, always before, he started slowly and increased his pace. Now, however, he moved quickly from the start, crescent kick flashing as he dropped into a foot sweep and breaking into a series of disarming moves that sent hands flying. He moved in a blur, leaving her almost unable to focus on him at all.

It was the most incredible sight she had ever seen. Samir's effortless moves flowed from one position to the next faster than she'd thought possible, even knowing what the herb could do.

Suddenly, his sword flashed into his already moving hand. Somehow, it appeared to pierce the air in several places at once as he summoned it from hand to hand in rapid succession.

"What is that *marvelous* herb?" the Wizard asked quietly, amazement putting a slight tremor in his voice.

"Twitch weed," she replied, knowing what he would say next. She wasn't disappointed.

"Isn't that dangerous?"

As hard as it was to drag her attention away from Samir's spinning grace, she looked the Mage squarely in the eye. "Do you think I'd endanger my boyfriend? Or anyone else?" she added. "It's safe if you don't use it too often. And I soaked it in redmoss tea overnight to minimize any ill effects."

"Which are?" he asked pointedly.

"Shakes, vomiting and increased stress," she admitted, "but the redmoss makes it almost unnoticeable. I tried it myself or I'd never have let him use it."

She managed a fair amount of defiance as she looked at him. Somehow, though, Jenaris' own stare made her feel like a little girl caught tracking mud in the house.

"How often can it be used?" he said, still plainly dubious, but also apparently quite curious.

Morena released the breath she hadn't known she was holding. "Twice a day, maybe. But *never* without a good break in between."

Applause and loud shouts of approval came suddenly from almost every direction. Returning her attention to Samir, she found him surrounded by a press of other men eager to offer their praise. He stood, somewhat glassy-eyed and sweating profusely, but not even breathing hard.

With a weary smile, he stepped clear of the last soldiers and made his way on wobbly legs back to Morena. He skin was a bit pale, she noticed, and his lips a little thin, yet he didn't appear ready to become ill.

"How did you keep from losing your balance?" she asked, more than a little amazed. "When I tried it, I kept throwing myself out of position."

Samir smiled, color returning to his cheeks. "Are you kidding?" he laughed. "Moving that fast, my balance was terrible. Why do you think I relied so heavily on hand techniques?"

Looking him over as subtly as she could, Morena found no signs of shaking. In fact, he already appeared completely recovered.

"You see," she insisted. "I told you it would help."

He nodded slowly, as if not entirely convinced. "It could definitely help in a pinch, but I wouldn't want that to wear off in the middle of a fight." His expression was troubled. "I'd be an easy target for at least a few seconds."

"My boy," the Mage broke in, placing a hand on Samir's shoulder, "the way you moved, I'd be very surprised if anyone could have survived that assault. But if Morena will give me one for study, perhaps I can find a way to help you."

Reaching into the pouch, she quickly pulled out two and dropped then into his outstretched hand. "Let me know if you need more," she offered eagerly.

"I'm sure this will do nicely," Jenaris replied, tucking them into a pocket of his trousers. He pointed at the sword on Samir's hip. "Are you finished with that?"

At the warrior's nod, the weapon instantly appeared in the Mage's hand. Turning wordlessly, he left.

"Well," Samir slipped an arm around her shoulders. "I'm famished, and *you* have training to do."

With a quick kiss, he wandered toward the wagons. She did need to get to the practice ground, but it would be a few minutes before he showed up. Sliding the small pouch back into her satchel, she headed off to meet Caleb for their session.

Chapter 29

To Set a Trap

Jenaris watched, stone-faced and unblinking as Kordel wove his hands in the gestures he'd been working hard to learn. The chants the apprentice voiced were just audible—more as a feeling than a sound—as if the air vibrated with a sense of building power. Unfortunately, it was a bit too much.

As expected, moisture condensed in the air above the viscous black tar, shifting rapidly from a mere mist into a thick, low-hanging cloud. Lightning flashed downward, igniting the tar and sending billows of acrid smoke into the sky.

Jenaris quickly released the spells he'd prepared, smothering the blaze immediately and dissipating the energy of the growing storm in seconds. He resisted the impulse to smile.

Truth be told, it wasn't a bad first try. If anything, he'd expected too little power instead of too much. Either way, control would come from practice just as long as he could form the necessary magics.

While Kordel watched, Jenaris blended movement and voice, keeping his fingers loose and subtle where the apprentice had been bold. The mist formed, gathering slowly until a light rain began to fall, pattering softly on the hot pitch. For several minutes he watched as water gradually filled the small, black lake.

Lifting his hands, he brought them together with a loud clap. Instantly, the moisture remaining in the cloud condensed, dropping with a splash that sent ripples spilling over onto the surrounding dirt. The mage grinned as he surveyed his work, finding not an inch of the sticky, dark ooze anywhere in sight.

At the next pool, Jenaris nodded to his apprentice once again, taking a few seconds to prepare more counter-spells just in case. Obviously, the younger man had seen where he'd made his mistakes and, though a bit sloppy, soon had a light sprinkle of rain falling slightly off center.

The Mage made a slow, sweeping gesture with his hands and a slight rush of sound from his throat. A gust of wind rose from the west and, in a blink, the cloud floated directly above the pitch.

With a nod of thanks, Kordel clapped. Water sloshed as it smacked the inky liquid, covering the pool entirely.

"Well done," the Wizard offered, seeing no reason to be less than honest. "Now, watch me on the other two at this end, then you can try the northernmost."

Walking a few dozen paces, Jenaris placed himself between the two pools at the southern end of the chain. Gathering a deep breath, he swept his hands around, moving them in slow circles. Again, the throaty sound came forth, this time erupting loudly. The air swirled, only lightly, bending the grasses in waving ripples across the surrounding plain. Slowly and gradually the winds built as they drew in more tightly, tearing grass from the earth as it began to howl.

The small funnel twisted as it came toward him, darkening as it moved. Only the barest twitch of his fingers was needed as he guided it easily back and forth over the ground. Little by little it moved closer until it hovered above the furiously rippling pitch.

He paused barely a second, then slashed his hand in a fast, cutting motion. The wind ceased abruptly, dropping a pile of dust and rocks onto the small piece of ground between the pools. Men immediately attacked the mound, casting dirt onto the watery pitch by the shovelful. Gradually, the Mage smoothed it down, working until it was level with the surrounding earth. Soon only the stakes indicated its location.

"Remember, Kordel," the Wizard nodded toward the lone remaining pool. "to drop it beside the pitch."

He watched the youngster trot off, knowing he needed to follow and supervise. But he was tired and, even with Kordel's surprising success, he was frustrated.

Two days of abortive attempts to perfect his own spell had done nothing for his mood. He was already on the ragged edge of usefulness in spite of the help he'd received to keep the links going. Exhaustion had been wearing at him, and that left him prone to careless mistakes. The previous night, he had finally expanded the sword's capacity enough to add the next Fixed Element, then immediately had a mental lapse that nearly lost him his work.

Of course, he could have simply put something—*anything*—into the blade, but he'd always been far too stubborn for his own good. Now that he had in mind to embed the new spell, nothing else seemed to fit. Eventually, he would make it work, if only from a refusal to let anything best him. Yet he couldn't shake the feeling he might need to prepare Dragon's Fang more than once before he did.

The maddening thing was that he was so close to his goal. He could already duplicate the herb's effect. That had been relatively easy. But he had also inherited the side effects, and he was sure he could eliminate them if he just kept trying.

He had spells that could calm, banish fatigue, and even energize people. All of them such basic magic they could be performed by the dullest apprentice, and all nearly the right one. Combining the effects of three spells into a fourth would be so difficult as to be virtually impossible, however. What he needed was a single spell that could provide for Samir's recovery. Like sleep without the involvement of time.

Time. How could he have missed something so obvious? He already had a spell to place the body into an accelerated state. Now all he had to do was take part of the duration and put it into recovery. He was fairly certain Samir wouldn't complain about having one minute instead of two. Not if it wore off without leaving him vulnerable.

"Kordel," Jenaris said with a smile. "Go and ask Samir if he can spare me the sword for a few minutes. We have work to do."

The Wizard was barely aware of his apprentice's retreating footsteps as his mind plotted the new intricacies of the job ahead of him. It would work, he knew it would. The only question was whether he could do it on the first try. Hopefully, Kordel wouldn't mind being used in another experiment, but this was too important. After all, placing a faulty spell into so perfect a blade would be a tragedy.

It had been tempting to try the sword's new power again as soon as he'd awakened, but he couldn't risk wasting it. For whatever reason, the Wizard had limited its use to only twice a day and, while twelve hours had passed, he wanted to keep it available. In a few hours, it might be useful.

Samir couldn't exactly feel the dragon getting closer, but he was aware of it now in a way he hadn't been before. At first, it was so subtle that only his unconscious mind had registered its presence. Over the last two days, however, it had grown noticeably stronger. The wyrm was getting closer, and quickly.

Judging by the reactions of the other men, his wasn't the nearest. Outwardly, Kulmar was relaxed despite the alert look in his eyes. But Samir had noticed that the man was keeping one hand on his knife hilt much of the time now, which was a very recent habit. So far, Hul, Gillis and Suppan seemed little more aware than they'd been in the beginning. It was Kessel and Alban who seemed the most on edge. He expected their dragons to appear at any time.

Of course, it was possible that their reactions were completely subjective, and no real gauge of distance at all. Yet with nothing else to go on, it seemed prudent to believe there was some connection.

The canvas top of the open-sided tent billowed and flapped as he entered, stirred by the warm breeze. While not especially bothered by the sun himself, it had driven Morena to find shelter. Her much fairer skin was susceptible to painful burns, and had even blistered once. Besides, the company was usually good under the pavilion.

"Kulmar," Caleb hailed the big Gotarran who lay in the grass a few feet away. "Do you mind if I ask you a personal question?"

Sitting up with a soft grunt, the older man smiled. "How did I get this scar?" he guessed.

"Yeah," Caleb nodded, propping himself up against one of the tall support posts. "If you don't mind."

Samir had been curious as well, having seen how the other barbarians gave the man a respect bordering on awe. Unlike Caleb, however, he had thought it best to keep his questions to himself—though it had evidently been a needless concern.

All around the tent people stopped to listen—Gotarrans and Acedians both. The huge warrior seemed amused at the attention, and more than a little pleased.

"I doubt you'll ever find a man who's reluctant to brag on his battle scars, lad." Kulmar began to slowly unlace his shirt, just enough to strip it off. Underneath, three more scars ran along his ribs on the right side of his lean, muscular frame. "Happened when I was just a bit younger than you, I'd guess. On a hunt with Gerrit."

He stood, dropping his shirt and looking around at his audience. "Now, Gerrit is a right fair shot with a bow, so it was no trouble for him to bring down a nice fat buck. Well, we got it dressed and were walking home when the bear stood up out of the bushes. Nine feet tall on his hind legs, he was, and roaring a challenge." He paused to look at Caleb a moment. "Like I said, we were young. That means we were smart enough to know all it wanted was the deer, but dumb enough to decide the bear couldn't have it without a fight. In other words, we were stupid young.

"It was Gerrit's turn to carry the buck, so I hefted my spear." The man mimed a two-handed grip as he adopted a fighting stance, milking every ounce of drama. "I charged in, thinking to go up under the ribs with one good thrust, but he doesn't just stand still. Paws the size of platters he had, and his swing bats me aside like I wasn't there. Gave me these." He fingered the scars on his chest.

"Anyway, I couldn't very well leave my closest friend unprotected, and he'd broke my spear, so I pulled my knife and dove in again." Wielding an imaginary blade, he stabbed at the air as if facing the bear. "Tried to squeeze the life out of me, but I could move my arm. Just kept sticking him till he fell over, but not before he tries to bite my head off. It's his teeth did this." Kulmar grinned as he stroked a broad thumb along his jaw. It pulled his face into an evil rictus.

His other hand lifted the leather thong around his neck, revealing the long white claw. "Took this to remind me not to be that stupid again. Course, I've come close a time or two."

Samir had known men to kill jungle cats on a hunt, but those weren't half again a man's height. Impressed, he offered the man a small bow from where he stood beside Morena's camp stool. One of the others was less cordial.

" You killed a nine foot bear with a *knife?*" a voice called. "Not likely."

Samir immediately spotted the sneering soldier who said it. It wasn't one of his students, thankfully, or he would have been shamed by the rudeness. As it was, if a fight started, his honor wouldn't compel him to take the man down, but he decided he would do so anyway.

"That's exactly the way my father tells the story," Huldrich said loudly, facing the Acedian and clearly ready to scrap. "Do you want to call him a liar, too?"

Samir could see cockiness in the other man's bearing as he framed a reply. He never had a chance to give it.

"That is an excellent question," Caleb spoke, coming to stand beside Huldrich, "*are* you calling my father-in-law a liar?"

The soldier's face paled as his arrogance dissolved. "No, Highness."

"Good," Caleb smiled. "In that case you may go and report yourself to your sergeant. *Go!*"

The man knocked several of his fellows aside in his haste to carry out the Prince's orders. Laughter followed him out of the tent.

Kulmar's unmistakable roar cut off abruptly, causing Samir to spin, alert for the cause. The Gotarran stared just east of true north, jaw muscles knotted tightly.

"It's close," he spat. "Too damned close."

It was more than enough for Caleb. "Captain Ward," he shouted, "assemble your men."

Soldiers immediately rushed for the weapons stacked neatly by their tents. Kulmar and Huldrich prodded their own warriors to their feet. The men rose drowsily, grabbing the spears and bows they kept close at hand.

In only a few minutes, rows of archers had formed ranks behind the two water-filled pools, arrows nocked and awaiting commands. A dozen cavalrymen sat calmly in the saddle, ready to split into squads to charge north and south.

The Majaran walked slowly toward the northern end of the pools, ready for the attack to come from that direction. Beside him, he watched as Jenaris strode staff in hand to the stakes at the edge of the loose earth that covered the uppermost pool.

The Mage's lips began to move in a silent chant as he closed his eyes. Impossibly slim tendrils of mist rose from the ground, nearly as fine as human hair—first in ones and twos, then in clusters. Gradually they thickened as the bare earth filled with them, covering the area with the image of thick, lush grass. Only the tops of the stakes showed above the illusion.

Jenaris didn't stop.

The chanting intensified, climbing to audible levels as he raised the staff before him. More mist rose, piling rapidly higher into a row of mounds across the now hidden pitch. Slowly, features emerged, giving the mist the form of foot soldiers, standing ready behind a wall of high shields.

The Mage ceased the chant, opening his eyes to examine his work with apparent satisfaction. "That should make him commit to the attack," he said, obviously excited.

The cheer that resounded was short lived as a cry split the air from the mounted ranks.

"I see it!" called a familiar voice.

A glance revealed Gillis pointing to the horizon. Samir had to wait, lacking the height advantage of the cavalry. Soon enough, however, he could see the black shape on the edge of vision but moving quickly. It wouldn't be long.

Chapter 30

The Trap Closes

Huldrich could just distinguish the bobbing of its tail in the far distance when the dragon saw them. It charged, putting on a burst of speed that belied its bulk and the shortness of its legs.

Given their preference for taking victims from ambush, he was actually surprised at its willingness to attack so many at once. It came on as fast as a horse at full gallop, closing the distance incredibly fast. But that was good news. Now the cavalry wouldn't need to try running it down, placing good men and horses at risk unnecessarily.

Seven hundred yards. All around, men drank the awful concoction Morena had given them. Huldrich followed suit.

Six hundred.

Alban's raised arm came down suddenly, signaling the archers to release their first flight. Two dozen humming bowstrings heralded the launch as the shafts sped skyward, wind whistling in the fletching.

Again the beast accelerated, leaving the arrows to fall harmlessly in its wake.

Five hundred yards.

Another flight launched as the archers quickly nocked more shafts. Another.

Three hundred yards. Several arrows struck the scaly back, bouncing off harmlessly. Another burst of speed. No horse could have come *near* to matching it.

One hundred yards. Another volley flew, followed immediately by the call to raise poles. Archers dropped their bows as arrows pelted the creature, ricocheting into the grass. Crouching, they quickly raised a hedge of long sharpened pikes, using booted feet to anchor the butts firmly in place.

Fifty yards. Twenty. Ten.

With a last lurch of extra speed it lowered its broad, armored head and launched itself. The drake was determined, intending to smash through the ranks of men standing before its charge. It struck nothing solid. Mist swirled as it passed through the Wizard's illusion, temporarily obscuring the images of men and grass. It nearly cleared the pitch-filled pool, covering much of the distance in its final leap. Yet, at the last moment, front legs slammed downward as the beast tried to drive itself forward yet again.

A scream pierced the air as claws pushed through the loose soil and into the thick tar beneath, sticking fast. Overbalanced, it heaved forward, nearly tumbling as its chest struck with a thud to plow up mounds of dirt and pitch.

With a jarring crack, head and jaws smacked solid ground as the dragon came to a stop on the near side. Struggling in vain to free itself, it thrashed, sinking its hind legs into the ooze as well.

A savage battle cry ripped from Huldrich's throat as he rushed forward, echoed by others all around him. The resulting surge of strength erased all traces of fear as it drove him on the last few yards. Beside him, Kessel ran to the left, so he cut right to flank the head.

Before they could cover the distance, the tail whipped forward, stabbing at Huldrich's chest and forcing him to drop and roll. He barely registered the sickening, wet thud behind him as he did. All his attention was on the dragon. Pushing himself back to his feet, he raised the spear in his hands to thrust it at a glaring red eye.

The head reared back on a neck that was limited, but still able to move, causing his blow to glance harmlessly away. Fangs bared, the beast lunged, missing only narrowly as Hul leapt back. Its attack left it vulnerable. Kessel stabbed, scoring soft flesh beneath the scales of the outstretched neck.

But the cheers were short-lived. Enraged, the dragon turned toward the source of his pain, ripping the spear from his grasp. Gaping jaws angled to snap closed around Kessel's chest.

Huldrich leapt, putting his strength and weight behind the sharp steel of the spearhead. The tip slid, scraping along the base of the creature's skull for an instant before slowing. With a jolt, it dug into the thick hide beneath the scales to sink through soft flesh. The wyrm shuddered, then dropped limply to the ground as Huldrich's spear pierced its brain.

It took two tries, bracing a foot against the muscular neck, before the spear finally came free. The motion brought him around to face the cheering men around him, but he paid them no mind. His attention was drawn to the Acedian soldier who'd been behind him when he'd dodged the tail. The man's chest was a gory ruin, the wound large enough to admit his closed fist.

He tried not to think how close that had come to being his own fate.

Well, he didn't know the man, but it was only right to pay him honor. Kneeling beside the soldier, Huldrich gently arranged his limbs, straightening the legs to give what dignity he could. It wasn't much.

Since the man had no spear, Huldrich was forced to use his own—laying it across the unmoving chest and folding the hands atop it. "Honor never dies, brother," he said softly. "See you in the next life."

With a deep sigh, he straightened, looking around for Kessel. It wasn't hard to spot someone that tall. The gangly youngster stood before the massive head, hammering with his knife pommel at the still open mouth. Wrapping a hand around one of the fangs, he pulled, straining the muscles in his arm and shoulder. It came free with a loud snap—a bone-white dagger that now ended in a jagged fracture at the root. He tossed it to Huldrich.

"Couldn't get you a claw," he shrugged looking to where the beast lay sunk to its shoulders in tar.

"It's all right," Hul admitted. "I think Suppan has a spare, but this'll do."

"I believe I can spare one," Jenaris offered as he surveyed the huge carcass. "Of course, under your traditions, I think the ones I have belong to Samir."

Without waiting for a reply, the Wizard turned his attention to the drake and raised his staff in both hands to hold it rock steady above his head. The rapid fire syllables that poured forth bore no resemblance to any human language, yet somehow they blended into smooth sounding phrases. Slowly the staff came down, looking almost as if it was meeting resistance. Equally slowly, the wyrm's body began to sink, pushing its way down through the thick surface of the pool. Sweat broke out on the Mage's brow as he fought to bring the staff toward the ground and the creature sank deeper into the pitch. Gradually it vanished, swallowed, until the tail finally followed the rest.

Dropping down in the short cut grass, Huldrich watched as men ran forward with shovels and began scooping dirt over the fresh tar. He didn't have the strength to help even if he wanted to. The fight hadn't lasted long, and he'd really put his full strength into only the one blow. But that wasn't the reason. The rush of excitement he got during a fight always gave him added energy, and when it was gone it left him drained and chilled. It felt like he'd jumped into a frozen river, right down to the shivers he tried to quell.

"I know that look, lad." The boots and buckskins in his peripheral vision were unmistakably Kulmar's, as was the voice. "Why don't you go back to the tent and take a nap? I promise we won't steal all the glory while you're gone."

Huldrich took the offered hand gratefully, and was jerked to his feet as if he weighed nothing at all. He was tired, needing the thick fingered hand on his back to get him started through the press of bodies. He might not sleep—probably couldn't with every moment of the battle running through his head—but it would feel good to lie down for a few minutes.

Reaching the shade of the pavilion he plopped down hard, beyond caring about dignity. As he lay back, he turned the enormous tooth over in his hands. It was his first good look at the trophy.

The thing was truly a wicked looking weapon, its curving shape tapering from a broad oval to a point that would put a good knife to shame. Curious, he held it against his palm. Its length was astonishing—stretching from his wrist to just past the tip of his middle finger. And *that* was from an incomplete example. Looking at it, it was hard to imagine anything more naturally deadly in all creation. But, then, the tail and claws were just as vicious.

On top of all that, those twisted things had more than enough hate to make it effective, fighting with an abandon that simply seemed evil.

There was no choice but to stop them—to wipe them out completely, even if it took their lives. Sadly, he knew it might take exactly that.

"Here it comes!" someone called.

With a grunt, Huldrich scrambled to his feet and moved to the edge of the tent. All eyes were pointed west, where a black shape grew on the horizon.

It wasn't his dragon, which seemed to be somewhere distantly northeast. Judging by their stiff postures, this one was probably linked to either Kessel or Alban. Both appeared to be reacting as though he were the one it sought, moving to put one of the hidden pits between themselves and the approaching drake. In either case, it looked to hit somewhere in the middle of the field. He needed another spear.

Tirza strained at the lead rope, forcing Morena to brace her feet just to stay upright. The rough hemp dug into her palms, but she could deal with that. What was difficult was keeping her balance when the dog lunged. But she'd promised that Tirza wouldn't get near the fighting, and she wasn't about to let go.

Not that the hound wasn't quick enough to evade an attack. The problem was in the chance Tirza would fall into the very trap set for the dragons. If she got stuck trying to enter the fray, retrieving her was most likely hopeless.

Of course, Morena was fairly sure that having her stay with the dog was Samir's way of keeping her well away from the danger. That was fine. She had absolutely no desire to ever get near a dragon that still drew breath. Not again. It was her intention to survive this and grow old with Samir—which meant she wasn't about to put up with his getting killed either.

Several volleys of arrows sped off in rapid succession as the dragon came into range. If any of them struck home, she couldn't see it from her current vantage well away from the pools. Especially with the monster still in the distance...for the moment.

After a glance at her surroundings, Morena made a decision. With a great deal of effort, she dragged Tirza backwards to the center of the pavilion, stopping beside one of the support posts. Her hands were raw, but she kept working, tying the dog to the thick wooden pole. A second knot followed, and a third for good measure.

The camp stool was exactly where she'd left it, near the eastern end of the tent. Careful of her balance, she stepped up, bracing herself with a hand on one of the tightly stretched ropes. From there, she could easily see above the milling soldiers.

She almost wished she couldn't.

The dragon's final charge was *insanely* fast, outpacing anything she could've imagined. It bore down hard, heading straight for the archers behind the water-covered pit. Again the bowmen dropped their weapons, reaching down to snap their pikes into position. The beast swerved, changing direction at fantastic speed, feet missing the water's edge by a mere handbreadth.

Jenaris' illusory grass vanished as the dragon's momentum carried it straight into the next tar pit. The thin pitch of the pool splashed and rippled as the surface gave way under the enormous weight.

The drake scrambled frantically, screaming as it tried to reach the edge and safety. Arrows peppered its scaled hide, a few even managing to find some small chink in which to gain purchase. Pitch flew in great, fat drops in every direction, cast by the desperate, angry thrashing.

"Another one," came a shout from the front.

A chorus of voices all rose at once, relaying frantic instructions as a dark shape appeared in the distance. Archers scrambled to form up again, ranks facing to the northeast. Fresh shafts went to strings, awaiting the command to loose.

The Wizard dashed forward to the near edge of the pool, staff raised as he faced the trapped wyrm. It clawed at the sides for purchase now, ripping away great chunks of soil as it dragged its massive upper body onto solid ground. Runnels of black liquid flowed into the dust, dripping from forelegs and chest.

Men broke into a run, following the line of stakes around the pit as they went to intercept the escaping creature. Morena's breath caught as she recognized Samir in the lead.

The tail swung hard just as he arrived. Effortlessly, the Majaran dropped low, into a ground-hugging stance, calling the sword to his upraised hand as he did. He was barely in time, the thick appendage missing his head by no more than inches as it slid the length of the unnaturally sharp blade.

A roar erupted from the beast as the long, sharp spike fell to the ground at Samir's feet, jerking its injured tail away from the sword. With a dull thud, the limb struck two of the other men and sent them flying. Both landed with a plop in the inky pool—one head first and unmoving.

Samir never hesitated. He darted in, blade licking at the serpentine neck as he sought to drive it back into the pitch. Instead, it lurched forward, jaws snapping the air just as the warrior spun to the side.

Spears stabbed from the other side as a pair of Gotarrans took the chance to strike. Claws raked at the new threat as the furious beast shredded the arm of the nearest man. The head swiveled, jaws opening to spit.

Venom struck the other barbarian—Kessel judging from his height—even as he dodged aside. Morena's heart froze for an instant. But the man continued to fight, showing no reaction to the awful poison plastering his chest.

A flurry of arrows drew her attention. The other dragon was close. Far too close and moving toward the battle already underway—where Samir had eyes only for the current threat.

Waving the others away, the Majaran became a flashing blur of motion, impossible to follow as he flowed between assault and defense. The dragon attacked in a rage—tail, teeth, and claws all in motion as it tried to reach the lone human. It never came close.

The sparkling blade parried every strike, flicking in continuously to puncture face and neck as he danced around its determined bite. Maddened with pain and frustration, the beast pressed forward, skirting the edge of the pool.

Morena screamed in spite of herself as the second drake ran hard and fast, straight toward the warrior's exposed side. The monster sprang, launching itself the final distance.

At the same instant, Samir lunged forward, taking the first beast through the eye nearly to the hilt. He didn't bother to extract the blade as he stepped and spun, ending poised on one leg. Immediately he summoned Dragon's Fang, driving it in behind the shoulder as the second wyrm swept past—straight through the space where he'd been a moment before.

Crying in outrage, the evil thing skidded, trying in vain to brake and turn. Unable to stop, it rolled, tumbling into the waiting pit even as it died of the puncture wound to its heart.

Samir strode quickly toward Kessel and his injured companion, his utter disregard for the dragons confirming the danger had passed. It was all she needed to know. The stool rolled under her foot as she jumped, nearly pitching her face first to the ground in her rush. Scrambling for balance, she clutched her satchel to her chest and ran, pushing through the milling soldiers without regard.

A momentary glimpse of the scene revealed little but blood soaked bandages. It was too much blood. With almost reckless abandon, she rounded the lake, barely avoiding the pitch but arriving quickly. Morena slid, scraping her hip on the hard packed earth just as Kessel eased the now pale man to the ground.

He'd lost a great deal of blood.

Shoving her hand into the bag, she dug furiously among the familiar pockets. Her hand emerged quickly. "Pour that on the wound." She tossed a small bottle to Kessel as she shoved a wax coated berry into the man's mouth. With her free hand she closed his jaws hard, releasing the juice to ease the warrior's pain.

An examination of the arm revealed horrific damage. Pearly white bone showed through where claws had flayed the limb from wrist to elbow, severing the muscle. The bleeding had thankfully slowed to a trickle as the bottle's contents constricted the veins. It would take a goodly store of her supplies, and several slow weeks, but she could heal it so long as he didn't bleed to death.

Morena wiped her hands on her pants as she stood, heedless of the blood. Her attention was on Samir, sweeping her gaze from top to bottom. He'd taken no obvious injuries that she could see—not so much as a scratch for all the worry he caused her.

She hadn't even been aware that she'd balled up her fist until it struck his short ribs. He barely uttered a grunt.

"How could you use yourself as *bait*?" she shouted at him, knowing he'd done exactly that. "How could you do that to me, you stupid selfish...*man*!?"

He just gazed at her with calm concern, gathering her to his chest to hold her for a moment. She wanted to hit him again. Too soon they were interrupted, however, as men arrived bearing litter and fresh bandages. Pushing away from Samir, she grabbed her bag and prepared to go to work.

Disorientation gripped her briefly as she whirled in the direction of the pavilion tent, eyes sweeping the horizon. To no avail.

How, she wondered, *could a thing like that just disappear?*

The answer waited with Kulmar.

Tirza stood at the end of the lead, tail wagging happily as she and Samir came around the oily pool. The tent post lay in the grass beside her. Morena just shook her head. Clearly the knots had held, but the dog had been determined.

Samir took the rope from a chuckling Kulmar, murmuring thanks as they passed on the way to where the expanse of canvas lay on the ground. At least there they could move the Gotarran into the shade once the soldiers had raised it again.

One man already waited there, covered in slick black goo and wearing what must have been an Acedian uniform. His breathing was slightly labored, but he was conscious. Most likely she would find several broken ribs when she examined him. She'd seen the blow that threw the men into the pit, and it had been brutal. Looking around, she found no one else.

"Where's the other man?" she asked, still scanning the approach to the rise.

"Never came up." The man's wince spoke of more than just the pain of broken ribs.

A sigh behind her caused her to turn. Kessel's head hung slightly as he came to terms with the unwanted news.

"Remembered in honor, Anton," he whispered.

Chapter 31

A Visitor By Night

Samir watched the progress of the narrow sliver of moon as it marked the vanishing hours for sleep. It wasn't the battle that kept him awake, though he had replayed it in his head many times already as he lay awake. What bothered him was Morena's coldness. He understood that she'd been tired after treating the injured men. But normally she would have dealt with the stress by coming to talk, or perhaps just sit together. Now she was keeping her distance.

He wished it was merely anger. That, he could deal with.

Oh, she had laid into him pretty well in the minutes after the battle, and her shot to his ribs had caught him completely off guard. Even then he'd known it wasn't about anger, however. Not really. Morena was afraid.

Strangely enough, he couldn't actually fault her for it. Her view of events, and the startling reality of the danger he faced, had left her badly shaken. He was just glad she hadn't seen it from his perspective. If she had, he suspected her reaction would have been much, much worse.

In truth, his overconfidence had very nearly cost him everything, and he couldn't simply ignore that because it was inconvenient. It had been a mistake to toy with that first dragon, no matter how easy it had seemed at the time. Certainly, it had posed no risk to draw the thing's attention to himself while Kessel got the other man, Brand, clear of the battle. It had even been a good idea—if not exactly *wise*—to give the other drake a clear target. It was his timing that had nearly gotten him killed.

Even with his speed enhanced by the sword, it had been too close a thing. The creature's muzzle had actually brushed his hip as he stepped clear. That he'd only been knocked off balance rather than into the pitch had been luck. He was just thankful no one else had been close enough to see it—or the bobble afterwards.

But as much as he could appreciate Morena's fear, he could not accept that fear himself. It wasn't that he would claim not to feel it. He was a warrior, not a liar. But he had learned to manage it and to act in spite of it. He *had* to.

Fear was a distraction and, in combat, distractions could kill. Majaran warriors trained to deal with their anxieties, and to fight aggressively, for the same reason—those who worried about getting hurt practically guaranteed it. To fight with any hesitation, or to seek his own safety, could only hamper his ability to end things quickly.

There was nothing Samir could do but to commit fully to each moment and trust his skills. He hoped she understood that. If she wanted to discuss it, he would be as open and honest as he could. Beyond that, she would have to learn to cope with who he was, because he would not—*could* not—change.

The sound of shuffling feet in the grassy stubble brought him instantly alert. Closing his eyes to mere slits, he waited, relaxing his body and breathing evenly.

A glint of light on bare steel revealed the sword, but he could make out Kordel's features well enough in the dark. He couldn't imagine a less threatening person in the camp. Still, he watched as the apprentice quietly bent to slide the blade into its empty scabbard a few feet away.

In moments the sound of retreating footsteps had faded to nearly nothing. Opening his eyes, he could see Tirza calmly watching the way Kordel had gone.

"Some bodyguard you are," Samir said quietly. "Just let someone walk up with a drawn sword."

For answer, she merely rested her head on her paws and closed her eyes.

At least someone around here can sleep, he thought wryly. But his good humor lasted only moments.

At Tirza's throaty growl, he was instantly on his feet, sword in hand even as he thought of it. Nothing moved in the darkness around him. Only a single man tossing fitfully in his sleep among the Gotarrans.

His blood ran cold.

"Up arms!" he shouted, trying to orient himself to the proper direction. A glance at the hound showed which way the threat lay. "Up arms!" he repeated.

All around him, people began scrambling to rise as they fumbled for weapons. He avoided them easily as he dashed toward the line of traps, Tirza beside him.

In the dark, he nearly didn't see them in time. Only the dim reflection of moonlight on the water warned him to stop.

Hackles up and clearly tense, Tirza sniffed the air suspiciously, as if the scent she expected was somehow elusive. Samir almost grabbed her as she began trotting up and down, parallel to the oily pools. But the hound didn't appear inclined to step any closer to the hazardous pitch as she listened and scented. How she could hope to hear anything significant with the camp in an uproar was beyond him, but she was plainly trying to do just that.

"It's mine," Huldrich announced, coming up beside the Majaran. He pointed a bit north of where Samir was looking.

The horizon was too dark, making it all but impossible to detect a black shape in the distance—even a moving one. Still, he strained to pick something out of that background.

"The archers will be useless in this," Samir growled.

"Too right," Alban returned. "But they haven't done much good so far anyway."

Men carefully crowded forward all along the line, scanning the horizon even as they kept an eye on the stakes. A glance told Samir that most were watching the wrong direction, and some pointed toward a non-existent enemy.

"Should have considered this." The Wizard's voice was critical, but seemed primarily self-directed. "*Stupid.*"

"None of us thought of it," the Majaran replied. "Warriors should know better, too."

A bark sounded beside him as Tirza crouched. He couldn't tell what she'd sensed, unable to see or hear anything above the chatter around him.

"*Silence!*" he ordered, holding up is hands.

The resulting quiet was immediate, leaving no sound other than the occasional scrape of booted feet. He listened, straining to catch...anything.

A rustling caught his ears close by. Damned close.

Light flared at the end of Jenaris' staff, casting everything in an otherworldly blue glow. It shot forward an instant later, a blue ball streaking over the grass, briefly illuminating a low dark mass as it flew past.

The dragon reared up, only twenty yards away and now dimly backlit by the receding glow of the spell. It was enough.

Tirza sped away, following the water south before cutting east along the clear path. Samir wasn't far behind.

He barely heard the guttural chain of syllables coming from the Mage, but the effect was dramatic. Intense green threads of light arced and skittered across the beast's entire body. The drake shook, looking like a mount trying to rid itself of annoying flies. Still, the jagged lines of energy didn't seem harmful, only surprising—and that briefly. It's glaring eyes continued to track Samir.

Arriving well ahead of her master, Tirza placed herself squarely in the creature's path. The wyrm ignored her, watching the blade in the warrior's hand as he closed the distance.

Without warning, the tail lashed forward, seeking to impale the hound. But, as fast as the beast was, the dog was faster. Tirza moved, jumping aside easily as the spike split the ground and whipped back, green sparks dancing.

Others arrived then, quickly circling the dragon and spreading out, ready to attack from several points at once. It was a sound strategy.

They charged.

The tail caught one through the side at almost the same instant as the jaws snapped shut on an arm. A pair of bodies dropped to the ground, unmoving, arcs of green light briefly dancing across their still forms. The other two men jumped back, one narrowly avoiding an impossibly fast swipe from a claw.

Samir paused as he watched for an opening, heartbeat steady. The creature stood rock still as it watched him, paying no heed to the other warriors moving to attack its flanks. It was a standoff, and that only made it more likely that someone would try something stupid. He couldn't let it come to that.

Three quick steps had him within striking distance, sword already moving for an eye. It jerked away even as he lunged.

Reflexes were all that saved him as the tail came in behind his lower legs, trying to take him off his feet. Springing backwards, he dropped to the ground, landing hard on hands and shoulders as he brought knees to chest. Uncoiling, he pushed off, bringing his feet beneath him once again—just in time to see the teeth streaking toward him. He twisted sideways desperately, barely evading the strike as his counterstroke shaved a ribbon of flesh from the massive lower jaw.

Thankfully, Tirza chose that moment to reappear, the hound a streak of white fur as she bounded off the dragon's snout. It was exactly what he needed.

Samir leapt away, tucking into a quick roll before coming to his feet again. There was nothing else he could think to do under these conditions.

The Wizard's spell was both a blessing and a curse. Their ability to see the dragon was critical, and yet the glowing threads of *whatever* this was were maddening. His mind simply could not interpret what he saw. On top of that, he was almost certain this wyrm was actually faster than any he'd faced before. A Gotarran ran forward, stabbing for the open mouth. He was too slow. The neck twisted, head swiveling as it snapped at the shaft, sending a shower of splintered wood to the ground. Rather than retreat, however, the man reached for his knife. It was a serious mistake.

A razor sharp claw opened the barbarian's thigh. The deep gashes poured blood even as the severed muscles failed, dropping the man to the dirt.

Samir rushed in, parrying the tail that lanced toward the Gotarran's belly, then stabbing for the thick, scaly neck. Others moved in as well, several jabbing with spears and swords as a pair of soldiers pulled the fallen man clear.

He took stock as everyone fell back, spotting another barbarian with claw marks and an Acedian with a limp arm. Probably from the tail. The battle was growing costly.

But the thing *was* fast. Only the one he'd faced in the woods, his first, was anywhere near the speed of this one. The others had been slow by comparison.

A thought struck him.

"Jenaris!" he called on impulse. "Give us *light*."

In seconds, a glowing ball of blue light swept toward them, followed by another and another. A steady stream moved slowly overhead, bathing the area in soft light. The dragon's eyes narrowed, pupils contracting hard.

Samir launched himself at the beast, covering the short distance in three quick strides. Around him, battle cries rang out to announce other warriors joining him. At the last instant, he jumped sideways, landing in a broad based crouch as the tail stabbed at where he should have been. He drove the sword upward, blade piercing the thick appendage and drawing a scream of pain from the drake.

Enraged, the creature spun toward him, jaws wide. But the Majaran had anticipated the attack, shifting swiftly backwards and causing the bite to fall short.

Hot breath washed over him as another cry burst from the dragon. On the beast's far side, Kulmar jerked free the spear he had driven into its side. Samir took full advantage of the moment, thrusting his blade through the soft palate and into the drake's brain. It collapsed.

"Nicely done, lad," Kulmar offered, nodding.

"A high price to find out they can't see well in bright light," Samir sighed.

Half a dozen men lay still in the grass, and a soft moan to his left indicated at least one badly wounded. He'd come very close to joining them this time.

"We have a problem," he announced as the Mage joined them, Alban at his heels. "I'm fairly sure *this* attack wasn't an aberration. The ones in broad daylight were."

After a quick mental tally, the Captain shook his head. "Three out of *four* are aberrations?"

"Three out of five, technically," Jenaris offered thoughtfully. "Samir faced one in heavily shadowed woods, and Suppan's was during a storm."

"Three of six," Caleb cut in. "The first group we saw hit us in the woods, too."

"And I'd wager a fair bit that most of the attacks we *don't* know about happened in the dark," Kulmar added grimly. They've chosen neither this ground nor when they arrive. Most times they can."

It was a valid point. The creatures had been operating secretly for who knew how long, and working in the dark was a good way to remain unseen. Besides, if their sight *was* worse in daylight, they'd be unlikely to accept that disadvantage willingly.

The flickering arcs of energy finally faded and died as the litter bearers headed back to camp with the injured warrior. Morena followed slowly, watching him from the corner of her eye, but saying nothing.

Samir sighed. At least she couldn't have seen the battle well enough to know how badly it had gone. Then again, the proof of it was there for anyone who could count the bodies.

Chapter 32

A Shot in the Dark

Pair after pair of red, bleary eyes greeted Samir as he looked from face to face. He was fairly certain no one had gotten any sleep after the attack of the night before, listening instead for some clue that another battle was imminent. Unfortunately, that included himself.

"What I'm saying," Jenaris insisted, "is that it won't do any good at that distance. It's easy to make a shield to cover a single person, but the farther it stretches, the weaker it gets."

"So if you set one to protect the camp," Huldrich surmised, "a dragon could walk right through it."

The Wizard smiled indulgently at the young Gotarran. "My boy, a mouse could walk through it. Stretch one to the horizon and it would be little better than a cobweb."

"Well, there has to be something you can do," Gillis objected. "How about some sort of alarm?"

Samir could see the Mage's irritation grow, had been watching it. The lieutenant's comment had been the capper, however. It was a look he'd seen too often on Shimei's face and always as a result of a student's thickheaded behavior. Not a look he wanted to have directed at him.

"Young man," Jenaris said with a smile that was anything but friendly. "Just because I'm a Wizard does *not* make me all-powerful. Nor do I wish to be. I have a good sense of my limitations, and what you ask is far beyond them. Any wards that extensive would be worthless."

Gillis glanced away from the Mage's stare, definitely uncomfortable with the scrutiny. No doubt he would speak more cautiously next time.

"Which brings us round to sentries again. May as well not even bother, little good as they do," Kulmar grumbled. He held up a restraining hand toward Alban. "I know it's good military practice, friend. You've said it often enough, and I agree. But not a man among them can see anything before it's on top of them, and sending them farther out will only get them killed."

The bleak reality of the situation had definitely dampened the mood of the camp. After the first three had fallen so easily, it had seemed the rest would be simple—merely a matter of waiting. Now it looked like a much more even battle, at least from where Samir stood.

In the dark, he lost much of his advantage over the creatures. Where his vision failed, theirs evidently improved, and their ability to respond to attacks strained his reflexes to the limit. He only hoped he'd actually seen the worst they could do.

Still, where Gillis insisted on a spell to end all their troubles at a stroke, Samir would take any small edge he could find. He turned a questioning gaze on the Mage.

"Can you make a spell that will *amplify* sound?" he asked.

"Yes." Jenaris expression was plainly curious.

Samir smiled. "Then I think the archers might be useful after all. Not that they'll appreciate my idea."

Briefly he explained what he had in mind, eliciting nods from Jenaris and comments from the other warriors. His own basic concept opened a floodgate of suggestions, providing not only a workable plan, but a fresh wave of enthusiasm to boot.

The Majaran felt bad about giving the Wizard so much extra work. Although he hid it well enough, Jenaris was as exhausted as any of them. Still, he insisted that Kordel could perform most of the basic magic and, with only three links to maintain, it wouldn't be a burden.

It was a good plan. At least as good as they were likely to find. Of course, even a perfect strategy would fall flat if they didn't get some decent rest. Excusing himself, he headed for his blankets.

The morning sun would be no problem. A folded cloth over his eyes would block enough light to give relief, and his saddlebags made a fine pillow.

The sun was past its noon peak when Samir sat up, letting the shirt fall into his lap. He'd have preferred to sleep longer, but a few hours would be enough. It would have to be. Hunger gnawed at him as the smell of smoking meat drifted to him on the breeze—smoked dragon, he assumed. He would need plenty of energy, probably sooner than he liked.

"Good morning, sleepyhead." Morena's voice cut through the fuzzy remnants of sleep that lingered, bringing him to full wakefulness.

"Good afternoon."

He glanced at the position of the sun before glancing back at her.

She held up a vial of purplish liquid as she came around in front of him, Tirza trailing. "Brought you another dose."

Something in her face told him there was more to it than that. But then, there usually was with her. It was one of her more...challenging qualities.

"How long have you been waiting?" he asked, eyebrows raised in question.

The sheepish look she returned answered his question. She'd been there a while already. Whatever it was, there was no doubt it was important.

"I had Tirza to keep me company," she said, avoiding the subject. He saw no reason to call her on it or make this difficult.

"I'm sorry." He stood smoothly, pulling on his shirt. "I should've killed that dragon as fast as I could. Toying with it was foolish."

"It *was* foolish," she agreed, nodding slowly. "But you wouldn't have done it unless it was necessary. I'm sorry, too. I was just...."

"Scared," he said matter-of-factly. "I understand that, but I can't avoid danger to make you feel better. You know that. I love you, but I *won't* be a coward for you."

She said nothing for several seconds, only looking at him with those magnificent green eyes. Finally she nodded.

"You have to be who you are." Morena's smile was warm. "It's part of what I love about you. But I will be glad when this is over."

Taking her hand, he pulled her gently into his chest. He'd be glad, too, but then he would have another job that was just as dangerous. She knew that, knew all about Kemal and Majar. Now, though, didn't seem like quite the right time to remind her.

"I love you," was all he said.

Slipping an arm around her waist, Samir started walking in no particular direction. It didn't matter where they were going, and he paid little attention. Just as long as he was with her.

He shivered, a chill running down his spine without warning.

He knew what had caused it. The link with the dragon felt like an itch he couldn't scratch now, having grown noticeably stronger since he'd gone to sleep. If it got much worse, it would feel like the thing was on top of him. He was definitely not looking forward to that.

"Gillis says his is a lot closer, too," she said, evidently noticing that his gaze had again wandered northeast.

"What about Kessel?" he asked.

Morena shook her head. "I haven't seen him, but I heard someone say he thinks it stopped."

"Stopped?"

"Just what I heard," she shrugged, apparently not giving the rumor too much weight.

They had come to the edge of the pits, facing east. Somewhere out there, a dragon was hunting him. He wasn't particularly worried. When it finally did arrive he could handle it, although he *would* ask the Wizard to break the link at the last minute. After all, trying to fight the beast with his skin crawling like this would probably get him killed.

Samir watched as Alban's scouts rode back and forth, zigzagging in from the horizon as they dropped arrows at regular intervals. Clearly Jenaris and the apprentice had been busy if they'd already prepared enough to cover the ground from north to east. With enough arrows they should be able to make this work, but all he could do was trust the Mage to know what he was doing.

The afternoon crept by as they watched Gillis slowly grow more agitated, pacing constantly. The lieutenant declined Morena's offer of something to soothe his nerves, however, in spite of an obvious desire to accept.

Personally, Samir sympathized but wished he had said, "Yes." In his present condition, the man was in no decent shape to lead anyone into battle anyway.

But eventually the Majaran could take no more of Gillis' company, his patience giving out in the face of almost constant reports of the dragon's progress. Finding a place on the other side of the pools, he began to work through his forms. He deliberately kept his movements as slow as possible, concentrating on every aspect of technique—fully aware at every second of his balance, his breathing, and his heartbeat.

Time ceased to exist for him apart from the moment, apart from *now*. The movement of the sun, the wind, and everything else around him were lost as he focused completely on the slightest motion of his hands and feet.

When he finished, slicked with sweat on chest and back, the sunset was almost a memory. All that remained was the lingering deep purple in the west surrendering to the black of night.

"If you moved any slower, you'd have been going backwards." Caleb stood up, dusting the seat of his pants.

"Maybe I should try that," he shot his friend a grin.

The other man's smile vanished abruptly. "Don't do it on my account. My decision making hasn't exactly been good lately."

He supposed it wasn't all that surprising that the Acedian prince hadn't managed to move past this yet. Until Caleb made peace with his father it probably wouldn't be possible. Still, even though Samir didn't approve of the way his friend had tricked Carlon, he wished the man would stop denigrating himself. Everyone made mistakes, and a single act could hardly define a life.

"Caleb, I'm going to say this once, and I want you to listen." Samir looked squarely at his friend, waiting until he was sure he had the other man's full attention. "*Stop it!* If you keep telling yourself you aren't good enough, you'll start to believe it. And if you question your leadership, so will everyone else."

Caleb was plainly less than pleased at the way he'd been spoken to, but he nodded once. "I hear you."

"Good," Samir smiled, trying to lighten the mood. "It's about time you figured out I'm always right."

The other responded with a small mock bow. "Of course, Master Samir. Your wisdom exceeds that of us mere mortals."

His reply died on his tongue as a loud crack sounded to his right. There was little doubt what had caused it. One of Jenaris' arrows had just been broken—which meant that he and Caleb were caught between a dragon and the trap.

Spinning toward the noise, he instinctively dropped to a crouch, ready to move in any direction immediately. Nothing moved in the dark. Or at least nothing that he could see.

Another crack, closer.

"Archers," Alban's voice boomed behind him. "Fire when ready."

Several bowstrings twanged simultaneously, followed by the sporadic release of many others. He heard only a hint of the whistling shafts as they sped in random directions, arced high.

Balls of light bloomed as they struck the ground, each hovering several feet above the tall grass. The effect left a wide swath of ground bathed in their soft blue glow, revealing the dragon as it crept slowly forward.

With a deafening, angry cry the thing charged.

Before he was even aware of summoning it, Dragon's Fang appeared in his hand. "Get back to camp," he told Caleb.

"Why should you have all the fun?" his friend laughed. "Besides, I'd never make it across the path with everyone else coming this way."

A quick glance revealed the simple truth of the statement. At least two dozen warriors were attempting to squeeze through the narrow lanes, doing their best not to knock each other into the pitch. They should have stayed back. The trap would never work with all of them on the wrong side of the pools. But, then, he suspected they were coming to protect Caleb.

So be it. They would stand and fight.

Men began to fan out around them as the drake bore down at incredible speed, its short legs eating up the distance. More arrows fell in the intervening space, giving light that would hopefully reduce the number of graves they would have to dig in the morning.

In the space of only a few yards, the wyrm skidded to a rapid halt, claws scrambling for purchase in the hard packed soil. As the beast's hindquarters slewed around to the left, a wildly swinging tail swept several men off their feet. Others dove frantically away, just avoiding the same fate.

Samir drove the point of his sword into the earth as the tail reached him, bracing the hilt upright with his own weight. The blow jarred him, but the weapon held, shaving off thick scales before burying itself in soft flesh.

The enraged creature spun, snapping at the air where he had just been. But the jaws closed only on razor sharp steel as the warrior rolled to the sword's other side. Blood poured from the deep lacerations in its mouth as the drake screamed, flinging the sword into the dark as it reared its head back.

Spears jabbed hard into both flanks as men took advantage of its focus on the unarmed Majaran. The tail's sharp spike stabbed to the right, scoring a deep gash across a barbarian's chest, while claws raked left after retreating targets.

Recalling the sword to his hand, he watched the dragon carefully, alert for any sudden movement. Its head and eyes swiveled restlessly, sweeping the circle of men to find anyone foolish enough to be in range. It waited, tail poised and shoulders hunched, hatred seeming to roll from it in waves as blood dripped from its jaws.

But they had planned for this, having learned their lesson well after the previous fight. The area had become a killing ground then, as warriors tried to rush past the creature's defenses in order to strike. Then, as now, the dragon had been waiting for them to do exactly that, and had used the opportunity to reap a deadly harvest.

Not this time.

"On three, men," Samir called. "One...Two...."

He took a deep breath. "Three!"

The drake lashed out as everyone rushed forward—tail, teeth, and claws all seeking human flesh. Yet almost immediately the men stopped, causing every attack to fall on empty air.

Neck and claws already extended to the full, the beast strained to strike again as men leapt forward. Whipping to the side, the tail took a soldier across the ribs, flipping him to the ground with a crash. Yet the others got through. Spears and swords bit, sinking beneath the scales and into the vulnerable flesh.

Samir didn't hesitate. In an instant he was alongside the outstretched head, driving the blade with every ounce of power into its temple. The glistening steel slid through easily, piercing hide and bone without resistance.

Soundlessly, the creature collapsed.

Wrenching the sword free, he wiped the blade carefully with a handful of grass. Several others worked hard to free their weapons, while a few helped the wounded limp back to camp.

It had definitely been a good plan. Perhaps most importantly, though, the suggestion had been Caleb's. He shot a broad grin at the other man.

"I suppose now you'll think all your ideas are brilliant," Samir rolled his eyes dramatically.

"Of course, they will be." Caleb assumed an arrogant expression. "When have I ever had any other kind?"

The Majaran couldn't help but laugh at the obvious revisionism. It was good to see his friend's sense of humor again, though.

"I see," he offered with deliberate sarcasm. "Remind me to ask Sorana how she remembers it."

Caleb seemed to have no reply to that as they walked back to camp.

Chapter 33

Hunting the Hunters

Samir had known when they started that it wouldn't all be easy. Not that nearly getting himself killed more than once had been *easy* exactly, but at least they'd had the choice of ground. Now he had a feeling it was going to get tricky.

Nearly everyone was already waiting under the tent when he arrived. Only Kordel and Kessel were missing.

"You cost me several days' work summoning the blade out of my hands last night." Jenaris disapproving stare followed him as he moved to take a seat beside Morena. "And you were only minutes away from having a new property."

"Sorry," he offered with a shrug. "I sort of needed it at the time."

The Wizard's frown softened to mild amusement. "I suppose you did at that," he said. "Besides, I was actually impressed. I was close to forty yards away when you summoned it."

Samir sat silently as the implications sank in. He hadn't thought how far away he'd been when he brought the sword to him. But the Mage's small tent was every bit of thirty yards from where he'd been. He had simply done it, and with no real effort. A far cry from the ten or so he'd managed that first day.

"Thank you for not taking it back in the middle of the fight," he chuckled.

Kordel and Kessel entered the tent together, though only the Gotarran moved to a seat. The other man moved quietly behind Samir, once again working to maintain the link between himself and the dragon. Presumably, he had just done the same for the barbarian, who had the only other such connection.

As always, he felt nothing from the magic being used. All he sensed was the wyrm's presence, somewhere to the northeast. It was a presence that was growing more troubling as the day wore on.

"Any change?" Kulmar looked to the younger Gotarran.

The question silenced any other conversation as they all awaited the answer. At this point, however, no one really expected any change.

"If you're asking whether it's gotten any closer, then no." The annoyance in Kessel's voice gave it a hard edge. "The damned thing is moving, though. I think it's following the treeline."

"Looking for a way to reach you without leaving cover," Huldrich suggested.

It was reasonable, based on what they knew of the beasts. Unfortunately, his own news made him absolutely certain that Huldrich was right. He didn't like it one bit, and he was sure nobody else would either.

"Well, at least one is still coming," Caleb put in hopefully, drawing nods from the others. From everyone but Samir.

"No, it isn't," he informed them. "It's been moving farther away ever since sunrise."

Only a grunt from Kulmar broke the stunned silence. The huge farrier looked ready to smash something.

"How sure are you?" Alban sounded resigned to the bad news he was about to receive.

"No question," Samir replied. "It's been nearly six hours, and he's moving away faster than he ever moved *toward* me."

Kulmar's hand unconsciously kneaded the hilt of his long knife, knuckles white. "Not that I doubt you," he said flatly, "but you can't be sure it won't turn right back around come nightfall."

Even the big man clearly knew that what he suggested was beyond mere unlikelihood. There was now no question that it was reacting poorly to the exposure of the wide open plains. Once it reached the cover of the forest, it wouldn't be coming back. They would need to go into the trees after it—on ground of its choosing.

"We were going to chase after Kessel's dragon anyway." Jenaris was plainly unhappy about the situation, but there was nothing to be done for it. He turned a questioning gaze on the Captain. "Do we pack up after lunch?"

Alban shook his head, barely considering. "First light tomorrow if there are no objections. Just in case the dragon changes its mind."

Samir didn't detect much in the way of hope as he scanned the faces around him. Still, he would be glad of a good night's sleep before spending a day on horseback. He knew there would be no battle to disturb him tonight.

They had actually been lucky to bring five of the creatures this far into the plains, but the Wizard wasn't about to complain when things worked in their favor. As it was, he just hoped it would be enough. After all, the knowledge that only two more Marqued dragons lived meant nothing. They could be met by a dozen more once they entered the woods. But even that wasn't his greatest concern.

The real question was how to find the lair and whether there could, in fact, be more than one such place. All he'd read pointed to a single location the wyrms would use as a breeding ground. But he had only one ancient mage—a man named Olandis—to use as an authority, and he could hardly credit everything from that source. Not when so much of the behavior he'd observed to this point disagreed with the texts.

They were hardly acting like the solitary creatures the books had made them out to be. A dragon's ability to survive had always depended on remaining hidden—on their being nothing more than a myth. Yet for some reason they'd made themselves impossible to ignore. He needed to know why.

It went completely against his nature to accept that wyrms had changed so completely. They were doing everything differently. Things like that just didn't happen without some compelling reason, some cause. Jenaris had spent a lifetime—*two* of anyone else's—studying the nature of things, the order of creation, and had yet to find a more difficult puzzle.

The truth was, too many pieces were missing. Before he could even begin to understand, he would need to find at least a few of them. But that was a problem for another time.

Right now he had to focus on what he *could* do, assuming either of the two remaining drakes would serve his purposes. He'd studied the bodies of the last few well enough to recognize the differences that signaled maturity and differentiated the sexes. Hopefully, he could make use of that information.

Weaving his way through the neat arrangement of the soldier's camp, the Mage soon found what he sought. Outside one of the larger tents, Samir sat calmly across a chess board from Alban, and at first glance, had a serious advantage in pieces and position.

"Excuse me, Captain," Jenaris interrupted. "Would you mind my borrowing your opponent for a few minutes?"

Alban's look of relief was almost comical as the man started packing up the pieces on the game board. "Not at all, Magus. I think we can call this game finished. Actually, I should have resigned six moves ago."

"Is *that* when you think you made the mistake?" the Majaran goaded gently. "No wonder you lost."

"Don't gloat." The depth of Alban's annoyance had plainly taken several games to develop. "It's nearly as irritating as the fact that you always win."

Rising smoothly, Samir offered the Captain a short bow before turning a curious expression on the Wizard. Without a word, Jenaris began walking along a route that would take them beyond the edge of the camp and any ears that might overhear. The warrior beside him kept silent, demonstrating a rare patience for one so young.

Reaching the edge of the cut grass north of the encampment, he stopped to look at the Majaran. Samir studied him casually but intently as he waited for Jenaris to speak. It was fairly obvious he expected to hear something he didn't like. Sadly, the man was probably right.

"How difficult would it be to...*not* kill a dragon? Just for a short time?" the Mage asked, not exactly hopeful of the answer he would receive.

Samir's stare was distinctly unpleasant as he considered the question, the deep brown eyes seeming to look *through* the Mage. "You want to *capture* one?" the warrior finally asked, voice deceptively calm. "I don't think that's even possible."

"I'm not talking about capturing one," Jenaris shook his head. "The question is, how confident are you that you could fight without actually needing to *kill* the dragon?"

The younger man's eyes widened abruptly. "You don't want much, do you?" he asked, tone practically dripping sarcasm. "Would you like me to render it unconscious or just start pushing soldiers in front of it?"

Jenaris had expected this reaction, and he couldn't actually blame the warrior. After all, the life at stake would be his and, although trained to face danger without flinching, it was only natural to want a reasonable chance at survival.

"Neither," the Mage dismissed the sarcasm. "I need to know if you, *alone*, can hold a wyrm at bay until I can get a good look. Our success may very well depend on it."

"How close a look?" Samir spoke slowly, not willing to commit himself, but at least not rejecting the idea out of hand.

He'd been counting on the young man's need to constantly challenge himself. Still, there was a very real possibility of refusal—especially if the Mage failed to provide convincing answers.

"It won't take long," Jenaris assured him, "but I *do* need to get fairly close to see the necessary signs."

It took only a minute to explain his intentions. While he couldn't be sure, he assumed Samir's nods were a good sign, at least conveying understanding.

"I can't promise anything," the Majaran said flatly. "If I need to end the fight, I won't hesitate. And I expect you to work as quickly as possible."

He didn't doubt that was as close to a promise as he was going to get. It would have to be enough. Murmuring his thanks, Jenaris went in search of his next answer.

Chapter 34

Into the Gap

It was strange to feel the link change so rapidly as they rode east toward the thickly forested hills. The dragon was still north of him, but was now moving with astonishing speed along the treeline.

Kessel, on the other hand, grew grim as the trees drew closer by the minute. Somewhere under their dense cover, he knew, a thing of absolute hatred waited to take his life. But it wasn't the barbarian who would go in after it.

The Majaran reined in a few hundred yards from the trees, not bothering to look at the Wizard. The man *would* be right behind him when he entered the woods, or Samir would simply kill the thing and be done with it.

Leaning to his right, he kissed Morena as he quickly handed her the reins and swung out of the saddle. They had already said all that needed saying on the ride and, as tempting as it was, he couldn't afford anything more prolonged. It would just be a distraction. As it was, most of the day on a horse had left him too stiff for the fluid movement he would need to survive.

"You're sure you won't take some extra hands along?" Alban offered as his gaze shifted rapidly between Samir and the forest. "I'd feel better knowing you had a few swords behind you."

He wished he felt better about his decision to do this alone. But worrying about someone else was the last thing he needed right now.

"I'm sure," he said, doing his best to put a humorous tone in his voice. "But if I'm not back in an hour, assume I've changed my mind."

Kulmar erupted in laughter, bringing echoes back from the nearby trees as Samir walked toward the waiting woods, long grass dragging at his legs. Beside him, Tirza bounded along easily, almost outpacing him. Thankfully, she hadn't caught a scent of the dragon yet. Once she did, he was sure he would need to run just to keep up—which would certainly mean leaving Jenaris behind.

The underbrush at the edge of the wood was thick, but only a little searching turned up plenty of game trails. Still, he hesitated a moment, tempted to ask the Mage to do something to keep Tirza from following.

"Something wrong?" The Wizard sounded unconcerned, but was probably just trying to get him moving.

"Nothing," he replied. "Just letting my vision adjust to the dark."

Summoning the sword, he stepped through into the forest. Ground cover was sparse in the low light under the canopy of leaves—mostly brambles and low shrubs to snag his ankles as he passed. In front of him, the earth rose in a gentle slope, limiting his sight as much as the thick trunks around him.

He kept his pace slow as he moved toward the hilltop as his mind noted rocks and exposed roots to complicate footing in a fight. It also allowed him to watch for any movement. Suddenly, he was glad to have Tirza along, since it would be nearly impossible for anything to approach without her notice.

A soft whine escaped the hound as she sensed his tension. Her posture, though, suggested no immediate threat.

Samir crept forward as quietly as possible among the brush and broken twigs littering the path. Trying not to alert the drake to his presence might be a scant hope, however. If the beast had senses anywhere near Tirza's, the damage was probably already done. It would know he was here long before he could see it, but he would take any advantage he could get.

A small, bowl-shaped clearing opened before him as he topped the rise, giving him a good view of what lay ahead. Across the depression, a massive stone ridge rose to half again his own height, leaving him only two options—a narrow defile or a climb up its face. But before he made that choice, he would have to expose himself in the open sunlit expanse. Until now, he'd thought only of how the trees interfered with his own vision, but he hadn't really considered what it would mean to leave their cover.

"You ready?" he whispered, glancing behind him to catch the Wizard's eye.

There was no sign of the man anywhere.

He was certain Jenaris had been right there the whole time. In fact, the man had been too noisy to ignore as they topped the rise. Now he seemed to have simply vanished into thin air.

"I'm right here," Jenaris' voice beside him was startling, very nearly causing him to strike. "It's a handy trick, isn't it?"

As the Majaran watched, he became aware of the Mage's presence, slowly recognizing that the man had been there the entire time. And it wasn't as if he'd been unable to see the man. More like he had *ignored* him.

"Yes. Very nice, until it gets you killed," Samir replied dryly. "I strongly suggest you avoid surprising me right now."

Consciously relaxing his grip on the sword, he started forward down the short slope to the clearing. Nothing moved but grass and leaves, stirred by a rare puff of wind. If the beast was here, it gave no sign.

He crossed the clearing at a trot, only too well aware that fast movement drew the eye but trying to minimize his time in the open. Either way, it would give the wyrm a chance to see him with exactly the same results—the very fight he'd come for.

Samir had already chosen between the rock face and the constricted path to the top. In the end it was an easy decision. Having his movement restricted was better than having his hands and feet unavailable.

The gap was only about two feet wide and fairly smooth—likely worn by generations of deer and other small game. It would be a little steep, but it was passable and the ground was dry enough to give good purchase for his feet.

Keeping his blade ready in front of him, he crept sideways into the crevice.

Without warning, Tirza darted past him, knocking him off balance into the rock wall. It probably saved his life.

The tail's long, sharp spike tore stones from the bluff only inches from his head, pelting him with dirt and rock as it withdrew. Unable to move forward, he threw himself back toward the clearing only a few feet away, rolling immediately to his feet as he hit the ground.

He ignored the trickle of blood past his right eye, neither knowing nor caring what had caused it. At that moment, he was only concerned with the creature that stood a few feet away.

The dragon perched motionless atop the low bluff, tail poised and shoulders hunched—a darker shadow against the backdrop of the forest. Pure hatred emanated from the beast as it watched him, unblinking.

Claws chewing up the rock face, the drake flowed forward onto the floor of the clearing with unbelievable speed. He moved with it, forward and down, as he swept the blade overhead and followed his target. The beast circled left, just beyond his range.

Reaching out with his will, he touched one of the now familiar runes etched deep in the blade, activating it. Time appeared to slow, the dragon's movements seeming merely quick as he watched it.

Matching it speed for speed, the warrior moved closer.

The tail slashed, sweeping for his body as he came within striking distance. Dropping to a crouch, front leg outstretched, he shifted forward under the blow. But the wyrm wasn't finished. Samir was forced to parry, easily redirecting a claw, yet missing his own chance to strike. Still, he knew he couldn't risk hurting it too badly. Not yet.

The dragon came on, attacking with every weapon at its disposal, refusing to be thwarted. Such coordinated strikes should have strained his ability to defend. But the Majaran fought effortlessly, reflexes seeming to direct the sword even before he saw the drake move.

Burning with anger and frustration, the creature attacked with new fury, redoubling its efforts. It slashed and struck, harder than ever before—yet Samir's blade met the blows and redirected them even as he danced aside.

Although the warrior continued to repel the lightning assault, a thread of concern crept slowly into his mind. With every passing second, his ability to match the dragon's pace threatened to vanish. He was only too well aware that the spell would expire, and soon. If Jenaris didn't hurry, Samir was likely to be in *serious* trouble.

More than once he considered simply killing the beast, removing the threat of losing his one advantage. Each time he chose to wait, giving the Mage a few more seconds, one more chance to learn whatever it was he sought.

"Kill it," the Wizard's voice called over the din.

It was all he needed to hear.

With a quick pivot step, he spun, coming inside the striking radius of the open jaws and stopping beside the thick, sinuous neck. Too late the dragon tried to pull back, swiveling its head to bite.

Dragon's Fang bit first, driving into the throat and severing the spine. Without a pause, Samir whipped the blade free, flicking his wrist to dash blood from the steel before the beast struck the ground.

"Took you long enough." The warrior made no effort to hide his displeasure as he gradually became aware of the other man's presence.

"I wouldn't be much good to anyone if I'd gotten myself hit by that tail," Jenaris answered with no little amusement. "Besides, you didn't cut it nearly as close as you seemed to think. You had nearly half your time yet."

The warrior had no time to reply.

A pained whine cut instantly through the rush of excitement, pulling his attention to the top of the small bluff. He was barely aware of crossing the distance, climbing the steep defile in only a few long strides.

Tirza lay in the flat stretch of rocky soil, whimpering as she panted in short, rapid breaths. With only a glance, the injury filled his vision—one hind leg cocked at a horrible, unnatural angle, obviously broken. Kneeling, he checked the rest of her, finding nothing else. The leg was enough.

"Hush, girl, hush." He stroked her gently, smoothing the short coat as he tried to soothe her. "I'm here now."

Tears stung his eyes as he scooped her from the ground, eliciting a yelp and a nip at his arm as he hugged her to his chest. The walk back seemed to take forever, moving as quickly as he dared while doing his best to avoid jostling the anguished hound as she whined. It felt as though every thorny plant snagged him and each tree root rose up to trip him or turn his ankle. He refused to slow further.

He should never have let her come. *Never*.

Finally, he broke through into the sunlight of the plain, tears rolling freely down his cheeks. Slowly, tenderly, he lowered Tirza, laying her in the soft grass as he tried to keep her still.

Morena was there in a flash, kicking her horse to a gallop to cover the quarter mile between them. Before Dawn Rose could stop, she threw herself out of the saddle, nearly sprawling herself headlong in the process.

"What's wrong?" Her eyes scanned Samir, with rapid efficiency, seeking some injury. In moments, her gaze shifted to the hound.

As gently as she could, Morena probed the break, assessing the extent of the damage. Her compassion for Tirza was written plainly on her features, reflecting his own pain. Still she did nothing, biting her lip as she stared frozenly down at the wounded hound. After a short eternity she met his gaze, head shaking slowly.

"I don't know what I should do." Tears formed in her eyes as she spoke. "I'm not sure what's safe to give her and what's not."

"Like horses and Jasper berries?" he said more than asked.

She nodded miserably.

Samir was torn and his heart threatened to tear as well. He couldn't let Tirza suffer, and he couldn't stand the thought that he could lose her because he made the wrong decision.

Could lose her. Right now, though, she was suffering.

"Do what you have to do," he said with a calm he didn't come close to feeling.

Hand softly stroking the dog's fur, he watched as Morena extracted several items from her bag, laying them in front of her. Hesitantly, she picked up a familiar looking wax-coated berry and held it out to him.

"Does anyone have water?" she asked.

Looking up, he was surprised to find a crowd surrounding them. Taking one of the offered canteens, the warrior set it in the grass beside Morena.

She handed it back. "Give her some with the berry juice," she told him. "*Only* the juice."

Uncorking the canteen, he poured water into his palm, losing more than he held. He didn't care. Holding the berry above the cupped hand, he squeezed, watching as several fat drops fell into the water, tinting it blue. Carefully he put it under Tirza's muzzle.

The dog lapped, splashing some but getting most. As he poured more water, she continued to drink.

"She's not going to like this part," Morena said apologetically.

The Majaran watched as Morena rolled a wide, red-veined leaf between her palms, sliding it into the end of a short tube. Holding it up to her mouth, she gripped the hound's lower jaw and put the other end down Tirza's throat. The dog struggled, gagging.

Without hesitation she blew and withdrew the tube.

"More water," she instructed.

He did as she told him, offering palmfuls of water until Tirza pulled her mouth away. Tossing the canteen aside, he went back to the work of calming her, knowing what was about to happen.

Gently, Morena reached for the broken limb, taking care not to move it unnecessarily. Gripping both sides of the break, she pulled hard, shifting the bone into place by feel.

Samir pressed Tirza down firmly as she fought to escape, crying piteously. Glassy-eyed, the hound looked at him accusingly, not understanding why he would hurt her.

Finally releasing the tension on the leg, Morena held it in place while Kulmar splinted and bound it. As the big Gotarran tied it off, she sank back to sit on her heels, a deep sigh escaping her. She looked completely spent, much like he felt himself.

Tirza bucked suddenly under his hands shaking uncontrollably. Samir could do little more than watch, helpless, holding the dog carefully as she convulsed violently. Finally, slowly, it subsided.

Reaching across, Morena peeled back first one eyelid, then the other, looking clearly concerned. At his questioning gaze, she shrugged weakly.

"If she wakes up, she should be all right," she offered, lightly laying a hand atop his.

With a nod, Samir sat in the grass beside Tirza, preparing himself for a long vigil. He would wait for as long as it took.

Beside him, he was vaguely aware of Morena's comforting presence.

Chapter 35

The Last Link

Samir awoke with a start to find himself staring up at a smirking Caleb. Head still fuzzy from sleep, he sat bolt upright and immediately regretted it as the world jumped in and out of focus.

Berating himself for a fool, he looked around for Tirza as soon as his vision cleared. She lay on her side only a few feet away, splinted leg stretched out, tail lightly thumping the ground as she met his gaze with complete unconcern.

"Why did you let me fall asleep?" he asked Morena, who sat nearby, knees hugged to chest.

"Maybe we should let you lie back down," Caleb joked, "until you can say that without slurring your words."

"Knock it off, Caleb," the healer told the Prince. Eyebrows arched, she returned her attention to Samir. Her mouth twisted in distaste. "*Let* you fall asleep? I had to *make* you fall asleep."

The last thing he remembered was Morena bringing him a hot cup of tea. The realization that she'd tricked him left the Majaran hurt and a little angry. She *knew* he wanted to stay awake until he was sure Tirza would be all right, and she had drugged him. At least now he knew why it was so hard to focus.

"I'm sorry," she offered sincerely, responding to his pained expression. "I wouldn't have done it, but you needed to sleep. Or do you think you could face another dragon after two days without rest?"

The look she gave him now was anything but apologetic. Oh, yes, his mother would definitely like Morena.

Her words instantly brought the other wyrm to his awareness. Apparently, the drug had fogged more of his mind than he'd known. He could still sense it, and it was close, but it felt almost like an echo of the usual sensation.

As slow as his wits were at the moment, however, he was absolutely certain of one thing—he would die if he went into battle like this.

"How long?" he asked, doing his best to focus on Morena.

She waved away his concern. "A couple of hours. Less, if you get up and move around."

Samir thought he might trip over his own feet if he tried to walk, but he held his tongue. As it was, he could barely talk anyway.

It would take *hours* for his head to clear. He couldn't tell with any confidence, especially not in his present condition, but he thought that would be cutting it close. Well, done was done and he would just have to deal with it, however it turned out.

Lifting himself on wobbly legs, he stood, swaying slightly. If walking would help clear the fog, then it was high time he got up. Besides, he needed to eat.

Hopping to her feet, Morena deftly tucked herself under his arm, steadying him without seeming to do so. He smiled his gratitude, despite the strangeness of the situation. True, he needed help because of the herbs she'd slipped him, but he had forced her to take such drastic action. If she hadn't, he'd have killed himself through sheer stubbornness.

A few steps brought a twinge of guilt. He looked at Tirza, unable to follow and watching him leave.

"Go on," Caleb said, seeing his hesitation. "I'll stay with her."

Waving his thanks, Samir headed toward the wagons.

Several pieces of sharp cheese and some of the smoked dragon meat—which was surprisingly good—did wonders for how he was feeling, and having an excuse to hold Morena close was worth a little dizziness. He did earn a stern look when, after finishing his breakfast, he casually wiped his hands on his pants. But, given the abuse they'd already suffered from the briars, they were already a lost cause.

"Oh! I almost forgot to tell you," she exclaimed. "Jenaris wants to see you. He said to meet him at the clearing."

Samir attempted a questioning look, but he lurched slightly as he turned his head. Chagrinned, he decided just to speak.

"About what?"

"I don't know," she said with a shrug. "And before you ask, I didn't wake you because he agreed you needed rest."

He could just see her expression out of the corner of his eye, daring him to deny the truth of it. He was wise enough not to argue. Instead, he drank the offered dose of Blackthorn potion before heading into the woods.

Without the pressure of impending battle or an injured companion, the walk to the clearing was surprisingly short. Once again, the Wizard had spent a great deal of time cutting away portions of the drake's anatomy, presumable learning whatever he could. The smell from the open belly was everything he remembered, and wished he could forget.

Beside him, Morena held a small kerchief to her nose. Jenaris himself leaned back against a thick-boled oak, shirtless and coated to the shoulders in dried blood. With a heave, he pushed away from the tree and walked to meet them, exhaustion clear in every line of his face. It was obvious he'd stayed awake all night, and regretted the necessity.

"You left this over there," he said, summoning the sword and pointing to the top of the bluff. He handed it, hilt first, to Samir. "I hope you don't mind my putting it to use."

"Not at all."

At least the Mage had cleaned the blade, which was more than *he* had done before leaving it in the dirt. Of course, he suspected Jenaris had used magic, considering how spotless he managed to keep his clothing—until now. Then again, even a simple spell was probably more trouble than it was worth when you were ready to drop from fatigue.

Morena studied the pieces of dissected wyrm strewn about the trampled grass. "So what exactly were you looking for?"

"What?" The Mage appeared momentarily confused by the question. "Oh, this is just curiosity. I have a theory that dragons aren't a natural part of our world, but were created magically."

"And?" Samir prompted, suddenly interested.

Jenaris considered for a second, then shook his head.

"I can't decide whether I've actually found proof, or if I'm simply seeing what I want to see. I wish Lorn were here," he added absently.

If true, it would be interesting, but.... "How does that help us?" he asked.

The Wizard didn't answer at once, evidently lost in thought. He came back to the conversation with a start.

"I'm not sure it does," he replied, abashed. "Sometimes I just get...fascinated by ideas. It's a gift and a curse most mages share."

"So, you wanted to talk about something?" Samir suggested.

Jenaris nodded wearily, beckoning them to follow as he approached the dragon. Carefully avoiding body parts on the ground, he squatted beside the hindquarters and pointed to a spot above the back heels.

"Do you see that bump?" He looked up, gauging their reaction. "In a mature male, that would be a spur at least two inches long. This was a juvenile."

"I'm sorry," Morena sounded as confused as Samir felt. "Why do we need to know this?"

Levering himself to his feet, Jenaris leaned back against the beast's flank while he considered his answer. "I thought you should know why I'm asking you to risk yourself." He met the warrior's eyes with a piercing blue stare that showed little evidence of fatigue. "I was hoping we could use one of the final pair to trace them back to their breeding ground. Unfortunately, this one wouldn't work."

"Because it's not full grown," Morena said thoughtfully.

Jenaris smiled. "If we want to trick its body into thinking it's time to breed," he replied, "a juvenile won't do."

Even though his mind was less foggy now, the Majaran still couldn't put his finger on what troubled him about the plan. It was definitely not a feeling he liked.

"So," Morena's eyes sparkled with sudden excitement, "Samir shouldn't have to fight this one. Right?"

"I'm afraid it's not that simple," the Wizard answered sadly.

The warrior's mind finally made the connection, and he didn't like the implications. "What happens if this one's a juvenile, too?" he asked.

"That," Jenaris agreed, "is the problem. Only three of the seven I've examined have been immature, but there's always a chance that this one will be worthless to us."

The warrior nodded. He'd been taught to always consider the worst possibility, and this qualified. But they had nothing better at the moment, so all they could do was try.

"Do you have a backup plan?" he asked hopefully, giving Morena a light squeeze as he felt her tense. "No." The Mage's lack of hesitation at least proved he didn't believe in providing false hope, but it wasn't the answer he wanted.

"Then I guess we'd better hope this works," he insisted, doing his best to lighten the mood. "What else do I need to know?"

Jenaris obliged, but did little to instill confidence as he spoke. Every teacher he'd ever had insisted that plans were better kept simple. Each new addition, each variable, was one more thing that could go wrong. Unfortunately, this plan depended on what appeared to be pure chance.

Well, he told himself, *we can only work with what we have.*

His head now almost clear, Samir bent down, catching Morena off guard as he put all of his passion into a long, deep kiss. Her surprise lasted only a moment before she returned it. When he finally pulled back, he had to catch his breath.

"What was that for?" she fairly purred, leaving her arms wrapped around his neck.

He smiled warmly as he paused to look at her, memorizing the loving expression on her face. What he had to do next was the hard part.

"It's time for you to go," he said quietly. "Jenaris and I have work to do."

For only a second, she looked afraid as she realized what that meant, barely keeping herself from looking into the trees. Without hesitation, she unwrapped her arms and smiled, giving him a good look at her beautiful green eyes before she turned and left.

As he watched her go, it occurred to Samir that she was definitely a warrior's daughter. Whether her mother had spoken to her about goodbyes or if it was just instinctive, she had more strength than some soldiers, and he couldn't help but admire her.

Now, though, he had to focus on the task at hand. The clearing was a mess of assorted dragon parts and would never do as a battlefield a second time. Regrettably, there wasn't time to find another—he was sure of that. Only one option remained. Easing his way through the narrow passage in the rock, he climbed to the top of the bluff. The small space between the edge and the first trees was a bit over twenty feet wide and perhaps twice as long. With the dragon in the middle of it, there would be little left for him. That was fine. Although it would limit his ability to maneuver, the beast would be more limited still. If all went well, he should only need to hold it for the minute or so Jenaris needed for a good look—which should be easier from the lower ground of the clearing.

The footing was fairly smooth and level, although several good sized stones were pushing their way through the soil. He would just have to leave them and try not to turn an ankle or hook a heel. After all, prying them out would only leave a hole that was every bit as dangerous.

"You ready?" The Wizard's voice came from just below his position.

Samir almost laughed. "It wouldn't matter if I'm not, would it?" he asked. "But, yes, I'm ready."

That wasn't exactly true. The link now felt like an almost constant itch that made it hard to focus.

"Don't hesitate to break the link," he told Jenaris, wishing they could do it now.

"The instant it sees you," the Mage assured him. "I promise."

He knew it had to be that way. Releasing the dragon now probably wouldn't make a difference, but leaving the connection until the last moment was only prudent. After all, enough things could go wrong already without risking more.

The loud crack of a snapping limb sounded through the woods only a short distance away. Not long now.

With the sword held lightly in his grip, the Majaran systematically relaxed his muscles from neck down to feet. Breath coming in a slow, steady rhythm, he waited.

True to his word the Mage broke the link immediately as the creature emerged from the trees—the feeling just vanishing entirely. It was as if hundreds of screaming voices had simultaneously ceased.

As he activated the rune, the world slowed around him.

Samir didn't bother to parry the spike as it shot toward his chest, choosing merely to turn sideways to avoid it easily. Still, there was no need to make himself a target. Two quick steps backward placed him directly beside a thick trunk, limiting the wyrm to attacking from the front and left side. The creature didn't disappoint, surging forward immediately.

Dagger-like teeth shot forward as the jaws opened impossibly wide. Samir slid one foot backwards, shifting to a position so low his hips barely cleared the ground. It would have been a simple matter to redirect the tip of his sword and stab upward, but he couldn't kill it yet—and hopefully not at all.

The chance passed almost before he saw it, as a set of razor sharp claws tore in from his left. Using the flat of his blade, he redirected the blow, jarring his arm with the beast's speed and power.

Feeling somewhat pressed, he attacked, thrusting the sword from half a dozen angles to gain room. He kept the strikes just fast enough, ensuring the drake would have time to dodge back as he rose to a more defensible stance.

The creature obliged.

Quickly avoiding a coordinated assault from jaws and tail, he became vaguely aware of the Mage's chanting. He almost regretted hearing the sound. It meant the drake would be allowed to live a while longer—but only until they could track it wherever it went.

A fountain of venom threatened to steal his vision as it flew toward his face. He ducked aside even as he darted in, smashing the flat of his blade against one of the long upper fangs. The wyrm roared with anger as a jagged end went flying.

"Now, Samir," the Mage finally called.

He dredged deep into himself, drawing on every ounce of strength and compressing it to a single, white-hot point. With a thought he triggered the rune, feeding it. All of his will channeled into and through the blade, pouring into the spell and driving it to incredible proportions. Impending doom radiated from the blade.

For the first time, Samir saw something other than hate in a dragon's eyes. He saw a mind-numbing terror, far beyond panic, forcing out any thought or emotion but the need to escape.

The drake's eyes rolled back in its head, exposing only the whites as it backpedaled, fleeing the Majaran's presence. With a spray of dirt and gravel, it threw its massive body around, causing Samir to dive aside or be struck by a wildly swinging tail as it tore wood and bark from a nearby trunk.

The sound of shattering trees echoed through the forest as the creature disappeared from sight, leaving only a spreading puddle of waste.

"Remember me, dragon!" he bellowed after it, heart pounding in his chest as he deactivated the rune. "I'm coming for you."

"Thank you." A quiver shook the Wizard's voice. "I don't think I could have taken much more of that, even with my own bond to the sword."

Surprised, the warrior turned to find a pale and shaken Jenaris looking back at him. It hadn't occurred to him that the Wizard would be affected by the fear rune. Then again, he hadn't thought to ask, merely assuming the man would be safe from his own spell.

"Sorry," he offered lamely, a little abashed.

"Are you daft? That was magnificent!" The old Mage dismissed his concern immediately, fixing him with a blue-eyed gaze. "I was afraid I'd have to throw my will behind yours to get enough power. My boy, you just proved to me that you deserve that weapon."

A swell of pride suffused him at the unexpected compliment. It reminded him of those rare moments when his Sóra expressed pleasure at his skill. Yet, at the thought, joy vanished in a twinge of homesickness.

With a sigh of regret he climbed down from the bluff and began the slow walk back to camp.

Chapter 36

Gotar

It was gratifying that their plan—and his spell—seemed to be working, but a week of hard riding had Jenaris eager to see it finished. No matter how fast they pushed their mounts or how many miles they covered, however, it was evident they couldn't keep pace with the wyrm they were chasing. Even leaving the wagons behind had done little to help.

The trail was easy enough to pick out for a competent tracker, and one of the Gotarrans was among the best. The old woodsman, Brand, never missed a sign, scrape, or claw mark that had been left by the beast's passing. The problem was that their quarry kept to no trail they could follow—scrambling up and down sheer cliffs with the ease of a squirrel in a tree. Their own route wound back and forth of necessity, taking what paths carried them in a direction to find the trail again.

There was absolutely no danger of the dragon getting away, however. Even if it ran to the farthest corner of the world, they would be able to find it again simply by linking someone to its Marque. No matter how many miles it put between them, it would eventually reach its destination and they would close the gap.

Of course, catching up was a slow process. But that was one of the hazards of traveling in a land with few established roads—and *none* where they were currently riding.

Few people other than the most determined hunters ever ventured into this part of the hills, but that had always been one of its charms. Jenaris knew the area well, having lived there for over half a century. He'd hunted its woods, fished its lakes and streams, and built a cabin only a few miles from where they were.

He had felt the gradual increase in his power and ability as they had ridden past the hills of his home the day before. It was a place he knew better than any other, and it had been tempting to detour a bit west just to catch a glimpse. But it would have been foolish to do so.

The party's route through the ancient forest was determined by the dragon—as it had to be. It was too easy to make a mistake when all you knew was the direction of your goal, but not the distance. Until the scouts came back with something definite, they had no idea whether the creature was a mile away, or a hundred—only that it had passed by about two days earlier.

Acedians and Gotarrans were working well together, having bonded somewhat in the past few weeks. In fact, they were hardly discernible as separate groups apart from the uniforms of the soldiers. The Acedians had even suspended the practice of riding in columns— though in this terrain it would've been single file—in favor of teaming with the barbarians, who were teaching them woodcraft.

Not that they lacked outdoor skills. The Gotarrans had been pleasantly surprised at their abilities, in fact. But even a Gotarran child could survive in the forest, and it only made sense to learn from those with greater skills.

Thankfully, their new friends were only too happy to teach.

Between that and Samir's training sessions, Carlon would soon have an elite troop of guardsmen among his soldiers. Of course, it was almost ironic that it was due to the formation of an alliance that would remove almost any call for their use. Oh, they would be needed in the present circumstances, but Acedia had nothing to fear from their neighbors—unless Brisia began acting with uncharacteristic aggression.

The sunlit glade was a pleasant change from the darkness of the thick woods covering most of the foothills. It also gave them a chance to leave the narrow trails and spread out enough to at least ride abreast and hold a rare conversation.

The Wizard watched as Samir pulled even with Morena, taking time to scratch Tirza as she lay uncomfortably behind the young woman's saddle. Morena insisted the hound would be out of the splint and walking again in only a few days, the bone somehow fully healed. It had been a clean break, but the claim was still nothing short of amazing—that a broken bone could heal in a week and a half. Whatever it was she had given Tirza, it was certainly effective.

Not for the first time, Jenaris wondered if she might loan him a few of her books.

"Someone coming, Magus," Kordel pitched his voice low, insuring that only the Wizard would hear. It was an unnecessary precaution, since the soldiers in the van would see the man in the distance soon.

"Thank you, Kordel," he replied, "but it's considered good courtesy to announce such news to *all* of one's allies."

The apprentice looked mildly embarrassed at the rebuke, reddening slightly. It was a sign Jenaris now knew to mean that the intended lesson had been learned—and he had yet to make the same mistake twice.

Now that he had actually begun teaching Kordel, he had to admit Lorn's choice had been a good one.

"Rider!" the call sounded from the head of the line, bringing all eyes to bear on the distant treeline.

Horses were reined to a halt as men eased swords in their scabbards or readied spears. It wasn't the man coming toward them they perceived as a threat. Even if he weren't one of their own scouts, he wouldn't be an enemy. The danger lay in what might be following.

Rather than continuing to watch the woods, the Mage watched the oncoming figure long enough to identify him as Brand. From the speed the tracker was urging from his mount, Jenaris assumed the man had something significant to report. Without waiting, he directed Keera toward Kulmar and Huldrich, knowing the man would deliver the news there.

Samir and Morena wasted little time in following his example, trailed by Caleb and two officers. Others began to crowd in behind and around them—mainly Gotarrans who could stand on their rights to hear what was said. Still, they were careful to leave a wide lane for Brand to reach the center of the crowd. The wait seemed to stretch as the rider dropped to a canter, and eventually a trot.

"It feels good to be popular," the man joked gruffly as he rode into the sea of expectant faces, "but I don't suppose someone brought me some food."

The broad grin showed a few gaps from missing teeth as laughter answered his greeting. Pulling up in front of the waiting leaders, Brand scanned the faces around him as he let anticipation build. Clearly the tracker enjoyed a bit of drama, as Jenaris himself did. Of course, in his case it tended to come with the title of wizard.

"So," Brand said loudly after milking the pause for all it was worth, "does anybody want to go to town?"

Kulmar snorted, a sound like ripping cloth. "Have you hit your head, man? There are no towns out this way."

Jenaris kept silent, knowing very well that no settlements existed out here but his own. That was exactly the way he preferred it, and most of the reason he felt drawn to the place.

"It's a town, all right," the scout assured them, meeting Kulmar stare for stare. "At least it was once, a long time ago. Now there's nothing but dragons."

"Where?" A light of excitement showed in Huldrich's eyes.

Brand smiled slowly, but didn't pause long. He seemed to accept that delay would be unwelcome. "Ten miles, more or less. Near straight north."

"Gotar." The voice that spoke sounded almost awed. The Wizard had no idea who said it, but it was almost as if a dam had burst among the barbarians—every man seeming to feel a need to repeat the name. Slowly, the hushed and reverent tones gave way to silence.

"What's Gotar?" Caleb leaned in to whisper to Huldrich.

It was the farrier who answered.

"A story," he replied loudly enough for everyone to hear. "Gotar never existed."

Angry grumbles came from somewhere in the crowd, but the big man stared them down, his scowl pulling cruelly at the scarred jaw. Gradually, the noises subsided. Kulmar's stony look didn't soften a hair, the glare continuing as he turned to face Brand.

"I never claimed it *was* Gotar," the tracker insisted, not intimidated for a second. "But you don't know for sure that it's a tale."

"What's Gotar?" Caleb repeated as the two barbarians continued to stare at each other silently.

"It's said to be the original home of my people," Huldrich said quietly, plainly not sure whether he believed—but wanting to. He raised his voice as he continued. "If it ever really existed, though, there can't be anything left after so long."

"I'd have to agree," Jenaris offered.

The stories he'd heard spoke as if Gotar had been lost only a few centuries ago. Yet the way it was described, as if practically made of silver and gold, indicated many generations of embellishments. If it had ever truly existed, he would have been very surprised to discover that less than seven or eight hundred years had passed. Probably much more. Given the span of time, any buildings would certainly have been claimed by the forest.

"Ten miles, you said," Samir called the discussion back to the matter at hand.

"Yeah. Just about," Brand agreed thoughtfully. "Couldn't promise, 'cause the trail's not straight. But close enough."

Jenaris glanced to the sun to gauge the time. Though it was early in the afternoon, a ten mile ride would take them into evening. It was no good. There were certainly more than a few who would gladly have pushed hard to get there hoping to wage an immediate assault. Worse, some would have camped directly outside the lair overnight, walking into the unknown at the time it posed the greatest threat.

"Best to make camp here and leave at first light," Samir insisted, apparently reaching the same conclusion.

"Nonsense. Plenty of time to get closer before dark," Gillis scoffed. He glanced at Brand. "Any suitable campsites near halfway?"

From the fiery look in the Majaran's eyes, the lieutenant was fortunate to be out of arm's reach. Gillis missed the expression entirely. Alban hadn't.

"Go and see to setting up camp, lieutenant," he said, clearly making it an order.

With a brisk salute, the junior man made his way through the crowd, his horse making slow progress.

"There are a few spots closer," Brand answered, obviously missing the significance of the exchange. "Good running water and level ground."

Huldrich shook his head decisively. "I'm not sure this is far enough not to give ourselves away," he announced. "We can't risk going farther today."

A consensus of nods greeted the pronouncement. It was the only sensible plan.

"I'm afraid I won't be joining you," the Mage asserted.

"What?" the Captain blurted. "Where are you going? We can use your help planning for tomorrow."

Jenaris chuckled softly. "I think one of us had better take a look around tonight. And, unless one of you has abilities I don't know about, I guess that means me. Planning requires information, Captain."

It wasn't exactly his first choice of how to spend the night, but the more they knew the more likely they could develop an effective strategy. Besides, he *had* to get a look at whatever this place was. That he could be so close for this long was simply unbelievable. How could he not have discovered it years ago? Decades?

First, though, he needed to make a few preparations.

This close to home, he felt strong enough to attempt something bolder than he would normally consider. The camp was large, but perhaps not so big that the right wards would be too weak. Walking the perimeter of the site, he dragged the butt of his staff in the grass. His chant wove its own counterpoint, subtle but nonetheless powerful. As the circle closed, Jenaris felt the protection snap into place. It wouldn't keep a determined enemy away, of course, but unless a drake was practically on top of them, it should help them avoid notice.

Samir's blade took only a few minutes and a great deal of concentration. He had managed to add another Element a few days earlier, but it had been so basic it hardly required much effort. The sword should, he thought, hold one more—the one that would make it a masterpiece. After that, he would be facing diminishing returns, with great effort adding nothing to the item's considerable power.

Swinging into the saddle, he took a moment to cast the same wards over the mare and himself, completely masking their presences. It would take power to maintain them, but as long as he did nothing fancy, it wouldn't tax his strength—especially this near his home. Brand had marked the trail well. The ride was hardly a difficult one, at worst requiring him to keep his feet dry fording a stream. Had it been any less eventful, in fact, he might have fallen asleep. For the most part, it was more of the same up-and-down travel under the dense forest cover.

As the hours wore on, however, he experienced the odd feeling that he was going the wrong way. The tracker's signs were there—notches cut into bark or a pile of stones to mark the route. Yet, each time, the thought occurred to him that he may have missed one, and should search in another direction. He dismissed it, always finding another in plain sight, pointing the way.

The eastern sky was fading to deep blue as he finally topped the last rise and looked across a wide valley. He almost didn't see it at first, covered thickly in ivy and nearly overgrown with trees of various sizes. Brand's "town" was certainly there, as he'd claimed.

Only it wasn't a town at all. It certainly wasn't Gotar, although he understood the barbarian's confusion. The sheer size of the place would have made for a fair Gotarran village, and wide gaps between sections made it seem comprised of separate buildings. But the Mage could see what Brand had missed—the mounds of rubble and the symmetry of its overall shape. What now stood, partially obscured by trees and vines, had once been a palace.

Chapter 37

Among the Ruins

The Wizard was waiting for them at the top of a steep hill. From the look of him, he evidently hadn't slept much—if at all—during the night. Hopefully, the man's deprivation had bought them the information they needed.

Samir had slept well enough, feeling quite good aside from some saddle stiffness. Unfortunately, the hours on horseback could affect his skills as badly as lack of rest. Still, he was ready to fight, having prepared as he rode—working his hair into a tight braid and arming himself with knives and fans.

Dismounting quickly, the Majaran wasted no time in helping Tirza down before joining Jenaris and the others. It felt wonderful just to stretch his legs on the short walk. That was driven from his mind almost immediately, however.

The view from the hill would have been breathtaking in its own right. A lightly forested glen stretched out below, nestled between steep ridge lines with a small lake at its eastern end. But there was more of interest than the scenery.

His attention was repeatedly drawn to the square corners and straight lines that would never appear in nature. Expanses of grey stone stood straight and true as they broke free of the trees and ivy around them. Here and there, pieces of a perimeter wall stood as well, though most of it had gone to rubble.

When whole, whenever that had been, it would have rivaled the royal palace in Toskar—for size if not splendor. Now all that remained was the barest hint of its former glory. Only bits and pieces stood, forlorn amid the quiet woodlands that would someday bury the rest.

Without a word, Morena slid her hand into his as they shared the view. At the simple gesture, the warmth and softness of her skin washed away a tension he'd been unaware of. Yet her very presence caused him to worry.

There was no question of her going into the lair—they had both agreed that she would remain outside. She would be safer there, but having her this close with only a few others for protection tied his stomach in knots. To be honest, though, it wouldn't have mattered how much protection she had. Unless he were the one between her and danger it would never be enough to satisfy him. Nothing short of Shimei himself would put him at ease.

Giving her hand a squeeze, he turned his attention to the Mage. "What are we facing, Jenaris? How many?"

"That, I don't know," the Wizard admitted with a deep sigh. "I didn't go that deep underground. But I *do* know where we'll find them."

It wasn't exactly a comforting answer. Samir had hoped to go in with at least an idea of what they'd be facing. Of course, given the size of the place, the man had probably spent hours trying to find an open entrance to the lower levels and a safe route through the debris. Still, even that knowledge would save them valuable time.

"So, what is that place?" Kulmar jerked a thumb in the direction of the ruins.

Jenaris shook his head absently. "I don't know," he replied, "but it's *incredibly* old, and it's still protected by magic more powerful than I could hope to do."

"Protected?" Alban said cautiously. "You mean trapped?"

"No," the Wizard assured them. "It's nothing like that. There are bindings and wards that have preserved some parts for centuries. Several have broken down, with the results you've seen. Others are still in place.

"There are also some spells I found rather interesting," he continued, a twinkle in his eyes. "You may have noticed feeling a desire to look elsewhere. A very good way to keep the place undiscovered, I think. Except that it wasn't *entirely* undiscovered. I believe stories about Gotar actually did originate here—spread by those who stumbled on it. But another spell keeps you from recalling where you'd found it."

A thoughtful silence followed. Samir had no idea what it would take to do what the Mage described, but he could see its effect on the old man. In addition to the excitement and wonder of his discoveries, the man was amazed and a bit frightened. Having seen what the Wizard could do, Samir felt a healthy respect for whatever lay beyond his abilities.

"Anything else you can tell us?" Huldrich asked, hopeful of at least a little more information to keep them alive.

"Sorry, no," Jenaris offered apologetically. "But if it makes you feel better, I'll volunteer Samir to go first." The Wizard's grin caused a few quiet laughs, breaking some of the tension.

Morena stiffened slightly at the comment. Samir wished he could say something to reassure her, but he couldn't promise to come back safe. Gently, he slipped an arm around her waist. She leaned into him.

The planning took surprisingly little discussion, since leaving things as flexible as possible only seemed prudent. Samir would take half the warriors into the lair—along with Jenaris, Huldrich, Kulmar and Alban. Caleb would keep Gillis and the other half to protect the camp and act as a reserve force. The only real difficulty lay in deciding who would stay behind—and enforcing it—with several Gotarrans asserting their right to go where they would. In the end, drawing straws seemed the only fair way to decide the issue.

In the meantime, the Majaran took Morena aside, finding a spot under a nearby oak. She looked at him expectantly as they sat on an exposed root, apparently waiting for him to kiss her. Instead, he called Dragon's Fang to his hand, laying it carefully across her lap.

"I need to teach you something," he said softly, eyes still on the sword. "I should have done this weeks ago."

"Should have done what?" she asked, confused at the significance of the gesture, and a bit wary as well.

"Taught you to use this sword."

Morena tensed, causing him to lift his gaze from the blade. She was angry, though she hid it well. When she spoke, her voice was quiet. Too quiet.

"Do you think I give a damn about this stupid sword?" she said, full lips thinning slightly.

The question caught him off guard, as did the coldness of her tone. All he had done was offer to share a secret with her. Why would she get mad at him for *that*? He'd have thought she would be pleased.

"What's wrong?" he asked. Suddenly concerned, his mind swiftly reviewed the discussion to this point, trying to grasp some reason for her reaction.

"Nothing," she answered flatly, looking straight ahead rather than at him.

Oh, yes. Something was *definitely* wrong, and he had no doubt that the next words out of his mouth had better be the right ones. Unfortunately, he didn't have a clue what those words should be. Somehow, it felt as if he were walking into a trap.

"I'm sorry." He reached to take her hand, which jerked away as she looked at him, brows arched.

"For what?" she said sweetly, a dangerous look in her eyes.

He was *clearly* in some sort of trouble.

Only one possible response came to mind. "For whatever it is I did that made you mad at me," he replied, a hint of frustration slipping through.

Now her anger was undeniable—her mouth thinning to a hard line as she crossed her arms beneath her breasts. "You don't even know, do you? You're just saying what you think I want to hear."

"Of course," he admitted, astonished. "But I wouldn't have to if you'd just tell me what's wrong!"

Morena stared silently at him as her hand curled tightly around the sword's hilt. For an instant, he wondered whether he should prepare to defend himself, or simply summon the weapon away from her. Instead, he merely waited.

She stood, throwing the blade into the dirt at their feet and rounding on him. Her eyes blazed as she placed hands on hips and leaned over him.

"You want to know what's wrong? *Fine!*" Her voice quivered tightly, on the bare edge of control as the volume of her words increased. "You're going to walk into danger, and you think you're just going to leave me a *sword*!?"

"I'm not...," he tried to reply, but she immediately cut him off.

"How *dare* you think I want some stupid piece of metal?" Morena's voice heated intensely as she spoke, taking on a sharp tone. "Do you think I'm just going to smile politely like my mother and be happy with that? *Do you*?"

Now he understood. At least he thought he did.

He'd seen Marius' sword above the mantle—the only thing her father had left them—and he knew how raw her grief still was. Samir had heard her crying softly in the dark some nights, and now he had thoughtlessly fed her fears. He felt like an idiot.

Standing, he gently took her by the shoulders, meeting her hard stare with a look of patience. She fell silent.

"I have no intention of *giving* you that sword," he told her calmly. "I plan to give it to our children many years from now. At the moment, I just want to teach you how to bond with it, so we can share that."

"Oh," she replied lamely, cheeks coloring as the anger drained away.

Briefly, he considered arguing Morena's point about her mother. Having met Laurie, he could picture her putting on a brave face in public—even with her daughter. But it was unfair to suggest that she hadn't wept as much or as deeply at the loss of her husband.

Not wanting another fight, he let the matter drop.

Guiding her back to their seat, he called the sword and again handed it to her, careful of the unnaturally sharp blade. Patiently, he talked her through the steps as she forged an indestructible bond with Dragon's Fang and cautioned her not to trigger the runes. After several long minutes, her eyes opened wide, punctuated by a sharp intake of breath.

When she finally looked up, he could easily read the wonder in her expression. He smiled as he summoned the weapon to his hand. With an answering grin, she called it back, delighted that it responded to her will.

"Thank you," she laughed, kissing him. "This is *wonderful*! How do you not do this all day long?"

Standing slowly, he recalled the sword and sheathed it. "Don't think I haven't considered it."

After a short goodbye and a long kiss, he joined his men at the crest of the hill. He was pleased to see Dane and Roland—two of his better students—as well as Suppan and Kessel. It wasn't his intention to take all of the most skilled fighters with him, but he did want to make absolutely sure this was done right the first time.

With a nod to Jenaris, the Majaran started down the slope, only vaguely aware of the warriors falling in behind him. His attention was fixed on the shadows all around, under every cluster of trees. Nothing moved but the occasional rabbit bolting from its frozen position as it sought the nearest cover.

It was nearly half a mile to the shattered palace, but it went by in an instant. His senses hyper-alert for any sign of a wyrm, each moment blended into the next. The worn and weathered stone inched closer, coming into clearer view with each step. He could see the details of what had been intricate carvings, rivaling the best he'd seen in Scara—delicate bodies of knotwork and spiral patterns gracing even the caps atop walls. Between the standing sections lay heaps of rubble, covered in tangled vines and giving root to stunted trees. As they crept silently forward, he passed close enough to see details of the outer wall—or what remained. What lay piled on the ground was littered with bright metal spikes, somehow unrusted amid the ancient wreckage.

Jenaris waved them to the right, climbing with great caution over a pile of stone from the crumbled fortifications. It shifted only slightly as dozens of feet picked their way across to the ground on the other side. The Mage continued, angling toward a pair of standing sections—one a tower almost entirely obscured by clinging greenery.

Most of the twenty foot gap in between was filled with collapsing material—rising nearly halfway up the three story structure. Just enough remained clear for him to see into some of the rooms. Amazingly, aside from a few blown leaves and roosting birds, everything seemed intact and nearly new. Whatever magic still preserved the building here, it apparently also protected its contents.

The Wizard gestured to a small door in the side of the tower, already open several inches. Easing it slowly, Samir was surprised that no squeal of rusty hinges shouted the presence of his small army of invaders. He smiled, thankful for the lingering power of whatever spells had lasted all these centuries.

Nothing but deep darkness greeted him, swallowing the last few steps that wound downward to his left. Willing the blade into his grasp, he activated the most recent addition—causing a soft white light to shine in a cascade of sparkles along its frosty surface. More stairs came into view.

Behind him, Jenaris and his apprentice summoned glowing lights of their own at the ends of their staves. It was nearly lost in the bright daylight at the foot of the tower. Others pulled out bundles of arrows, all that was left of the hundreds the Wizard had enchanted to produce light when struck.

Samir moved onto the stairs, balanced on the balls of his feet. Step by step he wound downward steadily, traveling deep under the castle. At each smooth movement, the light of his sword slid forward to illuminate more of the curved wall and another tread in the staircase.

Occasional carvings decorated the walls on both sides—intricately woven knots cut into the smooth, clean surface. Even a momentary study showed sharp edges in what appeared to be new stonework. He was certain Jenaris would give his eyeteeth to know how it had been preserved so well for so long.

Finally, a landing appeared—a broad, flat stretch of stone without a speck of dust. Before him a heavy wooden door hung on wrought iron hinges, tightly closed against the jamb. A few feet beyond, the stairs continued deeper into the earth.

A small, shuttered window in the door was closed, forcing him to listen with an ear to the oak. Not a whisper of potential danger reached him through the thick, dense wood.

Expectant faces met him as he looked up. A line of men stretched back up the stairs, all armed and waiting for whatever came.

Placing his left hand on the door, he pushed.

It swung easily on well-oiled hinges, revealing a wide, high-ceilinged room. Bunks lined the walls to one side of the door, a long table and benches to the other. A guardroom.

Stepping inside, he glanced quickly around. Again no dust on any surface and furniture that still appeared new.

"Three," Huldrich said beside him, snapping him out of his own thoughts.

"What?" he asked, trying hard to grasp the barbarian's meaning.

"Three doors."

Following Huldrich's outstretched arm, Samir saw what the other man had noticed already. One door stood directly across from them, and another at each end of the room.

Three exits led from the room, and they had no idea which—if any—would take them where they needed to go.

Chapter 38

Underground

"It's the door straight ahead," the Mage said in Samir's ear as the men pushed their way inside. Spreading out, they stood against the walls or sat on the table. "The two on the ends lead to cells."

It was good to know Jenaris had at least gone far enough to point them in the right direction. The last thing they needed to do was wander aimlessly until after dark, when the dragons would likely go out to hunt—and find the camp.

The center door was barred from inside the room, but the thick wooden plank lifted cleanly and easily from its brackets. Leaning it quietly against the wall, the Majaran turned to scan the faces watching him with eager expectation.

"One man stays here to bar and guard this door," he announced, inspiring a chorus of grumbles. It spoke well of the heart in the men present, but they had no time to waste arguing. He swept the room with a look, fixing each one briefly with his gaze. "I don't care how you decide, but it's going to be done within five minutes. Got it?"

Resentful nods answered him as he leaned back against the door, watching as Jenaris conjured half a dozen glowing spheres. Around the room, men matched up furiously to shoot odds and evens on their fingers, the winners grinning while losers matched up again. In remarkably little time, two men remained in the middle of the room, both in Acedian uniforms.

Samir didn't wait to see who won. Grabbing the door's wrought iron ring, he paused. "I want arrows dropped every fifty feet, starting on the other side of this door," he told them.

He pulled slowly, peering around the widening gap. Dim light leaked through into the corridor beyond, but revealed little for the moment. The foul odor that rolled into the room nearly made him retch—though not everyone managed to resist, judging by the wet plops that sounded from several directions. No one said a word or cracked a joke. After all, either option would bring a need to inhale again that much sooner. Forcing himself to breathe through his mouth, he tried to put it out of his mind.

The light radiating from the sword shone forty feet beyond the door, revealing more of what he'd seen above ground. Perfectly preserved, seamless walls extended for a dozen feet beyond the doorway. After that, it seemed an entirely different world.

Cracked and broken sections of stone tilted crazily as the wide tunnel settled under the weight of the earth above it. Gravel and dirt littered the uneven floor, and patches of lichen and mildew were everywhere.

"I'll shore it up," Jenaris whispered. "We'll be safe enough."

Samir nodded, continuing on.

From somewhere ahead, a noise that may have been a yawn reached them as it echoed down the hallway. There was no question what had made that sound.

He crept forward, the glow of his blade advancing ahead of him. A few feet at a time, the darkness retreated to reveal more of the collapsing tunnel. The view appeared unchanging for several hundred feet until, suddenly, only jagged edges showed at the limit of his light. Beyond the corridor's end, the glow was swallowed by a greater darkness.

Moving gingerly through the last bit of the broken section, he stepped carefully. Although the massive slabs appeared to balance precariously, nothing shifted, aside from a trickle of dirt. The experience made him grateful for the Wizard's presence. While he was now fairly confident there would be no collapse, he set his feet well clear of any hazards.

The jagged end of the hallway grew in his vision, drawing nearer. His light still revealed nothing at all beyond.

Finally, Samir caught sight of a far wall and a rough ceiling as he reached the entrance to the broad open space. What lay before him was a large natural cavern—dagger-like stones hung from the roof and were fixed to the floor, their surfaces like melted candle wax. Piles of fallen rock and soil littered the floor, leaving only a few clear lanes in which to move. In several places, tunnels branched off to vanish into darkness.

Beside him, Kulmar grunted disgustedly. The Majaran had to agree with the sentiment.

"What do you think?" Alban asked quietly of no one in particular. "Split up?"

It was the last thing Samir wanted to do, giving up the numbers they might need for the sake of time. But there was no telling how long it would take to search this place, even with several groups. With only one, it could take far longer than they dared. It was a trade-off plain and simple, but a necessary one.

Looking around at the others he saw the same conflict on their faces. He also saw the same grim resolution. One by one, they nodded their agreement, Huldrich showing his frustration and distaste by spitting dramatically.

It was a futile gesture even if he did sympathize. They would do what was needed because that's what warriors did. Liking the situation had no relevance whatsoever.

"We've got three men who can make light," Kulmar observed. "That limits us to three groups."

The Wizard gazed long and hard at his apprentice as he considered. Finally, surprisingly, he nodded.

"All right," the Mage agreed. "Kulmar, if you'll take Kordel, Huldrich can come with me, and we can split the men three ways."

No one voiced a better suggestion. Soon enough, the two dozen or so men formed groups around Kulmar, Huldrich and Samir himself. Dividing the arrows between them, it suddenly seemed like there were far too few.

Seeing no reason to wait, the Majaran took his group and headed down the center tunnel.

Kulmar watched the young Wizard from the corner of his eye as they moved down the right hand tunnel. Nervous wasn't the half of it. He could appreciate Jenaris' desire to keep his apprentice with an experienced leader. The Mage had seemed grateful to have someone to watch over the youngster. That was fine. In a way, he shared the feeling, knowing Huldrich had the more able Wizard to help him. But he would have to tell Kordel to keep clear of any fighting and let the warriors handle things. The lad was a good sort, he supposed, but it was better to depend on proven men.

With his people spread out across the wide, rocky corridor behind them, he shifted Kordel to the left so the light would reach as far as possible around the curve ahead. Given the irregular shape of the caverns, they would more than likely have little or no warning when they came face to face with one of those things.

It was bad enough that the wet limestone of the cave floors would offer poor footing in a battle, and that puddles of vile smelling filth were everywhere. What really bothered him was that the very light they needed to see would give away any chance of catching a dragon unprepared. It would probably be safer hunting bears with a stick but, then again, none of them had come thinking it would be safe.

The smell of decay was strong, tickling his nose. He had no doubt of the source. Water clinging to the stone sent shimmering blue reflections dancing around them, highlighting the piles of animal bones strewn around the large open space.

Entering a larger section, he peered through a forest of fang-like stalactites that appeared to have dripped and flowed into place. The stalagmites, however, were a ruin—gouged and ripped by claws that had been raked through the soft, wet stone. More scratches and scrapes marred the floor.

Every hunter in the group knew the signs. They'd seen trunks rubbed clean of bark by bears and elk, or used as scratching posts by wildcats. At least one dragon frequented this cave and had marked it as his territory. But none of the creatures would live here. This was its dumping ground—the place where it left its waste.

Scanning the possible routes in and out immediately told Kulmar which way to go. Wear marks on the stone surfaces from continual traffic, as well as the rubs from scales on stone, left no question.

Staying close to the walls, the men crept toward the tunnel mouth, weapons ready.

The big farrier clutched his spear tightly, hands low and ready to thrust. Against these monsters speed was critical. So was precision. There were so few vulnerable places where a blow would matter, that every strike had to count. From what he'd seen, drakes protected those spots incredibly well.

It was a blind corner that twisted immediately back toward them, at least from the angle Kulmar had. Heart pounding like a drum, he stepped away from the wall, moving far enough to see around the turn. He could feel something soft under his foot as he did so, but he refused to look or allow it to distract him. When you had a wild pig cornered, you *didn't* look away.

It was dark inside, with the light coming from the wrong angle and reflecting only a little. It was no good trying to strain his eyes. Kordel would just have to come closer, like it or not.

He saw it as he turned toward the Mage, just inside the tunnel they had just left and poised like a stalking cat. It knew it had been seen.

Screaming a deafening challenge, it charged, the noise echoing madly.

The last man in line never had time to raise his spear as the tail smashed across his chest with bone-shattering force, driving him into the wall. It went little better for the next man, who managed to swing for the beast's head too slowly. Dagger-like teeth punctured the Acedian's breastplate and the soft flesh beneath it, slinging the body away as its neck whipped back.

Men scrambled away from the wall, trying to fan out for some semblance of a coordinated attack. In the process, one man slipped to the wet floor only to be pinned as the wyrm leapt forward atop him.

Running forward at top speed, Kulmar knew he would be too slow by half even if he kept his feet. Time seemed to crawl as he watched the tail's spike dart forward, angling directly toward his chest. With every ounce of strength, he flung the weapon in his grip, aiming for the palm-sized eye that glared hatred at him. He knew as it left his hand that the throw was *perfect*, but it would do him no good. The lethal spike would have him.

His momentum worked against him as he tried to veer sideways, still moving toward the striking tail. The big man tensed.

The tail stopped with a jolt as it struck...nothing.

An invisible wall met Kulmar's shoulder as he reached the place where the tail had been halted. With barely a glance back at the young Wizard, the farrier drew his long knife.

Men stabbed at the beast's flanks, spears and swords striking with powerful blows. But Kulmar had a better target in mind.

The drake thrashed its head wildly, its screams now born of pain and fury as it tried to dislodge the spearhead in its eye.

Kulmar dashed in as the barrier dropped, blade held at his waist and angled upward. With all the power in his arm, he drove the point forward—coming up under the chin to pierce the softer scales. The shuddering beast collapsed as the blade sliced into its brain, jerking the hilt from his grip as the head fell.

Wrenching his spear loose, the big man stood over the lifeless hulk of the dragon's corpse, staring down at it with a powerful sigh. He barely noticed the celebration around him.

"What's wrong?" Kordel asked, confused at his lack of enthusiasm. The Wizard's own face was split ear to ear in a triumphant grin.

"Nothing, lad. And thanks for the help." Kulmar clapped the other man on the back, nearly knocking him off his feet. "I'm just trying to figure out how to roll this thing over. I need to get my knife back."

A distant roar reverberated from the walls, coming at Huldrich from several directions at once. Whoever it was that had found what they sought, he wished them luck. But whether they won or lost, he couldn't worry about that now. He had hunting of his own to do.

The walls to either side were smooth, the ceilings arched. It was almost as if someone had added a hallway to connect existing caverns, and it wasn't the first such passage they'd found.

As silently as he knew how, Huldrich slunk through the tunnels at a half crouch, spear raised and ready. He was somewhat discomfited by the Wizard, who strolled casually beside him as though completely unconcerned by the possibility of attack. Still, Jenaris made no more noise than he as they moved.

The chamber that opened up before them was the largest they'd seen yet—the Mage's light failing to reach either its roof or the far end. But it wasn't a problem for long. A gesture from Jenaris split the glowing ball at the end of his staff, sending the new light drifting out into the enormous cavern.

Only the lower tips of the stalactites were illuminated as the light revealed the rest of the space. Great worn pathways, like bizarre game trails wound among the stalagmites, connecting numerous entrances around the perimeter. Not far to their left, a single wide passage angled upward steeply, its gouged and worn floor showing the heaviest use. Perhaps its most remarkable aspect was the slightly fresher air—carrying less of the awful stench of corruption that had nearly gagged him.

Slipping away from the group, Brand glided from one thick pillar of stone to the next, covering the distance to the sloping tunnel in moments. The man moved with a strange grace, belying his advanced age—a skill born of life in the woods, where game spooked easily. After only a quick peek the man darted around the corner, leaving the light behind. He was gone for only seconds before returning.

"Good, sweet air, Hul," the tracker winked. "That's the way out when we're finished here."

"That's welcome news at least," Huldrich replied. It never hurt to have another exit handy, after all. "Thanks, Brand."

The information would be helpful, but it was the other passages that concerned him now. With a hunter's trained eye he looked them over, hoping to find the greatest signs of wear. It didn't take long.

Glancing from face to face he pointed with his spear, making sure all saw where he meant to go. He never finished.

A soft scraping sound interrupted him, drawing his gaze back to the cavern as he pressed himself tightly against the wall. Jenaris' staff winked out as all the men froze, as perfectly silent as they were still.

A dark snout eased from one of the tunnels moments later, sniffing the air. The eyes followed cautiously as the wyrm studied the magical light hovering at the far end of the cavern. It stared suspiciously for several seconds, drawing a long, deep breath.

With a loud snort, the head withdrew.

No one dared to move. Too many hunts had been ruined by some impatient or uncomfortable fool scaring away the game. Despite the cramps in his back and legs, Huldrich stood motionless. He wasn't about to assume it was safe to move.

Minutes passed as sweat beaded on his face in the cool, damp air. His legs began to tremble slightly. He *would* have to move soon, but he would do so as slowly as he could.

"Follow me," Jenaris whispered, simply fading into his awareness. Without waiting, the Mage strode to the tunnel where they had seen the dragon.

Huldrich shrugged in response to the questioning looks of the others. If Jenaris thought it safe to move, then it must be.

With a grateful sigh, he pushed away from the wall. The relief was only partial, however, stiffness making his movements uncomfortable as he moved to follow the Wizard. He did his best to hide it.

A light shone from the end of Jenaris' staff once again, though much smaller this time, just enough to see by. He was glad of that much. Still, the young Gotarran put a hand against the wet limestone wall as he entered the tunnel. Light or no light, he felt better with the wall to guide him in the gloom.

Jenaris' hand on his chest stopped him cold, but the Wizard said nothing. Huldrich watched, waiting silently as the tiny light receded toward the end of the line, then gradually returned. Finally, the older man stood next to him, soft breath falling on his ear as the Mage leaned in.

"When the light increases to full strength, it may hurt your eyes, but don't hesitate," he said. "She may only be blinded for a few seconds."

Jenaris withdrew, leaving him alone with his thoughts as he anticipated the need to charge. His hands caressed the haft of his weapon unconsciously, callouses rubbing roughly as he crouched.

A blinding flash stung his eyes, causing him to blink hard.

The dragon crouched angrily in a wide dead-end chamber, only twenty feet away. Standing directly before it, Jenaris held his staff mere inches from its eyes, the unexpected brightness forcing its pupils to pinpoints. Thin, jagged flakes of various sizes littered the floor all around them.

With a wordless cry Huldrich ran, muscles bunching in arms and shoulders as he drove the spear forward to strike an eye. He saw the jaws open as a hiss erupted from the beast.

Perfect.

Reflexes straining he changed his aim, angling the point down as he put his weight behind it. The long spear vanished as it thrust straight down the drake's gullet for more than half its length.

Ashwood broke with a barely audible snap as the head recoiled, bending the neck in a sinuous curve. With a violent wracking breath it exhaled, doing its best to cough out the splinters obstructing its throat. Jenaris stepped forward as the head withdrew, keeping the light in front of its eyes.

Exultation surged through Huldrich at the results of his strike. It took several seconds to realize he was unarmed. *Almost* unarmed. Grinning wildly he drew his knife as the other men fell on the creature's flanks. He never got to use it.

One of the Acedians shoved his sword point beneath the scales of the wyrm's side. Prying the blade to lift the thick plates, he jammed the hilt forward to plunge sharp steel through heart and lungs.

Men retreated quickly, throwing themselves to the ground as the beast thrashed. But it was no longer a threat. Heart ruptured and bleeding internally, it weakened rapidly. In moments it was still.

Samir couldn't shake the feeling that he'd gotten turned around in the winding passages. Twice they had come across a tunnel already marked with arrows. Since they were already running low on the enchanted shafts, he could only shake his head with regret over the waste as they backtracked. Reaching the last unexplored corridor, they began the search again.

Several muffled roars had reached them, but there was no way to judge their source or how many drakes had made them. Worse, if battles had been fought, he couldn't say who had won. The only thing he could be sure of was that at least one of the beasts was down here with them.

A quick series of hand signals brought the men fully alert as he indicated a side passage ahead. They had been through this several times already and were set almost as soon as he signaled. A nod to Dane sent the scout running across the entrance as the rest waited, ready to attack anything that merged to give chase.

Nothing.

Still wary, the man returned, watching the tunnel as he passed in front of the opening. The strategy seemed sound, but so far they'd found nothing despite a great deal of effort.

Samir had also lost all sense of time. He knew that it had been hours—or thought he did—although whether it was day or night he had no way to tell. There was only the steady blue glow and the seemingly endless view of limestone on every side.

Slowly and quietly, they moved on.

A few more twists and turns brought an almost surreal change in the passageway illuminated ahead of him. Within a matter of yards, the strange melted look of damp stone became a smooth and straight hallway—ten by ten. The Majaran felt an odd sense of displacement. The passage was far underground, extending from a complex of caverns, yet it would have fit perfectly well in Carlon's castle.

Only thirty feet away, the hallway split into a blind T that vanished out of sight in both directions. It would be a cozy size for a dragon, hardly requiring a special effort to turn around while protecting its flanks. If they met one here, two men could attack it at a time—perhaps three. He didn't like it a bit.

Samir remained cautious as he moved forward, his back to the right hand wall. It was slow going as his light revealed the left hand branch. Opposite him, one of the barbarians mirrored his movement.

The glow from the sword reached far enough to show him an archway perhaps ten feet beyond the corner, a staircase spiraling up. Across from him the other man shook his head. There was no danger. Pivoting smoothly into the intersection, Samir looked down the corridor on the right. A narrow wooden door, hung on iron strap hinges and set with a small window stood only twenty feet away.

The window was useless, darkness ending his hope of seeing anything at all. Attempts to angle Dragon's Fang and light the interior would be equally futile. His only possible accomplishment, he knew, would be to give away his presence to anything on the other side.

With a glance at the men behind him, he grabbed the iron ring and pulled.

Light flooded the room, striking highlights from glass and steel in a room twenty feet square. Cabinets, shelves and tables lined the walls—mostly empty from what he could see. Jars and other glassware sat abandoned, resting where they had been left who knew how long ago. The center of the room was occupied by a single table, apparently of the same bright metal as the spikes atop the outer wall. Alongside, a much smaller table held a disturbing arrangement of curved blades, saws, and sharp hooks—all shining as if recently polished.

Directly opposite was another door, slightly ajar.

Crossing the floor quickly he peeked through the four inch gap, shielding the light with his body to allow it to shine through gradually. Another glint of steel threw back glittering reflections, this time from wrist thick metal bars.

"Keep your hands to yourself, corporal," Roland's voice hissed softly behind him.

Over his shoulder, Samir could see the sergeant and another man, Rayburn, beside one of the tables. The soldier's hand recoiled from a pile of mottled looking flakes. Stepping closer, he could see clearly what they were—fragments of giant eggshell scattered on the table. Something for the Mage to worry about.

"We have work to do," the Majaran whispered sternly, drawing all eyes instantly. "Someone drop an arrow and let's go."

Within moments the room brightened behind him as he returned to the second door. It was hung to open outward, into the next room. Taking a deep breath, he set his feet and pushed. The thick wood glided away from him without a squeak.

It opened into a circular chamber sixty feet across and lined with enormous cages. There was no doubt about their intended use. With bars anchored firmly in the floor and ceiling, the construction was certainly sturdy. Stout enough to hold a dragon.

At the moment all were empty. The center of the room was not.

The dragon curled up in the floor came instantly awake, mammoth head swinging toward the source of light. Eyes blazing with fury, it screamed.

Darting through the narrow space between cages Samir crossed the open floor as fast as he could, taking only a few long strides to cover the distance. He fairly flew toward the beast. But even with his speed increased by the sword, he failed to catch it in a vulnerable position.

The creature uncurled as if by magic, already on its feet before he was halfway there. Forelegs crouched and neck curved back, it stood waiting—ready to meet him as he came within range of snapping jaws.

The Majaran threw himself aside, heedless of the filth coating the floor as he rolled back to his feet. It made no difference to the drake. Glaring angrily, it slashed at him, sinuous tail cutting across to open his belly. He barely had time to react.

Shifting his back foot, he leaned back just enough to avoid the sharp point. Immediately he pushed off, turning aside a set of slashing claws as he charged and slicing open the wyrm's leg.

The others had surrounded the creature as quickly as they could follow. Doing their best to force its attention away from Samir, they attacked where they could— seeking any weakness in its defenses. But their best efforts could do no good in the few seconds they had.

The second dragon was inside the chamber almost before he saw it, scrambling through the tunnel mouth with blinding speed. Its bull rush trampled one Acedian underfoot, never giving him a chance to react. Others *had* seen it coming, yet were still caught by the tail as it whipped for their legs.

Suddenly finding themselves trapped between a pair of the creatures, the others pulled back and left him to face the first drake alone. He hardly noticed. Focusing only on the battle before him, he fought on.

Left hand reaching to his sash for one of his knives, he jabbed the glowing blade toward an eye, forcing the head back. Almost as fast as the sword withdrew, the jaws sped toward him. He had known they would. The warrior spun to his left, coming alongside the outstretched neck as he extended the knife. Momentum slammed the perfectly angled blade all the way to the hilt as it was driven beneath the scales.

Blood gushed from the wound as he stepped away, leaving the blade stuck fast in the fatal puncture. The dying wyrm still struggled to attack him in its hatred and pain, but only weakly—allowing him to step over a sweeping tail.

But he was already focused on the other monstrosity as it squared off against the remaining warriors. Most of the men appeared to have avoided serious injuries in the initial attack, and Roland had somehow inflicted some light injuries. Still, the little they had learned from him had only been enough to keep them alive.

Samir had covered only a few yards before the beast's head swung toward him, drawn by the death throes of the first. Suddenly the other warriors were forgotten. Its sinister gaze watched him, anger almost palpable as it opened its mouth in a hiss.

His pulse quickened instantly as he saw it—the shattered stump of a left fang. He *knew* this dragon. It had been the reason he'd smashed the tooth at their first meeting, to be absolutely certain he would recognize it.

It knew him as well. He could see it in the creature's eyes—a terrible rage mixed with fear.

The drake backpedaled as he advanced, its bellowing cry filling the room. Ignoring everyone but Samir, it moved slowly away, its unblinking stare locked firmly on him. He fed on its fear as he followed.

With a jolt, its hindquarters struck the thick cage bars behind it. Samir smiled. The thing stood, frozen, watching as he stepped forward.

Maddened with fright, it threw itself at him in a violent frenzy. Now it was the warrior's turn to retreat as he dodged savage claws and teeth—the attacks coming faster than he'd even believed possible. A claw strike nearly landed as he parried another. It was all he could do to stay alive, but it couldn't last. Even with his sword-enhanced reflexes he couldn't match this pace for long. Thrusting to pierce an outstretched claw, he turned aside barely in time to avoid the snapping maw that threatened to impale him. Quickly he raised the sword, moving as fast as he could to turn aside the spadelike tail tip.

He almost succeeded.

Scales rained to the stone floor, sheared off by the sword as he parried. Yet he barely slowed the lashing tail. The air left his lungs in a rush as he was knocked back, pain almost too great to register. Knuckles slamming the ground, the hilt popped free to skitter across the floor.

The room plunged immediately into darkness as the steady glow of the sword winked out. Even as it left his hand he felt himself slow, returning to his normal speed as his connection with the rune was broken.

But as awful as the blinding darkness was, the sound was worse. The harsh scrape of talons on stone reached his ears at almost the same instant as the screaming. He couldn't tell pain from panic as the voices echoed, and he wasn't entirely sure he wanted to.

Agony lanced through him as he pushed himself up from the cold floor, battered muscles protesting. He ignored it. With all the self-discipline he could muster, he forced himself to stand in spite of the pain in his chest.

Light flared as Dragon's Fang leapt into his hand, giving him a fraction of a second to react. Neck arched back, it reared, claws of both forelegs sweeping toward his head. Reflexively, he dropped to a crouch as the wind of the blow caressed his cheek.

Directly in front of him, the dragon's belly stretched out, fully exposed. He didn't hesitate. Samir's hand lashed out, wrist and arm angling to drive the blade up and through the beast's solar plexus. The strike was perfect. Thick hide offered little resistance to the impossibly sharp point, parting easily.

Yet the warrior lacked the reach to drive it home. After only a foot, the blade stopped.

It was enough.

Releasing the hilt, the Majaran rolled aside as the dragon came crashing down with claws extended. It was the beast's last mistake. Momentum already driving it forward, the wyrm was unable to stop as the pommel struck the floor, stopping the sword. A cry of rage escaped the creature as its massive weight forced the blade farther in.

But Samir didn't stop, didn't waver. Rolling to his feet, he turned to strike even as he summoned the sword to his hand. It bit deep as it struck, sinking to the hilt and slicing through heart and lungs.

With a final shudder, the dragon stopped.

His chest an agony with each heaving breath, the warrior looked around him. Along with the pair the wyrm had killed on its arrival, three more lay dead in a scene of horrible carnage. The light had been out for mere seconds, but the monster had done awful damage in that brief span. A Gotarran lay eviscerated in a spreading pool of his own blood, eyes staring emptily. Another man lay in a crumpled heap where he'd been thrown against one of the cages, body torn by deep puncture wounds.

The worst hadn't been done by the beast, however. Rayburn stood in shock, a dripping sword clutched numbly in his fingers as he stared at Roland's lifeless body. It was fairly clear what had happened—striking out in the dark at something he thought was a threat. Unfortunately, that something had been Sergeant Roland.

"It was an accident, corporal." Sympathy welled in Samir, but there was no time for grieving. "I'm sorry, but we still have a search to finish, and you just got promoted."

Given the choice, he would have liked to call it a day. He had only three men left of his original eight and felt as if he'd been smashed by a boulder. Holding the sword up to light the chamber, he rubbed absently at his chest with his free hand. It came away wet and sticky with blood.

Looking down, he was amazed to find a deep gash slanting across his ribs. If these weren't the last dragons, he was definitely going to have a problem.

Epilogue

It felt good to finally step out of the broad, sloping tunnel and into the sunlight. Completely exhausted, Samir was actually surprised to find that it was still daytime.

They emerged onto a wide stretch of road threading south between the cliffs they'd just exited and the lake at the valley's eastern end. It would be a long walk back to the camp—especially burdened with a man who had wrenched his knee in a dark corridor. Still, the sooner they got back, the sooner they could wash and rest.

Of course, that also meant letting Morena see how badly hurt he was—and it *was* bad. He'd managed to wash the long cut on his chest, but the blood soaking his torn shirt made him look half dead. In truth, part of him felt like he was.

The road ended at the foot of the steep hill, apparently reclaimed now by the forest. It left them a formidable walk uphill on the stony soil. Thankfully, it wasn't as hard as he expected.

Before they had gotten halfway, men scrambled down to help them, making the climb much easier for the battered warriors.

Morena met him at the top, though without the anxious fawning over his wound he'd anticipated. "I'm fine," he offered, appreciating the brave face she put up for his sake.

"I can see that," she replied a bit sarcastically. "I'll get to you in a minute."

With that, she immediately began examining the leg of the Gotarran they'd been carrying, asking pointed questions and probing gently. In short order, she had dug several items from her bag and given precise instructions about their use.

Soon enough she was back, peeling off the shirt that was now plastered to his skin with dried blood. The edges of the gash were slightly swollen and reddened, looking more than a little angry. Given the nature of the cave floor he'd rolled in more than once, he hoped he'd gotten it clean enough. But he would be fortunate if it wasn't becoming infected.

Lips compressed, she glanced up from the cut. "Do you want this to scar a little, or a lot?" she asked.

He understood the question. Some warriors wanted scars, thinking them a sign of toughness. In Samir's opinion, they were a better indication that the man's fighting skills needed improvement. "I don't need scars," he said with a smile.

"Good. My father never approved of men who boasted about getting hurt." She smiled back. "Did you kill them all?"

He nodded, catching her hands as she examined the deep cut. "All that were here," he reassured her. "Who knows if that was all of them?"

Leaning down, he kissed her softly, very glad to be able to do so, considering the fight he'd nearly lost hours before. No, he didn't need scars, but he did need her. As for the rest, time would tell them if he still had dragons left to hunt.

Jenaris stared at the four immense, mottled eggs on the table before him. A foot tall, each weighed nearly ten pounds unhatched, and yet he'd almost missed them entirely with the body of the female wrapped around them. Though it hadn't actually registered during the battle, he'd begun to wonder why she hadn't moved in response to the assault. Now he understood.

She'd been protecting her babies.

Using his knife, he gently scored one of the shells several times around the middle. With a sharp rap, he brought the hilt down on the new seam. It split cleanly, giving him a good look at the unborn dragon.

The thing would have looked pitiful if it weren't so evil. Nearly the size of a cat and fully scaled, it was still being nourished by a rapidly diminishing egg sac. From the look of it, the little abomination would have hatched before too many days had passed. Thankfully, that would never happen now—nor for the other three when he was finished.

Using the knife already in his hand, he stabbed into its chest. An unnecessary indulgence to be sure, but satisfying nonetheless.

Setting the blade aside, he picked up the pieces of shell and set them gently on the balance scale he'd found. Almost exactly two pounds of shell. The math wasn't difficult at all.

"Eight," Kordel said uneasily as he stood watching the process. He was right to be uneasy.

"Eight," Jenaris confirmed. "More or less."

Kordel had carefully collected every fragment and speck of shell on the floor of the birthing cave, weighing it all in batches. Another four pounds were gathered from the very table they were currently using. The total had been very close to forty pounds. Now they knew that meant twenty dragons, and they had killed only twelve.

"Of course," the apprentice put in, "the question is whether the remaining dragons have clutched."

"Yes," the Wizard sighed heavily. "We can hope they simply haven't survived. But we have to assume they're out there somewhere. What we have to figure out is how to find them without knowing where to look."

In the grim silence that followed, he couldn't help but notice that Kordel was once again fingering the string of large, black beads around his neck. Apparently, the things had been a gift from Kulmar. Quite a remarkable gift.

As a man with a share in the kill, the big man was permitted to offer presents to those who had helped. Such a trophy from a bear would be worn proudly, but from a *dragon* it would clearly be a symbol of great status.

Many of the barbarians had begun to wear the beads carved from dragon scales in astonishing numbers already. After only a day it seemed nearly everyone had strung dozens to adorn their necklaces—sharing the leather thong with the claws or teeth of bears or wild pigs.

In fact, even the Acedians had adopted something of the practice. By approval of the Captain, every soldier present would be entitled to a beaded cord hung from the shoulder. Well, they had certainly earned them.

Jenaris glanced up as the door opened to reveal a young and somewhat anxious Acedian. "Lieutenant Gillis' compliments, sir," he said quickly. "He's found something you might like to see when you have time."

Interesting. And it wasn't as if he was terribly busy at the moment. With a shrug to Kordel, he waved for the young soldier to precede him.

Leaving the room, it was only a short walk down the hallway to the spiral staircase. The entire long climb had been more or less permanently lighted now by his apprentice, bathing it all in a soft blue.

As they had quickly discovered, the stairs emerged in a portion of the palace that was still standing. It was a stroke of good fortune. Nearly half had collapsed with no discernible reason behind the disjointed nature of the destruction—at least not so far.

Jenaris had only passed through the section once before, and had been reasonably impressed by the fine furnishings and craftsmanship. Emerging into the ground floor hallway, he was again taken by the plush carpeting and carved tables as they passed through.

It was a roundabout route, leaving through the western end of their current section only to circle back the other way. Although it added a considerable distance to the walk, it was much easier than climbing a veritable mountain of rubble. Still, it wasn't long before they reached a fair-sized section mounted with roughly made ladders—a product of the Gotarrans' craftsmanship. At the prompting of his Acedian escort Jenaris scaled one, entering through the window of a second floor room.

The Wizard had always considered his own little house to be comfortable, if a little rustic. Yet what he had seen of this place so far had forced him to reconsider his definition of comfort. The room was plush—with canopy and curtains of red velvet on the enormous bed, and thickly upholstered chairs before a broad fireplace. Dark wood paneling graced the walls, and gilding decorated the small tables. Everything about the place spoke of wealth. No, opulence.

On the far side of the room, Gillis stood next to an open door, conferring with several of his men—most older veterans. At the Mage's approach, he suspended the discussion to wave him over.

"I thought you'd best see this for yourself," the lieutenant offered with a mixture of excitement and anxiety. He pointed through the doorway before him.

Several tall bookcases lined the walls of a medium sized room—its appointments as fine as any he'd seen yet. Desk and chairs were masterfully carved and the carpets thick. Standing next to Gillis, he could now see a great deal of glassware on another table near the wall.

"A study?" he asked, cocking an eyebrow at the officer.

"We don't know." Gillis' reply contained more than a hint of frustration. "We can't get in."

To illustrate, he reached out a hand toward the doorway. It stopped at the threshold.

Surprised and curious, Jenaris took another look at the room. The lack of emotion in the other man's tone said they had found no danger, but he remained cautious as he pushed toward the barrier. His hand stopped as well.

"We found this next to the bed." The lieutenant held out a small book, bound in rich black leather and embossed in gold leaf.

Taking the volume, he turned it over to examine the writing on the spine. Though small, it was clearly printed in fine script.

"Oh, my," he blurted, understanding Gillis' excitement perfectly. "The Secrets of the Wizard Olandis."

Without waiting, he plopped down in one of the cozy chairs nearby to read. If they were *very* lucky, it would tell him what they needed to know.

The following chapter is an excerpt from

Dragon Spear

The Majaran Trilogy
Book 2

by

Peter Rogers Stark

Chapter 1

Unexpected Lessons

"Again!"

Without hesitation, Suppan threw himself into the maneuver, working the spear in a dizzying blur. The stocky, young Gotarran had quickly learned to combine his natural power with speed. As his teacher watched, the barbarian battered the air—razor sharp point and rough, wooden butt attacking the ankles, knees and head of his imaginary opponent in rapid succession. Immediately, the butt traced a broad circle, dipping toward the elegant, patterned carpet in a foot sweep as Suppan stepped forward.

"YAAAA!" The wordless shout rose from deep in the gut and echoed through the room as the young warrior jammed the spearpoint forward to end the exercise.

Excellent.

The man had made surprising progress since he'd learned to rid himself of all the needless tension that had slowed his motions. Now that he understood that power wasn't merely about strength, Suppan was well on his way to becoming a truly formidable fighter—with his knife as well as the spear.

There was still one thing he needed to work on, however.

"Again!"

For perhaps the twentieth time, the barbarian shifted his balance, centering himself to face the unseen enemy before him. Instantly, almost automatically, the weapon began to move against its assigned targets.

Samir pivoted smoothly, coming to rest in the precise spot where he knew Suppan had imagined his opponent. There was no time for his student to stop or even slow the brutal strike whistling toward his head, but that was fine. He was in no real danger.

Completing his pivot step, the Majaran planted his lead foot hard to shift his balance just as his hands gripped the spear haft. With a twist of his upper body, he jerked Suppan forward to crash into his hip. The muscular barbarian flipped easily, flying several feet to land heavily on his back.

It took all of Samir's effort to resist the smile that threatened to break across his face. But, that would have spoiled the lesson's effect—something he couldn't allow. After all, he knew from his own hard won experience just how important it was.

"What was *that* for?" Suppan grumbled as he stood, dusting himself off.

No Majaran would ever have *dared* speak to a teacher that way. Of course, he was not a Sòra, and none of his students had so much as set foot in his homeland of Majar. It was hardly what he would have preferred in the student-teacher relationship, but he was prepared to accept a certain...informality.

"Just a reminder," Samir replied seriously, using the same flat tone he'd heard countless times from Shimei.

"It's easy to expect your opponent to behave a certain way. It's also a mistake. I wanted to be sure you understood that an enemy isn't obligated to cooperate with your assessment of his skills."

Now the Majaran *did* allow a hint of a smile as he laid a thickly calloused hand on the other man's shoulder. For this, he wanted the Gotarran's full attention.

"I'm not sure you take my full meaning, A-Saír," Samir said frankly, using an informal term for a younger brother, despite the similarity in their ages. "It's true that you don't always read your opponent correctly, but I'm not just speaking of *your* expectations. What we sometimes forget is that he has also made an assessment of you, and that his actions will be based on what he thinks of your abilities."

Suppan's eyes narrowed thoughtfully as he nodded. "And I should make sure he underestimates me."

Credit where it was due, the man displayed a certain sharpness of mind. But, that was exactly what they had to fix—not that it should take much effort.

"You're a good fighter, Suppan, so don't take this the wrong way." He offered a grin to take the sting out of his next words. "When people meet a Gotarran, especially one built like you, it's easy for them to think *barbarian*—big, dumb and slow. I know that can be a drawback to being taken seriously, but it can also be an advantage, an asset." The warrior paused for effect, letting his point sink in. "It's a weapon you shouldn't be afraid to use when you need it."

"I understand," the other man replied, adopting a blank look before continuing in somewhat broken speech. "Me know how to fight good."

"Don't overdo it," Samir laughed, "but I think you have the idea."

Samir knew only too well that the most dangerous opponent was one you didn't see as a danger at all. It had cost the young Prince a broken arm and a painful slash to the ribs to learn that lesson—and he considered it cheap at that price. A drunken beggar had taught him early on that looks could be deceiving when the man had turned out to be an assassin. From that time on, he'd been extremely careful never to underestimate *anyone* if he could help it. After all, even one time could easily be once too often.

Of course, no one wanted to be seen as less than they really were, and people could put great effort into appearing to be *more*. Hopefully, Suppan could use that to his advantage.

A quick glance out the windows revealed lengthening shadows. He'd done what he could with the lesson for now, he knew. If he left soon, he wouldn't be late...but he wouldn't be early, either.

"That's all for today, Suppan," he said in dismissal. "Tomorrow we'll work on disarming techniques."

His student offered a hasty bow. Although poorly done, the move was obviously intended as a sign of deep respect.

Samir returned it easily.

Straightening, the stocky Gotarran hesitated. "If you don't mind, I think I'll stay here and practice."

"As you wish," the Prince acknowledged, bowing to the room as he stepped outside.

Formalities done, he quickly slipped into his shoes and hustled down the broad hallway. It was a short walk to the exit, a large hole in the wall where one of the numerous sections had collapsed over the centuries. Manpower and magic had cleared most of the rubble from the gap, leaving nothing more hazardous than a few large stones.

It had taken days of near continuous work to clear the most commonly used exits—working several shifts of Alban's soldiers with Kordel and, rarely, Jenaris helping with the largest stones. For the most part, the Gotarrans had simply melted away into the hills, wanting to reach their homes in time to prepare for winter.

Alban had done much the same once the heaviest labor was done, taking most of the Acedian soldiers back to Varella to report. Now only a handful of the men remained, under the watchful eye of Lieutenant Gillis.

That was fine. Just as long as he could count on more help arriving come spring. By then he would be anxious to hunt again, he was sure.

The only real surprise had been Caleb and Morena. Samir had merely assumed they would go with Alban, if not back to Acedia, then at least as far as Scara. Yet here they remained. Not that he wasn't grateful for their company, but he suspected that Caleb was putting off the inevitable meeting with his father.

As he walked, Samir was once again struck by the drastic drop in temperature as he stepped through the gap. At first, he had thought he imagined it, but Jenaris had assured him it was genuine—a simple step through the curtain of magic that kept the place at a constant temperature regardless of the weather outside. Somehow he'd gotten the impression that the aging Wizard was more than a little impressed himself.

Of course, Jenaris seemed to be impressed by nearly every aspect of the ruined palace. Not that Samir could fault him.

It had taken time for the Majaran to get used to the stunning beauty of the place, and in a very real way he still was, as the scene continued to change. In the first weeks, the trees had undergone a breathtaking transformation. Where the forests had once been an almost uniform, lush green, they had flashed into incredible and vivid reds, yellows and oranges almost overnight. The brilliance of the hues could almost make a fire seem muted by comparison. There was certainly nothing like it in his own land, where the change of season meant only a bit less heat and humidity...or a lot more rain.

He could almost have been content here. Almost.

It was still far colder here than he liked, especially at night. Unfortunately, he was told that it would get colder still—much colder—before winter, when deep snow would blanket everything for months.

Snow.

The idea of it fascinated him. Many times he'd seen the shining, white caps of the mountains in Majar, but it still seemed incredible to think of it as frozen water. Yet whether he understood a thing or not made no difference whatsoever. If his friends were right, and he had no reason to doubt their word, he would see it for himself soon enough.

The trail he followed was well worn after so many trips, across the grounds and up the hill to their now long abandoned original camp. While most of the soldiers who'd made it were well away—and most likely home by now—it still served Samir on his daily treks.

In the shade of the trees, the air was slightly cooler, and not merely because of the wind rattling the dry leaves overhead. Still, the walk kept him warm as he climbed the steep grade.

Once at the top, it was only a short walk beneath the thinning cover of the forest. Fallen leaves had begun to form a carpet of sorts, crunching underfoot as he navigated the trail.

"It's about time," Morena said teasingly as he came in sight of the tree.

In spite of himself, the young Prince glanced over his shoulder to gauge the position of the sun. It was difficult to tell even through the sparse canopy, but he knew he'd arrived on time.

"I'm not late," Samir smiled at the sight of her. "You're just impatient."

"Oh?" she raised a neatly arched brow, hands on hips as lips curved in a gently mocking smile. "You think I just can't wait to see you. Is that it?"

The warrior chuckled as he closed the final distance between them, Morena stepping carefully up onto an exposed root to place their eyes on nearly the same level. Setting a hand lightly on her hip, Samir leaned in until their noses almost touched.

"Of course you're eager to see me," he brushed her sweetly curving mouth with a brief kiss. "How else could you get me all stirred up?" Bending his head down, he allowed his lips to linger on her neck as he breathed in the scent of her hair. "What is that smell?"

"Like it?" she asked, obviously pleased. "It's honeysuckle. I found some a few days ago...in a room in the castle. Whoever built it had a pretty nice herb garden."

Morena watched him carefully while he thought about what she'd just said. She seemed to be implying....

"So there's been no need to look for your herbs? No need to come out here every day?" he asked, more amused than annoyed.

"I wouldn't say *no* need," the woman replied, almost laughing as she leaned against his chest.

He took another sniff, nuzzling her ear as he did. Very nice, indeed. Almost as nice as the orchids he would, he hoped, one day fill her rooms with. She deserved to be surrounded by beauty, and he would definitely enjoy making that happen.

It would be nearly as much fun as this was.

Samir kissed her deeply, savoring the delicious feeling as she pressed against him to twine her arms around his neck. It would have been easy—far too easy—to get carried away, as they nearly had several times already.

Placing his hands on her waist, he lifted her from her perch, lowering her feet gently to the hard packed soil.

Slowly, reluctantly, he straightened as they broke from the kiss.

Not surprisingly, it took him a minute to catch his breath. Taking her hand, the Prince drew her down to sit beside him on the thick, gnarled root. It was where they always sat when they met—a natural place, given its history. Here, beneath the towering oak, he had taught her to bond with his sword, Dragon's Fang, which had bonded the two of them as well.

Thinking of the blade brought a momentary twinge of longing. Normally, the Wizard returned it to him during the day. Yet it had been several days now since he'd even caught a glimpse of the man. Of course, he knew where to find the Mage. Everyone did. It was no secret that Jenaris spent nearly all of his time staring silently into a room he couldn't enter. And *that*, in a nutshell, was the problem. Because of the seemingly unsolvable puzzle, the Wizard had become rather moody—particularly when he was interrupted.

Unfortunately, if Samir wanted to see the sword again any time soon, he would probably need to go get it. That would have to wait, however.

"What was that?" he asked somewhat sheepishly, realizing he'd missed her last comment. "Sorry. I was thinking about something else."

"The sword?"

If she knew to ask the question, she obviously knew the answer already. Still, he nodded acknowledgment.

"I'm going to have to ask him for it. *Not* a conversation I look forward to," Samir admitted, winking to show that he was at least half joking. "Anyway, what was it you said? Something about Caleb?"

Morena nodded. "Tirza went with Caleb and Hul. She needs more exercise if the leg is going to get strong again." Seeing his concern, she gave him a slight moue of disapproval. "Don't worry. She'll be *fine*."

She was right, he knew. Huldrich and Caleb were more than capable of taking care of the hound. Still, since she'd been hurt, he couldn't help but worry...just a little. After all, Tirza had nearly *died*, and that wasn't something he could just forget. The injury had noticeably slowed her, and that left him more than a bit concerned.

"I know she will." He gave the healer's hand a light squeeze. "She'll be around to look after our children. Unless, of course, you're one of those people who believes in *extremely* long engagements."

"Not too long," she answered, shifting closer as he slid his arm around her waist. "Just a decent period. After you've retaken Majar, of course. But, your mother and I will decide all that later...if she approves of me, that is."

Samir failed to fully suppress a shiver that wasn't entirely due to the cool mountain air. Morena's quick glance let him know that she'd felt the slight shudder.

"You really should bring a cloak if you're cold," she smiled with light amusement "I'm sure Gillis will lend you one. Or any of the others."

"I'll ask," he assured her, kissing her forehead, "as soon as we get back."

It was a good idea, and one he would definitely have to follow up on. After all, while it was always warm inside, he had no intention of spending months cooped up indoors. Besides, better she think he was merely cold than tell her the whole truth—that if his mother didn't approve his choice for a wife, he would no longer have a family...or a country, for that matter.

If his mother took offense, which was entirely possible, he would simply be disinherited. He could live with that possibility, painful as it would no doubt be, just as long as Majar wasn't left in Kemal's greedy—and unstable—hands.

And, as long as he had Morena.

A sudden chill hit his spine, this time actually due to the cold he seemed to feel much more acutely than his friends. While he could deal with a little discomfort, he also realized it could become an issue.

"We're going to need to meet somewhere else soon," he said softly in her ear. "Someplace indoors. Where did you say this garden was?"

"Mmm," she murmured, huddling closer into his side. "But not too soon. This is good snuggling weather."

The Majaran had to admit the truth of that, and any excuse to hold her was something to be appreciated. In a way, it would be a shame when the approach of winter kept them inside the elegant ruins of the palace below. Then again, the place was so sparsely populated now, that finding a bit of privacy in some out-of-the-way room would be no problem at all.

Perhaps later there would be time for a quick look around. At the moment, though, he needed something to eat before his session with Gillis.

"What did you bring today?" He turned his gaze on the large leather satchel on the ground by her feet. "I am definitely...."

The young warrior was on his feet in an instant as the figure popped into existence only a few feet away. Instinctively, his sword appeared in his hand, drawn by magic as he spun to face the unexpected presence.

Beside him, Morena also stood ready.

"I didn't mean to startle you, m'boy," Jenaris chuckled easily, pointing to the weapon in Samir's hand, "But I hardly think you'll be needing that."

Peter Rogers Stark

About the Author:

His time as a U.S. Marine and being raised a diehard Chicago Cubs fan have taught Mr. Stark the value of perseverance as well as the ability to endure extraordinary frustration. Both of those lessons were useful in earning his PhD and in writing this novel. The Mensan and self-professed aviation nut relieves stress playing the guitar, watching anime, and reading whatever he can get his hands on. He someday hopes to read Tolkien's *The Hobbit* in the original Klingon.

As with all authors, he reserves the right to name his characters after his friends...and then threaten to kill them off.